The Keepers Of
The Sunken Way

Mirador Publishing
Mirador
Wearne Lane
Langport
Somerset
TA10 9HB

THE KEEPERS OF
THE SUNKEN WAY

R. S. FRECKLETON

Mirador Publishing
www.miradorpublishing.com

To Richard Smalley

Chapter 1

Even the most peaceful market town in England has dark corners and unsavoury spots where evil deeds are done and malicious plans are plotted. Behind the facades of grand Georgian buildings or ramshackle half-timbered Tudor cottages lay alleyways that seethe with the detritus and misery of modern living. Shrewsbury is full of narrow passages that criss-cross the town like the pastry lattice on a treacle tart, full of character and thronging with tourists and shoppers by day, but menacing and threatening once darkness takes hold.

Gerald Tasker, chairman of the Telford branch of the Family Unity Party, stood nervously at the entrance to one of these passageways one dreary Wednesday evening in November. There was hardly anybody about; the odd car passed cautiously down the narrow, semi-pedestrianised road that ran between the medieval shops. Nobody seemed to be watching him, so he moved into the shadows and walked purposefully along half the length of the alley. He turned and knocked sharply on an old wooden door that could easily have been missed by a less attentive traveller. There was just a hint of a breath in the air as Gerald waited for a response. He turned sharply – Surely he was not mistaken in his belief that he had not been followed? Peering into the darkness, there was nothing to be seen or any sound to be heard. "Get a grip," he said to himself.

With a creak and the rattle of a latch, the door opened and light briefly poured out. Gerald recognised the man inside as a colleague from a different branch of the Party.

"Come in, Gerald," the man said almost in a whisper. "He's here!"

"Have all the constituency reps arrived?" Gerald enquired in a voice that was dry and cracking.

"They're all here apart from Dorothy. She's coming from Bishop's Castle, so we'll give her another five minutes, but then we must begin."

"Yes, I agree," Gerald said eager to get on with proceedings. "We cannot stay here long, especially with the guest we have with us tonight."

The two men made their way up a rickety staircase and entered a large upstairs room. The building was poorly furnished with bare wooden floorboards, whitewashed walls and large beams of oak stretching the entire width of the building. At no point did two planes meet at anything like a right angle. In the room there was a large table, rather roughly finished, around which everyone was sitting. Gerald took his place and started looking around the table, mentally ticking off the names of the people as he went. He soon came to someone he did not recognise. This must be him. The man, unknown to Gerald Tasker, leaned forward and the light just caught his face. Gerald gave an involuntary gasp. There was nothing wrong with his face; he was balding in an unexceptional way for his age and he had a beard that would have graced a benevolent professor. It was his eyes that had shocked Gerald. As the man had moved, a sharp glint had illuminated a pair of blue eyes. They were not happy or friendly. Indeed, they were icy cold, hard as steel and without compassion. These were eyes that had seen torture and murder. They had seen people beg for mercy and yet witnessed their owner showing none. They were windows into a soul that had lost all sense of love and fairness, pity and clemency, and had only a bitter determination to fulfil an unswerving cause.

Gerald again had to pull himself together and realise that everyone was expecting him to start the meeting.

"Good evening, ladies and gentlemen," he began. "It gives me great pleasure to introduce, er..." He suddenly realised he'd forgotten the name of his guest.

"Call me Michael O'Grady," the stranger immediately said in a soft voice with only a hint of an Irish accent. "It's not my real name – but it is better you don't know *that*, maybe."

"Oh, er... It gives me great pleasure to introduce Mr O'Grady." Gerald was, by now, very discomfited. "He is going to give us some idea as to how we can move our vision for a more orderly and disciplined society in a God-fearing environment forward."

"Thank you, Mr Tasker, or can I call you Gerald?" A chill went down Gerald's spine as he realised that Michael O'Grady knew an awful lot about everybody in the room. The stranger with the soulless eyes continued, "Your organisation has made a good start in many ways. You have managed to create areas in some towns and cities where the majority of the inhabitants have rejected the authority of the establishment and you have been able to fill this void with your Neighbourhood Protection Committees. I am impressed with what you have done in Telford. You have managed to create 'no-go' areas for the police and have taken over the role of law enforcers, and hence, become *de facto* lawmakers.

"However, you cannot maintain this grip forever with what you've got. People are not so stupid that they will blame the gays and immigrants unceasingly when they see that their lives are no better under your stewardship than they were before. At that point, your control will crumble unless you can impose your will with an iron fist and deadly force. You need to arm your NPC's and be prepared to execute summary justice against anyone who steps out of line. You must keep your ghetto in check and against the rest of the world."

Gerald inwardly winced at this prospect. He was a hard man who believed in meeting out harsh justice to criminals. However, what this man was proposing went much further than he was comfortable with. He looked round to see if he could gauge the reaction of his fellow F.U.P. reps; some were moving uncomfortably in their chairs, but not all. Michael O'Grady continued:

"I gather you have links with the USA. If they can provide the money, I can provide the guns and the training for your foot soldiers, so they can become as hard and dangerous as my boys in Belfast."

The meeting continued with a more mundane discussion about the ways and means such an outcome could be made to come to pass. After more than an hour, the conversation was almost complete when there was a sharp tap at a skylight window which Gerald had failed to notice was there. The effect on Michael O'Grady was electric. He looked up immediately, whilst simultaneously, his hand went inside his jacket. Gerald now realised he had a gun in a holster strapped across his chest. O'Grady rushed out of the room. Seconds later a single gunshot was heard that made everyone in the room jump out of their seats. This was followed immediately by the miaowing of a startled cat, somewhere in the vicinity of the roof.

O'Grady sauntered in. "Just a cat or a pigeon I expect, but it's best to be sure."

"What would have happened if you'd shot someone?" Gerald asked querulously.

"They'd be dead." O'Grady said in a matter-of-fact way. "In any case, that wouldn't be my problem. I'm the guest and you're the host. I'm sure you'd be able to dispose of the corpse. Now, I must be going."

"Do you need a lift to the station?" one of the other reps volunteered unenthusiastically.

"How do you know I came by train? No thank you, I think it best to slip out into the night unobserved. If you need to contact me, your superiors on the F.U.P. National Executive know how to get in touch. Good evening."

He picked up a briefcase, which had been by his seat, strode purposefully across the room, down the stairs and left the building. The front door creaked shut behind him, and that was that!

Twenty minutes later Gerald Tasker was out in the street again. He was deeply disturbed by the evening's turn of events. All he'd wanted when he got involved with the F.U.P. was for the world to be more orderly and disciplined, for people to go to church on Sunday and respect the teachings of the Bible, for children to be obedient and respect their elders, for the young to aspire to be doctors and vets. It was all accelerating horribly out of control. If this latest venture failed he would be complicit in sedition at least, and possibly treason. He could be facing a long jail sentence. But what if it succeeded? What sort of society would he be helping to create? Deep down he knew it would not be the happy and orderly Garden of Eden he had dreamed of. It would be more like Germany under the Third Reich, or Afghanistan under the Taliban – or perhaps, in view of the evening's meeting, Belfast during the time of 'The Troubles' was the best analogy.

Then of course there was his son, Nathan. Why the hell couldn't he have just towed the line? He'd given the boy everything he needed. He'd mapped out a good life for him that would have seen him prosperous and content. Why had the boy provoked him to so much anger? Why had he done the most evil and wicked thing imaginable, and why, oh why, had he gone off with that Holdencroft boy to join that despicable band of renegade homosexuals hidden somewhere in London? His wife Daphne had never been the same since Nathan left. She had sunk into depression and then later lapsed into a full-blown nervous breakdown.

In a rage, Gerald Tasker marched down the hill to find his car and drive home.

Chapter 2

The very next day, Darryn Harcourt-Smith, one of the most respected and admired Guardians amongst his colleagues and friends at Rainbow House, decided to go and have a coffee in Shrewsbury. It was just after the lunchtime 'rush', although 'trickle' might have been a better term to use. The town centre was no busier than Gerald Tasker had observed the previous evening. The choice of venue was deliberate – a small independent coffee shop in an ancient Market Hall sited next to a small independent Arts Centre and cinema.

As Darryn entered, the reassuring smell of fresh coffee hit his senses. Why did it always smell so much better than it tasted? He looked around. The old 15th century walls and roof were starkly contrasted with a modern counter and coffee making equipment. As you would expect, there were a number of comfy, well-worn leather sofas and chairs with low coffee tables to match and, for the less fortunate when times were busy, a number of functional sturdy chairs surrounding no-nonsense pedestal tables.

There were two people serving behind the counter. One was a pretty girl, probably about twenty, with shoulder-length light brown hair and deep brown eyes to match. The other was a handsome young man of about the same age, with curly fair hair which was short at the back and sides and with just the hint of a beard. He was six foot tall with an athletic build. Darryn could not help but notice his arm muscles rippling through his white shirt. It was the girl who came over optimistically to take his order.

"What can I get you, sir?" she said, flirting as outrageously as she dare.

"A large cappuccino please, and I'll have a slice of that chocolate cake too, as I've had no lunch."

Darryn chuckled to himself. If only she knew that he was far more interested in her male colleague than he was in her. She would probably jump up on the counter and slap him round the face for making her waste all that effort on him.

When she returned with his coffee, he said rather mischievously, "When your colleague has a moment, tell him to come and join me. Here you are – There's some extra money for another coffee, if he wants one."

The girl looked extremely puzzled and disappointed, but Darryn was already turning to find somewhere to sit. Fortunately there were very few people in; an elderly couple who had taken a break from a shopping expedition and two Japanese couples in animated conversation over a map. Understanding Japanese was one of the few skills Darryn had failed to pick up. He made for a sofa in the far corner where he hoped he could have a quiet conversation without being overheard. After a few minutes the handsome man from behind the counter came and joined him, with a cup of coffee in hand.

"Hello, Sean. How are things panning out for you at the moment?" Darryn enquired, obviously very well acquainted with the man.

"Not bad," said Sean with a lilting Irish accent, "I'm doing a few 'odds and ends' jobs at the moment until something more permanent comes along. How are you doing, Darryn?"

"I'm fine, thanks. Actually I'm on Alliance business, which is why I've come to see you – although it's always a pleasure to see you, of course," Darryn added rather hastily.

Sean laughed and said, "It's alright, Darryn, you don't have to 'soft soap' me with flattery. I guessed there was some business involved. It's a long time since you paid me a purely social call."

Darryn considered why he had not paid this handsome and charming young man more social calls lately and could come up with no good reason. He moved hastily on:

"I had a very busy day yesterday. Firstly, I was down in Bishop's Castle visiting a cantankerous old dear who is signed up to the hanging and flogging brigade."

Sean raised an eyebrow, "Was that your idea of a fun day out?"

"Not really," Darryn replied, "But the old battle-axe was harmless enough and didn't deserve to be caught up in a dangerous plot with murderers and psychopaths. I think I persuaded her it would be better to stay at home rather than attend the meeting I was interested in last night, here in Shrewsbury. In fact, I think she will be scared witless enough to resign her position as an F.U.P. rep."

"So what was this meeting all about?" Sean asked expectantly.

"Ah yes, well that is the reason I have come to see you. My intelligence was a bit vague about where it was to take place, so I tailed Gerald Tasker and followed him on foot into town. He went into a building down some dark alley. I got on to the roof and was able to catch what was going on through a skylight. I had one of the new improved listening devices as well, so I was able to get a pretty clear indication of the conversation going on in the room.

"There was a guy who said he was from Belfast there. A nasty piece of work by the look of him, he said his name was Michael O'Grady. He was offering to arm and train the Neighbourhood Protection Committees. Have you ever heard of him?"

"I can't say I have," Sean said after considering the question very carefully. "However, if he's a commander of one of the loyalist or republican brigades, he's likely to be a very dangerous man indeed."

"I can well believe it." Darryn interjected with feeling. "I accidentally dropped my earpiece onto the skylight, and the next thing I know, the crazy idiot is out in the alleyway taking a pot shot at me without a thought for anyone who might be about."

"Bloody hell, Darryn. How did you get out of that one?"

"I was lucky. There was a cat on the roof as well. The shot startled it so much that it scampered away making an almighty din. Mr O'Grady was satisfied that the cat had made the noise on the skylight and I just remained silent and motionless with my fingers crossed."

"One day you are going to run out of luck, my friend." Sean added gravely.

"Well when my number's up there's nothing I can do about it," Darryn replied rather dismissively. "I was hoping that with your experience of living in Northern Ireland, you might know how these paramilitary groups might work."

Sean raised his eyebrows in disbelief: "Are you mad?" he said, "Anyone with any sense would stay as far away from those guys as possible. In most countries lunatics and criminals are locked up; over there, they are given guns and are respected as community leaders. I couldn't wait to get away from the place. The one thing the Catholics and Protestants agree on is that they hate the gays even more than the hate each other, and that, my friend, is an awful lot of hate!"

"Are you happy here?" said Darryn, suddenly changing tack. "You could always come and join us in Rainbow House if you wanted."

"Are you propositioning me, Darryn? What are you going to do to me once you get me all alone in your secret headquarters?"

Although this was said in jest, Darryn was beginning to think of some very interesting things he'd like to do to Sean if he had the chance. He hastily expanded on his previous statement: "I just thought you might find life a bit more exciting working for the cause - and yes, I'm not going to deny that I find you very attractive."

Darryn gulped. Had he *really* just said that? Sean smiled sympathetically and lightly put his hand on Darryn's knee: "You're a fine looking man yourself, Darryn, and if you'd asked me out a month or two back, I'd probably be asking you back to my place pretty damned quick. However, I'm seeing someone at the moment and it's going okay. If it all ends in tears, I'll come and cry on your shoulder."

Sean became more serious, and as a result his face probably looked more beautiful, "As for joining the operation at Rainbow House, you know some of us have serious reservations about all of that. I really think there's a danger you're all going to be caught in a trap down there in London. I say it's better to have small independent cells fighting the F.U.P. all over the country."

Darryn sighed, "You know I don't agree with you on that. You would never get the resources and equipment to do anything meaningful if you left everything to small groups."

At this point an athletic woman bounded over to join them. Her entrance was not observed by Darryn, who had been looking too intently at Sean to notice alterations in the surroundings.

"Hi, Annabelle," Darryn greeted her. "Did you have any luck following our mad Irish paramilitary friend last night?"

"You two look very cosy there," she began, and instantly Sean and Darryn edged a little further away from each other. "I followed him down the A5 as far as Chirk. He took the Wrexham road there. My guess is he's heading for Holyhead to get the ferry to Dublin. I've messaged our agent there to keep an eye open for him boarding."

"Hi, Annabelle," Sean greeted her. "Take a seat and I'll get you a coffee; then you can tell me all the news that's going on down in London."

Sean got up and went behind the counter to fiddle with the coffee making equipment. The girl had a few sharp words to say to him, obviously not happy that she had been left to mind the shop while he was socialising. Sean laughed and waved his hand dismissively, muttering something about good customer relations. Meanwhile Annabelle and Darren brought each other up to speed with the latest developments following last night's clandestine meeting.

The elderly couple and the Japanese tourists had gone, but were replaced by an even more elderly couple who were sitting in silence in a corner of the room and two young women in their late twenties, each with a young toddler in tow and anxious to catch up on the latest news outside the bubble of their day-to-day existence of rearing children. Sean came back over with coffee in hand.

"Thanks, Sean." Annabelle said, accepting the cup and saucer. "So you want to know what's going on in Rainbow House. I guess the big news is what happened to Martin Bradbury when the Guardians brought him in after the fracas down in Dorset."

Darryn shuddered and said, "Annabelle will have to tell you all about that. I was forced to take leave while all that was going on. I still don't know whether I've been told the truth about everything that happened."

Annabelle smiled and said, "Darren, sometimes you are just *too* paranoid when it comes to matters concerning your ex. Anyway, it was quite an event when he turned up as it was the first time we had ever brought a captive or hostage back to Rainbow House. Word got around that he'd been captured and people lined the social area to see him come out of the lift as if he was a celebrity. There was utter silence as he passed through the room. People just stared at him and he said nothing in return. He was taken to the living quarters by the stairs rather than the lift and two guardians were posted outside the door of his room, effectively placing him under house arrest.

"All the Numbers met in convocation, breaking the rule that at least one of them must be away from the house at any one time. They were locked together in conversation for hours and it was clear they could not decide what to do with him. Eventually, after almost a week of intermittent deliberation, Martin was summoned before them. I was one of the Guardians assigned guard duty the day he was called for, so I got to see what happened firsthand.

It was the first time I had been in the Room of Benign Decision and seen the Great Crescent Table completely occupied by the Numbers. N°1 was sat in the centre flanked in order of decreasing seniority by the others. It was a very impressive and noble sight, and yet Martin had the temerity to stand in front of them and smirk.

"I remember N°6 was the first to say something to him: 'Give me one good reason why we shouldn't just lock you in a room in the basement and throw away the key.' he said.

"I have to say that Martin was very cool under pressure and I had forgotten how attractively eloquent he could be:

'What exactly am I supposed to have done that would warrant such a punishment?' I recall him saying, 'As far as I'm aware, I have been driving a minibus for an organisation you don't like very much, and, okay, I did supply some recording equipment to tap into your communications, but you didn't seem too concerned about that when I met up with a couple of your heavies in Old Compton Street. You seemed to be more concerned to get at the youngsters we were trying to protect. Well you got them, so you won. Congratulations, but how does that make me guilty of a crime?'

"I think it was N°10, who then chipped in and said, 'But you betrayed us – You went and worked for the enemy. That in itself is surely bad enough to be considered a crime.' Martin remained cool as a cucumber and replied, 'Betrayal is a strong word and assumes I had some loyalty to your organisation and your ideals. Don't forget, I had already turned my back on you and walked out, as you said I was always free to do. No compulsion, No coercion, everyone is here by their free choice – That was your mantra. Well, I exercised the get-out clause, and so the question of loyalty and betrayal does not arise.'

"I remember Martin laughed at that point in such a sarcastic and cynical way that I was quite chilled by his whole persona. He continued, 'You woolly middle-class liberals are all the same. You have angst-ridden discussions about morality while the claret is being swilled down at some dinner party, but the moment you are actually challenged or threatened in the real world you behave just as badly as the pettiest dictator of some third world country. So you are going to incarcerate me here, or worse maybe, based on some charge that would not stand up in a proper court of law. I think I was right to turn my back on you. I hope you do lose the war that's coming and then there's an end to your sordid little ways.'

"There was the sound of awkward shuffling by some of the lesser Numbers at this point, but N°1 remained fixed, staring with piercing and unblinking eyes at Martin. It was time for him to speak and he did so with a sigh: 'You are quite wrong Martin,' he said like a long-suffering parent who is still trying to do the best for his wayward child. 'We have deliberated for days and are well aware of the moral problems involved in holding you here against your will. I'll be honest with you; we cannot decide what to do for the best. With great reluctance and much against my better judgement, I have finally acquiesced to the unanimous demand of all my colleagues that I and I alone, should make a decision and judgement which they will then endorse without argument. Before you condemn me as being the ultimate ruthless dictator, hear me out. You are not entirely guiltless despite what you say. You have manipulated the situation to put us in this moral dilemma and I believe you are enjoying watching us squirm. When you left us – and we did not stop you, although some of us were genuinely sad to see you go - you could have simply found a job with a computer firm or gone into Education and our paths would never have crossed again. It was a deliberate choice of yours to ally yourself with a group who you knew to be our sworn enemy and whose appalling effects we were trying to mitigate. You did deliberately attempt to thwart our efforts and try to prevent us rescuing frightened teenagers, so whether you betrayed us or not you placed yourself in the position of being our enemy. Now you are right that we do not have the power or authority to act as judge and jury, and in that sense, to hold you captive would not sit with the law of the land. However you pose a real threat to us. You know enough about us to endanger the lives of everyone here. All you would have to do is tell your F.U.P paramilitary friends where we are and how to get in and we are done for. But if we hold you here we will indeed be going against our ideals. You will not be with us freely. We would be keeping you against your will and we would be as bad as the F.U.P. trying to impose its ideas by force rather than persuasion. I am not going to allow you to put us in that dilemma. I am going to throw the moral conundrum back at you. I am simply going to let you go. *You* will have to decide whether you are going to risk the lives of everyone here. *You* will have to decide whether you hate the people who were once your friends so much that you are going to fight for their destruction. When the moment comes for decision I think you might surprise yourself with the choices you make. Annabelle and Rakshi, would you be good enough to escort Mr Bradbury out of the building? Give him five pounds so he can get the train back into central London and then make sure all the pass codes into Rainbow House are changed.'

"Well," Annabelle continued, "you can imagine the gasp that went round the room. Some of the Numbers nearly fell off their seats, but such was their respect for N°1 that no one questioned his decision or reneged on the assurance to back him. Even Martin was taken aback and the wind seemed quite taken out of his sails. I and Rakshi moved to escort him, first to his room to collect his belongings, and then through the social area to the lift. Martin said nothing, and to be honest we didn't feel like saying anything to him. As we moved across the social zone, crowds once more had gathered in silence to watch. The lift doors closed on a million questions that these people wanted to ask him but didn't dare voice. I was more than relieved when we reached the shop below. I half expected Martin to finally be awkward and demand to buy something from Vijay, who was checking stock behind the counter, but he didn't. He walked out of the shop and looked as if he was just going to move off when he unexpectedly turned and said, 'N°1 is either the wisest man I know or the biggest fool in the world. I'm not quite sure which at the moment.' I have to say it was hard to disagree with him. He walked off a lonely and pathetic figure."

"Ah, N°1 is a wise man indeed. Unfortunately wisdom seldom wins out when faced with brute strength, greed and envy," Sean chipped in as if some wise soothsayer.

"Don't be so gloomy," Darryn replied cheerfully, "If it's brute strength you want... there's always Annabelle and me to contend with. Well, Annabelle's got the brute strength and I've got the charm and devilish good looks, of course!"

"You don't half fancy yourself" Sean said smiling.

"Oh for goodness sake Darryn, let's go and do some work. I suppose I shall have to do all the fighting as usual, while you're checking your hair in the mirror." Annabelle added with some exasperation.

As they left, Darryn gave Sean a very warm hug and a peck on the cheek, much to the consternation of the elderly couple who now had something to talk about. The girl behind the counter had her coat and tapped her watch sharply before departing immediately behind Darryn and Annabelle, leaving Sean to manage the coffee shop on his own.

Chapter 3

Jake woke up. It was a Sunday morning just before the start of the Spring Term. He was in his apartment, room 42 in the accommodation area. He was not alone. There next to him was the warm and inviting body of his boyfriend, Nathan Tasker. Jake slowly caressed Nathan's arm with the lightest of touches. His skin was the softest thing imaginable and Jake could just sense the hairs that were almost invisible to the eye. Nathan stirred and made a slight groaning sound before reluctantly waking up.

"Morning, Gorgeous!" he said to Jake, and then turned round to hug him tightly and give him a kiss, "Morning, Handsome!" Jake replied when he finally disengaged his lips from Nathan's.

Nathan lay there contentedly, smiling and caressing Jake's hair for a moment before a spasm of panic suddenly overcame him, "My God, what's the time? I'd forgotten I'd arranged to meet up and rehearse with Sarah this morning. She will kill me if I'm late again and we've got our assessed performance on Tuesday."

Jake looked lazily over to his radio–alarm clock, "It's just gone ten," he said.

Nathan considered this for a moment, and relaxed, "That's okay. It gives me about an hour to get dressed and get over to her house. I'll have to miss out on breakfast though. Do you mind if I use your shower?" Then he added with a twinkle in his eye, "You can come and join me if you like."

Jake seriously considered the offer, but he was still well and truly worn out from everything they'd been up to during the previous night. He finally replied, "You haven't got time for funny business in the shower, or you definitely will be late."

"Spoilsport!" cried Nathan in mock horror, before playfully tweaking Jake's right nipple and jumping out of bed.

Jake lay back with his head resting in his hands and his elbows sticking out, watching the naked figure of Nathan recede to the bathroom. He was so damn lucky – and he knew it. Twenty minutes later Nathan, smelling fresh and clean in a combination of his own clothes and some of Jake's that fitted him (Nathan was slightly taller than Jake, as well as being a few months older), prepared to leave Jake's apartment.

"Right, I'll need to go and fetch my cello and then if I catch the bus from outside the tube station I shouldn't be more than a few minutes late. I'll see you later, babe."

Jake finally got out of bed and wandered over, still in a state of nakedness, to give Nathan a hug and a kiss, "Okay, matey, I'll see you when you get back."

Nathan left and the door closed behind him. There was a moment of perfect calm and quiet while Jake stood and felt sensations run up and down the inside of his thighs. He always got these feelings for a few hours when he had spent the night with Nathan. It was as if his body was remembering with pleasure the intimate contact it had just shared with a fellow human being. Jake at last found his own way into the shower and took his time over all the essential activities, ensuring that he'd cleaned his teeth so his breath didn't smell, and meticulously checking that every hair on his head was in exactly the right place. It was nearly 11 o'clock by the time he emerged into the world.

It was too late to be worrying about breakfast, so he decided to go and see how Matt was getting on with his art project. Jake decided to use the stairs rather than the lift and made his way down to the Art Gallery which was on the same floor as the cinema, theatre and 'Club Tropicana'. There was a little studio room that the gallery keeper, who was also the school art teacher, had allowed Matt to use to assemble his latest masterpiece. As Jake entered, he was most struck by Matt himself. He had always been an individual and meticulous dresser, but since starting at college and getting stuck into his art A-level, his fashion sense had exploded into something approaching the bizarre. Today he was wearing a bright pink shirt and yellow trainers, with trousers that looked as if they were made out of patchwork squares in clashing combinations of different colours. His hair was now shaved at the sides but on top was gelled to stand erect; this was dyed bright blue. He had also had his ears pierced. In one he had a stud which looked like a diamond, but bearing in mind his finances, was unlikely to have been, and in the other was a hollow ring; the result of a determined gauging process. Jake winced every time he saw this, but it seemed to cause Matt no pain.

"Hi, Matt, how's it going?" Jake said, announcing his arrival.

"Hi, darling, I'm just doing the finishing touches here and then hopefully someone with a car will help me take it into college next week."

The two of them embraced easily and Jake gave Matt a little peck on the cheek. Things had become much easier since it had become 'official' that he and Nathan were together. Jake had relaxed in his dealings with Matt, no longer concerned about giving signals that might give him the wrong idea. Maria was also in the room, but compared to Matt she looked positively camouflaged against the walls. Jake embraced and greeted her also.

"Well what do you think of it then?" Matt enquired eagerly.

"Yes do tell us what you think," Maria added mischievously, "Perhaps you can give us an insight about what it says to you. What is its deeper meaning?"

Jake groaned inwardly. He was not a fan of modern art and knew that whatever he said was likely to upset Matt. He could have cheerfully throttled Maria for having stirred things up at his expense. With caution he examined the large and impressive canvass. Just off-centre, tilted clockwise and attached firmly was a plain black toilet seat. Within the area enclosed by this were several cylindrical towers, projecting out from the canvass at eccentric angles and made from the inside cardboard tubes of toilet rolls stuck together. There was then a riot of white, pink and green toilet tissue arranged like a stormy tempest as if emanating from the bowl of the idealised toilet. Around the edge of the canvass, which had a gothic feel with a black background, were shadowy grey figures clearly in torment and pain. Finally, close to the corners but clearly designed to be asymmetric, were further towers jutting out towards the viewer, but this time made out of crushed pop and lager cans.

Jake took a gulp, "Well...It's very bold," he began, looking carefully at Matt to gauge if he was saying the right sort of thing. "It clearly has something to do with waste and sewage and causing pain to people."

Matt's beaming smile and Maria's look of disappointment caused him to overreach himself. He continued, "I'd call this the 'revenge of the dodgy curry'. Clearly these people have all had an excessive evening of drinking and debauchery and well... eating too much curry. The next day they spend all their time running back and forth to the loo and eventually they run out of toilet paper. That's why the figures round the edge are screaming so much. They are worried they are going to mess their pants. The moral is that they should all eat more healthily and drink less so we don't have to cut down lots of trees to make toilet paper."

The expressions on his two friends' faces had reversed instantly. He floundered on, "Good ethical use of materials I see. Cheap recycled toilet paper and a pretty bog standard toilet seat... Ouch!"

At this point the cardboard inner tube of a used toilet roll, thrown by Matt, hit Jake on the head.

"You are a Philistine, Jake Holdencroft." Matt said with haughty disdain and somehow his camp nature added to the degree of that disdain. "Any fool can see that it represents the cesspool of humanity and the way our materialistic society forces us all down the toilet pan in the end."

Maria laughed and said, "Come on boys let's not get into a silly argument that leads to a duel with handbags at dawn. It's very good, Matt, and you're an extremely talented artist. I'm sure it will impress your lecturers and get a good grade. Now why don't we go and find Jenny; by then it will be lunchtime."

So they went to see if Jenny was waiting for them in the social zone. As they were climbing the stairs, Jake continued to muse on Matt's art. Philistine or not, he could not help but be a little disappointed at the direction Matt's work seemed to be taking. He had excellent drawing skills and had dashed off a pencil sketch of Jake back in October. Jake had mounted the sketch in a photo frame and sent it to his mother as a Christmas present. Rose Holdencroft had raved about it and said that Maisie, Daisy and all the relatives had thought it an uncanny resemblance. They certainly would not be so impressed with his latest creation.

Jenny was waiting for them and all four made their way up the next flight of stairs to the dining area.

"What have you been up to this morning?" Maria asked Jenny when they had all settled down at a table by the window.

"I've been doing some work on that old banger I'm trying to get ready. I've got plans to learn to drive as soon as I'm 17, so I'll need something to get about in." Jenny replied enthusiastically.

"Is this old banger called 'Greased Lightning' by any chance, and do we get to do a big dance number clambering all over it?" Jake asked rather sarcastically.

"Listen, pal, no-one is going anywhere near it that's got dirty shoes or sticky fingers, so you'll have to be nice to me if you want a ride," Jenny retorted emphatically. "Where's Ashok by the way?"

"I think he's on kitchen duty today," Jake suggested. "I have to say, I haven't seen a great deal of him over Christmas. He left Rainbow House for a couple of days and he's been very mysterious about it since he's been back. We'll catch up with him at defence training this afternoon, Jenny."

Jake had finished his main course and decided he fancied a pudding. He took his plate and cutlery to the hatch, where he could just make out Ashok with his back to him in the kitchen peeling vegetables. In normal circumstances he would have called over and at least said 'hello'. Today he did not bother. One of the few things that had not gone well since Nathan's arrival at Rainbow House was that Ashok had not taken to him. When Maria had uncharacteristically and undiplomatically let slip that Jake had rather fancied Ashok in the past, Nathan began to reciprocate the animosity. Jake had tackled both of them about it but neither would give what he considered to be a convincing answer. Nathan would say that Ashok didn't seem committed to 'the cause' and was not therefore trustworthy. Ashok would say that Nathan seemed arrogant and was likely to put people at risk to satisfy his ego. In the end, Jake had given up trying to engineer situations where he could socialise with them both at the same time, and so Ashok was fading rapidly from his circle of close friends.

As it was still just the festive season, he decided to have a slice of mince tart and custard. He returned to join the others and looked out at the serene, steady flow of the Thames with the occasional river boat slowly moving one way or the other. It was grey and gloomy outside.

"What are you and Matt doing this afternoon while we are at training?" Jake asked Maria.

"Well, Matt is going to have a go at making me a dress. I'm hoping I can wear it for my birthday do. We're going to have a look at some fabrics and see where we go from there."

Jake refrained from making any comment, but thought Maria was putting an awful lot of trust in someone who seemed to think blue hair, pink shirt and multi-coloured trousers was a refined and restrained fashion statement.

After lunch, they went their separate ways. Jenny and Jake went back to their respective rooms and got what they called their judo kit. The training session began at 3pm in the sports zone near the bottom of Rainbow House. It was an essential part of the 'Guardian Training Programme' which Jake, Jenny, Nathan and Ashok had all eagerly signed up to in September when they became eligible to enrol. So far they had focused mainly on fitness and self-defence, but they had also done some first aid and tactical psychology. It was increasingly obvious to Jake that they were being trained to fight some kind of war and that everything they were doing was in deadly earnest. Jenny had mastered the various Japanese and Chinese martial arts techniques extremely well and was a match for students who were considerably older and more experienced. Jake was therefore not disappointed to be partnered with her for the afternoon's activities. As was usual, the teacher or sensei, took them through a couple of new moves which they practiced repeatedly. The remainder of the session was then devoted to rehearsing all the other moves they had already learned. The aim was that eventually they would simply become second nature. Nathan had rushed in at the last moment, but he was partnered with someone at the far end of the hall so there was no chance for Jake to talk to him.

The session lasted for an hour and a half and Jake's muscles were beginning to ache sufficiently for him to register that it had been a strenuous work-out. The sensei gathered them together in the middle of the hall to make an announcement:

"Students, because there are so many of you this year, we have had to split you into two groups to do your outdoors survival training. I will put lists on the notice board outside the changing room at the end of the session. It will be a full week's training away from London, so please make a note of the dates carefully. Now keep a calm mind and a balanced body and we will meet again on Tuesday evening."

With that, the students bowed to each other and the sensei and filed out calmly to get changed. The rush for the notice board was far less orderly. Jake and Nathan went together to look at the list.

"There I am in group one," Jake shouted excitedly. "That's going to be during the Easter holidays for me. There's Jenny's name, and Ashok's too, but..." his expression changed to one of disappointment, "You're in group two, Nathan."

At that moment, the teacher was passing and Jake pressed to intercept him, "Sensei, is it not possible for me and Nathan to be in the same group?"

The teacher smiled and said, "It was a deliberate decision to keep you apart. Everyone in Rainbow House knows you two are drunk on love for each other at present. You would never be able to concentrate on the training properly if you were together. That week is probably the most important for preparing you to be a true Guardian of the Rainbow, so you must have no distractions."

With that he moved away and Ashok suddenly appeared to look at the list, saying quite unnecessarily, "It'll do you good to get away from Nathan for a week. Maybe you'll be more like your old self again."

Nathan was incandescent with rage. "What the hell has it got to do with you?" he shouted at Ashok. "Keep your grubby little nose out of it."

Ashok looked as if he was preparing to square up for a fight. He responded threateningly, "Is Jake incapable of speaking for himself? Do you run his life completely now?"

"Shut up both of you," Jake interjected tersely, "if you are going to behave like Neanderthals, wait until I've gone before you start beating each other up." With that, he picked up his bag and flounced out of the room with as much dramatic gesture as he could muster. He was furious with both of them.

Nathan and Ashok remained eye-balling each other for a few seconds, seriously considering whether a scrap was a good option. Finally, they both thought better of it and simply walked off in opposite directions.

Chapter 4

It was later the same day and Jake was in his room finishing some chemistry homework before his first day back tomorrow. This was the other thing that had not gone as well as he'd hoped since Nathan had arrived. He had opted to do 'A'-level sciences and maths and was frankly finding it a lot harder than he had imagined. He had expected Nathan to do more or less the same and was looking forward to sharing lessons with him again, just as in those innocent days at The John Madin Academy when they were 'aspiring to excellence' side by side. Much to Jake's surprise, and indeed disappointment, Nathan opted instead to follow his dream and study music. To compliment this, he had also opted to study English, ICT and maths. The result was that they were never in the same lessons together.

Jake did most of his lessons at the local FE College where they had sat their GCSEs last summer. There were neither the numbers or facilities to run practical 'A'- level science courses at the school in Rainbow House. The status of the Rainbow House students was ambiguous. Jake was never quite sure how much the lecturers knew about their situation and so, like the others, he was always guarded in his comments relating to non-academic matters. The six of them who were doing chemistry also had a weekly session with Mr Devonshire, which Jake had found essential to keep on top of things. Even so, he was now struggling to calculate the volume of 2.0 mol dm^{-3} sodium hydroxide solution required to completely dissolve 150 cm^3 of chlorine gas at room temperature and pressure to make bleach.

There was a knock at the door. Jake shouted out, "If that's either Nathan or Ashok, go away. I'm still mad at both of you."

There was a pause and then someone tentatively tried the handle. Discovering it was not locked, the person slowly and gingerly opened the door a fraction. A head with a mop of floppy hair poked around the side.

"I said go away, Nathan." Jake restated firmly.

"Aw...Come on, don't be like that. I've come to apologise." Nathan said softly.

"I've got work to finish for tomorrow. Not all of us can play around on a cello all day and think it's a hard day's work, you know."

Nathan crept closer and wrapped his arms around Jake from behind, "I said I'm sorry, babe, but you've got to admit Ash was deliberately provocative and, okay, I shouldn't have risen to the bait."

Jake gave up any pretence of ignoring Nathan and now addressed him directly:

"Why can't you and Ashok just be civilised?"

"Me, civilised? I'm a Barbarian and a wild animal, don't you know."

Nathan was clearly not in a mood for being serious just yet. He embarked on what Jake described as a 'play fight'. In the past, Jake would have succumbed, but since he'd been doing his Guardian training, his levels of fitness and stamina had risen to match those of Nathan and Ashok. He ended up pinning Nathan down on the bed when the contest was deemed over.

"Well, aren't you all manly and masterful tonight," Nathan breathlessly opined. "Maybe I'll let you be king of the jungle later on."

"There's not going to be any funny business tonight. It's college tomorrow and I need a good night's sleep. You'll be going to your own room, matey. Now, why can you and Ashok not get on - and I want a proper answer."

"Well I've told you about a million times already. Ashok started it. I was quite prepared to be friendly. I get on with all your other friends okay, so let's be honest; I don't think I've done anything massively unreasonable. I admit that when I found out that you had a thing for him, I was a bit jealous and said a few things I shouldn't, but we weren't exactly best buddies by then anyway."

"But it's not just that. You keep saying he's untrustworthy. Why?"

"Look, I keep saying I have no evidence, and I wish you'd stop thinking that there has been some dramatic scene between me and Ashok that you don't know about, because there hasn't been. It's just a gut feeling. There's something bogus about the guy. Maria, Jenny and Matt, they are all what they seem to be, but he isn't. He's like that Martin guy – You know, the one who used to be Darryn's boyfriend and became a traitor. But look, for your sake and because I love you very much, I will keep quiet and won't make a fuss. I'll try and keep my temper and even force a smile."

"Well, that will have to do," sighed Jake who could scarcely comprehend the idea of Ashok being like Martin. "Now it is time for you to go. I've still got to try and do this chemistry question."

"You are cruel. Will you not let me stay and be your slave?" Nathan put on a mock sad expression.

"Go!" said Jake throwing a pillow at him, but also laughing under his breath.

***

Meanwhile, Darryn and Annabelle were sitting down to a late supper with Digby Forester and Janice in the kitchen of Digby's substantial country residence. Janice had been creative with the turkey leftovers and made a mild curry with some subtle flavours. They were discussing business:

"Our mister O'Grady didn't make it to Holyhead, or at least he didn't try to board a ferry to Ireland." Annabelle stated while the rice was being passed round.

"You said he'd gone up the Wrexham road, which means he could be anywhere in North Wales, Chester, Liverpool or North West England. I wonder what he is playing at," Darryn mused. "Is there any chance that he caught the ferry from Liverpool?"

"Our agents there have not picked him up, but it is more difficult to monitor comings and goings there." Annabelle responded.

"It's a shame you weren't able to get a picture of him, Darryn, I doubt very much whether Michael O'Grady is his real name, but I might have recognised him from the files that passed through my hands when I was at the Northern Ireland office." Digby suggested.

"He would have been a baby then." Darryn said teasingly,

"Don't be so rude, you young whippersnapper, it's not *that* long ago since I retired and even though I spent the bulk of my time at the Home Office there was always close liaison with NIO and MI6 over people who might pose a security risk. If he's who he claims to be, we will have picked him up on the radar."

Annabelle was keen to move the discussion on. She said, "We can't do anything about Michael O'Grady if we don't know where he is, so what are we going to do next?"

"It's clear to me that the F.U.P. in Telford intend to arm at least some of their Neighbourhood Protection Committees. I suggest we monitor their training regime and look for any unusual changes," Darryn said assertively. "Then, hopefully, we can find out who is doing the training and providing the hardware. We can then act, if necessary."

"Would you like some more rice and curry, dear?" Janice asked rather incongruously.

"I think so, Janice. That was delicious as always. Annabelle, have we got any teenagers on the 'at risk' list at the moment?"

"We've got one in Telford and two in Walsall, but none of them seem to be in imminent need of extraction."

"Good. We'll let a couple of the trainees keep an eye on them for a bit and you and I can give our full attention to the F.U.P. training methods,"

Suddenly a klaxon went off and bolts could be heard automatically sliding shut on all the doors, while exterior metal shutters closed on all the windows. The four of them sat motionless with their mouths open for just a second. Then Digby quickly rose to his feet and said, "The alarm has picked up an intruder close to the house. Quick, let's get to the control room. You come along too Janice. If the intruder wishes to do us harm, I want to have you close by."

They moved swiftly across the hall, passed the Tudor-style staircase and entered through an insignificant looking doorway that might have belonged to a broom cupboard. However, the room opened up into a technical buzz of activity, with TV screens, computers and banks of switches, dials and knobs. Digby flicked one of these and immediately the klaxon stopped. There followed an eerie silence in which all four of them strained to hear the sound of a pin drop.

"Has anything been picked up on the TV cameras?" Darryn asked.

"It's dark, so it's unlikely unless they've come up close to one of the doors," Digby replied. "Let's see what the infra-red cameras have to tell us."

Digby flicked another switch and the views on the TV screens changed to ones of ghostly black and white outlines.

"There!" exclaimed Darryn, pointing at a little white blob moving across the screen in a jerky up and down fashion. "Is that our intruder?"

"Probably not," Digby replied calmly. "It's too small and moving like a four-footed animal, not a human being. It's probably a fox."

Darryn was beginning to think a fox or a badger had been responsible for setting the alarm off, when all of a sudden the white spot darted off the screen and a bigger, stationary blob became apparent. "There he is. He must have startled the fox," Darryn whispered breathlessly. "Where exactly is he?"

"He seems to be stationed behind a yew tree about fifty feet south west of the front door," Digby replied.

"Right, I'm going out to investigate. Can you release one of the doors temporarily to let me out?" Darryn enquired.

"Yes, the kitchen door has a manual override. Once you're outside it will automatically lock behind you."

"Good, you three stay here and keep in radio contact with me." Darryn made to go but paused to give Annabelle a quizzical look, "Aren't you going to tell me to follow protocol and not be reckless?"

Annabelle sighed wearily and said, "What's the point. You never listen anyway. I guess you'll be expecting me to come and rescue you when it all goes wrong."

"That's my girl!" Darryn said cheerily and bounced out of the room. He quickly rushed upstairs to put on his black Guardian uniform shirt to match the black trousers and regulation black leather trainers he was already wearing. He put on a black balaclava so that only his twinkling eyes were now visible; he checked that his pistol was loaded and that he had spare ammunition in his pocket. As he made his way across the kitchen, he had a thought. He opened the fridge door and noticed a bowl with cold leftover gravy in it. He smeared some of this across the small portion of his face that was still visible to act as further camouflage, and then promptly left the house.

He moved quickly away from the door, which he heard locking behind him, but then he took a moment to become accustomed to the cold black surroundings, so different from the warm inviting house that he'd just left. He paced out about thirty metres from the house and then started to move in a circular fashion, keeping the house at the centre of the radius, so that he could approach his enemy from the rear.

Now that his eyes had adjusted, he could make out the yew tree in front of him but he still couldn't see if anyone was there next to it. He started to close in with pistol in hand:

21

"Annabelle, is he still by the yew tree?" Darryn whispered into his radio mike.

"Yes, he hasn't moved. You are closing in on him. If you can't see him yet he may be concealed or even in the tree. Don't lose the element of surprise."

Darryn halted to have a good look, scouring the undergrowth and the tree canopy as well as the more obvious ground level; then he saw him, crouched down in a little ball at the foot of the trunk, occasionally looking round to see if anything was going on in the house.

Darryn crept up on him noiselessly, mustering all the woodcraft his training had given him. He crouched to the man's level and then in a flash held the pistol against his head making sure that the sound of the gun cocking could be heard so there was no doubt that the next movement of Darryn's finger would result in someone's brains being splattered across the lawn.

"Get up very slowly, please, with your hands above your head," Darryn instructed in the sternest, most authoritative voice he could manage. The stranger did as he was ordered, rising slowly to his feet. He was dressed in almost identical garb to Darryn, so remained completely anonymous. Darryn matched his movements so the gun was always in contact with his enemy's head.

"Now..." said Darryn, but got no further. His adversary, at the point where he guessed correctly that Darryn would momentarily lose concentration, ducked and violently backed into him while simultaneously bringing an arm across to sweep his gun to one side. A shot rang out, but it ricocheted harmlessly against one of the metal window protectors. Before he could recover, Darryn received another crunching blow to the midriff and the gun was shaken from his hand.

The two of them now embarked on hand-to-hand combat. Darryn's adversary was a serious opponent who was able to parry the standard moves and put in some well-timed blows of his own.

"What the hell's going on?" Annabelle barked in his earpiece. "I told you not to lose the element of surprise. What was that shot?"

"Shut up!" Darryn responded tersely and breathlessly. "You're not exactly helping. Just stay put and I'll brief you when I can."

The more the evenly-matched fight went on, the more it seemed to Darryn like one of his standard training sessions at Rainbow House. It was almost as if his opponent was mocking him by going through the routine by the book. On schedule, his opponent swept his feet from under him and wrestled him to the ground. Darryn felt the full weight of his opponent on top of him. He had the strange sensation that the body was not totally unfamiliar; he recognised the curves and contours of the legs and arms. What was he up to now? His opponent seemed to be making a concerted effort to put his hand in his trouser pocket. Darryn was struggling to know what to do next. He obviously had to do something unexpected. He suddenly went limp as if he had passed out. His opponent was so surprised at this that he let go his grip. Darryn took the opportunity to suddenly reanimate and throw his opponent off. He then went aggressively at the stranger and got him in a head-lock, but he did not have the advantage for long. He was thrown over the shoulder of his opponent and, despite the grass being soft and forgiving, was quite winded.

Then all of a sudden, just as Darryn was at his most vulnerable the assault stopped. His assailant licked a finger and muttered, "Mm... Janice's gravy is not what it used to be," then rushed off across the lawn heading for the long drive that connected the house with the road. It took Darryn a few seconds to get his breath back and work out what was going on before he set off in pursuit. He was a good fifty yards behind and was not hopeful of catching him. The gates were closed at the end of the drive, but then he noticed there was a hole in the hedge several feet to the left. The stranger made for this, and with great alacrity passed through. By the time Darryn had forced his way through the same hole, he could hear a car starting up. Across the way an anonymous-looking Ford Fiesta was just moving off, its number plates deliberately covered over. Darryn stared helplessly as the car sped off up the road.

Chapter 5

Digby, Annabelle, Darryn and Janice were once more seated around the kitchen table and the security measures had been relaxed. On the table lay a crumpled letter with Darryn's name on the envelope. On his way back up to the house he had instinctively put his hand in his pocket and discovered the letter which could only have been put there by his assailant. It had taken him a further twenty minutes of searching in the dark to find his gun, but now they were ready to look at the contents of this letter. Darryn opened it as if he was nervously opening his 'A'- level results. It said:

'Darryn,
>   Your secret is safe – but I'm not.
>   Beware! The last tree can fall.'

"Bloody Martin, again!" exploded Darryn. "Why does he have to turn everything into a second-rate detective novel with his pathetic little puzzles?"

"Well if it's so pathetic what does it mean?" Annabelle enquired trying not to be too abrasive. She realised she'd given Darryn an unnecessarily hard time over the last hour or so. "I think he's been quite clever. No-one would think twice about this note if they found it lying around."

"But why deliver it here, and why all the cloak and dagger nonsense?" asked Darryn.

"I don't know," admitted Annabelle. "Maybe he just wanted to make us realise how vulnerable we were, or maybe he just wanted another tumble with you for old time's sake."

"Well we'd better contact Rainbow House with the details," Digby interjected, "and then we can consider what it all means over a game of billiards, maybe. Are you going to join us Annabelle?"

"No, you're alright. I'll give Janice a hand tidying away here. You boys go and play with your balls - After all it's where you seem to keep your brains most of the time."

Digby Forester winced visibly and said, "You've become a good deal less refined since you've been on active service, Annabelle."

Janice laughed and retorted, "For goodness sake, Digby, don't be such a prude and a hypocrite. You and your golfing friends are much coarser when you've had a few to drink – I do hear you, you know."

Flustered, Digby shuffled off in the direction of the control room muttering that he must get in touch with HQ now.

Later on, while Darryn was comprehensively beating Digby at billiards, they both had to admit they could make very little of the message. Maybe the 'one tree' referred to Rainbow House and maybe Martin was working for the F.U.P. again, particularly if he did not now feel safe. There seemed to be nothing, however, in this simple message to justify the events of the evening.

***

February arrived after a dull, grey tedious January. Jake's 17th birthday again fell during the half term week. He recalled his adventure in Paris the previous year with Darryn, Annabelle and Jenny and the abrupt way it had all come to an end. This year he was planning a more sedate affair; a meal with Nathan in a reasonably upmarket restaurant in Soho followed by a concert at the Royal Festival Hall. Jake still had a phobia of parties so he was pleased that Nathan had not only acquiesced to his plans but seemed positively enthusiastic.

When Nathan called on Jake to pick him up, he'd made an effort with his clothes and looked really smart. When Jake saw him he thought he looked older and more mature and thought none the worse of him for that.

"Happy Birthday, babe," he said, presenting him with a single red rose and swooping in to give him a prolonged kiss.

"Cheers, matey." Jake responded. He assumed Maria had been giving Nathan some lessons in how to be romantic, but was nevertheless touched that Nathan should want to go to all that trouble. He was glad now that he had decided to dress up smartly to match Nathan's demeanour.

"Oh yes... Here's your present. Sorry it's not more exciting, but I'm a bit strapped for cash at the moment."

Jake tore off the wrapping paper and saw that it was the music for Debussy's violin sonata. Nathan had worked on his cello sonata with his pianist friend, Sarah, from college. Jake had gone to the recital given by the students after their assessments were complete and had been bowled over by the beauty and sad gravity of the first movement. Nathan had explained later that Debussy had intended to write six sonatas but had died after completing only three. The last one was for violin and piano which led to Jake's interest in finding out more.

"That will do just nicely. Thanks Nathan."

The restaurant was just off Old Compton Street, so despite the times, they still felt themselves to be in a reasonably gay-friendly environment. They were seated in the window at a table for two, so could see the world go by as well as enjoy their own company.

"So another year and you will be a man without question." Nathan said while sipping a glass of red wine.

"It'll be less than that for you. But do you think you should be broadcasting our ages to all and sundry when you bought a bottle of wine illegally?"

"Whoops, point taken. It's your eighteenth if anyone asks."

"I wonder if we'll still be together in five years time." Jake pondered rather wistfully.

"I don't see why not, unless you irritate me so much that I murder you in a fit of passion." Nathan replied cheerfully.

Nathan had originally suggested paying for the meal as part of Jake's present, but Jake had wanted to pay because it was an alternative to having a party. In the end they agreed to split the restaurant bill, but Nathan had insisted on buying the concert tickets.

The concert was one Jake had been looking forward to immensely; he particularly wanted to hear Vaughan Williams 5th Symphony played live as he'd only heard a recording of the work previously. He was not disappointed. As he sat there holding hands with Nathan in the third movement 'Romanza', Jake thought he was listening to the most beautiful thing he had ever heard. He knew that if he hadn't been as happy as he was, he would have been sobbing huge pools of tears by the end.

When they came out into the dark night, it was mild and windy, but the clouds were scurrying so quickly across the sky, there was very little danger of rain. The lights were twinkling enticingly and reflecting with dappled harmonic motion in the water.

"Let's walk back along the river," Jake suggested. "We can go as far as Westminster Bridge and then go and catch the Tube from Waterloo Station."

"Okay, that sounds a good plan," Nathan agreed.

As they ambled along, Nathan put his arm around Jake and they talked about which pieces they'd liked the best, about the competence of the conductor, and which members of the orchestra they had fancied.

Although Jake was no longer studying music as a subject, he was continuing to have violin lessons with Mr Simmonds. In fact, he was preparing to take grade 8 in the summer and was already conscientiously practising lots of very hard scales and arpeggios. Mr Devonshire had found a very good local amateur orchestra which had been happy to take on both Jake and Nathan. Nathan had soon found himself on the second desk of the cellos, but Jake was happy enough to sit at the back of the second violins.

As they emerged from underneath the Hungerford Rail Bridge and made their way towards Jubilee Gardens, a few more people were about. The London Eye was just disgorging its passengers from its final rotation of the day.

"Get your hands off him, you queer faggot!" An unpleasant, withered old man in a cloth cap shouted at them as he was passing in the opposite direction.

"And a Merry Christmas to you too!" replied Nathan, making a gesture with his finger which was far from polite.

"Is that what you do with your *boyfriend*?" the man sneered as he receded into the distance.

"Yeah, it's good fun. You should try it some time!" Nathan shouted back at him.

"Yuk! We could have done without that bit of nastiness." Jake said to Nathan when they'd moved on a couple of paces.

"If we were a straight couple, everyone would go all gooey-eyed watching us hold hands – even the withered old toad that's just shouted at us," Nathan responded, bristling. "I don't see why us gay boys shouldn't have the same rights to show modest affection to each other in public."

"Even so," Jake continued cautiously, "There are a few more people about now. Maybe we ought to be a bit more discreet."

Nathan removed his arm from Jake's shoulder and said in a voice that was meant to be mocking, "I shall be very proper and respectable." He extended his arm and took Jake's hand, shaking it vigorously. "I am delighted to make your acquaintance Mr Holdencroft; I hope to be more familiar with your manners and foibles in due course."

Jake gave Nathan a playful little slap on the cheek. Nathan responded by laughing and running off. Jake followed in hot pursuit. They ran past the London Eye and on past County Hall. As they were coming up to the steps that would take them onto Westminster Bridge, Nathan halted breathlessly and went to lean against the concrete balustrade protecting people from falling into the river. Jake caught up with him a few seconds later. Nathan turned to face Jake who moved closer and pressed his body firmly against that of his boyfriend. He couldn't help himself; Jake went in for an all-tongues-blazing kiss that lasted for goodness knows how long. Several people, fitting a variety of descriptions, passed by while this was going on; they all looked the other way and pretended not to notice. That is, all except one middle-aged woman with glasses who had a good look and went on her way with a smile. When he re-emerged, there was a tear in Jake's eye:

"I love you *so* much!" he said in a quavering voice.

"And I love you too," Nathan replied much more firmly and cheerfully, "But come on, don't get maudlin. I'm supposed to make you happy, not sad. Now, I'll race you to the station and the last one there has to brew the coffee when we get back to Rainbow House."

So the two boys ran off up the steps and on down the road to the station. Their shouts and laughter echoed around the tall buildings and eventually evaporated into the river, murmuring its way to the sea in a slow inevitable progress, forever unchanged and unchanging.

Chapter 6

There is usually one day in February that harbingers spring; a mild, sunny day the like of which has not been seen since the end of October, when you can literally sense the sap rising. On such a day it is almost impossible not to be optimistic. Darryn was certainly not going to buck the trend and he was humming tunelessly to himself as he walked along Parks Road, past Wadham College, on his way to the Clarendon Laboratory. He had temporarily left Annabelle monitoring the Telford F.U.P. training regime to return to Oxford. He was however, still engaged on Rainbow Alliance business, even though he had taken the opportunity to catch up on some paperwork and fit in a tutorial with one of his students.

Darryn entered the stern, angular building that reeked of institutionalism. He climbed two flights of stairs and then went to find the laboratory of a Dr Palmer. It was not difficult to locate and he tapped sharply at the door.

"Come in." A voice beckoned from within. "Ah... You must be Dr Harcourt-Smith. How is the maths department doing these days?"

"We're all getting on splendidly together – but you do realise I'm here in a different capacity? I've come to assess progress on the shield development programme. I'm working for the group that is putting up the money."

"And we are very grateful for that," Dr Palmer said hastily. "It has allowed us to carry on with some other research as well. Come, I'll give you a demonstration. That's probably the best way of showing the progress we've made."

He led the way into a rather larger room. A good deal of technical equipment was scattered about and thick wires of all colours lay tangled like living spaghetti that had just died. At the far end on a table lay several sheets of flexible, thick transparent plastic.

"It has been quite a collaboration to make this," Dr Palmer continued. "We needed the help of the chemical engineering department across the road to manufacture it and some organic chemists to come up with a way of making the monomer molecules. Now, if I hang this piece here, we'll go back twenty paces and perhaps you would like to do the honours by firing this air pistol at it. Have you fired a gun before?"

Darryn nodded, not wishing to elaborate on his vast experience, and fired the pistol. They then went to examine the plastic. As expected, there was a neat little hole where the pellet had easily penetrated.

"Nothing to write home about there!" observed Darryn.

"Indeed not, but watch what happens when I subject the material to a high voltage." Dr Palmer continued his demonstration by clipping two wires to opposite ends of a second sheet. He then turned a dial on a box to his left and

28

as if by magic, the flexible sheet became hard and solid. Dr Palmer turned off the high voltage supply and hung this second sheet up.

"Would you like to fire again?" Dr Palmer enquired.

Darryn aimed and fired. There was a distinctly different sound, almost like a bell being rung. On inspection, it was impossible to tell where the material had been hit; there was not a scratch on it.

"Impressive!" admitted Darryn. "Can I try something a bit more demanding?"

He got out his Guardian service-issue revolver. Dr Palmer looked highly suspicious and not a little anxious. He said, "You do have permission to use that, I hope."

" Of course!" Darryn reassured him.

Darryn aimed and shot with the much more powerful revolver. Again there was the ringing sound and again there was not a scratch left on the material.

"Now that is *very* impressive! What force do you think it can withstand?"

"Well..." Dr Palmer took a moment to speculate. "It should easily be able to deal with a tank shell and also a bomb dropped or fired from a plane. It would not stand up to a nuclear explosion and would probably crack if subjected to multiple ground-to-ground cruise missile strikes."

"Very good," Darryn said cheerfully. "How do you make the material go flexible again?"

"Ah... now that is the problem we've only managed to solve in the past few weeks." Dr Palmer's eyes lit up with excitement as he felt the moment to launch into a full explanation had arrived. "The flexible plastic is no different in many respects to polythene. There are crystalline and amorphous regions. The more crystalline areas there are the harder and denser the material is. The difference is that *this* polymer molecule has positively charged groups down one side and negatively charged groups down the other. When the molecules are subjected to a strong electric field, they rotate to line up all in the same direction."

"You create a super-crystalline structure!" interjected Darryn.

"Exactly!" Dr Palmer continued, pleased that Darryn was following his discourse. "Not only do you get a super-hard and super-dense material, but the strong forces between the molecules make the material extremely hard to penetrate.

"So I guess the problem is that simply reversing the polarity of the electric field is not good enough to pull the molecules apart again," Darryn surmised.

"Yes, you've got the problem of making the material flexible again in a nutshell; the process is not reversible. For many months we thought this was going to be an insuperable problem, but by a stroke of good fortune we discovered that if you subject the material to a slow alternating electrical field for about twenty seconds, it seems to wiggle the molecules free enough that a strong reverse polarity can then finish the job. Look, I'll demonstrate."

Dr Palmer connected the solid sheet of glass-like material back up to the power supply, flicked a switch and turned a couple of dials. The sheet quivered rapidly for a while and then suddenly flopped and became flexible.

"That's excellent," Darryn said delightedly. "How long do you think it would take to get this into mass production?"

"A span of four or five years is normal."

"We haven't got that time – a year at most is all we have." Darryn moaned almost despairingly.

"Well we've done our bit. The chaps over in chemical engineering will assist in scaling up the laboratory equipment, but it's down to your backers to create a plant that will manufacture it."

Darryn had plenty to chew over as he bade farewell to Dr Palmer and made his way down the corridor. His phone rang; it was Annabelle. He stopped in his tracks to concentrate on the call.

"Hi, Annabelle, how are you?"

"Listen Darryn, there is definitely something odd going on here. Twelve of the NPC wardens were held back after their regular training session last night and they spent an extra forty-five minutes inside the hut. Guess who emerged with them at the end? It was none other than Gerald Tasker himself!"

"Mm... Maybe these are to be the first to get arms training. Twelve good men and true – How prosaic, don't you think?"

"It did look like twelve of the more intelligent ones, although I know that's not saying much." Annabelle grudgingly added.

"Well done. It looks as if you're on to something. I'll be back in a couple of days. Keep monitoring and keep me posted."

Darryn cut the call and was about to move on when he noticed and open door to his right. What really caught his attention was an animated conversation going on between two white-coated scientists.

"...but is it moral?" he heard one of them say.

"Blow morality! If we don't get this funding we're all going to be out of a job," the second one replied.

"But if we get this thing to work, nobody will ever have any privacy again."

Unfortunately, he was spotted by the scientist who was having a crisis of conscience. "Can I help you?" he said officiously in Darryn's direction. "This is a restricted area, you know."

"You're okay" Darryn replied emolliently, "I was seeing Dr Palmer at the end of the corridor and was just on my way out."

The laboratory door was shut in Darryn's face as if to make a point. He read the label on the door. Department of Quantum Optoelectronics, it said. This was definitely something to file away for future investigation. Darryn made a third attempt to leave the building but was hijacked by a strange looking man in a grey overall with wild white hair and bent over, as if suffering from a permanently twisted spine. This man grabbed Darryn by the sleeve and tugged him towards another room at the end of the corridor.

"I have been expecting you, Dr Harcourt-Smith." He said in a gravelly, cracked voice. "Come with me please!"

"Oh dear, do I have to?" Darryn said with a good deal of feeling.

"Yes you do, especially if you want to find out something of interest," the strange man insisted.

Darryn followed him into the room which was dark except for the eerie glow of a functioning cloud chamber. White illuminated streaks appeared and disappeared as random background radiation came and went.

"I can foretell the future using this cloud chamber." The man said confidently.

Darryn almost collapsed in disbelief as he suddenly realised who this strange man probably was.

James Grimwold was one of the most precocious talents of his generation. He easily obtained a double first in physics and maths and his PhD thesis on the forces holding the nucleus of an atom together was so brilliant that the authorities seriously considered awarding him a professorship on the spot. For a time his career continued to sparkle. He was the only person in the world to understand some of the strange mathematics that governed the world of leptons, quarks, bosons and other strange subatomic particles. This, however, was the root of the trouble. He would spend days and days locked away in sunless rooms, struggling with incredibly knotty mathematical equations, finding weirder and wilder behaviours for his subatomic particles, that in the end he lost his grip on the reality experienced by ordinary people and became quite mad. People first became concerned when he suggested that he didn't need to use the door because his particles were quite capable of quantum tunnelling through the wall. He finally had to spend some time in hospital after he insisted that he was in two places simultaneously. Out of a sense of duty, pity and guilt, the physics department had kept him on as laboratory assistant rather than see him become destitute.

Darryn decided the safest thing to do was to play along for the moment, "I'm surprised that an eminent scientist, such as you, would have anything to do with fortune telling."

"It's blindingly obvious," said James Grimwold, clearly roused. "As scientists, we believe in cause and effect. The force of gravity causes the effect of an apple to fall to the ground. Clearly everything that has happened has been caused by something that happened earlier. Hence if we could only understand it, we could predict everything that has happened or is going to happen by simply studying the way particles and energy came into being at the beginning of the Universe. This conversation we're having is the direct result of the Big Bang. Everything is predestined."

"Okay," said Darryn warily, "So how does this cloud chamber fit in with all of this?"

"Yes, yes," Grimwold shouted excitedly almost clapping his hands, "I have found out that the more random or uncertain the cause, the more certain is the effect. It's sort of like Heisenberg's Uncertainty Principle, but with cause and effect instead of position and speed." His eyes lit up manically, "Grimwold's Uncertainty Principle – I shall get that Nobel Prize after all."

"But the cloud chamber?" whispered Darryn, trying to bring his companion back to the point.

"Well isn't it clear, young man? You really are very stupid, you know. The traces in the cloud chamber are caused by background radiation, which is one of the most random effects you can have. I've learned to interpret the trails to be almost certain of the events that will happen as a result. Now, I've never seen that before."

Grimwold peered closer at the chamber. Darryn thought he was looking at a streak which seemed to have no middle. Grimwold interpreted:

"That means you will be in the world, but not part of the visible Universe. There's another. You won't be alone then, but maybe you will be one of the first."

This made no sense at all to Darryn, so he decided to have a punt on Martin's riddle, "What do you make of this? *Beware! The last tree can fall.*'"

"The only way the last tree can survive is by shedding its fruit far and wide and hoping some of it will grow, there is no hope for the tree itself. It will die as all things do." Grimwold was beginning to sound like an Old Testament prophet. But then he had a moment of shocking lucidity which took Darryn's breath away. "I know, of course, all about your headquarters in Canary Wharf. If that is the 'one tree' you're eluding too, you don't stand a chance. You will be up against the might of the British Government. It's what happens afterwards that's interesting. All hope may not be lost there, but the pattern is too fragmented and complex for me to be certain. Now let me try and read your personal future. Which radioactive isotope will match your eyes, I wonder?"

He seemed to have crossed the border into another world again as he sorted in the dark through a vast set of plastic rods, each tipped with a different radioactive isotope and capable of being inserted into the cloud chamber.

"Ah yes...Americium-241 is the one, I think." Grimwold slotted the rod into the cloud chamber and immediately fan like projections came and went from around its tip. He groaned as if taken aback, "That is not good. I can see a great deal of pain and suffering there. I think you will survive and come through it though. Betrayal is your greatest fear - and with good reason!"

Despite himself, Darryn was now thoroughly caught up in the atmosphere. His mouth was open and his eyes stared in wonderment at the hypnotic white streaks and patterns that danced in front of his eyes in the darkness. However, the magic was completely obliterated a few seconds later by a shout in the corridor.

"Where the hell is the cloud chamber? I need it in twenty minutes time for a lecture. If that fool Grimwold has squirreled it away somewhere I'll have his guts for garters."

The effect on Grimwold was dramatic. He recoiled like a dog that has suffered a history of beating. "Eek... Nasty master will be cross with me," he whimpered in a terrified voice. He removed the radioactive source and desperately tried to arrange it neatly with the others. Darryn had not liked the voice in the corridor and he did not like the effect it seemed to be having on James Grimwold. He decided to intervene. He decisively opened the door and moved into the corridor to confront the owner of the voice, a brusque and portly man with a moustache and heavily receding hair, unfashionably slicked flat with Brylcreem.

"I do apologise," Darryn began, trying to sound as official and knowledgeable as possible, "I chanced on Professor James Grimwold and had to take the opportunity to talk to him about his theories of nuclear binding. He was kind enough to offer me a demonstration and I'm afraid it is my fault that he was detained."

"I am Professor Jenner," the moustached man in the corridor said, clearly incensed by Darryn's reference to Grimwold as a professor. "Who the hell are you and do you have permission to go wandering around some of the most sensitive areas of the building?"

"I'm Doctor Harcourt-Smith." Darryn made sure he emphasised the word 'doctor'. "And yes – I do have permission to be here. I'm just on my way out now, as it happens."

Grimwold emerged, wheeling the cloud chamber on a trolley. "I'll just take this to the lecture room and set it up for you, master," he said in grovelling obeisance.

"Good, you better come with us too Dr Harcourt-Smith and I'll show you out."

Darryn nodded and followed, disliking Professor Jenner more and more as each minute passed. They pushed against a set of handle-less doors and found themselves by the demonstration bench of a large lecture theatre with tiered seating heading to the back of the room. On the blackboard behind, inscribed in chalk, was a set of impressive equations, pre-written to avoid wasting time in the lecture.

"Your equations are wrong," Darryn said trying to disguise the triumph he felt at the discovery. "It should be two thirds theta squared on the second line, not theta cubed over three."

Professor Jenner went bright red and was clearly about to explode at Darryn's impertinence. "How dare you! Who do you think you are coming here and cheekily challenging my teaching notes? I checked them through very carefully before writing them down. Oh..." His tirade suddenly came to an end as he realised that Darryn was absolutely right.

"I lecture at the Mathematical Institute," Darryn replied coolly. "I'll see myself out, thank you. Good day."

As he left, he heard a gurgling sound which could only have been James Grimwold chuckling quietly to himself.

Chapter 7

Darryn ordered a coffee and a pasty from one of the small cafes that had sprung up along Broad Street. It was one o'clock and time for lunch, besides which he needed to stop and mentally digest the extraordinary encounters of the morning. The day had continued its early promise and was warm enough to allow Darryn to sit outside; it looked as if this first spring day was going to last until dusk. A very well-dressed woman in her late forties or early fifties emerged from Balliol College and crossed the road towards him. The woman continued to approach until it was obvious that he was her intended destination. Then, at last, Darryn recognised her. He got up and pulled the chair out next to him and settled the woman in this seat.

"N° 2, this is an unexpected pleasure. I didn't realise you were in Oxford," he said politely.

"Very much a business trip, I'm afraid Darryn, and a rather depressing one at that." N° 2 looked every bit the chief executive of some powerful corporation. "I'm sure you will be discrete if I tell you I've been involved in some top-level Treasury discussions this morning. It looks as if the UK credit rating is going to be downgraded to junk status in the next day or two. This will be so humiliating that it will immediately worsen our debt crisis and lead to further swingeing cuts in government spending. The cabinet will be in disarray. The chancellor is already a defeated man. His officials are making all the policy now while he just says nothing; he is totally out of his depth. What's more, there's another by-election coming up. If the F.U.P. wins that one, then the Government majority will be down to two. A general election before the end of the year is very likely and circumstances are going to favour a breakthrough for Lord Bernard of Agincourt and his bunch of lunatics and psychopaths."

"You don't think they would win?" said Darryn in astonishment.

"I don't think they could manage that, but with the state of public disillusionment for the main-stream parties and the lack of any ideas about how to get us out of this economic mess, they could quite easily have a block which would hold the balance of power. Anyway, enough of these dismal thoughts, I really came over to see how you got on with Dr Palmer."

"Well, the shield works. We've now got to somehow set up a manufacturing plant in record time. Have you ever come across a James Griswold?"

"I can't say the name rings a bell," N° 2 replied after a moment's thought. "We can check him out at Rainbow House."

"He knows about our HQ. I'm hoping that he's been there, because the alternative is just too weird to contemplate. Thank goodness he's completely barking mad, so at least no-one will pay any attention to him."

The sun continued to shine down on them oblivious of the doom-laden news they were discussing. Bicycles rushed hither and thither as they had done for generations, and students rushed by either as serious, pasty-faced individuals or in earnest groups discussing some matter that was clearly of the utmost importance. The broad thoroughfare bounded by ancient colleges on either side, with Blackwell's Bookshop and the gawping stone heads outside the Sheldonian Theatre at the far end, was a scene that had remained unchanged for over a hundred years. Only fashions in clothes and transport would have changed. N° 2 and Darryn eventually parted, she to go back to Balliol and he to make the short journey on foot to Christ Church.

***

The day had finally arrived when Jake was to go off to Wales to do his Guardian outdoors survival training. He was not good at getting things ready. Maria and Anne, the student overseer and frequent surrogate mother, nagged him endlessly to prepare. However, he still found himself in a blind panic throwing things into his rucksack minutes before he was due to leave. They had been told to wear their outdoor kit to save space in their bags. Just as he was about to quit his apartment, he stopped to look at himself in a full-length mirror. His black shirt with rainbow epaulettes fitted snugly into his action trousers and his chunky leather walking boots made him look very rugged. If only he could convincingly grow a bit of stubble, he would look really hot.

"Come along, Jake!" Jenny called from the corridor, destroying his daydream.

They made their way down to the basement car park where the others were waiting. Ashok was there but rather awkwardly kept his distance from Jake. Another seven students, all dressed in exactly the same way, were set to depart in a minibus that was parked in a bay with the doors opened ready to receive its occupants. The tedious job of loading the luggage had already begun. From around the back of the minibus a handsome young man in his early twenties with short cropped ginger hair appeared.

"Hello, Jake," he said, "I was beginning to wonder whether I'd have to leave without you."

"Don't exaggerate, David," Jake replied. "Are you driving us and is Danny coming too?"

"Yes I am doing the driving, but no, Danny's not coming. Your mate Darryn has given him some new puzzles to solve, so he will be spending the next week or so in the operations room trying to find a solution."

Finally, all the rucksacks and camping equipment they needed to take with them were stowed and the ten would-be Guardians took their seats. Jenny and Jake persuaded David to let them sit in the front.

The procedure for leaving the basement was routine for Jake now. David drove up to what appeared to be a blank wall with a set of traffic lights by the side. He waited patiently until they turned green; then silently the wall slid back revealing an apparently identical car park on the other side. David drove through and the wall slid back behind him. They were now in the car park used by all the office workers and managers who worked in the interleaving segments of Rainbow House, totally unaware of the true nature of the building they spent their working lives in. David drove the minibus up the ramp and into the drizzle of an unimpressive early April morning. It was slow going through central London as one might expect, but after an hour they found themselves moving along the Edgware Road on the approach to the M1. Once on the motorway, David was able to put his foot down so that the minibus cruised along with the heavy Lorries on the inside lane at a steady 60 mph. The suburban monotony of identikit houses gradually gave way to some green spaces and when they passed through the belt of the M25 there were even some real fields with real cows and sheep.

"What are you up to these days?" Jenny asked David.

"I'm leading up the patrols in the East End of London. It's obviously one of the bigger operations, so I've got twenty people under my command. Funnily enough, the F.U.P is only making progress in small pockets there; they don't seem to have developed a strategy for taking over as they've done in other parts of the country."

"Have you had to rescue many people lately?" Jake asked.

"Well again, there doesn't seem to be quite such a problem there. London is still quite a melting pot of cultures and tends to be more liberal than the rest of the country. There are a few who still need our help, though."

"Have you had any news from Darryn lately?" Jake continued with his interrogation. "I don't think I've seen him since Christmas and his texts and e-mails have been very brief."

"Well he's been back roaming the West Midlands - and also doing some academic work in Oxford. It's a good job he does maths. I can't see he'd get away with spending most of his time being a Guardian if he had to write lots of essays and books, or spend days doing experiments in a lab."

"I'm sure it's a bit more complicated than doing a few sums," Jake said, feeling obliged to defend his rescuer and good friend. "I do wish he had a bit more time to help me with my homework though," he added wistfully.

"You heard about the fight he had with someone in Digby Forester's garden?" David continued. "It's all very strange. It seems that all the palaver was about sticking a letter in Darryn's pocket. It would have been easier to post the wretched thing."

"I gather Darryn is convinced that it was Martin," Jenny chipped in.

"Yes, he didn't get a good look, but he reckons it was. Anyway, that's why my Danny is so busy in Ops. Darryn reckons it was one of Martin's silly little codes, but what it means is anybody's guess. When we met a few weeks ago, Darryn told me about some nutty professor he'd met in Oxford who reckoned the message foretold the downfall of Rainbow House. Apparently, this guy seemed to know an awful lot about the place. Danny's got to check him out as well."

"I wouldn't have put Darryn down as someone who believed in fortune telling," Jenny said with some surprise.

"No, neither would I," agreed David, "But doing maths problems in the City of Dreaming Spires all day probably gives you a strange outlook on life. Now, we're coming up to the Watford Gap Services. Does anyone want a toilet break?"

Ten people very eagerly made it clear that they needed one. David pulled off the motorway and parked up in the spaces allocated for caravans and larger vehicles. He gave his passengers strict instructions not to be longer than twenty-five minutes and not to leave any money on the bus; he then wandered off to buy himself a coffee.

Ten minutes later, Jake awkwardly found himself emerging from the men's toilets side by side with Ashok. He couldn't really just ignore him, but on the other hand it would look extremely odd if he tried to start up a casual conversation as he used to do when they were still best friends. Fortunately, it was Ashok who decided to break the ice:

"Look, I know we've not been getting on well lately but it's going to be a very difficult week if we're not speaking to each other."

"Well there's only one topic that's causing friction between us," Jake responded, "And that's Nathan. If you stop doing him down, we can get on well enough."

"Okay, I promise not to mention his name." Ashok acquiesced.

There was an almost audible relaxation of the tension. The two boys wandered around the newsagents together picking up sweets and a magazine to pass the time away on the rest of the journey. Jake asked how Ashok's A-levels were going (he was doing languages) and Ashok reciprocated.

The journey began again with Jenny and Jake maintaining their position in the front next to David. It was still grey and misty, although there was the promise of the drizzle stopping and it becoming brighter later on. David took the M6 junction, continuing the journey until grinding to a halt just outside Birmingham. It took them forty five minutes to crawl their way through the elevated section and on past Wolverhampton. When they turned off on to the M54, Jake began to feel some strange sensations. Everything was now very familiar as he approached the town where he had been born and raised. Everything looked normal and untroubled as it always had done when his parents used to go on shopping expeditions to Birmingham. You do not see a lot of Telford from the motorway; a few oblong sheds used as factories or warehouses, and the Retail Park on the hill to your left are all that catch the eye of the passing motorist. What was going on in the area where he had lived? What had happened to his school and teachers? What had happened to David Peters? How much did the F.U.P. really control the lives of the people who lived here?

Even before he'd had time to think about this, the far more impressive landmark of The Wrekin loomed up on his left, its summit shrouded in light mist. The sleeping form of a giant, or his discarded load, depending on which legend you preferred, Jake recalled some happy times that he and his family had spent walking up to the top of this hill and admiring the views to The Malverns, to The Wirral and to Mid Wales. He also recalled that some of the boys in his class would go up there on summer evenings with cans of lager and bottles of cider to drink to excess without being disturbed by disapproving adults. Jake had only done this once, but it now struck him more clearly how everyone had become much chummier and how everyone had seemed more vulnerable and sad. There was a lot of drunken hugging and people telling each other that they were the best mate in the world. Jake muttered to himself as he was remembering this incident, "What's the difference between a straight lad and a bisexual? About four pints of lager, I should think."

"What's that you're saying" David said looking in Jake's direction.

"Oh nothing, I was just reminiscing."

"Oh yes, this is your neck of the woods, isn't it. It must seem strange coming back in these circumstances."

David drove on up the A5, past Shrewsbury and on towards Oswestry, but before he got there, he turned off into a village and stopped at the local pub.

"It is lunchtime folks," Darryn announced. They all eagerly left the minibus and filed into a room that was kept separate as a dining area at the back of the building.

David greeted a homely, well-built woman in her sixties. Some might have described her as buxom, but whatever, she was a cheerful soul with a caring and motherly attitude. She wore a checked dress and a white apron.

"Hello Bessie, I've bought another hungry load of gannets to be fed," David said.

Bessie laughed and replied, "I'm used to that, my dear. I see you've got ten with you this time; the numbers are going up all the time. I've been making one of my soups and some crusty bread this morning, then there is flan or cold meats and salad to follow and if they're still hungry, there's some apple pie and ice cream."

"I'm so pleased we have to stop in here on our way up to Wales," David beamed.

"Get away with you," Bessie said modestly going red. "How's Danny? Are you two still together?"

"Yes we're still solid. How's your husband George?"

"Yes he's well, dear. The pub's ticking over, but of course with all the extra trade we're getting from you, we're financially well set up. The F.U.P. is getting a foothold round here, though. Their message goes down well with the locals. They've never liked strangers and foreigners in these parts and they hate ramblers tramping over their fields. They don't seem to realise we don't actually make anything here anymore, and we can't all go back to working on the land. That dreadful Tasker man was poking his nose round here the other day."

When they had finished, it was quite late in the afternoon. David hugged Bessie and she told him to take care. They boarded the minibus and set off to rejoin the A5. Onward they went, though Chirk, Llangollen and Corwen. They turned left, taking the Bala road, before Jake became totally disoriented as they left the main road and slowly progressed through ever smaller lanes. Eventually they were crawling along a potholed gravel track before coming to a halt by two barns that looked like cowsheds.

"This is it - your home for the next week!" David announced gleefully. He could tell that the ten youngsters were not that impressed. Groaning, they disembarked and gathered their belongings from the bus. The sun had finally made an appearance just as it was about to bid farewell. The remaining clouds were turned a vivid red offering much delight to shepherds for the following day. Jake was wondering what they were going to do next when the most mismatched couple of people came out from one of the barns to greet them. The one was a slender well-proportioned woman in her mid-twenties with beautiful brown skin and long hair which was at present neatly tied up to match the perfection of the rest of her uniform. Jake thought she would look at her best in a sari and felt that she would be calm and poised in even the most harrowing of circumstances. The other was a rotund jolly-looking figure with an enormous handlebar moustache, but virtually no other hair on his head. Although fit for his age, he must have been at least in his early fifties. His uniform, though correct in every detail, was struggling to cope with the shape of its occupant.

"Good evening," the young woman addressed them. "My name is Rakshi and this is Mr Williams. Together we will be organising your training for the week. As you can see there are two buildings here. The one on the left is a dormitory block and in a moment we will take you over to sort out where you are all going to sleep. The accommodation is communal, but there are separate rooms for the boys and girls. This is mainly to protect the girls from the dreadful smells the boys produce rather than any major concern that you will suddenly turn straight in the middle of the night. The building on the right contains the kitchen and a communal area where we can have teaching sessions and also relax. There is very little free time and I expect at the end of each day you will be exhausted."

On that cheery note they all set off for the dormitory block and made decisions about where they were going to sleep. Jake decided to bury the hatchet further with Ashok by sharing a bunk bed with him. Jake had a fear of falling out of the top bunk, but fortunately Ashok was more than happy to go on the top. The other boys were familiar to both of them. Jake was on quite friendly terms with Tim, a long, lanky lad who said very little and always seemed grave and serious. He chose to sleep in a bed on his own. The other two lads knew each other well and didn't seem desperate to extend their circle of friendship to include Jake and Ashok. They shared another bunk bed.

Rakshi and Mr Williams had prepared a simple but filling supper for them all, but it was clear that everyone here was expected to muck in and afterwards Jake found himself doing a stint of washing up and tidying away.

Eventually the students found themselves in the communal area being given a refresher course on First Aid. They practiced bandaging and resuscitation and also how to carry an injured person if it was absolutely essential to move. It had gone past 10.30pm by the time they finished.

Rakshi concluded the session, "Now, we have reminded you about First Aid procedures tonight, because from tomorrow we will be out in the wilds and you will not always be under direct supervision from one of us. Accidents happen and it is important that you know how to cope. We won't let you go out in groups of less than three, so someone must stay with an injured person at all times while the other goes for help. You cannot rely on mobile phones around here, I'm afraid, because the reception is very poor. If anything does go awry, your first duty is to summon help from anyone you can. You are only trainees; you are not expected to be able to cope like fully credited Guardians. Are there any questions?" There were none so Rakshi continued, "You can have half an hour to yourselves before bed time, but lights out by midnight please."

Later, as Jake lay in bed waiting for sleep to take him, a number of things were passing through his mind. The most trivial was that he was desperately hoping none of the other four boys would start snoring. So far, so good, but he knew that Ashok was capable of sniffling if he ended up on his back. He then thought that this was how he had expected his life to be when he was rescued by Darryn, cooped up in some dingy dormitory, eking a living by hard graft and wits. He now realised that he had an extraordinary lifestyle at Rainbow House and was extremely privileged. His final thoughts were ones of worry. He was going to have to do some pretty horrible things as a Guardian. Maybe he was even going to have to kill someone. Had he got the stomach to do this? Would it change him as a person? He wasn't sure.

Chapter 8

The next day was, thankfully, sunny and bright. They had been told the previous evening that they were going to be split into two equal groups and that Rakshi would take one and Mr Williams would take the other. Jake was surprised to find that he, Jenny and Ashok had all been put in the same group. He had expected that they would have been split up. Tim was also in their group as was a very feisty-looking girl called Louise. Jake was desperately hoping that Rakshi would be taking their group, but of course, it turned out that Mr Williams was to take charge of them.

"Good Morning, my lovely boys," Mr Williams greeted them in a melodious Welsh accent, his moustache positively bristling with excitement at the prospect of what lay ahead. "The key things we are going to learn this week are shelter, food and travel. If you are in the wilds you will not survive without shelter, you will need food and water to sustain you and you will need to know how to travel so that you can avoid detection and reach your destination."

"Why did you call us 'lovely boys' when two of us are girls?" Jenny butted in rather rudely.

Mr Williams looked wide-eyed in disbelief as if such a question was sheer folly, "Why, there is no such thing as a 'lovely girl'. I am doing you the courtesy of making you honorary boys. You should be pleased."

Jenny opened her mouth and was about to respond when Jake gave her a dig in the ribs and whispered: "Don't say anything, Jenny."

Mr Williams, or Taffy as he was known to his friends, continued, "It's always best to be prepared if you can. We're going to take a large plastic sheet each. If you fold it up, it is light and takes up little room in a rucksack and yet could be invaluable in building a shelter. Similarly, why waste time with flints or a magnifying glass to light a fire; if you have a box of matches it'll take a few seconds. Get some packets of dried food, some chocolate and maybe the odd tin as well, and you won't need to gather as much food in the wild. Now follow me and we'll consider what makes a good spot to build a shelter and how we go about it."

Taffy Williams strode off with his five 'lovely boys' in tow behind him. They soon left the centre behind them and it became clear to Jake that they were climbing at quite a rate. The trees began to thin out and soon there was only thin stubby grass clinging on to bare rock. Taffy explained that the worst place they could try and shelter was on the very top of the hill; they would get a good view but would be dreadfully exposed to the elements.

"On the other hand," he explained, "If you pitch camp in a hollow down there in the trees, you run the risk of being flooded, or even having branches fall on you during the night. Now, it is always good to assess the weather and the general climate of the place before making decisions. It's a pity none of you have fair curly hair. I'm told that it becomes tight and difficult to control when a storm is approaching. Unfortunately my moustache doesn't respond in the same way."

They moved around the hill, using various signs from the sky and the landscape as they went, until Taffy was convinced they had a good spot. He got out his own plastic sheet and asked his companions for some suggestions of other items they might need as well. They collected some large stones to act as weights and, after a lot of difficulty, procured some fairly straight branches by backtracking into the woods.

"Right, now we'll throw into the mix a couple of other things to make life easier," he threw down a small roll of extra strong gaffer tape and a reel of what looked like cotton thread. "These are both items you will find in your standard issue Guardian survival kit. The thread is as strong as a rope and the tape can stick even in the wettest of conditions. Now, we can build a frame with the branches and then place the plastic sheeting over it, using the stones to hold it down. We can use the thread to act like guy ropes and the tape to stick various bits together for extra strength and security."

Taffy demonstrated various different designs, showing great alacrity in assembling and dismantling each structure.

"Right, my lovely boys, it's your turn. You've all got a piece of plastic sheeting. You know now what else you need, so off you go. Each of you, build me a shelter of your preferred design."

They all went off to find some stones and branches. Jenny and Jake agreed to help each other and both opted for a similar design, making a traditional tent-shaped structure. While they were constructing the frame for Jenny's effort, Louise came over and in a very matter-of-fact way said, "That will be blown down be the slightest gust of wind. You haven't got your triangles sorted out."

"Can you mind your own business, please," Jenny retorted, bristling with indignation.

"Okay, I was only trying to help," Louise countered. "I could help you make your frame a lot stronger, if you like."

"I can cope just fine, and Jake will help me if I need assistance." Jenny responded coolly.

"Suit yourself!" Louise said, shrugging her shoulders and walking off.

"That was harsh," Jake observed, giving Jenny a stern stare. "She was only trying to be friendly,"

"She was being a nosey cow and trying to get one over on us."

After about twenty minutes Taffy came and inspected their efforts. He looked at Tim's tent first. This was a triangular structure that would only accommodate one person. Taffy shook the frame quite vigorously, but the shelter remained sturdy and intact.

"Well done, Tim. A good shelter, but you're obviously not expecting visitors."

"When am I likely to get a visitor?" Tim muttered morosely.

Next he went over to Louise's. Again he shook the frame fiercely, but again the structure withstood the assault.

"Well done, Louise. Your shelter would withstand a hurricane."

He then viewed Jenny's attempt. Jake sidled away trying to disown any responsibility for its construction. Taffy merely touched the structure which then collapsed with startling ease.

"Oh dear, Jenny, I don't think you got your triangles quite right."

***

Annabelle was watching the Scout hut very carefully. Once again, after the other NPC wardens had left, the chosen twelve had remained behind for an additional training session. Annabelle was content to sit in her car parked on the opposite side of the road. She was more concerned today with what happened when they came out. She had picked up that one of the twelve was going to be met by his mother to do a special shopping expedition. Annabelle was going to attempt to follow and see if she could glean any further information.

A small car pulled up opposite her. The driver was a neat, well-dressed woman in late middle age. Having stopped the car, the woman took the opportunity to check her hair in the driving mirror and apply some additional lipstick. A few minutes later the twelve emerged in dribs and drabs from the scout hut. Annabelle had been struck by their varied ages from the start. The youngest was probably still at school whilst the eldest must be drawing his pension. Only two were woman however, and they all, not surprisingly, came from very Anglo-Saxon stock. It was the youngest lad who made his way to the car. He greeted his mother in a very matter of fact way and made himself comfortable in the front passenger seat. The car drove off.

Annabelle gave them a few seconds head start and then cautiously set off after them, maintaining a healthy distance so that she could not be recognised. She had a good idea where they were likely to be going, anyway, but she was not disappointed. Fifteen minutes later the woman and her son pulled into the car park at Blake's, a large out-of-town supermarket. There were plenty of parking spaces, so Annabelle went two rows further along and parked well away from her quarry. Keeping the mother and son in view at all times, she followed them into the store, picking up a trolley as she went. What sort of shoppers were they likely to be? Were they going to flit from one aisle to another or were they going to systematically work their way down the store, picking up their purchases as they walked by?

Annabelle sighed with relief when she saw they were in the second category. It was far easier for her to stay close and pretend to be shopping in exactly the same way.

"So you've got to take some tins and dry provisions, dear. Are they providing you with any meals at all?" Annabelle heard the mother enquire.

"I think we are going to be out in the wild most of the time, so we will have to make do as best we can." The son replied. "I'd better remember to take some teabags and a small jar of instant coffee. Do the still make that dried milk powder stuff?"

The store had clothes as well as groceries. This section of the store proved the most fruitful from Annabelle's point of view. The mother noticed some thick walking socks on special offer.

"Ooh...You could do with a new pair of those. Perhaps I ought to get you several."

"For goodness sake, Mum, I'm only going for a weekend." The boy complained.

"Yes, but it's the Easter weekend; you may not find any shops open in the middle of Wales on Easter Sunday."

"Mum, I'm going to be miles away from any shops. I'm not useless. I'll survive, clean socks or dirty socks."

Annabelle had got her intelligence. The twelve were off to Wales for a training expedition that would last a couple of days, and they were going this weekend coming. She maintained her vigil a little longer in the hope that they would let slip the exact time of departure, but frustratingly, that information was not forthcoming.

As the mother and son were about to move to the checkout, Annabelle disengaged herself as smoothly and invisibly as possible. She looked down at the items in her trolley which she had been accumulating subconsciously while straining to pick up tit-bits of conversation. It was an odd assortment, much of which she would probably not use. She considered retracing her steps and returning most of the items to the shelves. However, this would have looked odd and drawn unnecessary attention to herself, so she gritted her teeth and purchased the lot.

When she got to her car, the mother and son had already left. She loaded her shopping and sat in the driver's seat. Before setting off she rang Darryn up on her mobile.

"Hi, Darryn, the twelve are off to Wales this weekend. I'm guessing this is the moment when they are going to get their firearms training." There was a pause while Darryn said something on the other end. "No, I don't know exactly when they are going. I'm afraid we'll have to keep vigil from early on Friday. I'll meet you at Digby's on Wednesday evening and we can make plans. Cheers." Annabelle cut the call and started the motor. It was time to call it a day.

***

The second day of the training had been in sharp contrast to the first. Heavy rain had started falling at day break and with it the temperature had fallen so that it felt more like the middle of winter than spring. Jake and the other four members of his team were all cocooned in wet weather gear. He had initially been wearing gloves but the need to do dexterous things had meant that he had quickly discarded them. His hands were now blue and wrinkled with the combination of the cold and wet.

They had spent the morning learning how to make and set traps. Taffy had then taken them through some of the plants that were safe to eat. Jake was surprised at how many seemed to be edible. Taffy warned them about fungi and suggested that it was probably wise not to risk picking mushrooms unless there were no other options. In a way, Jake was hoping that the traps would remain empty. He did not fancy the prospect of having to dispatch some poor animal and then skinning it to get the meat. By this time, all five of the trainees were cold and miserable and all conversation had ceased. Only Taffy was remotely enjoying the experience.

"Of course, if you are trying to catch a variety of different mammals it's better to set your traps at night. We might just be lucky and catch a rabbit though. Fishing is another way of getting animal protein. We'll look at using a line and hook tomorrow, and in any case I'll show you how to prepare a fish for cooking tonight when we get back to base camp. Oh look... we're in luck."

At the entrance to a burrow, a small rabbit had been caught in one of their traps.

"Now, there is no room for sentiment. If it's a case of survival, you have to be as harsh as Mother Nature." With that, he bashed the rabbit over the head with a rock a few times to finish it off.

"If we are going to save the meat, it is important to bleed the animal straight away. If you are in dire need it might be worth saving the blood." Taffy then with great expertise showed them how to bleed, skin, gut and joint the animal. "You must be careful with rabbit. It is probably the easiest meat to come across in the wild, but it does not give you all the nutrition you require. You must always supplement your diet with vegetable material. It is also very rich in protein, but if you eat too much too quickly you can actually poison yourself; having said that, nothing beats a nice rabbit stew. Ashok, there were some primroses and tender dandelion leaves on the edge of the wood. Would you go and collect some please? If you can find anything else that would go well with our rabbit, by all means collect that too. Now, I've done quite enough work. Let's see if the rest of you can light a fire. Remember the conditions are not good, so you'll need to think about sheltering the fire and finding dry wood."

Tim and Louise went off to look in the woods for dry kindling, while Jake and Jenny started building a platform of stones, as the ground was wet.

"Can we use matches, Mr Williams?" Jenny asked.

"I should think so – as long as you've remembered to keep them dry in this awful weather." Taffy replied.

"Mr Williams," Jake asked in turn, "What are you supposed to do if you are a vegetarian?"

"But you are not, are you?" Taffy said raising one eyebrow.

"No... But just supposing," Jake persisted.

"Well, let's hope you remembered to bring plenty of cheese and dried packet food when you were cast out into the wild. You could survive in late summer for a while on berries, and maybe mushrooms would give you some protein, but I wouldn't rate your chances of survival in the middle of winter without resorting to meat."

Ashok returned with a selection of leaves and flowers. He had been unusually quiet, even accounting for the weather. Jake could tell that he had not enjoyed the killing and skinning of the rabbit.

"Well done, Ashok" Taffy commended him, "I see you have some wild thyme and garlic there. That will definitely enhance the flavour."

Tim and Louise returned with a bundle of fire wood which was surprisingly dry. They set about building a fire. Jenny muscled in to make it clear that she was in charge. However Louise soon had to make her point too:

"No Jenny, it won't light if you put the wood on like that."

"Look I know what I'm doing. Stop interfering." Jenny was getting very irritated by now.

"Oh yes, just like your shelter was perfect yesterday I suppose," Louise retorted sarcastically.

That was it. Jenny saw red in front of her eyes and went for Louise. Louise was not just going to sit back and take it though; she gave as good as she got. From a spectator's point of view, the whole fracas was comical. Because both girls had layers and layers of warm clothing and wet weather gear on, they looked like two balloon men trying to have a fight. Neither could get a grip on the other and the whole fight seemed to be in slow motion.

Taffy, trying not to laugh, revealed unexpected strength by lifting each with different hands and placing them a yard further back from each other.

"Now, my not-so-lovely boys, what's all this? We can't have dissension in the ranks."

"She's an interfering bitch," Jenny said, still seething with indignation.

"And she's a pig-headed arrogant cow," Louise retorted with equal vehemence.

Jake, Tim and Ashok looked on, not quite sure whether to be aghast or entertained by the spectacle.

Taffy decided now was the moment to offer the Wisdom of Solomon, "Jenny, you should really listen to Louise. She picks up what to do very quickly. Louise, you are not helping by being so abrasive. You need to learn how to handle people and show a bit of empathy."

The fire was eventually lit. Taffy improvised a frying pan and seared some of the meat and vegetable matter. Ashok and Jake went to collect some water from one of the streams on the hillside, as they had been taught to, and boiled it in a pot that Taffy had produced from somewhere. All the

47

ingredients were then added to the pot and allowed to simmer for an hour or more.

Jake felt a bit uncomfortable when they came to test their stew. It was the first time that he'd eaten anything that he'd personally seen killed. However he had to admit that the stew tasted surprisingly good. He looked at the others and suspected they were all going through a similar turmoil of emotions. The exception was possibly Tim, who always looked sad and looked no different from normal.

After their meal, Taffy took his charges through the procedure for putting out the fire and covering their tracks. If they were being pursued, it was important they left as little trace of their presence as possible. He then insisted that they go round and dismantle every trap they had set in the morning.

"If you were out in the wild and having to move on, you wouldn't have time to do this, but there is no point in killing or harming animals unnecessarily. The hunters of old were well in tune with nature and respected their prey,"

Eventually, they trudged their way back to the centre where Rakshi had already got her group to stoke up the stove. Jake only appreciated how wet and cold he'd become when he approached its life-giving warmth. It had rained non-stop all day. The only variation had been how heavily the rain had come down. Low grey cloud had scudded across the sky with not even a hint of sunshine. Jenny put the kettle on and the five of them sat around the stove drinking tea and eating cake for twenty minutes.

Taffy, as promised, showed both groups how to slit and gut a larger fish. The trainees had a go at this and the results of their efforts ended up as the basis for supper that evening.

When it finally got to that period of the day when they had half an hour to themselves before bedtime, Jake went and sat by Ashok and said, "You've been very quiet today. Is everything okay?"

"Yes, I think so," Ashok replied. "It's just today has made me think more clearly about where our food comes from. I mean, when you buy fish fingers in the supermarket you don't really think about the fish that's been bled and gutted and all the mess that goes with it, or the killing involved in making sausages."

"Has it put you off eating meat?" Jake enquired,

"I'm not sure." Ashok mused. "Most of my family are vegetarian anyway; I only started eating meat really when I came to Rainbow House. It's more the shock of realising how separated we've become from the means of our survival. If the food supply chain were to fail, most of us would die of starvation very quickly."

"Yes but isn't that the great thing about what we're doing this week? You and I would have a chance of being among those few who would survive."

"Yes, but what would the world be like that we were left with? A fairly grim and unforgiving place, I would imagine. I'm not so sure it would be a blessing to be one of the survivors."

Jenny walked by at this point and Jake decided to change the conversation from this rather gloomy discourse he was having with Ashok, "Hey Jenny, what was all that business with Louise about?"

"What business?" Jenny replied in all innocence.

"You know, that fight you had with her. It looked as if you really hated her guts."

Jenny had a twinkle in her eye and said, "I really don't know what you mean Jake, I think Louise and I are going to get on just fine. She's got some real drive and sparkle."

Jake sat there open-mouthed not knowing what to say. Could it really be that these deadliest of foes had suddenly become the best of friends? He would never understand women, and lesbians were at least three times more inscrutable than the normal female population.

Chapter 9

The next day was thankfully brighter and more spring-like. It was breezy, but with small cotton wool clouds scurrying happily against a blue sky, it looked set fair for the rest of the day. Taffy spent the morning showing his five trainees how to fish.

"Don't expect to be able to survive on fish in this country, especially if you are on the run. There are few rivers that are large enough to support decent sized fish, and it would only be safe enough to fish most of those at the dead of night. Still fish is a good source of protein and a useful supplement to the diet." Taffy Williams was once again in his element. He had found a quiet spot on a small river flowing through a field. Whether they had the right to be there or not seemed a bit dubious; Taffy seemed to take the view that he had the right to roam anywhere. He showed his students the spots where the fish were likeliest to be and how to use a line and hook suitably baited to make a catch. They did catch a few 'tiddlers', but Taffy put them all back making the point that it would have been possible to eat them if they had been desperate.

Jake had not dreamt Jenny's sudden change of heart over Louise. The two girls were chatting very happily, mainly about car engines and their favourite football teams. They had worked enthusiastically together on their fishing task, but made too much noise to be very successful. This meant that Jake was forced to seek companionship elsewhere. Ashok was still in a strange frame of mind and although not deliberately ignoring his companions, was not talking very much and brooding a great deal. In desperation Jake turned to Tim in the hope of some light relief. He opened in a general sort of way:

"At least the weather is better today. I'm glad we don't have to wear all that wet-weather gear again."

"It makes no odds to me. It might as well rain as be sunny."

Jake looked at Tim carefully. He was a tall lad, well over six feet, with brown eyes and slightly under shoulder-length brown hair. He was probably a little older than Jake, but somehow, he didn't seem to have any greater maturity. He had been quite thin, but like Jake, the Guardian training had bulked him up, and he was really beginning to look quite handsome. Tim's face was always very serious; he only spoke when he was spoken to and Jake, in all the time that he had been acquainted with him, had never seen Tim smile.

"Why do you never laugh?" Jake asked him, immediately realising that this was a stupid thing to say.

Tim raised an eyebrow and replied, "What is there to laugh at?"

"A joke, an idiotic thing said by a friend, just the joy of being alive," Jake suggested.

"There is no joy in being alive, only pain and struggle and loneliness." Tim was now surprised by what he had said and looked a bit apprehensive.

"But you are okay at Rainbow House? Surely you are happy there?"

"Life is almost bearable there," Tim replied in a dispassionate and matter-of-fact way.

"You must have friends and you can be open about who you are," Jake persisted. "I'm your friend," Jake asserted boldly.

"No, Jake, you're an acquaintance. You say 'hello' and ask me how I'm doing from time to time, but you have eyes only for Nathan and you have your little circle of close friends. Don't get me wrong, I'm not complaining. I'm quite jealous of what you've got going with Nathan; I think a lot of people are. You're a nice guy and I wish you were my friend."

Jake was on the point of replying and then stopped. He realised that Tim was absolutely right; he knew nothing about this tall, taciturn and serious young man.

Unexpectedly Tim continued, "Darryn found me trying to commit suicide. That's why I'm at Rainbow House. I'm at least at the point where I don't think I'd try it again."

Jake did not know how to respond to this. He had no words, so he put his hand on Tim's shoulder and gave it a little squeeze, hoping this would convey some empathy and understanding.

The gloomy atmosphere was shattered by Taffy's enthusiastic voice ringing through the air, "Right, my lovely boys, it's time to move on to the next stage of the adventure." With that he set off at full pace with his five trainees struggling to keep up. Jenny and Louise were still chatting together in animated conversation while the three boys trotted behind in silence.

"Do you believe in luck, Mr Williams?" Jenny asked as they were moving through trees.

"Things happen in a random fashion as far as I can see, so if you prepare ahead you can sometimes make your own luck." Taffy replied.

"I think that sometimes you can foretell the future," Louise chipped in.

"Well I suppose in terms of reading the clouds and predicting people's behaviour there is something in that, but portents in the sky or reading Nostradamus is all rot."

Jake was listening to this and told Taffy about the incident with the magpie and the cat the day he was chased away from Telford.

"Now that was surely some kind of sign that something dreadful was going to happen," Jake concluded.

"Well, first of all, Jake, I think it's very unlikely that a magpie would be caught by a cat, so it must have either been on its last legs anyway or else you misidentified it. It seems to me that you have made the scene rather more dramatic with the benefit of hindsight. Ah... here we are."

51

He made them stop at the edge of the woods and continued:

"We are now going to move on to the third element of this week's training, finding your way, especially when being hunted or tracked. The most important thing to remember is that as soon as you emerge into the open you become very vulnerable and can be seen from a long way away. You should always take a moment to assess your surroundings before leaving cover. Ashok, what do you make of the open land ahead?"

"Well there is obviously a quarry just up ahead and we are going to come out at the top of it. If we wanted to get to the other side we would probably have to walk round the edge."

"Good - is the quarry still in use?" Taffy enquired further.

"I'd have to go to the edge and look in," Ashok said.

"Use your ears as well as your eyes," said Taffy becoming quite animated. "Do you hear the sound of machinery? No, but what you can hear is the noise of gulls and you can see the birds swooping in and out. This suggests the quarry is no longer in use and is safe to approach. Moreover, you can see vegetation clinging to the top of the far rock face suggesting it hasn't been blasted for some time."

While he had been saying this, Taffy had been walking backwards towards the quarry edge and was now dangerously close to it.

"Mr Williams, be careful!" Jenny shouted, but it was already too late. Taffy realised he had over stepped the edge and was desperately whirling his arms in anti-clockwise motion to restore his balance. He fell from sight, shouting, and then only a matter of a second later a dull thud was heard and all noise stopped. The five students, still on the edge of the woods some twenty yards back, looked at each other in shock, none of them quite knowing what to do next.

***

Maria emerged from her bathroom with the prototype of the dress which Matt was making for her birthday. The fabric was dark purple and very striking.

"Come over here, dear, and we'll begin to put some shape to the thing." Matt said, gathering the tools of his trade.

"Ouch, be a bit gentler. You just pricked me with one of your pins," complained Maria as Matt set to work.

"Don't be such a Diva!" Matt retorted. "Honestly, I wish the pins were magically poisoned and would send you to sleep for a hundred years, like Sleeping Beauty. Then at least I'd be able to get on with doing this job in peace." He gathered in the fabric around Maria's waist firmly in retaliation.

Nathan popped his head round the door to see what was going on, "Hi guys," he said cheerily, "Is this the latest fashion, to be dressed in a shapeless sack of material?"

Matt thrust his nose in the air in irritation, "It is not finished yet, as you well know. I am surrounded by ignorant fools."

Nathan laughed and said, "If you say so. Didn't I see you out with some old geezer the other night?"

Maria looked troubled and interjected, "You didn't go out with your art teacher after everything we talked about the other night?"

"I'm sorry, Maria," Matt replied, clearly not sorry at all, "But it's what my heart says is the right thing to do. You can give me a thousand and one logical reasons why it's wrong, but he is the loveliest guy I've ever met."

"You're infatuated with him more like," Nathan added.

"You're a one to talk," Matt hit back at him, "Everyone can see you're totally infatuated with Jake."

"Yes, but at least Jake is gorgeous and the same age as me. Your art teacher is creepy, old enough to be your father and going bald."

"That just shows your lack of maturity, I'm afraid," Matt replied in a haughty fashion. "James has life experience and a lot to teach me. I find that all very sexy."

Nathan shrugged his shoulders in incomprehension. Maria frowned in concern and added, "Well do be careful, Matt. I can only see it all ending in tears."

***

After a few seconds of inertia, the five trainees ran to the edge of the quarry. Jenny was the first to look over the edge. It was not as far down as she had feared, only twenty feet or so. At first she couldn't see Taffy, but then she caught sight of a prone body lying to her right.

"Oh my God," she shouted. "We've got to get down there quickly, he's not moving."

"Wait, Jenny," Louise interrupted, holding her arm. "We've got to find a safe way down. When the quarry was worked there must have been a way to get in and out easily."

Ashok roused from his stupor, "Jake, you work your way clockwise and I'll go the other way and see if we can find a way down."

They rushed off in opposite directions. It seemed like an age to the other three who remained. Jenny kept an eye on Taffy. He was lying, face up, on his back. Ominously she had not seen him move from the moment she had first clapped eyes on him.

"I've found a way down," Ashok shouted, "Quickly this way!" The others followed at a run, but obviously Ashok with his head start was first on the scene and likewise, Jake was the last. Ashok checked for breathing and a pulse and was immensely relieved to find both.

"He's alive. Has anyone got a mobile phone on them?" Ashok barked as the others arrived. Jake and Louise both had theirs with them despite being told that they would not be able to use them. Unfortunately, neither of them could get a signal. Jake ran back up to the top of the quarry and shouted back that he was unable to get a signal from up there either.

"Right, well what do we do?" Louise said looking hopefully at the others.

Jake spoke up and said, "We must be careful not to move him until we are sure that he's not broken his back or neck. Which one of us knows the most about first aid?"

They decided that Tim was probably the one to give the most accurate diagnosis, despite his diffidence:

"He has no breaks in his legs. In fact considering the fall, they seem to be in remarkably good condition. His spine is harder to assess; I can't get underneath without moving him. His neck doesn't look broken. I say we leave him like that unless he's sick and we have to get him into the recovery position."

"Right, the most obvious thing to do would be for one or two of us to go and seek help or at least find a spot where we are in phone range to call the emergency services," Jake suggested decisively.

"The problem with that is we don't really know where we are." Ashok commented. "One of us could wander about for hours before finding help and then would we be able to retrace our steps or describe where we are to the emergency services?"

Taffy groaned and moved his head but did not regain consciousness to any greater degree. "So we could be sitting out here for the whole night if we're not careful." Jake added thoughtfully. "Is there any way of contacting Rakshi?"

Tim checked Taffy's pockets and jacket in the hope of finding a mobile phone or a wallet that might have details such as addresses and phone numbers. He found nothing. He then took the sheet of plastic out of his kit bag and laid it over Taffy for extra warmth. Mercifully the weather had maintained its early promise and was warm enough. They were also sheltered from the breeze down in the quarry.

"Look Jake, you go back up to the top and have a wander around up there," Ashok suggested "It's just possible you might find somewhere where you can get a weak signal, but don't go too far. Make sure you can always find your way back."

Jake scampered off again, but after half an hour it was clear that the exercise was futile. The quarry was just about at the highest point of the hill. The further you moved in any direction the lower you got, so it seemed that the odds of picking up a signal became less not greater. The track out of the quarry was no help. It petered out as soon as it met the trees. Obviously the area had not been worked for a very long time. He returned with the bad news.

"Well folks, we've got to make a decision. It's getting on for half past five. I think we are going to have to move him. We've got the plastic, the thread and the gaffer tape. If we could find ourselves a couple of sturdy poles, we could construct a stretcher. Let's see if we can break off a couple of straight saplings in the woods and use those."

Tim and Louise stayed with the patient, who seemed to be murmuring and mumbling a bit more. Jake, Ashok and Jenny went to find some wood that would do for their stretcher.

They quickly came across an area that had been regularly coppiced. They easily found some shoots that were fairly sturdy. In their kit bags they had serrated knives which they could use like saws. They soon found that if they made a substantial knick in the wood they could then snap the sapling trunk off. Within twenty minutes they had gathered six straight wooden poles. They raced back to the quarry.

"How is he doing?" Jake enquired anxiously.

"He doesn't seem to be getting worse, and he is mumbling and murmuring a bit more" Tim responded. "There is no sign of fever, which is good, but I do wish he'd regain consciousness."

With Louise's help, the wood gatherers lashed the six poles into two sets of three for added strength. They then used more of the thread in their kit bags to create a crude lattice framework between the two poles. Jenny, Jake and Ashok then laid their emergency plastic sheeting over this and secured it with the gaffer tape.

"We really ought to test this first," Jake observed. "Ashok, you're the heaviest out of all of us. Lie on the stretcher and we'll try and pick you up."

Ashok muttered something about not being fat, but complied with the request. Jake, Jenny, Louise and Tim took the four corners of the improvised stretcher and lifted. To Jake's immense relief, the stretcher withstood Ashok's weight.

"Great, it works. I think it should cope with Mr Williams, even though he is bigger and bulkier." Jake said this with some pride in their work. "Right, well this is the moment where we have to move him. We can do a four-man lift just as we were shown. Tim if you stay at his head you can try to make sure his neck moves as little as possible."

"Just a second," asked Tim as he leant close to Taffy's right ear. "Mr Williams," he whispered, "We're going to move you. If this is the wrong thing to do, moan or make a grunt or something."

Tim waited for a response for a few seconds, but there was none. He sighed and said, "Right, let's do it."

They got Taffy onto the stretcher with the minimum of movement and cautiously lifted it. It held. They then moved slowly along the track out of the quarry. When they got to the top, they had to put the stretcher down to have a rest.

"We'll have to take it in turns," Ashok said. "Four of us on the stretcher, the other acting as nurse while taking a rest. If we get too tired we all take a rest. Agreed?" The other four nodded their assent.

They set off to retrace their steps. They remembered the point where they had emerged from the trees, but they had not followed a well-trodden path through the woods. The best they could remember was that they had been steadily climbing for a good half an hour. They therefore did their best to follow the contours downwards, although they couldn't be absolutely sure of their direction.

Jake said to the others, "If only we could find the river where we were fishing this morning, I think I could find my way to the centre from there." It was still light, but the shadows were beginning to lengthen and the never-ending vista of conifers in all directions was ever more menacing.

Suddenly the trees ended and they were confronted with a barbed wire fence and pastureland beyond.

"I don't remember this," Louise said, failing to hide the anxiety in her voice.

"Okay, let's not panic," Ashok said quickly in response. "Everyone think for a moment how we entered the woods when we came up from the river."

There was a moments silence and then Jenny said, "We walked through a metal gate at the edge of a field. There was a track that led into the woods but it turned sharply left almost immediately and we just continued walking uphill through the trees."

"Right, so probably what we've done is just missed the gate and hit the fence instead. We need to walk along it to find the gate, but which way to go?" Ashok said in a perplexed manner.

"We'll have to send out scouts to try and find it," Jake suggested. "The gate is not visible from here."

"We can only afford to let one person go," Ashok replied. "We must have four people to carry the stretcher, and I'm concerned how long we've taken already. If Mr Williams is suffering from a brain injury he will need urgent hospital attention."

"I'll go," said Jake. "Five minutes in either direction, and if I don't find anything we'll cross the barbed wire here and just keep going until we see something familiar or come across a house where we can get help."

Jake set off to his left. It wasn't all that easy making his way through shrubby undergrowth with the trees constantly to his left. There was no sign of a gate. The barbed wire fence just went on and on. After two or three minutes he could see another fence making its way up the side of the field to meet this one. It didn't look at all promising and there was no sign of the river down below. He turned back. When he met the others again, he could see the disappointment in their faces.

"How is he?" Jake asked.

"He doesn't seem to have changed much," Tim replied.

Jake went off in the other direction, this time with the trees on his right. The going was just as difficult and the barbed wire fence was equally unrelenting. He was about to give up when he caught a glimpse of water in the valley below - the river maybe? He followed the line up the fields and thought he could make out a light track heading for the woods another quarter of a mile further on. He carried on further than he originally intended. Yes - it was there, the gate and the track turning sharply to the left could be made out now. They had gone off track by a considerable margin on their descent. He hurried back as quickly as he could, realising he'd already been longer than agreed. Four worried faces greeted him as he returned:

"Jake, where have you been, we were beginning to think of going on ahead without you."

"Sorry, but I found the gate and the track and it leads down to the river just as Jenny remembered," Jake blurted out.

They set off again. The going was really quite challenging and it took them more than half an hour to make their way, with the stretcher, to the point where the gate was. When they got there however, they all remembered passing through it on their way up to the quarry and their spirits were considerably lifted. They carried on down the rough field towards the river, leaving the dark woods behind them. It was past eight o'clock by now and the sun was on the point of disappearing behind the horizon. Jake realised it would now not be long before darkness enveloped them and so he urged his companions on with renewed vigour.

Suddenly he heard a bleeping coming from his pocket. It was probably Nathan sending him a text. Slowly the significance of this dawned on Jake.

"I've got a signal, I've got a signal," he shouted. They put the stretcher down immediately.

"Thank goodness," Ashok exclaimed, "Ring 999 and let's be done with this business."

Jake was already dialling, when a muscular adult hand grabbed his arm, and a melodious Welsh voice said, "That won't be necessary."

Taffy Williams, like Lazarus rising from the dead, emerged from his coma and stood up from the stretcher in extreme good health. The five trainees looked as if they had seen a ghost.

"Well done, my lovely boys. Not bad for a first attempt."

Chapter 10

Darryn was not in the best of moods. He'd had to get up extremely early and was only half awake. Annabelle had no idea when the twelve were going to set off and they dare not risk the possibility of an early start which they missed. Fortunately the weather looked set fair, but even so, at half past six in the morning it is still cold in April. It was Good Friday, so it seemed a little bit like a Sunday morning. Only a few cars passed them by, and they had no sense of urgency or rush.

Annabelle and Darryn were studying the Scout hut in great detail. They were now in the back of a white van, viewing the scene through a periscope which was hardly visible from the outside. To all intents and purposes it looked as if the van had been parked by the side of the road and left. Earlier, when it had become clear that no one was about, Darryn had a furtive look around the back of the hut and looked in through the window. Twelve sets of kit had been set out neatly in order, ready to be picked up and loaded.

At 9.00am a lone figure made his way up the drive to the main door. It was clear from the large bunch of keys in his hand that he was opening up for some reason. Over the next twenty minutes the twelve all arrived as well as four others who Annabelle recognised as regular trainers for the NPC groups. The youngest of the twelve, the one Annabelle had followed around the supermarket, was the last to arrive. He'd been driven there by his mother. As he got out of the car, he was given a kiss on the cheek. Annabelle couldn't help but smile as she saw the son's appalled reaction as he desperately tried to wipe it off.

At 9.30am a small army lorry appeared and stopped in the car park of the hut. It was the type that had a canvass roof over a metal frame and was designed for carrying troops about.

"That's unexpected," Darryn commented. "I was anticipating a minibus. I wonder where they got it from. You don't think they stole it from Donnington, do you?"

"I think it's unlikely they have the skill to infiltrate an army base just yet," Annabelle replied.

"We'll have to be careful when following them. There will be people looking out of the back all the time. They will notice if there is a vehicle following for any period of time."

At just after 10.00am, the lorry was loaded and everyone had boarded. The diesel engine sprang into life and they slowly moved off. Annabelle could make out that the trainees were sat equally partitioned, five on either side, in the back of the truck along with two of their trainers. The other two sat in the front cab with the driver.

Annabelle and Darryn waited for the lorry to disappear round a corner before emerging from the back and taking up their position in the van's cab. Darryn then set off at a steady pace in no hurry to catch up with the lorry. Annabelle noticed that the man with the keys was locking up again and had shown some interest in them as they moved off.

***

Jenny was absolutely furious with Taffy Williams for his deception. She sulked and was uncooperative for all of the next day. In the end, even Louise was forced to tell Jenny to snap out of it and just get on with things. Taffy, on the other hand, didn't seem to care or notice what Jenny said or did. He was his normal cheerful self and all criticism was like water off a duck's back. They had spent Thursday learning how to move about unobserved; Jake had enjoyed learning how to hide in a hedge and evade dogs. The moment had now come for the climax to the week. They were to be dropped off somewhere unknown and were to make their way back to the centre. It was Good Friday, the weather was glorious, and the minibus journey to the drop off point took them through some very beautiful countryside.

When they got out at the other end of their journey, Taffy was particular in taking them to the summit of a hill which commanded a good view of the land around. He addressed his students:

"Now, this is not as difficult as your final Guardian assessment, where you will be given no help and have to evade capture as well, but nevertheless, it is challenging enough.

"I can tell you that you are twenty miles from the centre. I'm going to give you a basic map with a suggested route. There are no place names on the map and you don't have to follow the route. You have your basic kits, a basic supply of food and a compass, but we have made sure you have no mobile phones or money on you.

"It's just gone midday. If you manage to find your way without mishap, you should be able to get back before sundown. However, if it gets dark, you must decide whether to continue in the dark or to pitch camp for the night. The exercise will only finish if you get back to base or twenty-four hours have elapsed - Any questions?"

The five trainees looked at each other but could think of nothing to say.

"Right, my lovely boys, I'll love you and leave you. Good luck!" Taffy marched off back to the minibus and drove away. Jake had a moment of feeling very isolated and inadequate, but then Louise's voice cut through the silence and said, "Well come on then, let's look at that map."

The map was hand-drawn and showed the route as a dashed line zigzagging across the page. The first obstacle seemed to be a hill. The dashed line almost reached the summit and then descended on the far side to meet a road which looked as if it was circumventing the base of the hill. The map also had a compass direction shown on it, so they were able see that they would have to travel in a northerly direction to get back.

"That has got to be the hill over there," said Jake pointing to an obvious feature in the landscape. "Look, I can make out a track going up which corresponds to the dashed line on the map."

Jenny checked the compass and found that the hill Jake had pointed out was in the right direction. The five of them set off optimistically towards the hill on a path that clearly seemed to match the map. They had to go down from their vantage point into a valley before they could then start climbing the hill in question. The map was not entirely clear as to whether they would have to cross a road in the process; however it soon became apparent that they would.

"Hang on," said Ashok, "Wouldn't it be easier just to walk along this road? It's got to be the one shown on the map which goes around the bottom of the hill. The track will meet it on the far side anyway."

"I say we should stick to the route," said Jake firmly.

"Taffy only said it was a *suggested* route. We'll take hours going up and down that hill and we'll wear ourselves out." Ashok reasoned in reply.

Jake was sticking to his guns and said in response, "Maybe it's a suggested route for a *reason*. We might not be able to pick out where the track comes back to the road."

"But even if we don't find it, the next bit is obvious. We simply go right when the road forks in two."

Jake was still being uncompromising and continued, "Did Taffy say he'd put all the roads on the map? I don't think so. There might be other forks and side roads not shown. We could easily get lost. I say we stick to the track."

Ashok sighed and said, "Jake Holdencroft, I'd forgotten how stubborn you can be. If I'm still out here in the middle of the night having to sleep under a piece of plastic because it has taken us hours to get up and down some mountain unnecessarily, I'll never let you forget it."

"Well, we could go round by the road, and get totally lost and find ourselves in Cardiff by the middle of next week, if you like. I'll never let you forget that either."

Ashok held his hands up as a sign of submission and all five of them crossed the road and passed through a dilapidated five bar wooden gate that marked the start of a faint track up towards the summit of the hill. The incline was slow and steady, but persistent so they were really feeling out of breath by the time they were halfway up. It was open and rugged land, with no trees and just a thin coating of grass to cover a jagged, rocky terrain.

Ever since his conversation with Tim when Taffy had been teaching them how to fish, Jake had tried to make a point of talking to him more. He had been stung by Tim's comment about him being merely an acquaintance and wanted to try and prove he was more than that. It wasn't always easy though; Tim could be very monosyllabic, making conversation a difficult and gruelling process. If anything, he had been slightly worse after their conversation, probably due to embarrassment at having opened up as much as he had.

"So, Tim, how do you think you'd manage to cope out in the wilds after what we've done this week?" Jake enquired as they were slowly making their way just to the right of the summit.

"The same as everyone else, I'd imagine," Tim replied tersely.

Jake sighed. It was going to be an effort but he persisted, "What have you enjoyed most about the week?"

"I think when Mr Williams fell over the cliff," Tim said. There was a pause and then much to Jake's surprise, Tim carried on: "Also I think I enjoyed it when Jenny went mental afterwards." There was a moment's further pause and then he continued, "What have you enjoyed, Jake?"

Jake was stunned. This was progress indeed. Tim had asked him a question for the first time this week. For some reason, he imagined himself to be like Professor Henry Higgins in 'My Fair Lady' and Tim to be his protégé, Eliza Doolittle. He was teaching Tim the art of conversation, and finally having some success. It was as much as he could do to prevent himself immediately bursting into a rendition of 'The rain in Spain falls mainly in the plain!' Instead he said, "I think the best bit was making the shelters. I certainly didn't like catching and skinning the rabbit, but I guess that's what you have to do if you want to survive."

"Life is cruel," Tim added in a monotone comment.

They had passed the summit on their left by now; the nature of the far side of the hill was beginning to become apparent. They all suddenly stopped dead in their tracks. Three-quarters of the way up the hill was a collection of temporary wooden buildings. Some were old and had been done up, but at least one looked brand new and recently constructed. The buildings were screened from the road by a thick copse of pine trees, but a substantial track, possibly newly made, led through to allow vehicle access to the camp. There were people wandering around, clearly doing some kind of work.

"Well, that's a surprise," Ashok said, "There's no indication of a settlement on the map. The track goes right through the middle of it and out of the other side. What shall we do?"

"We're on a public footpath," said Jake, "So we must have the right to go through there."

"Are you sure about that?" Ashok asked in a concerned way. "I didn't see a footpath sign back at the road and we don't know if this line on the map represents a public right of way."

"Well, we have the right to roam on land like this, don't we? Anyhow, they haven't fenced the buildings off which suggests they don't have the right to. Let's just walk on through. What's the worst that can happen? They tell us off, we say we're sorry, and they send us on our way."

So, rather self-consciously, they continued down the track towards the buildings, making sure they were all together in a tight-knit group. As they passed by the first building, they became noticeable to some of the people who were walking to and fro. Suspicious and none-too-friendly stares greeted their presence.

"I don't like this," whispered Louise to Jenny, "I get the distinct feeling we shouldn't be here!"

Jake overheard this and whispered back, "Just brazen it out. No one's actually said anything yet and we've only got another hundred yards before we're in the woods and on our way to the road."

They all desperately wanted to run; it was agony having to keep up the pretence and walk at a slow pace as if nothing were amiss.

Louise gave a little gasp, and whispered to Jenny, "That man over there is wearing the F.U.P. insignia on his shirt. We're walking through an F.U.P. training camp."

Jenny feeling beads of perspiration developing on her forehead replied, "Just keep calm and keep going. We've nearly made it through."

Indeed all five of them now realised their predicament, but were hopeful of bluffing their way through. Only another twenty feet and the track would enter the trees and they would be hidden from view.

"Hey, you..." A voice rasped through the air. Jake's heart was in his mouth as they turned to view their assailant. There was no point in running now. Their only hope was to protest their innocence. Ashok whispered to the others as they turned, "Let me do the talking. We must have a single consistent story."

The man who had shouted at them had narrow, mean eyes. He was overweight and had little hair. He was probably in his mid-forties and looked used to ordering people about. He continued, "What do you think you are doing wandering through here as free and easy as you like?"

Ashok remained as calm as he could and replied, "We're on a Duke of Edinburgh expedition. We simply followed a track shown on our map and it clearly comes down through your buildings and on to the road."

"The track is not a public footpath." The man said officiously.

"There's nothing to indicate that it's private land, and in any case, we surely have the right to roam. Why haven't you fenced the compound off, if it is so sensitive?"

"Maybe we will need to. Now show me your map."

Ashok apprehensively handed over the map. He felt he had no choice.

"What is this?" the man said aggressively. "It's not a proper Ordnance Survey map. It's just a scribble on a piece of paper. There's no way you can tell what a proper right of way is from this?"

"Our college is very poor; they cannot afford to buy us real maps." Ashok said rather desperately. Jake winced and wished he'd said anything rather than that.

"There's something not right about you five. I'd like you to come along with me so we can sort this out."

Ashok and Jake looked at each other but they realised the only course of action at the moment was to comply. They were led to one of the older buildings and shown into a room that seemed to serve as a social area of some kind. There were cheap easy chairs such as you'd find in a school staffroom, a sink, coffee making facilities and a TV mounted on the wall.

"Right, would you mind emptying out your pockets so we can see if you have anything to prove your credentials." The man said, ordering them like a sergeant major.

Jake was thankful that they had no mobile phones or wallets on them. Under the present circumstances it was best to remain anonymous.

"Why have you got no means of identification on you?" The man said in evident frustration.

"We were specifically told not to bring mobile phones, wallets or cash with us, so we left all that stuff at our base camp." Ashok said.

"So where are your instructors?" The man asked.

"We're on our final expedition, so they left us at the start point and will pick us up at the final destination. If we don't get there in time, I expect they will come and look for us."

This was a clever thing for Ashok to have said. For the first time, the man looked a little worried about what he had done.

"I better consult with some of my superiors. Wait here and I'll be back shortly." The man strode towards the door, still carrying Taffy's hand-drawn map. All five of the trainee Guardians heard an ominous click after the door shut, indicating that it had been locked and the key removed.

Jake hit his fist in frustration and said to the others, "We've got to get out of here and we've got to get that map back. They'll be able to trace our camp with it, and Rakshi and the other five may well be in danger then."

Chapter 11

Darryn was driving the white van along the A5. He had managed to get four cars between himself and the army lorry. Even so, he was desperately worried that someone in the lorry was going to notice that he'd been behind all the way from Telford. They were now working their way along the Oswestry by-pass. The traffic was quite heavy, especially with caravans. People had obviously decided to make the most of what promised to be a glorious Easter weekend with a trip into Wales.

"Look," said Annabelle sitting in the passenger seat, "They're indicating to go down the old road into Chirk."

"Right, we'll take a risk," Darryn replied. "It really will look suspicious if we follow them through the town. I'm assuming they'll carry on down the A5 eventually. Let's stick on the main road and let them catch up."

Darryn continued to proceed on the main road and let the lorry go. It was only a matter of minutes before they passed the junction where the lorry would rejoin the A5. There was no way that they could have been beaten to this point; Darryn knew he must be ahead now. He continued driving into Llangollen and pulled in at a petrol station. He took the opportunity to buy some more diesel fuel and a chocolate bar as well. He then pulled over to a parking area near the air and water station where he and Annabelle simply waited.

After half an hour there was still no sign of the lorry and Darryn was getting anxious, "I haven't gone and cocked this up, have I, Annabelle?" he said somewhat uncertainly. A non-committal grunt from Annabelle was far from reassuring.

A further fifteen minutes elapsed before Annabelle almost shouted, "There they are, just coming up to the traffic lights." A moment later she added "What's this? There's a second one behind. What's going on?"

"They must have arranged to meet with another group in Chirk before moving on," Darryn explained, "But where are they from? Chester, Wrexham, Oswestry, Welshpool?"

Darryn calmly moved off to rejoin the traffic heading west. He found it difficult to squeeze into the line of traffic snaking through the town, but he was not unduly concerned. Once they climbed into the hills and snaked their way backwards and forwards through the mountain pass, there were few options for turning left or right. They could make out the trucks ahead of them from time to time when the road straightened out for a moment. The journey mirrored that which David had taken with the trainees just over a week ago, through Corwen and taking the road to Bala. In fact, Annabelle was becoming concerned that they were going to end up very close to their own training camp. However, the trucks continued on the main road to Bala itself, and then on past the lake.

"We've got company," Annabelle noted. "There's a blue Fiesta on our tail."

"Damn," said Darren, "The caretaker must have been working for the F.U.P. after all. He must have tipped someone off; you said he looked at us suspiciously as we got going."

The two trucks ahead of them slowed down to turn left into a narrow road that only had patches of tarmac at a village called Pont Fronwydd.

"Have you logged, this spot?" Darryn asked Annabelle. "We'll have to come back later. They can't go far in vehicles like that up those narrow lanes. We'll carry on to Dolgellau. I know a nurse who works in the veterinary practice there. We can park in the car park and throw our follower off the scent. Have you got a signal on your mobile?"

"Yes, a very good one," Annabelle responded rather surprised.

"Good, give Paul a ring and tell him to meet us there; it's just on the main road before you get to the bridge into the town."

***

The five trainees crouched beneath the broken window on the outside of the hut. Once they had decided what to do, it was amazing how quickly they were able to execute their plan. Ashok had stuffed some gaffer tape in the lock of the door so the key could not be placed in the keyhole to unlock it. Tim had then held up a sheet of plastic from his kit bag against the window while Jake had used the wooden leg of a chair to smash the glass in the main window. Fortunately it was an old fashioned frame with single glazing, so it gave quite easily. Jenny and Louise then helped push out as much of the glass as they could. They all took up their kitbags and gingerly left through the window, being as careful as possible not to leave anything or cut themselves on any remaining shards of glass.

"Tim, Jenny and Louise," Jake whispered authoritatively, "Make your way to the road and wait for us by the fork in the ways that was shown on the map. If necessary, hide in the hedge. Don't be seen by anyone while you're waiting." Jenny opened her mouth, but Jake continued tersely, "Don't argue Jenny. We can't afford to be all captured again. If we don't manage to rendez-vous with you in half an hour, do whatever you can to summon help from someone in the Rainbow Alliance."

Tim and the girls sloped off onto the moor to give a wide berth of the buildings and circle round onto the road. Their training with Taffy about moving discretely through the landscape was going to be put to the test sooner than expected.

There was a fumbling at the door to the room they had just left. Jake whispered to Ashok, "Right, matey, I reckon we've got no more than two minutes before they break the door down and realise we've gone."

They light-footedly moved along the length of the building looking in at each of the windows as they went, hoping they might discover the whereabouts of the map or at least the location of the man who had taken it.

"If he is on his own, do you think we could take him down and force him to give it back?" Ashok enquired optimistically.

"That's a last ditch scenario," Jake replied. "We want to try to be as discrete as possible. Let's hope he's put it on a table somewhere and we can just grab it."

Then, joy of joys, in the last room in the hut they saw that this was exactly what had happened. The room was an office with a substantial old-fashioned desk and chair just in front of the window. There were several metal filing cabinets set against the wall, as well as a sturdy looking safe. A few wooden cupboards completed the business-like air of the room. Unmistakably, there in the middle of the desk lay, flat and unfolded, their hand-drawn map.

"I think there's a door into the corridor at this end of the hut on the other side of the building. I've got a good chance of slipping in unobserved." Jake said excitedly.

"Okay, I'll wait here and try to give you cover if you need it," Ashok said in reply. "You can open the window from inside and escape that way."

Jake was now high on adrenaline and his heart was pumping. He slipped around the end of the building. There were a few people moving around nearby, but none were looking in his direction or paying attention to that end of the hut. With one smooth continuous movement he flowed deftly through the door. In little more than a second he assessed that the corridor was empty and continued his movement into the office, closing the door silently behind him. He picked up the map from the desk, folded it and put in his trouser pocket. He was about to exit through the window as Ashok had suggested, when a thick file, also lying on the desk, caught his attention. The title said, 'The systematic long term plan for the removal and the elimination of the strategic threat posed by the gays.'

Jake thought about removing this too, but then his psychological awareness training started to kick in. If he took the file, then the F.U.P. would know it had gone and they would change their plans. There would have been no point in taking the file. Maybe he could look at it and memorise the gist of the detail. There was little chance of that as he could see the document ran to hundreds of pages. He opened the file up and saw there was a three page summary at the beginning of the document. He looked around and there in the corner of the room, which he couldn't see from the window, was a small photocopier - and it was on. Ashok was now getting very agitated outside the window, but Jake disciplined himself to think clearly. Although every second seemed like an hour, he placed each page, one at a time, on the glass platen of the photocopier and waited for each copy to come out. He was expecting someone to enter the room at any moment. As the third copy was removed, Ashok gestured a 'thumbs down' sign through the window followed by a motion with his hand across his neck. He then pointed to his right and moved rapidly away. Jake was sweating with fear now. He put the file back on the desk, the copies in his pocket, and after a moment's hesitation, turned the photocopier off. He had lingered just a little too long. He heard footsteps and voices fast approaching down the corridor. He did the only thing he could, which was to hide behind the door. He braced himself and tensed his solar plexus just in case the door was thrown open with violence. Fortunately it wasn't, and fortunately the two people whose footsteps he'd heard, did not enter the room.

"There's no one in here," a voice said. "It's unlikely they would come up here anyway. I expect they've scarpered onto the moor and are running away as we speak."

"Maybe we should just leave it. To be honest they were just kids, and they may well have been telling the truth," The other voice said.

Jake heard a weary sigh and the first voice said, "I doubt the new boss man will let it rest. I expect he'll have us scouring the area all afternoon and evening to try and find them."

The door closed gently and the footsteps receded. Jake started to breathe again as his mind raced, trying to work out how he might extricate himself from the present situation. After thirty seconds or so he cautiously poked his head into the corridor. There was no one about, so he slid lithely out of the room, shutting the door behind him quietly. He opened the outer door a few centimetres. There were three people in view, none of whom were focusing on Jake's part of the building. He risked leaving the building, trying to put into practice everything he had been taught about moving silently and inconspicuously through a group of people. His first thought was to retrace his steps completely and try to find Ashok on the other side of the hut. However, he heard a considerable noise coming from there and guessed that the search party was still looking up and down for the five fugitives from the locked room. There were some large waste bins which might afford some temporary cover across the yard. The only problem was that he was going to have to get past the three people he'd seen from the corridor.

There was nothing for it. He started walking across the yard as inconspicuously as he could manage. Two of the three people walked off together towards a building on the far side of the yard without looking in his direction. Maybe he was going to get away with it. He had passed the third when once again he was pulled up short by a voice addressing him.

"Hey, who are you?" the third person shouted.

"I'm new here," Jake offered. "I'm just going to find out what I'm supposed to be doing."

"So where's your identity badge?" the third person asked suspiciously.

"Here it is," said Jake, holding up a Blake's supermarket customer loyalty card, which he had in his pocket, simply because it had fallen out of his wallet at the centre and he'd forgotten to put it back.

The third person, who was a thin young man, only a couple of years older than Jake, leaned forward and said, "What's this..."

Before he could utter another word Jake had sprung. He used a move he'd been taught in his martial arts classes to incapacitate an opponent. This was the first time he had ever attacked anyone in earnest. He was shocked to see his enemy sprawled senseless on the floor.

Jake checked to see that the young man was still breathing, and was mightily relieved to find that he had not killed him. He dragged the boy quickly to the bins and obscured him from view, leaning up against a wall. Ashok unexpectedly appeared from behind one of the other bins and said admiringly:

"Bloody hell, Jake, I didn't know you had it in you!"

"We haven't got time for mutual congratulations. We've still got to get out of here," Jake responded realistically.

The two boys crouched behind the bins from where they could now get a view of the track they had rather unfortunately travelled down earlier. The trees which covered the track's last fifty metres or so to the road were frustratingly close, but there were too many people about simply to make a run for it.

Out of the blue, Jake saw an opportunity. First of all he heard a low rumble and then, bursting through the trees, he saw one army lorry followed by another, crawling up the track towards the buildings.

"Quick," he rasped, grabbing Ashok's shirt and pulling him to an upright position. The two boys sauntered as casually as they could until they were on the far side of the track. Jake's timing was pretty much impeccable. The first lorry was just about up with them and so was providing a shield between them and the camp.

"Walk quickly but don't run," hissed Jake. "We don't want to appear suspicious to the driver of the second vehicle and there may be people in the back of the trucks as well."

There was a small gap between the first and second truck when they were briefly exposed for all to see. They tried to remember their training and pretended to be in conversation with each other while not looking towards the camp. They dared not look up to the cab of the second lorry either so had no idea if the driver was reacting in any way. The lorry kept moving at a crawl, while Ashok and Jake quickened their pace. It was a race against time. Every second, the second lorry was moving further from the trees. There was still a gap of about five metres to cover although they would still be partially obscured from the main part of the camp.

"We're nearly there, Ashok," Jake whispered, "Keep walking, and if anyone shouts, just pretend you can't hear them. As soon as we are in the trees and round the corner slip into the trees on the left and we'll regroup."

There was one moment when their hearts were in their mouths as a shout came from the vicinity of the first truck, but they quickly realised the shout was not addressed to them and they continued as casually as they could. They reached the canopy of the trees, they reached the bend in the track and they slid as silently as they could into the trees. When there was ten metres or so of trees between them and the track they stopped and relaxed for a moment.

"Jake you're a genius," Ashok exclaimed. "I never thought we'd get away with that in a month of Sundays."

The relief was short lived as Jake heard another vehicle coming up the track, through the woods from the road. It was a lighter vehicle than the trucks they had just used as visual shields. It turned out to be a standard four-by-four Range Rover.

"Quick, crouch down behind a tree so you can't be seen and keep completely still." Jake ordered.

The Range Rover agonisingly came to a halt just adjacent to their position. The engine continued to idle and neither Jake nor Ashok dared turn round to see what was happening. Two minutes of fearful ignorance reignited their adrenaline rush before, to their great relief, the engine revved up and the car moved on. As soon as it was clear that it had entered the area of the camp, the boys got up and Jake said, "Come on, we mustn't dawdle. I've got a feeling we're not in the clear yet. Let's go and meet up with the others."

There was no need for restraint now. They released their pent-up energy by rushing through the trees in a line parallel with the track, but ten metres in. They quickly came to the road, a narrow single-track road with only patchy blotches of tarmac. Nobody was about and there was no sound of an approaching vehicle, so they continued to run down the road as fast as they could. Within two minutes, Ashok and Jake had reached the fork in the road. There was no sign of Tim and the two girls, and for a moment Jake was worried that they hadn't made it.

However seconds later the three of them emerged from the hedge as if dryads suddenly taking human form.

"We wondered what had happened to you," Jenny said concerned. "We had to conceal ourselves when two army trucks came up the road and then a car came up too. We were only going to give you another five minutes and then we would have moved on."

"Well, so far it's worked out okay. I got the map back and I also found some F.U.P. plans that they might be interested in back at Rainbow House," Jake replied. "But we mustn't hang around here. There's a very strong possibility they will come looking for us. I think we should continue on the route shown on the map. It's the only way we can be sure of finding our way back to the centre."

They set off at once following the badly made-up road. They soon discovered that the slightly bigger road that the map showed it meeting was in fact the main Bala to Dolgellau road. They were in a small village, which they hadn't expected. They stopped a moment to consider whether it might be quicker to follow the main road. Louise pointed out that they hadn't a clue where their centre was in relation to the main road, while Ashok added that they would be sitting ducks to any pursuers chasing them in vehicles. They therefore crossed the road, passed through the village, and went into the fields on the other side, continuing towards some impressively high mountains.

Chapter 12

Two things happened back at the F.U.P. camp which had a bearing on future events. Firstly, a female operative entered the office, which Jake had vacated some minutes before. She looked aghast when she saw the sensitive folder lying on the desk and realised that it was she who had forgotten to put it away. The woman quickly gathered it up, opened the safe and deposited it there, hoping that no one would realise her breach of security. Therefore all of Jake's difficult decisions worked out in his favour, and no-one in the F.U.P. became aware that the 'gay elimination plan' had been compromised. Secondly, the camp quaked with fear as the driver of the four by four stormed into the control centre. The door nearly fell off its hinges as Michael O'Grady, his eyes looking particularly murderous, burst in.

"What the hell has been going on?" he thundered. "Why is the window smashed in the end hut, and why have you got people running around like blue-arsed flies?"

One of the people in the room timidly responded, "We had some kids coming down the track. We apprehended them, but they escaped. They were probably on a Duke of Edinburgh expedition..." The man tailed off realising this was not going down well.

"You witless fool!" Michael O'Grady continued at considerable volume, "How many Duke of Edinburgh hopefuls do you think would have the knowledge or the gumption to try and escape from a military training camp? They were probably associated with those Rainbow Fairies that we need to crush. Why haven't you sent people out to search beyond the camp? There were two sets of footprints leading into the trees on the track up to the camp."

With that, everyone rushed around a lot more, orders were barked and search parties were quickly convened. Michael O'Grady had two other people with him. One was a handsome looking man in his late twenties with blue eyes and blond hair who he called Andrew and who seemed to be acting as O'Grady's right-hand man. The other was Martin.

***

Darryn and Annabelle had returned to the village of Pont Fronwydd. Their contact in Dolgellau, Paul, had driven the white van back to Telford. The blue Fiesta had followed it like a brainless sheep, leaving Darryn and Annabelle to go about their business unhindered, and using Paul's white Suzuki Alto to get about.

Darryn and Annabelle were about to get out of the car, when a group of ten or so men and women dressed in combat fatigues burst down the lane. They paused, a little uncertain of what to do, and then carried on across the main road, making their way to the other end of the village.

"That's interesting," Darryn noted. "They seem to be looking for someone or something, I think it might be interesting to follow them and see what's going on. Can you reconnoitre the camp by yourself?"

"Of course," said Annabelle rather testily, "In fact, I'd be happier doing it on my own as I usually have to come and rescue you when you're involved."

Darryn blew Annabelle a little kiss as he got out of the car and said, "I love you too, darling. Look after the car keys and keep in touch. The phone reception seems reasonable around here."

Darryn was also dressed in combat fatigues so that he could blend in with landscape if necessary. He followed the group at a distance. They came to a wooden stile and again paused, as if uncertain what to do. Darryn watched as the group looked around and argued. Then one amongst the group pointed to the hills very excitedly. This seemed to galvanise the other members who rapidly crossed the stile and started at a vigorous pace along the clear track which meandered gently upwards towards the foothills of the mountains beyond. Darryn trained a pair of binoculars on the track and following it into the far distance, he could make out five figures. He estimated they might be as much as a couple of miles ahead, and they did not seem to be aware of their pursuers. A rather troubling thought was forming in his mind and he tried to call Taffy and Rakshi on their mobiles before crossing the stile himself. Taffy's phone was on voicemail, so he left a message making it clear that Taffy should get back to him as soon as possible. He did manage to get hold of Rakshi but was not terribly reassured by her response.

"Hi, Darryn," she said, "My group are miles away from there and I'm watching them from a distance as we speak. I haven't a clue where Taffy's dropped his group off, but one of his routes does go that way. "

"Who's in Taffy's group?" Darryn asked.

"Jenny, Louise, Ashok, Tim and Jake," Rakshi replied.

"Right, well if you hear from him, tell him to get in touch immediately."

Darryn crossed the stile aiming to keep a good half mile behind. They were walking fast but not running. He could no longer see the five figures ahead so he had no idea whether the pursuers were gaining or not.

After an hour he got a call from Annabelle. He lay flat on the ground while he was taking it.

"Darryn," Annabelle said anxiously, "There's a whole military base being built up here. There must be over a hundred people milling around. Anyway, that's not the point at the moment. Something has happened here, the place seems in uproar. One of the windows in the end block seems to have been smashed and it looks as if they are sending out search parties."

"I've got a horrible feeling that Jake and his friends have somehow upset them. Leave the camp for now. We can have a proper look round later. The priority at the moment is to make sure Taffy's group come to no harm. See if you can have more luck in tracking down Taffy. We need to know where he sent them."

***

"Can we have a rest now?" Jenny complained. "We've been going uphill for ages and my legs are starting to ache."

"I think we ought to keep going," Jake replied. He was being troubled by a sense of impending doom.

"We will have to take a rest eventually," Ashok pointed out sensibly.

"Alright," Jake said rather hesitantly, "Let's at least make for that wooded area and then find somewhere away from the track."

So that is what they did. They made the effort to reach the trees and then moved to their left, off the track and further up the slope, until they found a fallen tree trunk to sit on.

"Let's have a look at the map again." Ashok requested. "There are no real features of any note marked until we get to a big lake. There seems to be another major road going by the side of that. Then we just seem to arc round on the other side of the road to get back to the centre."

"How far have we come?" Louise asked.

"There's no knowing if it's to scale, but I'd guess we we're about halfway. Now it's getting on for five o'clock and we were delayed at the F.U.P. camp, so we might just be able to get back before it's completely dark."

"I say we review the situation when we get to the lake," Ashok said. "That might be a good place to camp for the night."

Tim had wandered a little higher up the hill and had come to a rocky knoll that stuck out from the trees and afforded a breathtaking panorama of the whole valley they had just climbed out of. In the distance Bala with its associated lake could be seen and as you swept round you could make out the village they had passed through, one or two of the buildings of the F.U.P camp and the hill just beyond it.

"Come up here," Tim shouted down. The rest were so surprised that Tim had forcefully requested anything that they obeyed instantly. After admiring the view, it was Louise who spotted them, "Look," she yelled, "Coming up the track behind us. There are some people dressed in army uniform, just as they were at the F.U.P camp. They can't be more than half a mile behind, and look..."

She tailed off because it was now obvious to all of them that in the distance another twenty or thirty people had just crossed the stile by the village and were following some distance behind.

"Right, let's not panic," Jake said, taking command of the situation. "They only seem to be following the trail. They cannot see us in these woods, although we must get down from this hill now. I say we hide and see if they simply carry on up the track, thinking we are still ahead. Let's spread out too, so if one of us is captured maybe the others can escape."

73

The other four were simply pleased that Jake was prepared to take command and fell in with his suggestions. The first ten pursuers eventually did do exactly what Jake hoped. They simply followed the track on up with little care to check about them. Having given them a few minutes to carry on, the five would-be Guardians reconvened,

"Right," Jake said, "We have about twenty minutes to decide what to do. Louise, just go up to the rock again and see what progress those other twenty or thirty are making."

Louise set off and was quickly back to report they were making rapid progress and that Jake's estimate of twenty minutes was about right before they would be too close for comfort. Ashok suddenly grabbed Jake's arm and whispered, "Something moved in the trees just below us."

"Quick back to your hiding positions," Jake hissed. Everyone returned to their places of concealment. A figure came partially into view dressed in army clothing similar to that worn at the F.U.P. camp. It was only one person. Jake, emboldened by his recent combat experience, sprang up and attempted the same move that had proved so successful earlier. This time he ended up flat on his back. He stared up into a face that was smiling with dimples either side and mischievous sparkling brown eyes staring back into his.

"Darryn!" he exclaimed.

"Nice try, matey, but just remember you're the trainee and I'm the master,"

There was a moment of hugging and general bonhomie as everyone was relieved they had encountered a friend and not an enemy. Darryn, however, immediately took charge of the situation.

"Right, you can tell me what's been going on later, but for now the priority is to get out of this safely. I'd like to know where that fool Taffy Williams is. He should never have let you lot get into this scrape." As if appearing from another dimension, Taffy Williams suddenly materialised from the undergrowth.

"Darryn, you disappoint me," he said with mock hurt. "Don't you think I was watching over my charges all the time? They were doing very well too. I especially liked the way you escaped from the F.U.P. camp – very ingenious."

"Taffy, they're only kids," Darryn protested.

"You're an old mother hen, Darryn. My lovely boys have got to learn to stand on their own two feet sometime. Anyway, enough talk. The centre minibus is down by the main road. I've contacted Annabelle and she'll meet us there."

"Okay, but we are going to have to evade these extra characters that are coming up close behind. Listen, we are going to move to the lower edge of the wood, but remain hidden. We will wait until they enter the wood and then break cover. They will not be able to see us because they will now be in the woods themselves. We must be as quiet as possible because we will be very close to them at the point we move. Let's hope they don't meet up with the group in front until we are well on our way."

All seven of them moved down the slope and crossed the track, carrying on through the trees until they could see bare moorland beckoning. Taffy followed up the rear and did what he could to obscure any sign of their tracks. They squatted down a couple of trees in from the edge. Only Darryn had a view of the track as it entered the wood, but the others could distinctly hear voices as the larger group of pursuers approached. Then at a signal from Darryn, they summoned up all the woodcraft they could muster to move silently into the open.

The rugged moorland sloped downwards at a gradient that was uncomfortable on the knees. There was no track and so they were dependent on Darryn to lead the way. So far so good, there was no sign of anyone following. They had to clamber over an abandoned stone boundary wall and then make further progress without startling a flock of sheep that were thinly spread across sparse grazing.

At last they could make out a speck in the distance that was the minibus. They had two rather more established fields to cross, again, both full of sheep. Taffy was looking anxious, "There are some people on the outcrop. They will be able to see us."

Noises could be heard behind them and then figures burst out of the wood.

"Run," said Darryn. He threw Jenny and Louise over a stone wall into the first field and came up last with Taffy. "There's a gate between the two fields. Make for that rather than clambering across the walls."

The youngsters were hampered by their packs so their running was barely more than a trot. Jake could see Darryn and Taffy looking at each other with concern and guessed that they were weighing up in their minds whether they could get to the bus before the F.U.P. search party, running at full tilt, overtook them.

They reached the gate. Fortunately it opened with ease. As Darryn closed the gate, the first chasing figure could be seen clearing the wall on the far side of the field they were just leaving. The five trainees, exhausted but fuelled by fear, continued to trot as fast as they could, Taffy and Darryn skipped along behind them, resisting the temptation to simply make a bolt for it.

"Keep going," urged Darryn. "Don't slow down." The minibus was an enticing spectacle now, like a mirage in a desert. Two hundred metres to go – Taffy turned around to see the first of the chasers come through the gate. One hundred metres to go - another three had come through the gate and the first one was bearing down on them rapidly. Fifty metres to go –Taffy waved the electronic key in the direction of the bus.

"Quick, get on board, kids. Taffy, start up the engine." With that, Darryn turned to face the first of his enemies. He was glad they had been so ill-disciplined. This first F.U.P. paramilitary, although he was the quickest, had no support and was completely out of breath. It was an easy matter for Darryn to incapacitate him, However, the second and the third were not far behind, and he could make out a number too numerous to count who had just passed through the gate.

Louise was the last of the five youngsters to board. As her legs disappeared through the side door, the engine spluttered into life. Darryn had to deal with the second and then immediately afterwards, the third combatant. The back doors of the minibus burst open with an exhortation from Taffy at the driver's wheel for Darryn to make a dash for it. He did so, just as the fourth pursuer grabbed his leg. Jake and Ashok pulled Darryn onboard. The fourth F.U.P. man was dispatched by a ferocious kick from Darryn, and slid out of the bus to the ground. The bus started to move as Jake and Ashok quickly shut the back doors.

"Lock all the doors," said Taffy calmly as he began to move away at an agonisingly slow pace. There were fifty metres of unmade track to negotiate before they could turn onto the main road and speed away. Half a dozen had now caught up and were banging on the back of the bus as it crawled down the lane. Then a sharp thud was heard and the glass shattered in the back window. Someone had thrown a stone.

"Keep down," shouted Darryn. The bus suddenly turned sharply to the left and then sped away. Darryn dared a glance behind to see a multitude of figures now waving angrily but helplessly behind them. Then a car hooted and drove past them nearly mowing one of them down. It was Annabelle. Unusual of her to be late for all the action, he thought.

"Well, my lovely boys, that was an exciting adventure," Taffy said with twinkling eyes and a bristling moustache.

Chapter 13

After they got back to the centre and had a meal, Darryn decided he wanted to set off back to London straight away with the three photocopied pages that Jake had presented him with. He'd had a quick look at them, but they were written in typically official language and his mind was still racing with the events of the day.

"I'll take Jake with me," Darryn said. "Danny and N°6 will want to talk to him anyway to put the document in context. Do you want to come along for the ride too, Tim?"

Tim was sitting nearby and seemed pleased to be asked; he gave his assent readily.

At ten o'clock Darren was ready to set off in Paul's car, with Jake sitting in the front passenger seat and Tim content to sit in the back. Although, the days were now rapidly getting longer it was dark as they set off. Darryn and Jake had a lot to catch up on and Tim, never one to push himself forward, was content to listen in the back.

"So did Taffy try that falling into the quarry routine with you?" Darryn enquired.

"Yes he did," Jake replied. "We dragged him more than halfway back before he owned up. Jenny was furious with him." Tim chuckled in the back recalling Jenny's rants and Taffy simply ignoring her.

"Taffy would have loved that," continued Darryn. "He has a soft spot for feisty girls."

"Really?" said Jake, raising an eyebrow.

"Yes, he likes to wind them up and get them really mad."

"Well, he certainly succeeded there! How did he do it though? We all saw him fall into the quarry. It was deep enough for the fall to kill him. He won't tell us a thing about how he managed it."

"Mm... I'm not sure I should give away Taffy's secrets."

Both boys protested so vehemently, that Darryn was forced to give in.

"Okay, I'll tell you. You say you saw Taffy fall in, but I bet you didn't. I'd imagine you were at least twenty metres back from the edge. He was counting on you taking a few seconds to get over the shock and then a few more to reach the edge and summon up the courage to look in. He had a big mat down there, like they have for the pole vault in athletics. Having landed on that safely, he would have pushed it up vertically behind some rocks and gone and lain down prone in another part of the quarry. I bet you didn't have a good look in the quarry itself."

"The sneaky toe rag!" shouted Jake.

Darryn just laughed and added, "Never take Taffy for granted. He's a wise old codger and he surprised even me when he turned up in the woods this afternoon,"

"So if he is so wise, why did he send us straight into the middle of an F.U.P. training camp?"

"He does admit he slipped up there," Darryn agreed with a smile on his face. "He knew some of the buildings were there, but the F.U.P. must have only taken it over in the last month or so. Anyhow, it is you being so stubborn that caused the problem. Every other group that Taffy's let out on that route has realised that it is much quicker to walk around the hill on the road. Trust you to be the one to insist on following the path on the map to the letter."

"Is that such a bad thing?" Jake asked rather hurt by Darryn's comment.

"In one way, yes, but in another it did cause you to do something unexpected. It's never good to be too predictable."

"So have we passed or failed our training?"

Darryn smiled and said, "Let's just say that Taffy will have to use somewhat different assessment criteria from normal to decide."

As they sped through the North Shropshire countryside, Darryn brought Jake and Tim up to date with his dealings with Martin in Digby Forester's garden and his encounters in the Clarendon Laboratory. Jake had only found out that Darryn was a maths tutor at Oxford just before Christmas, but it had explained the mystery of why he was always going off there for days at a time.

"Now, I'm going to have to give Paul his car back and pick up mine. This will mean an unwelcome detour through Telford. I'd like you two lads to keep a very low profile please, especially you, Jake. There will be hardly anyone about at this time of night, but even so, if you recognise anyone avoid eye contact and try to ignore them."

They left the motorway at junction 4 and turned left. Darryn turned left again after a mile on to a well-maintained estate that seemed free of F.U.P. influence. He stopped outside an ordinary, but well-appointed house.

"My car's over there. Just go and make yourself at home and put your belongings in the boot," Darryn said, giving Jake the key. Meanwhile he knocked on the door of the house, which still had a downstairs light on. Jake noticed a brief friendly conversation between Darryn and the person who opened the door, but in a couple of minutes they were on their way again; once more Telford was left far behind.

As Darryn whizzed through the Birmingham section of the M6, a feat only possible because it was now after one o'clock in the morning, he decided to go on the M40 rather than the M1. The conversation was flagging now and Tim was beginning to doze off in the back seat.

"I could do with a toilet break, lads. I'm going to pull in at the next service station," Darryn announced, somewhat startling Jake, who was himself just about to drift off. The service station just south of Leamington was almost deserted. All the shops and the self-service restaurant were shuttered up, but the toilets were still open and there was a coffee machine just inside the door. Tim was taking his time in the toilets and so Darryn decided to buy himself a coffee.

"Do you want one?" he asked Jake.

"No you're alright. What is it with Tim? He told me you'd stopped him committing suicide."

Darryn raised an eyebrow before replying: "Did he, now! That is most unusual for Tim."

"So what's the story?" Jake asked impatiently.

"Come, come, you know better than to ask me to reveal another person's rescue story. It's for Tim to tell if he wants to, not me. All I will say is that he is a fragile and very unhappy soul. Please be gentle in your dealings with him and don't say a word to anyone about him trying to commit suicide – not even to Nathan." Darryn nudged Jake in the ribs as Tim reappeared at the entrance to the toilets, "Hi Tim, are you ready to go?" Tim nodded affirmatively.

They finally slid into the secret car park at the bottom of Rainbow House at four in the morning. Jake made for his room, simply removed his clothes and slipped into his bed. The sheer bliss of a comfortable mattress after a week of rough living was enough to send him into the land of sleep.

***

"Hi, babe," Nathan greeted Jake the next morning.

"Hi, matey, I've missed you loads," Jake replied grasping Nathan in a passionate embrace and giving him a long lingering kiss. Slowly, they made their way down to the social zone where Jake made himself a coffee. He had got up far too late to get any breakfast. It was Easter Sunday and the area was quieter than usual.

"You caused quite a stir in Wales. They've moved my training session to Scotland because of what you got up to," Nathan commented.

"Well it wasn't my fault we were directed into the middle of an F.U.P. training camp. I did find some vital intelligence, you know. I've got to go and see N°6 later on."

"Aren't you just the daring secret agent," said Nathan mockingly, punching Jake playfully in the ribs, "So, where's Jenny and the rest of them?"

"They'll be back later today. Darryn brought me and Tim back in his car last night."

"Special treatment for my special boy," Nathan said as if talking to a baby.

"Shut up, Nathan. So what's been going on here while I've been away?"

"It's been as dull as ditchwater. I've been working on my composition for my A-level music and practicing the Elgar cello concerto like mad. Mr Devonshire's orchestra might do it with me if I can get it ready by

September. Oh yes, and Matt is having an affair with his art teacher at college."

"For heaven's sake, has that boy got no sense or taste in men?"

"You don't have to tell me that. The man is a sleazy creep from what I hear. James Wellby's his name. I think he is married with kids as well. I'll have to ask the art teacher here if he knows anything about him."

Both Jake and Nathan ruminated over the spectacle of Matt and his new lover. After discussing some other trivial gossip, Nathan returned to the subject of his music project, "Now, are you going to help me with my composition? I really need someone to play through the first violin part to check it fits."

The two boys collected their instruments from their rooms and went to use a small practice room in the school area. Nathan's composition was a movement for a string quartet. He was hoping that when it was finished he, Jake, Maria and Mr Devonshire would play it through, as they occasionally got together to play through some Haydn and Mozart string quartets which Mr Devonshire had parts for. The two of them played through from the beginning.

"Mm... The first bits okay," Jake said, "But then this next bit sounds completely wrong. Are you sure you wrote it down properly?"

"Well I was trying to be modern there. I can't work out from my teacher whether I'm supposed to produce something that sounds like bad Mozart or something that sounds as if it's been mangled in a car crusher." Nathan responded.

"I'd stick to the bad Mozart, if I were you. It's only A-level after all. They can't expect you to be both Jaqueline du Pré and Beethoven, all in one and the same person."

***

The operations room was humming quietly. As it was Easter Sunday, only skeleton staffing was in place. A few lights were flashing and in the corner a lonely female operative had a pair of headphones on, presumably listening to incoming calls. The scene in N°6's office was in stark contrast to this, however, as N°6, Danny and Darryn were examining in minute detail the text of the three pages that Jake had photocopied and smuggled out of the F.U.P. camp. N°6 was an intelligent, articulate and avuncular man with a hearty build who had managed to retain a full head of hair even though he was now well into his fifties. By comparison, both Darryn and Danny looked like his sons or young apprentices.

Darryn squirmed as he read the first few paragraphs as they alluded to his escapade in Paris just over a year previously and did not paint him in a particularly good light. The document began:

'*Our efforts to eradicate the homosexual threat have so far been thwarted at every turn. Suspicions that a well-organised and funded group lay behind this sabotage were confirmed when an agent of this group was briefly* captured in Paris. He had some sophisticated listening devices, a gun, and other items which may have assisted him in espionage. The fact that he escaped and overcame the attempts of two of our agents to prevent him leaving the country, suggests that he had training and support from a much more highly accomplished assistant.'

Even though he was red-faced, he bristled at the idea of his assistant being more highly accomplished; he determined that Annabelle would never get to see this part of the transcript. The manuscript continued:

'So far, our political success has not been matched by our attempts to create a professional paramilitary force. The fiasco in Dorset last summer, when we lost seventeen teenagers to the gay desperados, only highlighted the deficiencies. There has, however, been one notable exception. The simultaneous bombing in London, Manchester and Birmingham caught the headlines and generated genuine terror. This event was outsourced to a group of dissident Northern Ireland terrorists under the leadership of someone who wished to be known as Michael O'Grady. Following the success of this operation, O'Grady was offered a position as Chief of armed operations and paramilitary training. His acceptance (on a free-lance basis) at the beginning of November initiated a move to set up a training camp in Wales and a programme to start training our more successful Neighbourhood Protection Committees. Money for this venture is being provided from the United States. Congressman Wayne Hackett remains our conduit and he will shortly be visiting the UK to discuss the discrete dispatch of funding without implicating the political wing of the F.U.P. which must remain independent and at arm's length.

At some point, when training and resources reach a suitable level, a second terror event will be launched, this time focussing on one venue, with the aim of inflicting death and injury on a massive scale. The terror effect will discourage the homosexual population, sow dissent in the wider general population and destabilise still further a weak and ineffectual government which is likely to fall at any moment. The details of this plan can be found later in the document (see plan A26b-operation "Gay Wipe-out").

In the longer term, our realistic political aim is to hold the balance of power after the next election and force one of the major parties into a coalition. Our priority will be to demand The Home Office and if strong enough, the Ministry of Defence as well. We can then extend our control over the police and armed forces. We need to infiltrate the gay organisation that is causing us such problems with a view to discovering their headquarters. When we discover its whereabouts, we can use the full might of the state to destroy it. We have a special agent who has been given special dispensation by the Vatican to help lure an enemy agent into indiscretion (see plan F34 – operation "Agent Entrapment" – and plan G2 – operation "Total Wipe-out").

At this point Jake walked in. The other three looked up and greeted him.

81

N°6 passed a photocopy of the three pages to Jake saying, "Here you are, my boy. As you went to so much trouble to get this, I think you have a right to view the contents." Jake took a few minutes to read the transcript while the conversation continued around him.

"I begin to see why that bombing last year was so out of keeping with the rest of the F.U.P activity," Danny said. "This O'Grady fellow seems like a dangerous piece of work. It's bad news that he seems permanently involved with the F.U.P now."

"Yes, I agree," commented N°6. "We will have to up our game if we are going to match the threat." He stroked his chin for a moment, despite the fact that he was clean-shaven, "It seems to me that we have three things to worry about. Firstly we have to neutralise the threat of another atrocity and save life and limb. Then we have to foil this attempt to compromise one of our agents. That all sounds very mysterious. What has the Vatican to do with it? Finally we may have to defend our HQ from a full-scale military assault."

"The shield is going into production soon," Darryn added. "We've found a little corner at the British Aircraft Systems factory in North London where we can make it without the bosses being any the wiser."

"That's good," said N°6 approvingly, "but I think our main worry, just at present, is to thwart operation 'Gay Wipe-out'. That seems to be first on their agenda; if only we had some idea of where they planned to strike."

At that moment, Darryn's mobile went off, "Excuse me," he said, "I'd better take it. It's Annabelle."

He left the room so he could concentrate more clearly on what Annabelle was saying, leaving N°6 and Danny to discuss possible targets and strategies for combating the threat. Jake felt a bit of a spare part and wondered whether he should offer to leave. However, he was curious to find out what Annabelle was going to say. She, Rakshi and Taffy had been charged with keeping an eye on the F.U.P. camp once all the youngsters were packed off safe and sound.

Darryn returned a few minutes later with a furrowed brow, "The F.U.P. has advertised for a part-time cook for the camp in the Bala Post Office; Annabelle has decided to apply for it to get cover for investigating the camp further. I can't say I'm very happy about that. She also says that Michael O'Grady has taken up residence in the camp, but that a rather attractive young man with blond hair seems to be acting as his right-hand man."

"Well if that isn't enough we still haven't cracked Martin's message," Danny added rather despondently. He put a photocopy of the note on the table. Jake now looked at it with interest. He had only heard oblique accounts of Darryn's encounter with Martin and had not seen the text before.

'Darryn,
        Your secret is safe – but I'm not.
        Beware! The last tree can fall.'

It seemed to him that the words 'last tree can' were in slightly bolder writing, but none of the others had commented on it. Jake remembered Darryn telling him that Martin had a weakness for cryptic crosswords and was always looking to change words and phrases into anagrams. He decided to speak:

"I think 'last tree can' is slightly more prominent than the rest of the text. If you change the order of the letters you can get it to spell Canal Street."

Danny leapt up in excitement, "Jake, you're a genius!" he shouted. "We all thought it was about an attack on Rainbow House, but it looks as if it's a clue to the location of the 'Gay Wipe-out' plan. So they're planning an attack in Manchester, at one of the venues on Canal Street."

"Yes, but which one and *when*?" N°6 added with an air of frustration.

"....And can Martin be trusted," Darryn muttered darkly.

"We'll it's the only clue we've got and Martin doesn't seem to have divulged critical information about us yet," Danny replied optimistically. "He does say in the note that your secret is safe."

Chapter 14

The start of the summer term was a return to hard academic graft for Jake. He had important exams in June and the fact that the Government couldn't decide whether or not they were going to count towards his A-level results only added to the stress. He had not really warmed to college and wished that he could have done all his studies in the friendly environment of the Rainbow House School. The FE College was cold and impersonal. It was full of long echoing corridors and sets of functional stairs with metal handrails. The classrooms were more or less identical rectangular boxes painted in a uniform magnolia colour. Even the labs were merely a variation on this theme. He had not really formed any attachment to his lecturers, or any students other than those he knew from Rainbow House. In fact he made sure he always made an arrangement to meet someone he knew (usually Nathan) at lunchtime, and it was this interaction which made the days bearable. He was indebted to Mr Devonshire who had patiently gone over work with him, not only chemistry, but physics as well.

On top of this, Jake was also now very close to taking his Grade 8 violin exam. Fortunately it was going to be at the beginning of July, which gave him a couple of weeks after his year 12 exams were over to really put finishing touches to his preparation. It was the scales and arpeggios which were causing a problem. He found it difficult to keep them in tune in the higher octaves while keeping them going at a reasonable speed. Mr Simmonds, his teacher was being very laid back about things and was being very positive about his pieces.

The spring had been a mix of warm days followed by periods of cold blustery showers. Now however, in the middle of May, came a weekend that was genuinely hot. Sunday evening found Jake, Nathan, Maria, Jenny and Louise on the roof of Rainbow house enjoying the tranquillity of a summer's evening. They were wearing tee-shirts and shorts and had cold drinks to hand. The roof was tended like a suburban garden with an extent of turf surrounded by flowerbeds, shrubs and even one or two small trees. Only the constant rumble of city life and the passage of boats up and down the Thames belied the fact that they were not sitting in some well-kept back garden. The three girls were sitting on the turf on top of a reed mat. Jake was lying on a bench with his head resting in Nathan's lap.

"Thank goodness we got graded for our training weekend," Louise said, "I was really worried when we didn't complete the final trek that we might have to do the whole thing again."

The students had just that day received notice of their results. All five of Jake's group had been awarded a pass with honours and were now entitled to be known as Apprentice Guardians. The citation had stated that although the five had not completed the final task, they had demonstrated the appropriate skills in escaping from the F.U.P. camp and, in Jake's case, acquiring vital intelligence.

"Apprentice Guardian Jake Holdencroft - That has a fine ring to it!" Jake said. "If we pass the next stage, we'll actually start getting paid. I wonder how much Darryn and Annabelle earn."

"Alright," said Nathan irritably, "I'll be joining you soon enough."

"Where's Tim, by the way?" Jake enquired.

"Did anyone ask him to join us?" Maria asked. She continued, "I think he's having one of his black moods at the moment. I haven't seen him at all at college this week and I don't think I've seen him about in Rainbow House either. Sometimes he prefers to keep his own company."

Jake now felt very guilty. It was his fault that Tim had not been invited.

"It's not good for Tim to be on his own so much, especially as he's..." Jake stopped himself just in time. He had been going to say, 'especially as he's already tried to commit suicide once.'

Maria looked at Jake suspiciously and said, "Especially as he's done what?"

"Nothing," mumbled Jake, who was now so conscience-stricken that he got up from his resting place and immediately went to try and find Tim. There was no reply to a knock on his apartment door and a quick tour of the social zone yielded no results either. After twenty minutes, he shrugged his shoulders and went back to the roof to rejoin his friends.

"While you're up, fill my glass again, babe," Nathan greeted him. Jake acted as barman and filled everyone's glasses with more fizzy lemonade.

The sun went down and the light gradually diminished, but it was still hot and they remained there as the lights about them started to twinkle.

"What are you planning to do in the summer holidays?" Nathan asked Jake.

"I was going to visit Mum, Daisy and Maisie in Malvern. I was hoping you might come too."

"Sure, why not? I haven't got any other plans. Are you sure your mum will be cool with it?"

"I think she's got her head round me being gay. As long as we are discreet about the house, she'll be fine."

Nathan laughed and said, "I shall be terribly, terribly discreet, dear boy!"

Jake and Nathan held each other, as did Louise and Jenny. Maria did not seem to mind being the only one uncoupled; she was genuinely happy that Jenny had found someone to love. They were about to call it a day when Maria had a call from Matt.

"Hi, darling, how's things?" Maria asked. Unexpectedly she was greeted with sobs and tears. "Matt, what's the matter?" She continued, rather more urgently.

It was difficult to get any sense out of Matt. In the end she simply asked him where he was, to which she got the reply that he was down by the river near the Tower of London.

"Okay, I'll come and meet you there," she said decisively as she ended the call.

"I'll come with you," said Jake. "You shouldn't be wandering the streets alone at this hour. The tube should still be running if we're quick."

"I'll come too," said Nathan.

"Alright," agreed Maria uncertainly, "But no more than that, it would be ridiculous if we all went, and I wouldn't be surprised if Matt is just being a bit of a drama queen."

***

Annabelle was cursing her luck as she was peeling the hundredth potato of the day. Why did she always end up with mundane tasks while Darryn seemed to get all the excitement? She had easily got the job as a part-time cook on the camp and had spent the last few days doing just that. She hoped that by now she had blended in enough to avoid suspicion. There were plenty of rules about where she was allowed to go and who she was allowed to speak to. In fact her employers seemed keen to restrict her access to just the canteen and the kitchen.

Since Jake's adventure there, they had tightened up security considerably with a barbed wire fence going all the way around the perimeter and a barrier and guard post across the track to the camp as it emerged from the wooded area adjacent to the road. Annabelle had been given papers which she had to present to the guard post both on entering and leaving the camp.

Annabelle saw very little of Michael O'Grady; a glimpse now and then, but he never came in to eat with the men and women in the canteen. His young assistant was another matter. He was very charming and often ate with staff of all ranks and positions. He had even had a brief conversation with Annabelle about the state of the kitchens. She had discovered that his name was Andrew and although he was from Godalming, had spent the last five years training in Rome. Exactly what he was training to be remained a mystery though. If she had been straight, she would have found his blond hair and blue eyes very beguiling.

She threw the one hundred-and-twentieth potato back in the sack. Enough was enough; it was now time to do a bit of reconnaissance work. She remembered Jake's description of the room where he had found the report. It might be worth having another look around.

She slipped outside as if to have a ten minute break. However, when it was clear there was no one else about, she ran across the yard and entered the building opposite by exactly the same door that Jake had used. Like him, she slipped smoothly into the office room and started to look about. Everything was quiet and she felt she had five minutes to have a quick look around.

"Hello, Annabelle," A still voice suddenly said from somewhere in the room. Annabelle jumped out of her skin and looked around to see a figure emerging from the shadow by the filing cabinet.

"Martin!" she screamed as quietly as possible.

"You seem surprised to see me. You really are getting careless being caught as easily as this."

Annabelle weighed up in her mind whether to take Martin on in a fight.

"Don't even consider it," laughed Martin, knowing exactly what she was thinking. Annabelle relaxed and Martin continued, "Do not underestimate Michael O'Grady. He is a ruthless, cold-blooded murderer. He has already stirred things up here and they are intending to train some seriously professional paramilitaries."

"So are you going to hand me over?" asked Annabelle, trying her best not to let her voice quiver.

"Good gracious, no," said Martin as if it was the last thing on his mind. "That would not be at all interesting. No, I want you to give Darryn a message. Tell him to be in the main concourse at Waterloo Station on the twenty-seventh of May at five o'clock in the afternoon."

"What is it with you and Darryn?" asked Annabelle unable to help herself.

"Maybe he's the only person in your organisation I can trust," he said shrugging his shoulders. "Now, I'd advise you to stick to peeling spuds for the next few days, and do tell Rakshi and that idiot Williams that I've been monitoring their every move around the camp. Run along back to the kitchens."

Annabelle looked quizzically at Martin for a moment and left the room.

***

They found Matt sitting on a bench smoking a cigarette and shaking rather nervously. As soon as he saw his three friends he got up and dramatically came forward to embrace one of them. The fact that it was Jake who received the benefit of his attention caused resentment and raised eyebrows form the other two for slightly different reasons. Maria felt she had a special bond with Matt and felt snubbed that he had sought solace from Jake and not her. Nathan had a jealous moment of thinking Matt was trying to muscle in on his boyfriend.

"What's up?" asked Maria rather testily, "What's all the dramatic stuff about?"

"My God, it's terrible," Matt said clearly very upset. "I thought I was going to be raped."

"Weren't you seeing that creep Wellby tonight?" Nathan asked in a none-too-sympathetic way. Unexpectedly, Matt did not contradict him but simply started to give an account, through sobs and passionate rage, of the evening's events:

"I thought we were just going out for dinner. He took me to this house near Fenchurch Street Station. Some older men were already there. I thought they were couples at first but then it became clear that they wanted me to

87

have sex with them - some kind of orgy. Well I didn't want to get involved, so I made it clear I wasn't happy. James turned really nasty and said I was a tease and a tart - and worse things. I thought he was going to get physical and force me into doing something really sleazy. I gave him a slap and rushed out of the front door. I've been shaking ever since."

"I thought you liked having sex with older guys?" Nathan said coldly.

"Nathan," interjected Jake with more than a hint of chastisement in his voice, "You can see he's upset. Lay off him, he's had a very unpleasant experience."

Nathan shrugged his shoulders, but Maria softened and said, "Come on then let's get you home. I really think you ought to tell someone about this. You've been taken advantage of by someone you really ought to be able to trust."

Matt put one arm around Jake and one around Maria. As they walked off into the night to catch a bus back, Nathan walked a few paces behind, clearly in the doghouse.

***

Darryn was in the middle of a video conference with Annabelle.

"So Martin was very definite about the time and place, but he wouldn't give a hint about what he wanted to meet you for," Annabelle said, concluding the account of her meeting with Martin.

"Will I never be rid of that man?" replied Darryn with feeling. "The galling thing is that I've no option but to comply with his request. You know, Annabelle, I feel like a puppet in some weird game he's playing, and I don't like it."

"Well just think of the problems I've got. My covers been essentially blown, but I can't *not* carry on going to the camp or that really would look suspicious. At any moment, Martin can decide to tell someone who I really am, and that's curtains for me. What do you think I should do?"

"I don't know," admitted Darryn, defeated, "You'll have to use your own judgement. If you've got the nerve, keep going in and ignore Martin. It might impress him in a perverse kind of way. I think he's also being a bit overconfident. He may know that Rakshi and Taffy are casing the joint, but Taffy especially is too wise and experienced for Martin to have tabs on him all the time. Anyhow, what else have you found out?"

"It's falling into a basic pattern that groups are coming in for two or three days at a time. They are given basic firearms and combat training as well as some kind of indoctrination programme. They seem to be trying to find the better recruits. Last week I noticed some of them had returned for a more intensive training schedule involving armed assaults on buildings. Michael O'Grady was personally involved with that."

"I wonder if this is the start of the attack on Canal Street," Darryn mused. "I wish we didn't have to depend on Martin for intelligence."

Chapter 15

Darryn was once again in deep conversation with Danny and N°6 in the operations room.

"It doesn't seem that the F.U.P. is ready to move just yet, if Annabelle's account is to be believed," Darryn reported. "Even so, I've been in touch with our Manchester brigade and stepped up patrols in the Canal Street area. We've alerted the bar and club owners to be vigilant too."

"Today's the day you've got to meet Martin." Danny observed, "Do you want back-up?"

Darryn smiled and said, "You mean will I need another shoulder to cry on if he messes with my head again. You can come along for the ride, but I'll need to go into Waterloo Station alone. I suspect he won't show if I've got company."

"What do you think he is going to tell you?" N°6 asked.

"I hope it is some more information about the attack on Canal Street. It's unlikely to be straightforward facts, however, so get ready to solve some more puzzles when I get back."

They spent hours talking about each of the venues on Canal Street and the likelihood or otherwise of them being targets. They considered how terror might be perpetrated and the possible ways in which the resources of the F.U.P. in North Wales might be projected onto the streets of Manchester. In the end though, it was merely speculation without more hard facts to go on.

They broke for lunch and Darryn decided to get himself something in the canteen. As he was passing through the social area he caught a glimpse of Matt Machin skulking in a corner. He thought no more of it for a second or two and then it clicked that he ought to be at college.

He called over, "Matt, what are you doing there? Shouldn't you be in college?"

Matt jumped out of his skin like a startled rabbit.

"Oh, I...er...I've got a study day to get on with my art project."

Darryn was not convinced, but said nothing more and continued on his journey to the canteen area. On further reflection, he remembered it was not the first time he had seen Matt about during the day in the past two weeks. As soon as he'd finished his meal he was resolved to ring the college and find out if everything was alright.

"Hello? I wonder whether it would be possible to talk with Matt Machin's personal tutor," he said as soon as he got through to the switchboard. "Yes, I'm Annabelle Jacob's partner; we are Matt's guardians," he explained when he was naturally quizzed about his interest in the student. Luckily, Matt's tutor was free and willing to talk on the phone.

"Hello, Mr...."

"Harcourt-Smith."

"Ah, yes, Mr Harcourt-Smith, I'm glad you've called really. Matt hasn't been to an art lesson for the past two weeks. He is always absent on those days when the lessons take place. Is anything the matter?"

"I'll check. I wasn't aware he'd been having time off. Is his art teacher available to talk to?"

"I'm afraid he's off sick today too. I'm sure he'll be happy to talk to you when he's back."

Darryn concluded the call and went off in search of Matt again. He wasn't in his room, nor was he in the social area. In the end, he tracked him down in the little studio room off the art gallery. He was toying with a surprisingly conventional landscape painting that was half-finished. Darryn didn't beat about the bush.

"Well come on then, tell me what's going on. Why are you skiving off college?"

Matt dissolved into tears and through sobs and anguish the whole sorry story of his affair with James Wellby spilled out. The only additional matter was that he was now too scared to confront his teacher and could not face seeing him in lessons.

Darryn sighed and put his arm round Matt to comfort him.

"Matt, you are a plonker of the first magnitude. Why do you never listen to your friends? I know Maria told you not to get involved with a teacher."

"I know, I seem to have a self-destruct button when it comes to relationships," sobbed Matt, "Do you think there's ever going to be anyone decent out there for me?"

"I'm sure there is, but really, you've got to start looking in the right places."

Darryn was silent for a moment and then looked at his watch. It was about two o'clock. He had three hours to kill before his appointment with Martin.

"Listen, I'll come into college with you tomorrow and we'll concoct some story about how you are getting stressed about your exams. Meanwhile I think I'll pay Mr Wellby a visit so that you won't have anything to worry about in your art lessons."

"You're not going to do anything violent, are you?" Matt asked uncertainly.

"I'm not making any promises," said Darryn with unusually grim determination.

***

Darryn stood outside the door of James Wellby's terraced house. This was his real house where he lived with his wife and two children, not the house near Fenchurch Street Station where he had taken Matt. Darryn rang the front door bell and waited. After a minute, the solid black door opened to reveal a thin man with spectacles and grey hair. There was nothing very handsome or prepossessing about him. What hold he could possibly have over a teenage boy, on the verge of his most attractive years, was beyond Darryn's understanding.

"Yes?" he said suspiciously.

"Are you James Wellby?" Darryn asked.

"Yes I am. Why do you want to know?"

"I'm Matt Machin's guardian, and I'm not very happy with the way you've been treating him."

Darryn could see that Wellby was now very uncomfortable.

"Now look," Wellby continued as assertively as he could muster, "if you are going to cause trouble, I'll call the police."

"If I cause trouble," Darryn replied calmly, "your wife and kids will know that you've been having it off with a seventeen year old boy, who you and your mates were eyeing up to gang rape the other day."

"Alright, alright," said Wellby totally agitated now. "Don't exaggerate. I wasn't going to force the boy to do something he didn't want to do. I thought he was up for it."

"You know," replied Darryn, trying to remain calm, "I'm gay too, but that doesn't mean I go preying on young lads who don't know any better, or abuse my authority to satisfy my lust. It is people like you who give people like me a bad name, and that makes me very angry. I hope you're not going to give me any of that crap about how you artistic types don't have to follow the same moral codes as the rest of us."

Wellby shrugged his shoulders and replied, "Well, what's done is done. What do you want me to do about it?"

With a great effort to maintain his composure Darryn said, "I want you to resign and leave the college immediately. I've discovered that it's not the first time you've had to do that in your career. I don't see why Matt should suffer for your indiscretions."

Wellby laughed and said, "You've got to be joking! Why on Earth should I do that?"

Darryn grabbed Wellby by the lapels, pulling him down two steps until they were eyeball to eyeball.

"You don't know who you are messing with here," Darryn whispered menacingly, "I have the power to damage you in so many ways."

"Are you threatening me?" said Wellby, all of a quiver.

"Yes - That's the general idea," Darryn replied.

The next day, when he accompanied Matt to college, Darryn feigned complete surprise when Matt's tutor informed them that Mr Wellby had resigned quite suddenly and they had had to call on a supply teacher to cover his lessons. Darryn knew that N^o1 would not have approved of his methods, nor was he entirely easy with what he had done himself, but he was wholly satisfied with the outcome.

***

It was ten to five. Danny dropped Darryn off just outside Waterloo Station. Not surprisingly it was extremely busy and the going had been extremely slow. Darryn would have been happy to take the tube, but Danny had insisted, thinking that Darryn might like the privacy of his car to talk things through afterwards. He still remembered with some alarm the state Darryn had got himself into a year ago when they confronted Martin in 'The George and Dragon' in Soho.

"I'll take a drive round the block and pick you up here. In this traffic, it'll take me a good twenty minutes"

"Okay," Darryn replied, "I can't imagine I'll be very long."

Martin had chosen his venue very cleverly. Darryn could hardly make his way through to the concourse for the crowds of suited bankers, lawyers and businessmen all wanting to head off home to the suburbs. He was a sitting duck and could be approached from any angle. The crowds were so deep that he could not clearly make out who was only a couple of feet from him. He decided to make things easier for Martin by standing under the clock, the most prominent feature around.

The platform indicator boards digitally recorded that it was exactly five o'clock. Darryn looked around, circling, trying to catch the slightest untoward movement. Then all of a sudden he felt a hand go down the back of his trousers and pinch his bottom. He turned sharply, but there was no-one there. He thought he saw a figure, about the right height for Martin, moving away towards the platforms. The figure wore a 'hoodie' so it was impossible to make out any facial features. Darryn set off through the crowd after him. It was difficult to keep track, but he caught up with him just as he was about to go through the gate to platform 12. Darryn put his hand on the figure's shoulder. To his dismay, the figure turned round to reveal himself to be a surly youth of about eighteen, Darryn mumbled profuse apologies while inwardly seething at Martin's cheekiness.

He now felt something uncomfortable and pulled out from the back of his underpants a note, Darryn rolled his eyes at the sense of déjà vu he was experiencing.

He went outside and did not have long to wait before Danny came round the block and picked him up.

"Well?" Danny asked enquiringly.

"Another note,"

"What does it say? Is it another cryptic clue?"

Darryn unfolded the note, dreading the sight of yet another tortuous statement.

The note said:

'Whether he's Bart or Nat, his day is not for a fair, but a massacre. I cannot say where, you'll have to prepare.'

"Oh for crying out loud," Darryn exploded in frustration, "Why can he not just write down a date? Why is he playing all these silly games?"

"It strikes me he enjoys being in control," Danny replied, "But look on the bright side. At least we are getting some information out of him."

The weather took a turn for the worse and a heavy shower burst on them as they crawled along the street back to the Rotherhithe Tunnel. Darryn was fed up with Martin and didn't want to discuss him any longer. He therefore made small talk with Danny about how he and David were getting on and what their plans for the future consisted of. He also determined in his own mind that it was high time he returned to Oxford to attend to his academic duties.

Chapter 16

The day of Maria's birthday party finally arrived. The weather behaved itself and so the original plan was adopted to have a marquee on the garden roof. Maria had been helped in her plans by Jenny and Louise and she had got some money for it from Millie, the Guardian who had brought her to Rainbow House. Millie was now based in Scotland, so was rarely seen in London, but she kept in touch with Maria. One of the students at Rainbow House called Geoff was at catering college hoping to start his own business one day, so he had offered to organise a buffet at a reasonable price as long as he was plied with some free booze. There was also a DJ booked for later and also a live band of dubious quality made up of fellow college students.

Maria had requested that people dress smartly, so the event had the air of a high society do. Jake and Nathan were there, dressed in smart shoes, dark trousers, designer shirts and jackets. Jake's was a cream colour one, very suitable for a warm summer evening, whilst Nathan was wearing one that was darker. Both of them wore their shirts open at the neck without ties. Jenny and Louise were there too. It was odd to see Jenny in a dress, and Jake was struck by how feminine she looked. He did not dare compliment her on this however for fear he might get a slap around the face for such impudence.

Maria was stunning in her purple dress. Jake had to hand it to Matt; he had created a classically eye-catching garment that showed Maria off as a beautiful, stylish and sophisticated young woman. Matt was acting as Maria's partner for the evening and never one to do things by halves, had donned full evening dress for the occasion. For a brief moment, Jake actually thought Matt looked quite sexy.

Most of their contemporaries at Rainbow House were there, as well as some of the older folk who Maria knew. There was an unwritten understanding that anyone over the age of thirty would gracefully retire before the proceedings got too rowdy later on.

Jake looked around and noted with some satisfaction that Tim had come along after all. He had badgered Maria to invite him, but was concerned that his efforts might come to nothing after he had spoken to him in the corridor earlier on. He seemed reluctant to want to attend, saying that he wasn't really Maria's friend and didn't like having to socialise with lots of people. He followed that up by saying that he hadn't got any decent clothes and was reading a good book at the moment. It took all of Jake's powers of persuasion to make him change his mind. Now that he was here, Jake felt a huge burden of responsibility to make sure he wasn't left in the corner all by himself talking to no one. He indicated to Nathan that he was going to mingle and then wandered towards Tim.

"Hi, Tim," Jake greeted him cheerfully. "You're looking cool this evening."

"Hi, Jake, you're looking pretty good yourself."

Jake looked more closely at Tim. He wore a dark suit, probably the only decent clothes he had, a plain white shirt and a thin black tie. On the one hand he looked as if he ought to be attending a funeral, but on the other he carried himself with some style and did look incredibly handsome – although always very sad.

"I'm glad you could make it," Jake continued, "Your book can wait for a day when it's raining."

Jake noticed that Tim had relaxed visibly when he came over to speak to him and felt that he was making some progress in becoming a genuine friend to this isolated teenager. He was determined to try and get him integrated into his circle of friends.

"Is there anyone you fancy here tonight?" Jake asked before realising the question had overtones he hadn't intended.

"No, not really," Tim replied after a pause. "I guess there's one person, but he's way out of my league and in any case, he's already spoken for."

Jake caught sight of Ashok. He called him over hoping that he might get him talking to Tim. Ashok was conspicuously underdressed for the occasion. He had some Jeans, admittedly new ones, a black shirt and some white shoes which looked suspiciously like trainers.

"Did you get Maria anything for her birthday?" Jake asked.

"Yes, I got her a couple of books she'd wanted to read. I know she could have got downloads, but it's nice to have a few physical copies of things as well. What did you get her?"

"I got her a CD of the Sibelius violin concerto" Jake replied.

"Well I'm sure she will appreciate that," Ashok said unconvinced.

"Anyway, you were going to take me to the Test Match at The Oval this year. Do you need money for tickets? Perhaps Tim would like to come too."

Tim looked perplexed at this suggestion and Ashok looked doubtful. Ashok responded, "I'm not sure I'm still going to be about in August."

Jake did not have time to digest the significance of this last comment as Nathan had come over and now intervened.

"Hey, babe, I think you've done enough mingling for the moment and in any case I've remembered there's something I need to ask you."

Reluctantly, Jake left Ashok and Tim together hoping they would continue their conversation. "What is it?" Jake asked with just a touch of irritation in his voice which Nathan didn't seem to notice.

"I've got a gig at a Gentleman's Club in Pall Mall – and before you say anything, it's not *that* kind of club. It's the sort where old fogies sit around drinking brandy and reading 'The Times'. The quartet I formed at college has got a regular spot playing in the foyer in the evening. The only problem is one of our violinists has had to drop out. Do you fancy playing with us? You'd play second, so it wouldn't be so hard and no-one is really listening. You'd get £100 for the evening."

"So when is it? You know I've got exams coming up in June and then I've got my grade 8 violin."

"Well, I've got to go off and do my Guardian training next week, so it would be on a Friday evening, the week after that. I'm sure you could manage it."

"Oh... alright, just as long as I don't have to spend too long practising."

The evening got to the point where the adults were tactfully withdrawing and the DJ had started his session. The youngsters were now in an upbeat mood and dancing with gusto. Maria seemed to be having a wonderful time, and rightly was the centre of attention. Jake had really not had a chance to talk to her except to say 'hello' and 'Happy Birthday'. The live band was about as bad as Jake expected. A lot of people took their appearance as a signal to take a breather and enjoy the balmy night air. He finally caught up with Maria for a moment.

"Are you enjoying yourself?" Jake asked her.

"Yes, very much," Maria replied with a satisfied glow about her. "I am lucky to have so many good friends."

Jake put his arm around Maria and kissed the top of her head saying, "You've been a very good friend to me. I'll never forget how kind you were when I first came to Rainbow House."

They watched the lights over London as the blue of the sky turned darker and the few clouds in the west turned to gold, illuminated by the invisible sun now well below the horizon.

"What are you going to do when our exams are over? You'll get some chore-free leave."

"I was going to go to Wales with Matt. N°8 has a holiday cottage not far from Portmeirion. She's said we can use it as long as we tidy up the garden for her. I think Matt would like to do some sketching around the estuary."

"You two have become very close," Jake observed.

"We have a lot in common. He is a very gifted individual, maybe even a genius, but he needs someone to help him. I enjoy his company."

"But what about you, what do you need Maria?"

Maria looked at Jake sharply. She was used to being the one dispensing advice and sympathy and was rather taken aback to be on the end of such a question.

"I don't know, Jake. Things will change and I will feel differently I am sure, but just at this moment Matt is my best friend and that is fine. I'm not daft. I know eventually he will find some guy that he wants to settle down with and then it will be time for me to move on. I don't want a full-blown romantic adventure like you're having with Nathan. It's all too much like hard work."

"Whatever you do, I just want you to be happy," Jake said, almost in a whisper.

The band finished and the DJ returned to put on some oldies. Nathan and Jake held each other tight and swayed around the floor as a love ballad from the 1970's played out across the marquee. A lot of other couples were similarly engaged in holding their partners tight and thanking their lucky stars that they had found someone to love.

Although the adults had been told that the evening would be alcohol free, some beer, cider and wine had mysteriously appeared once they had gone. It was now the early hours of the morning and the party was winding down. Jake was feeling very mellow and happy with everyone.

"Right, before we call it a night, I want to take a picture of you all so I can remember what has been one of the best nights of my life," Maria announced.

The assembled crowd insisted on placing a chair in the centre for Maria and in the end Geoff who was finishing tidying up, took the photo. Jake and Nathan were locked with their arms around each other's shoulders. Just before they were ready, Jake noticed Tim skulking in the background.

"Tim, come on - come over here and be in the picture."

Tim reluctantly consented and Jake put his other arm around his shoulder, Tim hesitatingly reciprocated the gesture. They were standing directly behind Maria, who was seated, and Matt who had propped himself up on one knee beside her. The resulting photograph showed Jake smiling sandwiched between Nathan, who was also smiling, and Tim, who was at least not scowling.

If Jake had known that such an innocent arrangement would foretell such grief and heartache, he would have probably left Tim on the sidelines. Jake could never look at that photograph again without shedding a tear, even when an old man.

***

Nathan's quartet consisted of two girls who were on Nathan's course at college, Jake and, of course, Nathan. The two girls looked very similar. Both were slender with long brown shoulder-length hair. They had completely different characters however. The viola player was jovial and accepted Jake without any difficulty. On the other hand, the first violin was rather snooty and made it clear that she thought Jake was a poor substitute for their regular player. It was clear though that Nathan was the boss of this outfit and she would have to limit her disapproval to a few sighs and scowls. Jake didn't mind as he had been warned by Nathan in advance what she was like. Nathan's theory was that she was really quite insecure and perhaps not quite as good a player as she would like people to believe. She therefore found it necessary to have someone to look down on.

Nathan had only just returned from his adventurous training in Scotland. His week had been far less eventful than Jake's, but he was still delighted that he now had equal status with Jake as an Apprentice Guardian. This was their one and only opportunity to rehearse before their engagement at the club in Pall Mall. They had a couple of the more famous Mozart string quartets, some Haydn and early Beethoven too. Once they had warmed up, Jake did not really feel out of place and was blending in quite well. Nathan had managed to find some lighter numbers as well to intersperse between the more serious items.

"Right, that will do," Nathan announced when they had been through everything they intended to play. "It's a formal do in a posh establishment, so you two girls will have to wear long dresses. We'll have to wear dinner jackets and black bow ties, Jake, and oh... don't forget to polish your shoes. Shall we meet by the college and get a cab in?"

They agreed that as they were getting £100 each for the engagement, they could afford a cab between them.

Chapter 17

Congressman Wayne Hackett breezed into The Corinthian Club in Pall Mall. He vaguely noticed the strains of a string quartet in the lobby as he passed straight through to one of the sumptuous lounges, tastefully dotted with leather arm chairs and sofas. Occasional tables were situated conveniently for glasses of brandy or cups of coffee to be put down between sips. A fat man with a miserly face and mean looking eyes stood up to greet Hackett as he approached.

"Congressman Hackett, very nice to meet you," the man said extending his arm for a formal handshake.

"Mighty glad to make your acquaintance too, Lord Bernard," Hackett responded jovially.

"I don't think you've met my colleagues, Michael O'Grady and Andrew Judgement," Lord Bernard continued, indicating O'Grady and his young apprentice who were standing to his right. Hackett nodded an acknowledgement in their direction and then they all sat down. There followed some inconsequential small talk about the relative merits of the English and American ways of life before Hackett, impatient to be getting on, said: "Well I guess it's time I and O'Grady went and talked business Nice to make your acquaintance, Lord Bernard. I'm sure we'll meet again soon. Who knows, you might even be Home Secretary by then."

O'Grady and Hackett left the room, leaving Andrew to babysit Lord Bernard of Agincourt, leader of the Family Unity Party. They went down a corridor towards the washrooms. Outside what claimed to be the disabled toilet, O'Grady punched in a four-digit code on a touch pad in the door which released the lock and let them in.

They did not find themselves in a disabled toilet however, but in the reception area to what was obviously a substantial complex of rooms and offices.

"Good evening, Congressman Hackett and Director General O'Grady, we've been expecting you," The woman receptionist, who could have equally doubled as an airline stewardess, greeted them. "Will you need anything for your meeting?"

"No, we'll just need to be left alone in my office for half an hour," O'Grady retorted gruffly.

The two of them made their way up some stairs to a well-appointed office, looking out onto the street with just the merest hint of Buckingham Palace in the background. O'Grady sat behind his desk and Hackett, still shamelessly sporting his ginger wig, sat in a comfortable chair on the other side without waiting for an invitation to do so.

"Well let's talk about money," O'Grady began, without beating about the bush.

"I have to say many of our investors back in the States are a lot happier now you've taken control of things. There were some pretty dumb foul-ups going on this time last year. I think you can rest assured that I can find the money to buy the weapons you need. Shipping them is slightly more of a problem, but we have our links in the Irish Republic and you have the capability to smuggle them across the Irish Sea."

"That's not a problem," O'Grady said confidently, "But we will need the extra supplies by the beginning of August."

"We can do that. We can smuggle the crates of rifles in with a consignment of cans of pink salmon that's due to dock in Dublin Port at the end of July. Can you arrange for your men to take delivery?"

"That's not a problem either."

"You're going to eradicate this gang of homosexual desperados, aren't you?" Hackett asked changing the subject rather abruptly.

"We have plans to infiltrate their organisation and locate their base. That is why I've got Judgement on board with me. Then if we can get into government at the next election, we can use the armed forces to take it down."

"I do hope so. They are becoming a major irritant and I don't want folks back home getting any fancy ideas about setting up resistance organisations there too. Anyway, we must publicly show the world that we can crush them. They must know that God is on our side and that he will not stand idly by while the filth of Sodom and Gomorrah pollutes his creation."

"As long as I get paid, I don't mind being described as a sewage disposal worker," O'Grady commented dryly.

"What do you think of this Lord Bernard of Agincourt?" Hackett asked, changing the subject yet again.

"The man is a pompous fool. Like most politicians, he deals in platitudes and generalised statements which have more to do with prejudice than hard facts. His greatest virtue is that he can articulate the 'Little Englander' attitudes of a lot of people in this country, whipping up fear of foreigners and people who are different, very effectively. He is our best hope of making a political breakthrough at the next election. We have deliberately kept him out of the loop when it comes to the military side of things. He hasn't a clue that this control centre exists, even though he's sitting less than a hundred yards away as we speak. He may fall to pieces in a crisis, but on the other hand he is highly suggestible and can be made to do what we want him to. "

**

Jake had settled down and was beginning to play quite confidently. The quartet had deliberately started with a couple of light, easy numbers to warm up.

Just as they got to the development section in the first movement of one of

100

the Mozart quartets, Jake had the fright of his life and nearly stopped playing altogether. His eyes had wandered to the main entrance door, to be greeted by the sudden and unexpected arrival of Wayne Hackett. He appeared just as Jake had remembered him on that February day back in Paris. Jake kept his wits about him and continued to play. There was nothing he could do without causing a distraction and it was clear that Nathan (who had never seen Hackett before) was totally oblivious to his sudden panic. Eventually the movement came to an end and Jake quickly requested a toilet break. The first violin frowned and sighed, and even Nathan was unimpressed by the inartistic disturbance to the flow of the music.

"Be quick," he said tersely.

"Do you want to go too?" Jake asked Nathan trying to give a sign.

"No you're alright. Some of us can control our bladders for more than five minutes."

"I think you *should* go too," Jake riposted more forcefully. Nathan finally cottoned on to the fact that Jake wanted to talk to him in private and the two of them headed towards the toilets. As they were passing one of the lounges, Jake got another shock as he saw Hackett seated with Lord Bernard, who he recognised from television appearances, and two other people.

Jake pushed Nathan into the men's toilet and had a quick look around to make sure no one else was there. He then positioned himself by the entrance door so that he would know immediately if anyone else came in.

"What on Earth is going on?" Nathan asked, not hiding his exasperation.

"I've just seen one of the enemy spies Darryn and Annabelle were investigating in Paris last year," Jake whispered excitedly. "He's the American one who seems to be controlling the money. He's talking to Lord Bernard in one of the lounges as we speak. This place is a hotbed of F.U.P. intrigue. Do you think we should contact Rainbow House straight away?"

Nathan was now very interested and gave a considered answer, "I don't think it would be wise. They might have electronic listening devices and we have to consider the safety of the two girls as well; we don't want to involve them in any nasty business,"

Jake was thinking he really would quite like to involve the first violin in some nasty business, but said, "Shall we just carry on then, but keep our eyes peeled?"

"I think that's best. Watch carefully to see who comes and goes. We can talk to Danny in person when we get back to Rainbow House. That's probably the most secure option anyway."

Jake opened the door and then very quickly shut it so he could only see out through a thin slit. In a panicky voice he whispered to Nathan, "My God, Hackett and one of the others are coming this way. I think they're going to come in here."

"Okay," Nathan replied in a voice that was meant to calm Jake down, "Get behind me and we'll leave as they enter. I've never seen this Hackett

101

guy, so it's unlikely he'll recognise me. He won't be expecting to see you either."

Nathan and Jake swapped places so that Nathan took over the vigil. After a few minutes he gave an audible sigh and said to Jake, "We're alright, they've gone into the disabled toilet together."

"Together? – That's very odd!"

"We can speculate on that later. Let's take the opportunity to escape back to the lobby."

Experts would have noticed that the remaining performances by the quartet had an edginess that wasn't present at the beginning. Even Nathan, who was normally very confident, muffed an entrance during a fugal section in one of the movements. Fortunately, there were no experts and, as background effect, the sound remained perfectly acceptable.

Hackett left forty minutes after they resumed playing. As he swished through the lobby and out into the summer night, Jake receded behind a date palm, trying to remain invisible. Later O'Grady, who Jake recognised only as the man accompanying Hackett to the disabled toilet, left also with a handsome young man with blue eyes and blond hair in tow. Lord Bernard did not leave while they were playing. Jake assumed he was either engrossed in conversation with fellow members of The Corinthian Club or dozing off in one of the comfortable arm chairs in the lounge.

When the quartet had finished, they packed away so quickly that Nathan almost forgot to go and get paid for the evening's work.

"Why are you suddenly so jittery?" the first violinist asked.

"I'm not, honestly..." Nathan said unconvincingly.

"Well it's your problem. As long as I get paid, you can do what you like. I suppose we have to do the same next week. Are we going to stick to the same programme?"

"Yes, for next week at least, we'll think about ringing the changes after that."

The four of them left the building and picked up a taxi to take them back to Canary Wharf. Nathan and Jake were very relieved when they were finally able to get rid of the girls and talk freely about the consequences of that evening's discoveries.

"I wonder what they were talking about," Nathan said as they headed furtively for Rainbow House.

"It's such a shame we didn't have a listening device with us. I bet they were talking about plans for further attacks on us," Jake said thoughtfully.

The two boys used an entry card to get into the shop, and gingerly made their way to the back in the semi-darkness, lit only by the emergency lighting and the familiar red light behind the counter. As they ascended in the hidden lift to the social zone they decided they should seek out Danny or someone else senior in Ops before going to bed.

***

Danny and N°6 were again in conclave in N°6's office digesting the news that Jake and Nathan had excitedly brought them the previous evening. The office was looking rather stale and tired. The furniture was scratched and from a former, more angular era; the brown carpet was fading and looked the colour of pale mud, while the wallpaper was stained with splodges of dried coffee. N°6, however, looked totally in keeping with this environment with his shabby nobility from an age now passed.

"I suppose they were talking money," N°6 mused. "Hackett holds the purse strings and is the link with the evangelical right in America."

"I'm intrigued by the other two. The description Jake gave of the one who went into the toilet with Hackett sounded very like our friend, Michael O'Grady." Danny added.

"Yes, well if that's the case, it does look suspiciously like they were having talks about providing money for arms."

"I'd really like to have a look behind the door of that disabled toilet. We've been trying to find the F.U.P. central base for over a year now. It's tempting to think that Jake and Nathan may just have stumbled on it."

N°6 stroked his chin and then said, "Nathan has organised a regular slot at The Corinthian Club with his quartet. We could get the two boys to do some low-level surveillance for us; they have the perfect cover. I'll have a word with Jake later and brief him."

Danny frowned, as if concerned, but did not question N°6's judgement. Instead he changed the subject, "Have you made any progress on Martin's latest message?"

N°6 paused and then said, "It all seems to hang on the significance of Bart and Nat. Bart is a short hand for baronet but Nat doesn't bring any honours to mind. Nat could stand for National Aids Trust, but then how would Bart fit in with that?"

"I must confess," Danny interjected with a smile, "when you say Bart I think of yellow cartoon characters."

"Well there is always the possibility that Bart is indeed shorthand for Bartholomew, in which case, Nat could stand for Nathaniel. I do seem to recall from my dim and distant studies in theology that St. Bartholomew and Nathaniel were considered to be one and the same apostle. Let's see if there is a Saint's Day associated with either."

Danny typed the relevant information into a search engine on the computer on N°6's desk. Neither of them was disappointed with what came back.

"Well it's all pointing to August 24th. Look at this reference to a traditional fair being held on that day. It fits in with the clue nicely. Oh this is even better - I'd forgotten about the infamous St. Bartholomew's day massacre, *'Whether he's Bart or Nat, his day is not for a fair, but a massacre. I cannot say where, you'll have to prepare.'* Yes it all works. So we'd better warn Darryn and the Numbers that the planned attack is on August 24th somewhere in Canal Street, Manchester. If only we knew which venue though. It looks from the clue as if Martin doesn't know either."

Later that day Nº6 tracked Jake and Nathan down in the commerce area, where they were buying a few essentials for their rooms. He briefly explained the idea of using Nathan's regular engagement as cover for a bit of spying. Jake was quite hurt by Nathan's protestations that he would have to come up with some very imaginative excuses for not allowing their regular second violinist back into the group. However, Nº6 had not risen to his exalted position without good reason. He twisted Nathan's arm most courteously and persuaded both of the boys to go along with his plan.

The following week, the priority was to position a microdot camera opposite the keypad for the disabled toilet so that Ops could try and work out what the combination was to get through. Having successfully managed to transmit all week without discovery, the boys' next task was to place a listening bug to a table as close to where Lord Bernard sat in the lounge as possible. This also continued to transmit, but merely proved the point that he was a figurehead being manipulated by others and not really the master of the game himself.

Meanwhile, amongst all this subterfuge, Jake had to take his AS exams. The chemistry went surprisingly well. Mr Devonshire's advice about listing and learning all the key definitions paid dividends. He had a sweaty moment in his maths mechanics paper when the collision of three snooker balls at a certain angle failed to yield the required mathematical relationship. However, with two minutes to spare he had a flash of inspiration and managed to tease out the proof.

By the time the next Friday came around, Jake was getting weary of his enforced spying duties. The novelty was beginning to wear off and the drudgery of playing the same things week in, week out, convinced Jake that a professional music career would not have been for him. They had been given no specific duties this week, but as always, they had to keep an eye open for anything unusual.

Jake soon spotted something very unusual. A small female figure dressed in a waitress uniform looked strangely familiar. It was Jenny. What was she up to? She'd clearly got herself a job here, but was it purely to make a bit of money or was she casing out the joint for Nº6 or someone else?

When the quartet took a break, Jake went to intercept Jenny in a quiet corner where neither of them would be noticed.

"What the hell are you doing here?" Jake hissed.

"I'm working here to make a bit of extra pocket money," Jenny said quite innocently. "It is allowed you know."

"I'm not sure I believe you," Jake continued suspiciously. "You know this place is a viper's den of F.U.P. big-wigs, don't you."

"Really," Jenny replied as if butter wouldn't melt in her mouth.

"Are you working for Nº6, or are you on some brainless freelance stunt of your own?"

Finally, Jenny gave a quiver of annoyance at this suggestion and said, "Well I've managed to find the code for that disabled toilet, which is more than you and Nathan have managed to do in all the weeks you've been here."

Jake was stunned. "How have you managed to get hold of that?" He asked weakly.

"Simple," Jenny said triumphantly, "one of the other waiters is an F.U.P operative who has such a dreadful memory that he has to write all his passwords in a little note book. I've managed to have a look in it while he was serving one of the diners. I was going to investigate when my shift was over."

"You can't go in there alone," Jake said aghast. "It might be the F.U.P. military headquarters."

"Well if you don't want me to go in there alone, you'll just have to come with me!"

Chapter 18

Darryn was sitting again in his favourite coffee shop in Shrewsbury. From time to time, he casually looked over to the counter where Sean was hard at work. The sweat on his brow only made him more attractive. Between furtive glances, Darryn was checking up on his contacts.

His first call had been to Annabelle. He had been concerned for her safety ever since she had had her encounter with Martin. He was relieved that she had finally decided to quit her menial job in the camp. To be honest, they had learnt all they could, now that Annabelle had been compromised by Martin, and Taffy and Rakshi were continuing to monitor the camp from a distance. The training regimes had become predictable; it was now clear that a crack body of troops was being trained to storm a building, eliminating all resistance inside and then laying waste to it by setting it on fire. During the past week Taffy had noticed a switch in emphasis to delivering the troops to the destination, the attack itself having been planned and perfected.

Darryn's second call was from Danny, informing him of the solution to Martin's puzzle. Darryn was immediately worried about the overreliance on this intelligence. He told Danny in no uncertain terms that they must not assume that the attack was going to take place on that day. A pre-emptive strike a few days before would leave them totally unprepared and likely to fail in their attempt to prevent it.

"We must trust the information coming from Taffy and Rakshi," he insisted. "They will know when the troops are ready to move out and we can then monitor their movements all the way to Manchester. We must develop a flexible and rapid response that can cope at any time, not just on the twenty-fourth of August."

Danny seemed to get the point and Darryn hung up reasonably reassured. He then called some of the field agents working in the West Midlands, partly to bolster morale and partly to update his picture of what the F.U.P. were up to. At present, they seemed to be moving into the run down parts of Walsall, Wolverhampton and Birmingham; by taking on the gangs peddling drugs and petty crime, they were making themselves very popular.

Sean came over to talk to Darryn. It was mid-afternoon on a working day and there were just a few regular customers in. No one was waiting to be served, so it was safe enough to take a few minutes break. Darryn was pleased that he came over, but tried not to make it too obvious. Darryn was sitting on one of the brown leather settees set into the corner of the whitewashed hall, with contrasting black-painted timbers criss-crossing the walls in no regular pattern. Sean came and sat beside him and said, "Hi, Darryn, how're things going?"

"Well the F.U.P. seems to be playing it very much to plan. I don't like the look of what it's building up to, mind you. I just hope we have the luck and the capacity to stop them."

"I'm sure you will, but how about you personally?"

"I've not got time to think about anything other than work or my Guardian duties at the moment. I've just spent two weeks marking exam papers, and my goodness; I've never seen such a load of rubbish in my life. I'm sure the students are getting worse. They all seem to be taking their A-levels at primary school these days, and yet some of them don't seem to understand the most elementary calculus."

Sean smiled and said, "It sounds as if you are overstressed. You need to find yourself a boyfriend and go off for a holiday in the sun for two weeks."

"That's the last thing I need at the moment," Darryn said, convincing neither himself nor Sean. "Anyway, how are things with your new man? Everything was looking very promising when I last saw you."

Sean sighed and replied, "It's all gone pear-shaped. The rat was two-timing me all the while. When I found out and confronted him, he said he needed freedom and if I couldn't accept that then we might as well end it. I'm unhappily single again."

Darryn tried his best to be sympathetic, but secretly his heart skipped a beat with joy when he discovered that this adorable, handsome and kindly man was now available again.

"I'll be coming down to London in a week or two," Sean continued. "Do you want to meet up while I'm down there?"

"Sure thing - Do you want to stay with me if you haven't made other plans?"

"That's sweet of you, but I've already arranged to stay with an aunt."

"Okay... well I'd better go. I'll keep in touch."

Darryn moved his head closer to Sean's and was about to give him a peck on the cheek as he normally did, circumstances permitting, when suddenly he got the urge to kiss him full on the lips. Sean did not resist and the kiss lingered long enough for Darryn to sense that his impulsiveness was being reciprocated. As their heads moved apart, they stared into each other's eyes for a moment, desperately trying to fathom the motive and intent of one another.

"Is anyone serving here?" a none-too-happy voice rasped across the room. Sean jumped up and rushed apologetically to the counter. Darryn hurriedly, and with some embarrassment, left.

***

"This is a fool-hardy plan," Jake wailed at Jenny.

"If you don't like it, go home and stop moaning," Jenny replied irritably.

"You know I can't do that. What would happen if you got caught? I dread to think what the consequences might be," Jake replied, desperately trying to turn Jenny from her proposed course of action.

107

Jake had made his excuses to Nathan at the end of their playing session, explaining that he did not like the idea of Jenny travelling home alone late at night. Nathan made some cutting comment about Jenny being more capable than Jake at dealing with unwanted attention, but agreed in the end to Jake's suggestion. He reluctantly took Jake's violin, stand and music as well as his own. Jenny and Jake had then hidden in the kitchens until the lights had gone out and the club had been locked up.

Jenny had come prepared with a torch, which made Jake wonder how long she had been cooking this plan up. His questions to Jenny about how she knew that this was an F.U.P. base were deflected or vaguely answered. They were now standing outside the disabled toilet door. The moment had finally come when Jenny could no longer contain herself and so she pressed the combination on the keypad.

A click could be heard as the bolt sprang open. Jenny looked at Jake with a manic air of triumph as she carefully pushed the door. Unexpectedly, harsh neon light flooded through the gap and too late they registered that there was someone watching the door on the other side. It was the woman receptionist who had been on duty when Michael O'Grady and Wayne Hackett had met a few weeks ago. She still looked as if she might be about to board a plane as an air stewardess, with her face made up and her hair done to perfection.

There was a moment of incredulity in her face when she did nothing but stare at the two teenagers who had appeared so unexpectedly at the secret entrance to the F.U.P. headquarters. Then she moved swiftly to try and press a warning button to summon assistance. However, Jake's training kicked in a split second sooner and he managed to rush over and grasp the woman's hand before she could carry out this deed. There was a brief struggle in which Jake was reluctant to incapacitate the woman completely. Somehow it seemed rather an unmanly thing to do. In the end Jenny came over and knocked the woman out cold with a fearsome punch to the jaw.

"What were you messing about for?" she asked Jake when they got their breath back.

"It didn't seem right to hit a woman," he replied rather apologetically.

"For goodness sake...what a sexist thing to say. Hit them hard, whether they are male or female. 'Equal rights for women' is my motto. Now we need to go this way."

Jenny set off, while Jake eyed her suspiciously. How did she know which way to go? What was she trying to find? There was an awful lot that Jenny had not told Jake and he was beginning to feel quite angry about that. Miraculously there seemed to be no one about, but even so Jake thought it highly probable that they were being caught on CCTV cameras.

Jenny darted into a room which had a desk, shelving and a modernist picture on the wall. Without turning the light on, she went immediately to one of the drawers in the desk and yanked it open. She desperately rummaged through the papers, using only her torch as a means of illumination.

"What are you looking for?" Jake now asked with a degree of urgency.

"It must be here somewhere..." Jenny was now becoming desperate.

Another more adult voice said, "I guess this is what you're looking for."

Jake's heart jumped into his mouth and both he and Jenny turned sharply to face a man moving out of the shadows brandishing a folder. Nathan would have recognised him quicker; Jake and Jenny had only seen him in photographs. Jake thought the man handsome, even in the half-light of the darkened room, and could see why Darryn would have been attracted to him. It was Martin.

Jenny made a move to snatch the folder out of Martin's hand, but he was too quick and dispatched Jenny without ceremony back across the room.

"Don't be even more foolish, than you have been already," Martin said to Jenny with a great deal of harshness in his voice. "If I was N°1, I'd kick you off the Guardian programme straight away for pulling such a childish stunt as this. Don't you realise that if the F.U.P. caught you they would be able to extract from you all the details about Rainbow House?"

"I wouldn't talk," said Jenny defiantly.

"Brave words, little girl," said Martin, mockingly, "I don't think you are familiar with Michael O'Grady's torture techniques, however." Martin paused for a moment and then looked at Jake and decided to carry on in the disapproving teacher mode, "I'm surprised at you, Jake, getting mixed up with such a harebrained scheme. I always rated you as being more sensible."

Jenny was not to be daunted. "I want that folder," she said with force.

"Well you're not going to get it! I've a good mind to let the F.U.P. do their worst with you, but, fortunately, you've caught me on a good day. I'll give you one chance to get out of here. The cameras have been disabled and the receptionist won't remember enough about you to give a good description. Go now. Oh... and Jenny, don't come back. Quit your job as a waitress immediately, for your own safety. Jake, you can come back and play with Nathan. It's rather nice having some decent music going on in the background. You have no idea how excruciating it was to have a tone-deaf boyfriend for all those years."

Jenny and Jake needed only one glance at each other. They rushed out of the room, ran down the corridor, passed the slumped figure of the receptionist and slammed the disabled toilet door shut. Now in darkness once more, they only had Jenny's torch to guide them. They made for an emergency exit, which surprisingly, was not alarmed. In a matter of a few seconds they found themselves in the empty car park at the rear of The Corinthian Club.

**

"Stop," Jake shouted at Jenny who was racing ahead of him. They were making their way to catch a night bus to Canary Wharf.

"Let's catch the bus first and then we can talk," Jenny replied reasonably.

Jake accepted this logic without reply and was rewarded by finding a bus ready to leave as they entered Trafalgar Square.

When they were seated on the top deck, Jake looked around to see there was no one but themselves. "Right," he said firmly, "you've no excuses now. Tell me what is going on. You haven't been level with me all evening and I resent being put in danger without knowing the reason."

Uncharacteristically, Jenny burst into tears. Jake was so startled by this that for a few minutes he did not know what to do. In the end he put a reassuring arm around her shoulder and told her not to be so soppy. Jenny, realising that her normal hard-woman demeanour was taking a serious knock, pulled herself together and dabbed her eyes dry with a handkerchief.

"I'm sorry about that unseemly show of emotion..." Jake took this as his cue to remove his arm. "It concerns Louise, you see. The folder had information about her."

"So why is the F.U.P. so interested in her?"

"She knows about their secret base. The folder and the information it contains is their guarantee that she'll not blab to anyone."

"She's obviously blabbed to you," Jake observed.

"That's different," Jenny responded testily, "we're partners and we've vowed to tell each other everything. Don't you and Nathan do the same?"

Jake considered this for a moment; he wasn't sure they did. He shrugged his shoulders and Jenny continued:

"Louise did something silly when she was younger. She stole a Mercedes from some millionaire and wrote it off. She was obviously far too young to be driving at the time, which only made matters worse. Her father was a police officer. He managed to get the charges dropped and spirit away the file from the police station. The owner of the car was told that the culprit was never found. Then Louise's dad got involved with the F.U.P. and he got posted to their headquarters. For some reason he kept plans for the layout of the Corinthian Club, which he left lying around the house. Louise often looked at these plans and got to know where everything was.

"One day, a colleague of Louise's dad in the F.U.P. caught her looking at the plans and went mental. He insisted on taking the file on Louise, which her dad had foolishly not destroyed, saying that if Louise ever said a word to anyone about the headquarters, he would release the file back to the police and she would be arrested.

"Soon afterwards, Louise and her dad had an almighty row about it, and Louise ran away from home to be found by a Guardian. She has been too frightened to say anything about it to anyone. I thought, if I could get the file and destroy it, the F.U.P. would no longer have a hold over my girlfriend."

Jake sighed. "Why on Earth did you not talk to Annabelle or Darryn?"

Jenny shrugged her shoulders and said, "I thought it would be quicker just to try and get the folder myself."

"Well you are going to have to tell someone now. If you don't, I *certainly* will."

Chapter 19

July began and just as the summer was promising to develop into something quite special, the weather turned and gales more akin to late October ravaged the Welsh hills.

Annabelle was sitting in the communal area of the training camp barn with Rakshi and Taffy. They had a fire on in the log burner because it was so cold. Taffy was particularly morose. All training activities had ceased following the setting up of the F.U.P. military camp on their patch, and he was missing putting his 'lovely boys' through their paces. The reconnoitring he was doing went some way to making up for this, but he still had to spend dull, boring hours simply watching not a lot going on.

"Well it looks as if a consignment of arms arrived last night," Annabelle commented. "That lorry turning up at two o'clock in the morning flanked by motorcycle outriders looked very suspicious."

"They are getting quite expert at storming that mock building they've set up," Taffy observed. "At least we'll know what their tactics are going to be though, even if we don't know exactly where they are going to strike."

"What do you think Martin is playing at, Annabelle?" Rakshi asked. "There seems to be no indication that he's said anything about you to the F.U.P. and yet he clearly had your number marked the moment you went snooping around the camp. He is obviously in the higher circles of the leadership these days; there are times when only he, O'Grady and his young acolyte Andrew are closeted together making decisions."

Annabelle couldn't help going red with embarrassment. Being caught by Martin was not one of her finest moments and she didn't thank Rakshi for bringing the subject up again, "If he is trying to use the F.U.P. for his own advantage, he's playing a dangerous game," she finally said. "O'Grady is not someone to be messed with. On the other hand, Martin doesn't seem to be wholly against us, if the clues he keeps dropping us are genuine. I know Darryn doesn't trust him an inch."

"...and I tend to agree with him," Taffy added. "He could be trying to throw us off the scent so that we will not be prepared when the blow falls."

"Well everything we've seen suggests the F.U.P. is going to be ready for an attack sometime in August, which fits in with the clue about St. Bartholomew's day. Anyway, I've got to go and monitor F.U.P. activity in Shropshire next week, so I'll have to leave you two to monitor the camp. You will be careful won't you? There's always Paul and his team in Dolgellau to call on if you need extra support."

Rakshi smiled and said, "Don't be such a fuss-pot, Annabelle, we'll be fine." Taffy looked even more morose at the prospect of reducing his social circle still further.

***

Jenny, Louise and Jake were having a very uncomfortable time in N°2's office. They were being interrogated by N°2, N°6 and Danny, about what they knew concerning the F.U.P. headquarters in Pall Mall. N°2 seemed particularly interested in the detail of their meeting with Martin and showed concern at the turn of events in which he again seemed to be at the centre. She was as smart and well-turned out as ever, but her demeanour, although calm and controlled, showed unmistakably that she was annoyed and disappointed with their behaviour. Jake had redeemed himself somewhat by being the one to come forward and reveal the extent and nature of Jenny's escapade.

N°2 finished her stern rebuke to the girls, "Jenny, after all the training you have received about the importance of working as a team, why on Earth couldn't you have confided in one of us? We would have taken the matter seriously, and Louise... why didn't you tell us about the headquarters? You could have saved us months of fruitless investigation trying to find it."

Louise looked down, thoroughly ashamed and on the point of tears, but Jenny was feeling unusually rebellious and couldn't stop herself saying in response, "Darryn and Annabelle go off and do things by themselves without consulting every Tom, Dick and Harry."

Jake couldn't believe Jenny's insolence and nudged her in the ribs, making it clear she should shut up immediately. N°2's eyes narrowed intently and focused on Jenny.

"Darryn and Annabelle have spent many years training and have earned the right to make some independent decisions. You don't seem to understand that it is a burden and not a luxury to be in that position. Unlike you, Jenny, they have to weigh up the consequences of their actions and consider how other people might be affected by their choices. Now I'm getting pretty fed up with this discussion. If any of you get involved in any more ridiculous go-it-alone adventures, you'll be off the Guardian programme. Is that understood?"

There was a murmur of assent from the three youngsters before they sheepishly filed out of the office. As soon as the door was closed, Danny said rather anxiously, "Do you think we should have a word with the Director of the Guardian Training programme and put Jenny on report?"

N°2 laughed and said, "Good Heavens, no. We expect a lot from our youngsters these days and sometimes we forget they are still teenagers with a lot of growing up to do. Jenny has a lot of spirit and she is very brave. Not many girls of her age would have walked into enemy territory and demanded that file back. We will need people like her in the years to come."

"There is also the question of what we do with this new intelligence," N°6 said, changing the subject. "Louise will be able to give us a detailed plan of the F.U.P. headquarters. We could attempt an attack ourselves and wipe it out."

N°2 looked pensive for a moment and then responded, "The pages that Jake brought back from the military camp in Wales clearly show that the F.U.P. will attempt an assault on our base here. It is tempting to try and pre-empt that by attacking their base first, but think where it is, right in the heart of London with all those Government buildings nearby. We couldn't send in an overwhelming force. Think also about the publicity. The cover for their base is a rich gentlemen's club. Goodness knows how many cabinet ministers, generals and senior civil servants use it. An assault would be portrayed as an attack on the very fabric of the State, making us appear like traitors and reinforcing the F.U.P.'s propaganda about us. We must be careful what we do next here. I think our first priority must still be to try and thwart their proposed outrage in Manchester."

***

Darryn had returned to Oxford for a few days. The middle of July always seemed a sad time in this city. All the undergraduate students had gone down and somehow all the life seemed to be sucked out of the place as a result. Japanese and American tourists crawled over the place as if it were an ancient ruin. The sudden turn in the weather with unseasonal gales and leaden skies only heightened this impression.

One of the things Darryn had to do while he was there was to make another trip to the Clarendon Laboratory. There were a few technical issues with the shield that he needed to discuss with Dr Palmer. The shield itself was being installed at Rainbow House that very week, and Danny was hopeful they could give it a proper test either in August or September.

Darryn was also secretly hoping he would bump into James Grimwold again. The precision of some of his predictions had been unnerving and he wondered whether he might get something more out of him. There was also the matter of what the Quantum Optoelectronics Group had been up to. He had not forgotten the urgent debate about morality and the statement that no one would ever have any privacy again, nor had he forgotten the rather unpleasant way he'd had the door slammed in his face.

His meeting with Dr Palmer was routine, short and satisfactory in outcome. As he was passing down the corridor on his way out, he couldn't help but notice that the door to the optoelectronics lab was open. Like a fly irresistibly drawn to a spider's web, Darryn inched towards the entrance. He poked his head in cautiously; no one was there. On tip-toes he silently entered the room, looking around all the time for any unpleasant surprises. It was a large room segmented into several workspaces, each with its own long bench and littered with wires, electronic boxes and computers. On one bench was an object which caught Darryn's eye. It was a sheet of what looked like plastic coated with thousands of tiny little silver dots. These gave the sheet an iridescent quality and shimmering changes in colour hypnotised Darryn as he moved closer towards it. He took the edge of it in his hand and was surprised that it felt as smooth as silk and not as cold to the touch as he'd expected.

"Ah, we meet again," A wild voice croaked from the far side of the room. Darryn jumped out of his skin and let the sheet fall from his grasp. He turned around to see James Grimwold smiling manically at him, still in a grey overall and with hair that was even whiter and more dishevelled than he remembered.

"Where the hell did you come from?" said Darryn visibly shaken.

"I popped by from an alternative universe," Grimwold said quite unremarkably.

"That's impossible," Darryn retorted irritably.

"Quite improbable, I grant you, but not impossible. It's amazing what *is* possible if you think quantum mechanically."

Darryn decided to make the most of his opportunity and not get distracted by Grimwold's scientific and philosophical strangeness.

"Can you really foretell the future?" he asked, "Because if you can, I need to know when the F.U.P. is going to try and murder hundreds of people in Manchester... and exactly where they are going to do it."

"Ah, so you are not so cynical about the predestination of The Universe now," Grimwold said with triumph. "I know that you know it will occur on Canal Street. I also know that you have been told that it will be on 24th August. You don't trust the person who revealed this to you, but his motives, although cloudy, do not look malignant. I cannot tell you exactly where on Canal Street they will strike. You *will* know before the day, but a great tragedy for you personally must occur before that information is revealed."

"What kind of tragedy?" said Darryn; now feeling even more uncomfortable.

"Ah, that is not clear. That is all I can say on that subject. Do you see this?" Grimwold pointed to the shimmering sheet which Darryn had been recently feeling. "This is going to be your salvation."

Darryn was utterly mystified, but he could not question Grimwold further due to the sudden agitation of his state.

"Quick, quick, you must go. The optoelectronics team will be back from their meeting with the F.U.P. any second. We must not be found here. You will have a chance to talk with me only one more time after this. You must make sure you ask me the right questions."

Grimwold hobbled off to the back of the lab and may well have dissolved into a parallel universe. Darryn did not hang about either. He quickly left the lab, shutting the door behind him. He continued at a fast pace down the corridor, passing a group of scientists going in the opposite direction. He recognised one of them as the man who had shut the door in his face on the previous visit. Fortunately, the man was engrossed in conversation and did not notice Darryn at all. Then, as he burst out into the grey autumnal July day, the significance of something Grimwold had said suddenly struck him.

Why was this group of scientists meeting with the F.U.P. and why was the F.U.P. so interested in their work?

***

It was the day of Jake's violin exam. Nathan had slept over and Jake was now lying in bed hugging him close, thinking about the day ahead. Nathan was dead to the world even though Jake was stroking his skin softly. Jake still loved Nathan very much. Even when he had had a curry the evening before and did one of his terrifically smelly farts into the bed clothes, or had forgotten to brush his teeth so his breath smelt rank, Jake still loved him. Jake was, however, concerned that Nathan might no longer be so enamoured with him. On the face of it, all was still well, but their love-making had become somewhat mechanical and less spontaneous, there were times when Nathan seemed distant and he was not always so insistent about being with Jake as much as possible. Whenever Jake asked Nathan if he still loved him, he always laughed and said Jake was silly for thinking anything else could be possible.

Jake lightly kissed Nathan's shoulder and then he rolled out of bed. He washed and dressed as quietly as possible. He checked he had his keys, wallet and phone and then left the room, taking his violin, stand and music with him. Nathan had a free period at college first thing, so did not have to get there until ten o'clock. Jake was happy to leave him asleep in his room while he had breakfast and did some last minute practice.

Mr Devonshire had agreed to accompany Jake in his pieces and met up with him an hour before they had to go to have a final run through. The small theatre in the arts and leisure zone had a very nice Fazioli baby grand piano and Mr Devonshire had obtained permission to use it for half an hour.

In the end Jake had decided to play the last movement of the Bach violin concerto in E major, the second movement of the Schumann Sonata in A minor, and the first movement of the Debussy violin sonata. The last of these had been a late decision following Nathan's presentation of the music as a birthday present.

Mr Devonshire gave the following advice when they had finished, "Try not to be too nervous. If you're going to start with the Bach, just watch the intonation, particularly the D-sharps, and don't set off at too much of a gallop. You played the Debussy very well."

The two of them did not have far to go to get to the venue, so they decided to catch the bus. The early morning rush had subsided, so finding a seat was not difficult.

"How are things going at college?" Mr Devonshire asked politely.

"Okay, we're not doing a lot at the moment as there's only a week until the summer holidays and lots of people seem to be off on trips since our exams finished."

"Have you had any thoughts about applying to University?"

"Not really, I'm going to wait until I get my AS results and see how well

I've done. I'll probably apply to one of the London colleges. I want to stay close to Rainbow House."

"We wouldn't leave you out on a limb, even if you applied to Aberdeen. Although, frankly, by the time you've finished the Guardian programme you're going to be more capable of looking after yourself than most."

They reached their stop and got off. Their destination was an imposing building used as an Education Institute and Meeting Hall. They followed the signs and were shown to a large waiting room. Jake got out his violin and tuned up, doing a few scales and arpeggios to warm up. After five minutes, a woman called his name and they went into the lion's den. Mr Devonshire whispered 'good luck' to him as they entered the examination room.

A very severe woman was sitting behind a table. She stopped writing notes on a pad in front of her to peer over her glasses at Jake.

"Good Morning, Mr Holdencroft. If you would like to prepare yourself we'll begin with your pieces."

Mr Devonshire sat at the piano and gave an A. Jake was relieved to find he was still in tune, avoiding the necessity for further heightening the tension by having to fiddle with his pegs and fine tuners. He put his music on the stand that had been set up for him and prepared to begin.

In the Bach, Jake made a quavering entry but settled down to give a reasonable performance. There was the odd intonation issue, particularly with the double stopping which he was rarely able to judge accurately, but other than that, it could not have been much better. By the time he got to the Debussy, he had relaxed and was able to think of Nathan while he was playing it. He even managed to hit the artificial harmonics spot on. The middle section, with its incessant quavers in the piano part gave a disturbingly restless feel that always made Jake think of the composer realising he had not long to live.

At the end of this Mr Devonshire smiled and left the room, leaving Jake to do battle with his scales and arpeggios. These went reasonably well; the only black spot being the double-stopped scale in thirds. He had been pleading with the unknown deity for weeks that this would not come up. Going up wasn't too bad. Coming down led to some excruciating intonation. Jake was convinced he caught the woman examiner wincing as he came to an end. He was good at sight reading and aural tests, so it ended on an optimistic note.

"Everything okay," Mr Devonshire enquired as Jake re-entered the waiting room.

"Yes, I think so; the only thing that went seriously wrong was that wretched double-stopped scale in thirds."

"The pieces sounded good. I'm sure you've got good marks on those."

"I hope so."

"I think we deserve a coffee somewhere before you go back to college. I'll take your violin and music back to Rainbow House, if you like."

Chapter 20

Darryn was propping up the bar in 'The George and Dragon' in Soho. Sean had sent him a message asking if he wanted to meet up as he would be in London that weekend with his aunt. Whilst trying to remain cool and casual, Darryn had secretly jumped at the opportunity. They'd arranged to meet at lunchtime when the bar would be relatively quiet and loud music would not be deafening them. Darryn kept thinking about that kiss the last time they met, and what it might lead to. In fact he was feeling ridiculously nervous, like a teenager going on a first date. He looked at his watch. It was already five minutes past the time they'd agreed to meet up. How long should he give him? He decided half an hour was reasonable, enough time to drink another half pint of lager very slowly. Surely Sean, of all people, was not going to stand him up?

He was vaguely aware of someone else coming up to the bar and ordering a drink. Anxiously, he looked at the entrance. There was still no sign of Sean.

"Do you come here often?"

Darryn was startled to be addressed directly. It was so rare that anyone actually talked to a stranger in a place like this that it quite took him aback. He now focused on the person who had asked the question. It was the guy who had just bought a drink next to him. He was a handsome man in his mid-to-late twenties, with sparkling blue eyes and fair hair that had been shaved in a close crop. Darryn had a secret desire to brush his hand against that hair and feel its spiky manliness. The stranger was almost exactly the same height as Darryn, which meant he could look directly into those irresistible blue eyes without either stooping down or peering up. 'Very tasty,' thought Darryn.

"No, I don't come here often. I'm not a great one for bars and clubs these days. I was hoping to meet a friend, but it looks as if he's not going to make it, how about you?"

"I'm new in town," the blond-haired Adonis said. "I'm just having a look round Old Compton Street; I'll probably go and have a look around the shops in Oxford Street this afternoon. My name is Alex, by the way... pleased to meet you." Alex extended his arm and he and Darryn shook hands formally. Alex continued, "Do you want to go and sit down? I don't know many people in London yet so it would be nice to have a chat. Perhaps you could tell me some good places to go and eat."

Darryn followed Alex over to a seat in the corner by the door. They talked easily. Darryn was careful to give his much-rehearsed and half-true life story about being a maths tutor at Oxford. Alex seemed very impressed by this and gave every indication of becoming interested in Darryn. Alex's story was that he had got a job working for the Treasury and had recently bought a flat south of the river. As is always the case with gay men, they had to explain how difficult their teenage years had been to each other, whether they were 'out' to their family and friends, and when they had first had a boyfriend. Alex's eyes seemed to twinkle when Darryn, with a degree of embarrassment, had to admit that he was currently single.

"Look, I'm going to level with you," Alex eventually said. "I came over to talk to you deliberately because I thought you were an incredibly good-looking guy. You're really hot."

Darryn was flattered by this and a little surprised. It was a while since he'd been referred to in those sorts of terms. Darryn replied, "Thanks, you're a very good-looking guy yourself."

"I hope you don't mind me being so forward, but I couldn't really pass up an opportunity like this. I'd like to get to know you a bit better. Why don't you come shopping with me and then we can go back to my flat afterwards? You can help me choose one or two small items for the bedroom."

Darryn hesitated and looked at his watch. It was long past the time when he was supposed to have met Sean. Obviously his interest was not as great as Darryn had imagined. Making a decision, he said, "Okay, why not... although I should warn you I'm not one of those gay men who are good at interior design."

Alex smiled and said, "No, but I can imagine wrestling with you, and that kind of makes me feel horny."

The two of them got up and left. Five minutes later, a bedraggled figure rushed in and went up to the bar. He looked around urgently, desperately trying to pick someone out.

"Have you seen a man on his own with brown hair and eyes?" he asked the barman. "He'd be about my height and build and a good-looking fellow. I was supposed to meet him in here an hour ago, but I got stuck on the tube."

"Yes there was a guy like that, but he wasn't alone," the barman replied. "He left with a very dishy young man about five minutes ago. You've only just missed him. Can I get you something to drink?"

Sean was crestfallen. He had been looking forward to meeting Darryn and now it seemed he'd gone off with another man. "No, I might as well go. There doesn't seem to be any point in hanging around here now."

***

For Jake, the summer of that year marked the start of a season of losses. Some of these were permanent whilst others had the possibility of restoration; some were life-changing whilst others tore at his heartstrings less keenly.

The first of these came unexpectedly on the penultimate day of term. Jake had returned to Rainbow House from college. After relaxing and listening to music for an hour or so, he had a wash and made his way down the grand staircase to the dining zone to get something to eat. Ashok was working in the kitchens and Jake cheerily hailed him. These days Jake rarely got more than a grunt in return. However, today Ashok acknowledged him and came over to sit with him by the window. Fortunately Nathan was not about, so there was no risk of a row.

"I have something important to tell you," Ashok said rather unexpectedly.

"You haven't got into some kind of trouble, have you?" Jake responded in a worried tone.

"Of course not," Ashok said with some irritation. "I'm leaving Rainbow House at the end of term."

This hit Jake like a bombshell. His mouth opened and closed several times before he could make any meaningful words come out:

"But you can't... you're gay... where will you go?"

Ashok smiled a little at these disconnected statements and decided to start with the last one, "Where do you think I was at Christmas? I stayed with an uncle and aunt who have slightly more liberal views than my parents. It went okay and they've said I can go and stay with them as long as I make an effort to re-establish myself within the family hierarchy."

"But isn't that what you ran away from?" asked Jake, becoming increasingly dumbfounded.

"No, not particularly, you don't know why I'm here Jake, because I've never told you."

"Aren't you happy here then?" Jake asked, floundering to keep up with this unexpected turn of events.

"I'm not unhappy, but then I'm not happy either. It's all turned out very nicely for you, Jake. You have a boyfriend, you've slotted into the routine, you're doing well on the Guardian program and you are certain of who you are. Do you see me with a boyfriend? Do you see me hobnobbing with celebrated Guardians? I'm less sure of who I am now than I was a year ago. The world is going to turn nasty, Jake. People are going to be like they used to be in the old days, hating the likes of us and making our lives as difficult and awkward as possible.

"The thought of having to live rough and eat off the land was the last straw. That training week we had... I know it all went wrong when we stumbled across the F.U.P. camp, but even so, I'd made up my mind before then that it was not for me.

"You don't have a choice, Jake. You're gay, and that's an end to the matter. For me, it's more nuanced. I could live with a woman; I could settle down and have children. I'm tired of being an outsider. I just want to be normal and blend anonymously into the background."

Jake looked at the person who had once been his best friend carefully. He did indeed look worn out with bags under his eyes, and very, very sad. Tears welled up in Jake's eyes and he hugged Ashok very tightly.

"I will miss you so much. Will I see you again?"

"It's unlikely," Ashok sighed, "But there will always be a bond of friendship between us."

There was nothing left for Jake to say. He suddenly wasn't hungry anymore and decided to leave without having anything to eat. Ashok returned to the kitchens, muttering under his breath, "and for God's sake, Jake, don't let Nathan ruin your life."

***

It was the first day of the summer holidays and Jake woke up in Nathan's arms. They were in Jake's bed once again. Why did they always sleep in Jake's room? Jake could think of no satisfactory reason to explain why they rarely stopped over at Nathan's flat. A faint moan and stirring indicated that Nathan was also about to emerge into the land of the living. He stretched and finally croaked:

"Hi, babe, you okay this morning?"

"I'm fine, matey," Jake replied before rolling out of bed naked and making his way to the shower. He stood under the hot water thinking about what had to be done that day. They had to pack and get themselves ready before noon, then head off to Euston Station to catch the train. Jake was looking forward to seeing his mother and sisters, Maisie and Daisy, who he expected to be waiting at the platform to greet them. It had been touch and go whether Nathan would be given permission to accompany Jake. N°6 in particular was worried that Great Malvern was in the sphere of influence of the F.U.P. and was concerned that Gerald Tasker would discover where his son was. However, a directive from N°1 himself gave Nathan permission, as long as he remained alert to danger and maintained a low profile.

Jake gave a start as he suddenly felt cold hands on his chest. Nathan had also got in the shower and was hugging Jake from behind. The sensation of Nathan's body close to his made Jake feel both secure and excited. Surely he would never tire of this, however long he and Nathan were together?

"Shall I put some shower gel on your back and rub it in? You can clean my back in a minute too."

"Alright, but we mustn't be long. We've got to pack, and you're even worse at that than I am. You get distracted too easily."

"Well when I've got someone like you to distract me, you can't really blame me."

"Shut up," said Jake going red with embarrassment. "You don't need to use cheesy chat-up lines now I'm your boyfriend. Now I'm serious Nathan, we can't afford to be late for the train. Our tickets are only valid for that one departure. I've got to contact Mum in a bit too, to check everything is okay."

Nathan hugged Jake just a little bit tighter under the constant downpour of the shower, but Jake was in no mood to be trifled with and did not succumb to Nathan's attempts to initiate what he often referred to as some 'dodgy business'.

As Jake, half-dressed, was still drying his hair, he turned on his desktop computer and called up Daisy on his internet video phone. Daisy responded on the other end and her picture came into view. Jake was always taken aback at how Daisy was growing up. She was now thirteen and had already completed two years at senior school.

"Hi, Jake," she said looking at the screen carefully. "Eew... you look gross. Put a top on, please. I can't believe Nathan fancies you looking like that."

"Thank you, dear sister," Jake replied sarcastically, "Is Mum there? I just want to check a few details before we leave."

This had become the standard way that Jake used to talk to his mother. He would video call either Daisy or, less frequently, Maisie on his computer or Smartphone and have a chat with them first. They would then call their mother who would continue the conversation without the technical worry of having to press buttons and choose menu options.

Rose Holdencroft came into view. She looked pale and weary.

"Are you okay, mum? You look a bit out of sorts."

"I've had a bit of a shock dear. I'll need to sort a few things out today that are going to be difficult."

"Do you still want Nathan and me to come? We could put it off if you like."

"No, no... What's happened concerns you anyway. You need to be here."

"Mum, what's happened? What's going on?"

"I don't want to say anything over the phone, dear. I'll tell you when you get here tonight. Can you remember where Aunty Violet's house is in Great Malvern? I may not be able to get down to the station to meet you."

The video link was cut rather abruptly and left Jake with many questions racing through his head. Something clearly was not normal, but he couldn't work out, for the life of him, what the problem might be.

"Everything okay, babe?" enquired Nathan, also in a half-dressed state.

"I'm not sure it is. We'll find out later anyway."

Jake found it particularly difficult to concentrate as they packed, his mind wandering with numerous scenarios of what the issue might be with his mother. They took a holdall each which they packed with clothes and washing things. They also took a rucksack each which they filled with other items they might need for their fortnight stay. Jake was convinced they did not have everything they required, but Nathan was beginning to moan and make comments about taking the kitchen sink.

They were in good time for the train and unexpectedly met Maria and Matt at Euston Station, also waiting for a train going north. Matt looked even more odd than usual. His central blue hair was limp and tied back in a ponytail with his shaved sides now dyed red. He wore a tweed jacket along with his jeans and a trilby-style hat. He looked like a cross between a hippy and a country gentleman. Maria was much more soberly dressed and didn't seem to be worried about being seen with Matt, much to Jake's surprise. All four of them stood on the concourse looking up at the display boards showing the departures.

"So you're going to see your mum," Maria said. "I bet she'll be pleased to see you."

"You and Matt are going to North Wales, I believe," Jake replied.

"Yes, Matt's planning to do some painting, if this dreadful weather improves. I've got some books to read for my English A-level. I might as well make a start on them and just hope I get the AS grades. Jenny and Louise are going to call by. You know Jenny passed her test last week? She and Louise are out driving in her car now. They're planning to drive out to Wales to see us. I guess they were given strict instructions, like us, to stay well away from Bala and that F.U.P. camp you stumbled across, Jake."

"Well we're going to Malvern, so we are going nowhere near there...Oh that's our train." Jake had heard the muffled tones of the announcer and seen the platform number flash up on the board. There were discreet hugs all round and Jake and Nathan moved down the ramp to board the train to Birmingham New Street.

Chapter 21

"So can we be sure it's going to be 24th August?" N°2 asked.

A group of the great and the good were sat around the conference table in the boardroom of the operations zone. It was rare that this room was used. Usually only a few people were involved in key decisions and the offices of N°2 or N°6 were big enough to host the necessary meetings. This room had a very corporate feel, smelling of industrial air freshener with a coffee machine in the corner. A thick beige carpet was matched by neutral colours on the walls and window blinds slatted vertically.

"It is looking very likely," N°6 responded, "Even Darryn is coming around to the idea after his visit to James Grimwold the other day. It's funny you know, I never thought Darryn would be one to be swayed by mysticism and prophecy. Maybe the scientific element has made a difference."

"The intelligence we're getting from Rakshi and Taffy Williams is suggesting that they're not quite ready yet," Danny added. "They've been training to storm a building, shooting everyone inside and then setting fire to the premises. It looks as if the assault team is going to be about a dozen, with another thirty or so acting as support and back-up. Taffy's most recent report suggests that they are going to embed themselves in the local area a day or two before the event and then emerge from the crowd only minutes before committing the atrocity. It may be very difficult to respond unless we know exactly which venue is going to be attacked."

"There are about five or six iconic venues along there that could be targets," N°2 mused. "Could we spare thirty people for each? That would be about one hundred and eighty Guardians in all."

"We could," responded N°6, "but it would mean using trainees and dispersing our experienced officers rather thinly."

"How many have we got there now?" N°2 asked.

"We have thirty Guardians patrolling the area, mostly under cover." Danny responded.

"I understand you've asked Darryn to lead the operation on the ground. I'm rather surprised that he's not here." The comment had a rather disapproving tone.

N°6 intervened and said, "He had some matters to attend to in Oxford, and in any case he was due some leave, so I thought it best to let him have a week off now so he is fresh and alert when the fireworks begin."

"Well I want to see him the moment he is available, and I expect daily briefings with you and Danny from now until it's over, N°6. I also don't want us to forget about some of the other issues raised by that document Jake Holdencroft acquired. I am concerned that we don't know more about *plan*

F34 – operation 'Agent Entrapment'. We need to put some resources into finding this special agent of theirs and discovering how he is planning to lure one of our agents. I suspect this is how they are planning to initiate their ultimate plan to destroy us."

***

It was a good day in Oxford. Alex had come up from London and was being shown the sights. They started in Christ Church. Because Darryn was a Junior Research Fellow there, they were able to gain free access to the cathedral, the picture gallery, the library and the Dean's Garden. They were now strolling around Port Meadow; the bright sunshine sparkling on the waters of the Isis and the intense green of the grass and the trees in full leaf matched Darryn's sunny mood. There was no question that Alex was an incredibly good-looking guy and they had already spent a couple of nights of passionate lovemaking which had lived up to expectations. Darryn's initial concern, after the way he had been approached in 'The George and Dragon', was that Alex might be a bit of a 'blond bimbo'. He was, however, delighted to find that Alex was a highly intelligent man with broad interests and intellectual curiosity. Could this be the one? Could this finally be his soul mate?

"You have a nice set-up here, I must say." Alex said cheerily. "Where do you stay when you're down in London?"

Darryn was wary when being probed about his movements in the capital, and said rather vaguely, "I have a flat out east towards Poplar, but I use it infrequently. I spend most of my time here in Oxford."

"Still it would be nice to come and visit you there when you're in town."

"Your place is much nicer," Darryn replied quickly. "My place is very small and the neighbours aren't friendly."

They continued their walk and ended up in the city centre, where they had a leisurely lunch. Afterwards, the day was so warm that they decided to take a punt out from Magdalen Bridge and head up stream. They took a cheap bottle of white wine and some cakes with them for an impromptu picnic at the furthest point of their journey. Alex spent most of the time lounged decoratively in the punt, while Darryn did most of the hard work with the punt pole. As they glided silently back down the river with the occasional splosh, Darryn couldn't help feeling like an actor in a budget version of 'Brideshead Revisited'. Wasn't this the sort of thing he was supposed to have done as an undergraduate, rather than lead a lonely existence pouring over intractable equations in dark basement rooms?

It was a warm evening and they sat out in the open until it had gone quite dark. There was nobody about, so Darryn had his arm around Alex, who was snuggled up close to Darryn's chest. A full moon was low on the horizon and so much larger than normal. Its light provided enough guidance to see by, even without the help of the street lights of Oxford.

"Are you going to stop over?" Darryn asked optimistically.

Alex smiled and replied, "I should think so. I haven't had a better offer. I'll need to head for the station early in the morning though. When are we going to meet again after that?"

Darryn sighed and said, "I'm going to be pretty busy for most of August so I may not be able to catch up with you again until the end of the month."

"That's a shame," Alex replied with genuine disappointment in his voice. "I'll keep in touch, obviously, and maybe you'll have the odd evening free? Now I think it's time to head back to your place, don't you?"

***

Jake and Nathan got off the train at Great Malvern. The small three-unit diesel they alighted from was a far cry from the mighty high-speed intercity express that they had set out from Euston in. The station was well kept but gave the impression of having seen grander, greater days in the past. Lady Foley's Tea Shop was about to close as they passed by on the opposite platform to exit the station. Each of the boys had their rucksack on as well as carrying a holdall. They were in shorts and tee-shirts because the weather was so hot. Nathan was all in white, while Jake had a red shirt and commando-style shorts. As they stood in the station approach, Jake had to get his bearings for a moment to try and recall which way he needed to go to get to Aunt Violet's house. He then confidently marched out with Nathan in tow. Jake had been unusually quiet on the journey. The disturbing message he'd had that morning was still gnawing away at him and he was half-dreading arriving at his destination to find out what the inevitable tragedy was to be. Nathan seemed to appreciate his boyfriend's state of mind and did not engage in banter with him as he normally did. So, in silence, the boys approached a large sturdy Victorian house, large enough to accommodate more than one family. Using the heavy old-fashioned doorknocker attached, Jake gave three sharp knocks on the door. Moments later scurrying feet could be heard and the door swung open to reveal two excited girls who clung to Jake, kissing him and making it clear they were happy to see him. Then realising they might be seen to be impolite, they repeated the whole thing in a more restrained way with Nathan. Jake's mood was temporarily lightened at seeing his sisters in such a happy frame of mind, but this did not last long as he entered the corridor that led to the stairs and the downstairs rooms to see his mother emerge from the kitchen. She was pale and clearly strained. Jake thought she might have recently been crying too. He hugged his mother in welcome and was shocked at the way she clung to him as if she was needing the support of her son, rather than the other way around,

"Maisie and Daisy, can you show Nathan up to his room. I assume you two boys will want to sleep together?" Maisie and Daisy looked at each other and giggled as their mother said this and Jake went as red as a beetroot. This was quickly forgotten, however, as she continued, "Jake, I'd like to have a word with you alone for a moment, if you don't mind."

Nathan and the girls disappeared up the stairs. Jake knew that Aunty

Violet had gone away for a few days and so he assumed that he and his mother were now alone. He followed her into a large kitchen and sat at the sturdy oak table that was the focus for most of the meals in the house and much else besides.

Rose Holdencroft carefully shut the door and said in as matter-of-fact a way as she could muster, "There is no easy way to tell you this, Jake. Your father is dead."

For a second or two, time stood still. Jake replayed the statement in his head in case he'd misheard it. Then he considered whether it might be a bad joke. Then the impact that it was the truth hit him.

"How...why...?" he fumbled.

"From what I've been told by the police, he seems to have committed suicide."

"But why...?"

"I don't know, dear. The police seem satisfied that there was no foul play involved. There was a note addressed to you, left by the body." Rose held out an innocuous-looking brown envelope.

Jake took the envelope, which had already been opened. He assumed the police had already had a look at the note before allowing his mum to have it. There was his name on the envelope, unmistakably written in his father's hand. He took out a single piece of unlined notepaper which had this simple message on it:

'Dear Jake,
I have probably done you an injustice, for which I apologise. I have left you two thousand pounds in my will for you to get that violin from Samuels that you always wanted.
Dad'

"Have you read this, Mum?"

Rose shook her head negatively, so Jake handed the note over.

"That is so typical of your father," she said angrily. "He never could express his true feelings and he could never admit that he was wrong. I mean, what is all this stuff about 'doing you an injustice'? He just about did the wickedest thing a father could do to his son."

"He says nothing about why he killed himself either," Jake added. "He just calmly says he's left me some money in his will. What's going on?"

"I'm not sure we'll ever know why the stupid man took his own life, as if he hasn't made things difficult enough for us already. He never did think through the consequences of what he was doing."

"Do Maisie and Daisy know yet?"

"No. I only found out myself yesterday, and I haven't found the right moment or the right words yet."

Rose suddenly couldn't keep up the act any longer. She sat in a chair and burst into tears. Jake, trying his best to hold back his own tears, did his best to comfort her. Small feet could be heard on the stairs and Rose gathered herself together, somewhat more in control for having unburdened herself to her son.

"Don't say anything to the girls just yet. We'll talk again in the morning and I'll decide what to do for the best," she whispered urgently, as the girls and Nathan were about to burst in.

Rose and Jake managed to put on a brave face for the rest of the evening. Fortunately the girls were in a bubbly mood which masked the sombreness of Jake and his mother. Nathan did eventually twig that something was up and Jake was forced to confess what his mother had told him, while they were lying in bed that night.

"Whatever you do, don't let on to Maisie and Daisy... and try to look as if you don't know anything when talking to my mum," Jake urged Nathan.

Jake thought about his poor mother lying in the main bedroom with no one to comfort her. At least he had Nathan to hold him tight and give him reassurance. This was his second loss of the summer and the first that was irretrievable.

The next morning, Rose Holdencroft had a grim determination about her. Gone were the tears and in their place was a steely determination to set everything in place so they could all get on with their lives. She caught Jake on his own for a few minutes while Nathan was in the shower and the girls had been sent on a spurious journey to the supermarket to get some more milk.

"I have to go into Worcester today to see the undertakers. I need to make arrangements for the funeral. I also need to get in touch with the family solicitor. Can you and Nathan look after Maisie and Daisy for me today?"

"Yes, of course," replied Jake, "and I'll tell them about Dad too, if you like."

Rose hesitated for a moment and said, "It really ought to come from me."

Jake however had a moment of conviction and said forcibly, "Look, I'm not a kid any more. You have a lot on your plate as it is and I'm the eldest man in the family now. I ought to be taking some responsibility at a time like this."

Rose looked at him and saw a mature young man for the first time rather than the baby boy she had always viewed him as previously. She relented conditionally:

"Alright, but don't say he committed suicide. I'm not sure I ever want the girls to know that. Say they think he died of a heart attack or something."

Rose walked off to the station leaving Nathan and Jake to mind Maisie and to a lesser extent Daisy. It was a glorious summer's day again and Jake hit on the notion of taking the two girls onto the Malverns to try and fly their kite, so that they would at least have some fun together before Jake broke the news to them.

Daisy was not keen at first, but was in the end persuaded. Their long trek up to the Worcestershire Beacon was rewarded with glorious views both across Worcestershire and Herefordshire. The wind, however, was not much more noticeable up on top than it had been at ground level, so efforts to fly the kite were mainly in vain. Nathan was aware of Jake's plan and so, when the dreaded moment came, Nathan's presence was a much-needed prop to help with the unenviable task Jake had taken to himself.

He sat everyone down on the grass. The town of Great Malvern looked like a miniature representation below. The abbey, the theatre and the showground were all clearly visible as was the railway line heading in a straight line towards Worcester, vaguely discernible in the middle distance. They were on the crest of an undulating set of hills that made its way south like a green sea serpent writhing across the flat fields of the Garden of England. The mid-afternoon sun was beating down, although the altitude and a gentle breeze prevented it from being unbearable.

"Girls, I have something sad to tell you. The reason Mum has gone into Worcester today is because Dad died last week and she needs to go and sort the funeral arrangements out. I'm so sorry."

The reaction he got from Daisy was not at all what he expected: "Jake, that's a sick joke to be making. If Dad had died, Mum would have told us herself."

"Poor Mum has a lot to do at the moment and she hasn't got anyone to help her. I said I'd break the news and she will talk to you about it when she gets home."

Daisy became really angry with Jake and shouted at him, "You're only my brother, Jake. What gives you the right to act like our Dad? You never liked him did you? It was probably your fault he died. I hate you... and Mum."

She stormed off down the steep side of the hill in the direction of North Hill. Nathan put his hand on Jake's shoulder and said, "I'll go after her. You stay here with Maisie and look after her. I'll bring Daisy back when she's calmed down." As Nathan set off, Jake couldn't help but notice that other people, making the most of the fine weather on the hills, had stopped to look at what was going on.

Maisie was now crying and although he was shaking and on the point of tears himself he put an arm around her and hugged her tightly.

Twenty minutes later, Nathan returned with Daisy.

"I'm sorry, Jake," she said.

"That's okay," Jake replied, after which there was more hugging and crying all round.

By the time they were ready to descend and return home, the shadows were beginning to lengthen and the number of people walking along the hills had declined. Rose had returned home before them, so there were more tears and hugs as she spoke to the girls about what had happened and tried to fill in

128

the gaps posed by their questions as tactfully and sensitively as she could.

Later that evening, Jake and Rose were once again alone in the kitchen. Nathan was being a hero and playing with Maisie, while daisy was in her room listening to music.

"Thanks for breaking the news to the girls, dear." Rose said gratefully.

"I didn't do it very well," Jake replied. "Daisy went mad at me and Nathan had to go after her."

"There's no easy way to give news like that. I'm sure you did it as well as anybody could."

"How did it go at the undertakers?"

"As well as can be expected, I suppose. Arthur's brother was there too. He wasn't sure whether I'd want anything to do with Arthur now we were separated. He's agreed to share the burden of arranging the funeral and sorting out the finances. He was really very sweet and it's taken a load off my mind. The funeral is going to be next Thursday in Telford."

"We'll all come, of course," Jake responded without thinking.

Rose became agitated and said, "What a fool Arthur's been. Now his own family can't even go to his funeral. Listen, Jake, a lot of Arthur's F.U.P. colleagues are likely to be there. Gerald Tasker himself might attend. Nathan certainly cannot go anywhere near there and I think you would be in danger too. I'll ask Daisy as she is old enough to make her own decision, but I don't think Maisie should be put through such an ordeal at her age."

Jake looked at his mother, concerned. "You can't expect to go through that alone with all those F.U.P. thugs in the congregation. I should be there."

However he couldn't argue with the logic of the situation and had to admit that his presence at the funeral would lead to a reaction of some sort from the F.U.P. They might even at this moment be hatching a plot to try and catch him or worse.

Nathan suggested they go for a run on the Malverns. It was another beautiful day and it was hard not to be slightly cheered by the bright sunshine showing the hills looming up above the town at their best. Since the end of term, they had not done any specific fitness training associated with their Guardian training.

They started jogging gently to warm up and so were able to talk to each other.

"Have you stopped playing at that club in Pall Mall?" Jake asked.

"Yes, thankfully... It was weird going there after you and Jenny had your run-in. It was as if we were all playing a game. They knew I knew that it was a front for the F.U.P. and I knew they knew I was with the Rainbow Alliance – or at least Martin did. That was the worst thing. Every now and then Martin would come in to meet Lord Bernard, he would always stop and wait 'til we got to the end of a movement. He would then make a big thing of clapping and say something like 'Bravo, well played. How's thing's going with the boys, Nathan?' He'd then wink at me and laugh. It was very nerve-racking to put it mildly. If they ask us to go back in September, I'll see if Lucy wants to do the cello part. Blow the money, it's not worth the hassle."

"Well now that Louise has provided a detailed map of the secret complex inside the club, the need for reconnaissance isn't so great."

"I've really not been able to find out anything useful since Jenny went bonkers anyway. Oh hello... What do you think those soldiers are up to?"

A group of soldiers had just jogged by them. They were in running kit but identifiable from the logo and markings on their running shirts. They were obviously out on a training expedition themselves.

"I don't think we should be outdone by a bunch of squaddies. Let's take them on, Jake."

"Let's not..." replied Jake plaintively, but it was too late. Nathan had stepped up a gear and was closing on the four soldiers in front. They saw him and responded. It became a full-blown race up the steep side of the Worcestershire Beacon to get to the top. Jake had given up the chase before it had even started. He was not at his best going up hills and was inwardly seething at Nathan for showing off and being an idiot. Jake staggered up and was at no more than walking pace by the time he reached the top. To his surprise, he saw Nathan with the four soldiers laughing and engrossed in conversation, standing by the trig point. As Jake approached they all slapped Nathan on the back and ran off. Jake thought he saw one of them slip Nathan a piece of paper which he quickly and furtively put in his back pocket.

"Hi babe, you took your time." Nathan greeted him cheerfully.

"Shut up," snapped Jake. "You always have to show off and make out you're better than everyone else, don't you?"

"Okay, don't get your knickers in a twist." Nathan said innocently enough. However this so enraged Jake that he flew at Nathan and the two of them ended up wrestling around the side of the hill. Nathan kept laughing all the time this was going on, but angry though Jake was, he eventually ran out of steam and gave up.

"Have you got all that out of your system now?" Nathan asked as they lay panting on the rather uncomfortable and rocky ground. Jake grunted. Nathan continued, "Good, because I've thought of a plan. You could go in disguise to the funeral. If you sat at the back of the church and the crematorium, they'd probably not notice you. You could wear glasses and maybe dye your hair or shave it off. If you had a female companion as well, no one would look twice at you."

"Where am I going to find a female companion? Don't tell me you're going to dress up in drag and come along too!"

"Interesting as that might be, I think your mum's right. If my dad and mum are there they will see through any disguise I have, but I have got someone in mind for you."

Chapter 22

Darryn was walking slowly along Canal Street. It was a Sunday morning, so the rubbish, the vomit and the repulsive alcoholic after-smell were still present from the revelries of the night before. Even so, the sunny weather did its best to put a cheerful demeanour on the scene. The sun even managed to sparkle on the dirty polluted waters of the canal that ran the full length of the street.

He had done a thorough check on the properties with his Guardian colleagues the day before, mainly with the active consent of the owners. He was particularly concerned about those which could be accessed from the rear through fire exits and staff entrances, thus making a dual-pronged attack a deadly possibility. He was also worried that they may have been too literal in their translation of Martin's note. Although the 'Gay Village' had shrunk in recent years, there were still juicy targets in the streets round about. He did not have the manpower to protect all of these as well.

He came to a halt outside 'The Sunken Way' and looked up and down the street. If they were to attack an establishment like this, halfway down between intersecting streets, they would have to coalesce almost directly outside the front of the building. Surely they would not risk shooting their way down from the end of the road, or were they that supremely confident?

August 24th, St Bartholomew's Day, was a Saturday and a Bank Holiday weekend at that. Although the Manchester Gay Pride event had been wound up several years before, the streets would still be heaving that evening. It would be so easy for a terrorist to move through the crowds unobserved, even with a rifle. Darryn shuddered at the prospect. Yes, it would be relatively easy for thirty armed men or women to gather in front of this building, even if he had a hundred men out on the street. He wondered whether the police would be complicit in the attack. He suspected that at the very least there would be plans to divert their attention while the assault was in play. Cuts in the Police budget had meant that officers were rarely deployed to maintain a presence on the streets anyway.

'The Sunken Way' was open so, as it was now time for a break, he went in to order a coffee. He sat inside at a table by the window looking out. A slender, over-thin young man bought the coffee over with a biscuit and some sugar. He acknowledged Darryn and asked how he was before heading back to do some cleaning duties behind the bar.

This was Darryn's venue of choice in Manchester. It was a cut above the others in terms of sophistication. It was an old warehouse which had been converted rather tastefully so that it was on several levels, retaining some link to its past use. Yes, it did have the ever-present dance floor, but at least this was downstairs in the basement and out of sight. There were plenty of little nooks and crannies where you could talk quietly with a friend or a small group of people and sit comfortably surrounded by wood panelling and soft fabric. The main bar was downstairs facing the large glass windows that fronted onto the street.

He was disturbed by a call on his phone. It was Annabelle giving an update by videophone.

"Hi Annabelle," He began, "how's things with you?"

"Fine Darryn," Annabelle replied. "There's not much to tell here really. They are still going through their attack manoeuvres. Taffy is convinced they are practicing to attack the front and the rear of the building simultaneously. They look to be trying to overwhelm any opposition in a sudden and swift operation. It's not clear whether they are expecting any serious resistance or not."

"I'm not sure that really helps us. Every venue along here has at least a fire escape at the back. I wish we could narrow it down somehow. You know I'm worried they may go for one of the places off Canal Street."

"Well, I can't help you there, I'm afraid. One thing that is odd is that O'Grady's young side-kick seems to have disappeared. It would be interesting to know where he's gone and what he's up to."

"Yes, I remember you were quite taken with him weren't you?" Darryn said with a smile.

"Well it is unusual to meet a man who is polite and courteous. He did show an interest in the staff as well."

"I'm sure he did."

"It's just a shame he's a fascist bastard and on the wrong side, really. Well, I'll let you enjoy your Sunday. I'll keep you posted."

The screen went blank and Darryn took another sip of his coffee.

***

"Veronica!" exclaimed Jake.

"Why not Veronica... She seems an obvious choice to me." Nathan replied calmly.

"Maybe the fact that when she last saw me she slapped me around the face and used every swear word known to man makes me think you might be wrong."

"You forget, I was at the school a few months longer than you. She was on your side, you know."

In the end Nathan called Veronica. Somehow he still had her number. Jake was astonished that she said yes to their plan immediately and even enquired after Jake with some fondness.

"See, I told you it would be alright," Nathan beamed when he'd finished the call.

The plan was that Jake would wear glasses (they bought a cheap pair with a minimal correction at the supermarket), cut his hair really short and dye it blond. For extra cover, Veronica was going to ask a few of her college friends to come along so they could all sit together at the back.

As it turned out, the church was of rather unusual design. It was designed by Thomas Telford himself and was octagonal in shape, having a balcony seating area three-quarters of the way round the inside of the building. This meant Jake and Veronica and half a dozen people that she bought along could sit upstairs without easily being noticed from below.

Jake had not levelled with his mother, who had been adamant that Jake should stay as far away as possible. He had confided in Daisy who had been equally determined to attend, but swore her to silence on pain of death. Maisie was dispatched to a school friend's home for the day. Aunt Violet had returned on the Tuesday afternoon and insisted on attending with Rose. As Aunt Violet had a car, this solved the problem of an awkward train journey for his mum and Daisy, for which Jake was very grateful. He saw them now, seated at the front on the right along with Arthur's brother and his family. Jake was also pleased to see one or two of his mum's friends and neighbours from her days living in Telford. Jake was not too happy to see one or two prominent members of the F.U.P. there, one or two quite outrageously wearing the military-style uniform of the organisation. Gerald Tasker did not seem to be present, but he was shocked when he realised that one of the uniformed members of the congregation was David Peters, his neighbour and best friend at school for many years.

The vicar entered ahead of the coffin reading verses of Scripture. This was a peculiar moment for Jake. He did not feel heartbroken or particularly sad. Yes, he had had some good times with his father which he remembered fondly, but the trauma of that day when his dad had stood by and let the angry mob chase him from his home and his life, had emotionally distanced him from any bonds of attachment. His main feeling as the service proceeded was one of guilt; guilt that he really felt no sorrow or loss for the man at the centre of the ceremony. His mother clearly was affected, shedding a tear or two and being comforted by Violet. Daisy was looking pale but was holding up well under the circumstances.

All too quickly the church service was over. The homily was of a very general nature and bore only a passing resemblance to the man Jake remembered as his father. Again, there was reference to his period with the F.U.P. which seemed more like a stain on his character than a distinguished act of public service. The coffin was taken out by the pallbearers and placed in the hearse. Jake was not going to push his luck by trying to attend the committal at the crematorium, where there would be fewer people present. He was now satisfied that his mum and Daisy would come to no harm.

Jake sneaked out via the graveyard when most of the other attendees had gone. He thanked each of Veronica's college friends personally and then turned to his ex-'girlfriend':

"It was very good of you to help out. I was surprised you agreed to do it."

"I've calmed down now," she replied smiling. "Anyway, how are you feeling? You've just been to your dad's funeral."

"I feel quite odd to be honest. It's as if I've been watching the last hour of my life as a detached spectator."

"I expect it's the shock. Listen Jake, I'm glad I've had the chance to catch up with you again. I didn't like the way we left things. I should have guessed there was something dodgy about you the way you were so easy to talk to. I do miss you as a friend, you know. I understand you're with Nathan now, and actually I think that's really cool. I'd like us to be able to keep in touch though."

Jake smiled and replied, "That would be really good." He gave Veronica a hug and a kiss on the cheek.

"Do you want to join us for a coffee? There's a place in the shopping centre where my friends go sometimes."

"You're alright, I'd like some time by myself. I'll be in touch though."

Veronica and her college friends left Jake to his contemplation of mortality. The graveyard sloped steeply down to the road. It was well kept and had a sense of peace about it. His father would soon be remembered, like all the other incumbents of this field, only by an inscription on a stone. One day he too would follow.

Arms from nowhere embraced him. Momentary panic subsided as he recognised them. "Nathan!" he exclaimed, "What on Earth are you doing here? We agreed you'd stay as far away from here as possible."

"I thought you might like a bit of moral support, babe," he replied. "In any case, I just got a feeling I wanted to see my old hunting ground again. How was Veronica?"

"She was really sweet. I'm glad I've seen her again."

"Hey, I've got some competition then." Nathan said in mock horror,

"Don't be daft!"

The two of them hugged and kissed, not really caring if anyone saw or not.

***

Annabelle had just finished checking the duty staff in the West Midlands area. It had seemed remarkably quiet. Obviously the F.U.P. must be concentrating on their big spectacular planned for the end of the month. There was only one thing that disturbed her. She knew about the funeral of Jake's dad in Telford and had asked Marcus, the Guardian Officer for the town that day, to keep an eye on proceedings. He reported that Jake had turned up in a ludicrous disguise that would not have fooled anyone, and even worse, Nathan had made an appearance at the end as well. Annabelle had frowned and asked Marcus to tail the boys and make sure they didn't cause any trouble. Darryn was having too much influence on those two. They were becoming as reckless as he was.

She sat in the coffee bar in Shrewsbury where Sean worked, sipping a latte and eating a chocolate muffin amid the mediaeval irregularity of the building. Sean came over to clear a table and give it a wipe.

"How are you?" Annabelle asked.

"I'm okay, I suppose," Sean said without conviction.

"How did your meeting go with Darryn down in London the other week? I'd put money on you two being an item by now,"

"Don't joke about it, Annabelle. It was a disaster. The tube got stuck in the tunnel and so I was an hour late. The barman told me he'd gone off with some blond airhead. I haven't spoken to him since."

"Interesting," said Annabelle, "He's said nothing to me about a new man."

Sean was clearly not in the mood for conversation, especially when it was about Darryn. He quickly gathered the dirty cups and plates and went to put them in the dishwasher behind the counter.

Annabelle was about to leave, when she got an unexpected call on her phone. It was from Rakshi. Within seconds, Annabelle could tell that Rakshi was in a dreadful state.

"Rakshi, what's up, darling?"

"I... Oh, it's terrible, Annabelle. I've got a 'code red' situation here. I need rescuing." Rakshi babbled on the end of the line.

"Okay, where are you?" Annabelle said, now fully alert and focused.

"I'm holed up in Corwen. They've sent a posse into town. It's only a matter of time before they find me."

"I'll come and get you."

"Be careful, Annabelle, they might recognise you. Make sure you have some cover."

"I will. Can you tell me where to meet you?"

"Opposite the car and van centre, before you get to the main high street, there's a road which leads to a small car park. Wait there and send me a blank text. I'll be nearby and try to get to you. Look out for anyone hanging about."

"I'll get there as soon as I can. Be strong, dear."

Annabelle hung up and made her way up to the counter.

"Sean," she said, "Do you know anyone who could drive me to Corwen now?"

Sean raised an eyebrow and replied, "That's a strange request. If you give me two minutes, I suppose I could. I've finished my shift."

"Thanks, Sean; I need someone I can rely on."

Ten minutes later they were sat in Sean's rather ancient mini, with Annabelle trying to hide as much of her face as she could with dark glasses and a rather unfashionable baseball cap. She told Sean as much as she could as they were driving down the A5. The weather had broken and some very big clouds were heading towards them from the west. As they got to Oswestry, the heavens opened in a tirade of water droplets. Sean was forced to turn the lights on and his windscreen wipers could barely cope, even on maximum speed.

"I hope water doesn't get into the electrics," he muttered to himself. The road was now covered in water and the speed of the traffic had slowed to a snail's pace.

By the time they got to Llangollen, it was beginning to ease off, but the rest of the day was going to be drizzly, dull and grey. As they entered Corwen, the car park Rakshi had directed them to was easy to find. The car and van centre was obvious and a sign pointed to the road where the car park was. There were plenty of empty spaces. On one side of the car park there were open fields; on the other were the backs of houses. A building which looked like a village hall was located on the third side furthest from the road.

"Where shall I park?" Sean asked Annabelle.

"It doesn't really matter, but make sure you can make a quick getaway and leave the engine running. Did you see anyone lurking about?"

"No, but there may be someone sitting in a car, just waiting."

Annabelle sent the blank text. The rain had subsided to a fine drizzle, but the leaden skies made the whole area look very bleak. Five minutes passed. Both Annabelle and Sean strained their eyes in every direction to look for signs of Rakshi or her pursuers.

"I'll give her five more minutes, and then I'm going to have a look round." Annabelle said in a worried tone. It proved unnecessary however, as within seconds of saying this, Annabelle noticed a figure dressed in black slip over the garden wall of one of the houses and crouch down behind a car.

"Flash your lights three times," Annabelle instructed Sean.

The figure noticed and started cautiously to proceed to the vehicle, slipping behind one car after another, trying to evade notice.

Sean suddenly caught sight of a man in his wing mirror just emerging from behind the village hall.

"Annabelle," he said with some urgency, "There's a man behind us... and he's got a gun."

No sooner had he said this than a shot rang out. Annabelle reacted instantly. She opened the passenger door while removing her own regulation-issue gun from its holster and, in one fluid movement, fired at the man who had emerged from behind the hall. She hit him. The surprise made him drop his gun and clutch his upper arm where Annabelle's bullet must have impacted.

"Rakshi... Quick, I've got you covered" she shouted. The figure in black scurried quickly towards Sean's car while Annabelle, unconcerned with secrecy now, held her gun up and circled through a full three hundred and sixty degrees. With hawk-like eyes she scanned the full panorama looking for any other assailants. Rakshi sprawled into the back seat and immediately Annabelle returned to the front passenger seat and closed the door.

"Drive!" she commanded Sean.

Chapter 23

Jake could not believe where he and Nathan were now standing. How had he been persuaded into such an idiotic venture? There to his right was the weeping willow tree that he had found Nathan under, drunk and dissolute, almost a year and a half ago. In front of him was the residence of Gerald and Daphne Tasker.

"Right, you've seen your house, can we go now, please, before we get caught? It's amazing there aren't any guards on duty."

"Hang on," replied Nathan as cool as a cucumber, "I just want to see if there is something in the garage."

"What?" Jake held his hands to his head in disbelief.

"Stay here then Jelly-Belly, while I go and investigate."

As bold as brass Nathan walked up the driveway and tried the garage door. It was locked, but he had a key in his pocket that opened it. Jake did not know what to do. He considered going to hide in the weeping willow; he considered joining Nathan for safety in numbers. In the end he simply remained transfixed to the spot. He was bewildered still further when Nathan reappeared a few minutes later wheeling a motorbike.

"Do you like it?" Nathan asked.

"Does it matter whether I like it or not? What the hell are you doing with it?"

"It's mine – or rather, it was going to be mine when I passed my A-levels. I thought I'd just take early delivery of it."

"Can you actually ride it?" Jake asked concerned.

"I think so," Nathan replied casually.

"You certainly haven't got the right to ride it. It's too big to drive on a provisional license."

"Don't quibble. Are you a Guardian of the Rainbow or a mouse?" With this he threw a helmet at Jake and put another one on himself that he'd found in the garage. He then checked the settings and turned the key (which he also just happened to have) in the ignition. He sat astride it and pressed the start button – there was no need to kick-start it. The engine purred as it idled and warmed up.

"Come on Jake, hop on the back and well go for a ride. It'll be fun. We can pretend we're like Keanu Reeves and River Phoenix in that soppy art film you like so much."

"More like Thelma and Louise," replied Jake with a degree of scorn, "or Wallace and Gromit, - and I'm the dog, by the way. He's better looking."

They had been pushing their luck and the sound of the motorbike engine idling away finally brought a response from inside the house. Gerald Tasker threw the front door open and his eyes nearly popped out of his head when he realised that it was his son who was standing astride the motorbike.

"Nathan!"

"Hi, Dad," Nathan responded as casually as you like. "Are you pleased to see me?"

"If you've come to your senses and decided to come back to your family and follow a sober Christian course, then yes. I am very pleased."

"Sorry. I've just come to take the bike. I think you agreed I could have it when I passed my A-levels. I'm not expecting to pass this way again for a very long time so, if you don't mind, I'll take it now. Don't worry; my college report is very good. I'm sure I'll get those A-grades you wanted. If I don't, I can always send it back."

"Wait," implored Mr Tasker with a sense of pleading which struck Jake at least as unusual. "Your mother has missed you. Does your family mean nothing to you?"

"Who is my family?" replied Nathan and as if to make his point, he put his arm round Jake and continued, "Here is my family." He gave Jake a kiss in full view of his father. "My brothers and sisters are those who love me, for who I am, not the tyrants who wanted me to be something to satisfy their own religious and moral beliefs. I renounce you as my father. My new family are the Rainbow Alliance. When I was hungry they gave me food, when I was thirsty they gave me something to drink, when I was a stranger they invited me in, and when I was in prison, at your behest I might add, they rescued me."

Mr Tasker went purple with rage, "You blasphemous devil! You will burn in Hell."

Nathan calmly turned to his father and replied, "Are you so sure that's not where you're heading too? I know some of the things your organisation's planning. I thought cold-blooded murder went against at least one of the Ten Commandments. Goodbye!"

With that Nathan engaged first gear and dramatically left the scene with Jake hanging on for grim life riding pillion behind. The reality of hanging on to Nathan astride a motorbike was not the erotic fantasy he had hoped for. He was expecting Nathan to crash at any moment and he felt very unstable.

"Do you have to go so fast?" he shouted when they had gone round the corner so that they were no longer visible from the Tasker's house.

"Don't be such a wuss," Nathan replied. "I'm only doing twenty-five miles an hour."

Jake wasn't quite sure where Nathan was going to take him, but he was suddenly distracted by the sight of what appeared to be a fracas at the side of the road.

"What's going on there?" he shouted at Nathan.

"I don't know. Let's go and have a look." Nathan replied.

A skinny lad of about fourteen or fifteen was being interrogated by two older lads in F.U.P. uniforms who were clearly throwing their weight about. One or two other unsavoury characters had also gathered.

Nathan stopped the bike and he and Jake got off.

"What's the problem?" Nathan asked as he approached the group.

"What's it got to do with you?" one of the uniformed lads said in a malicious and officious way.

"Maybe nothing, maybe everything... It depends," Nathan retorted enigmatically.

Just then a third figure in uniform appeared from an adjacent street and walked towards them.

"Well, well... If it isn't David Peters!" exclaimed Nathan.

"Nathan ... and Jake!" shouted David in return. "What have you done to your hair, Jake, and when did your eyesight get so bad?" Jake made sure he stayed out of sight at the funeral so that David wouldn't recognise him, but he still wore the glasses which he now took off as superfluous and placed them in the pocket of his jacket. He still had a close crop dyed blond though.

"Are these the two homos who went to live together in Benderville?" one of the other uniformed lads enquired sneeringly.

"Yes that's right," Nathan responded cheerily, "we didn't want to stay here in Lobotomy City where the average IQ was in negative numbers."

David looked uneasy and the other two uniformed lads squared up, looking aggressive.

"What do they want with you, kid?" Jake asked.

"It's okay, don't cause any trouble," the boy responded anxiously.

"I hope you're not bullying the weak and the innocent." Nathan said furrowing his brow.

"I think you should just go before there's any trouble," David said almost as nervously as the kid.

"I'm afraid we can't do that, David, because unlike you, Jake and I have developed a backbone and we're prepared to stand up for what we believe in. Now you lot, just leave this kid alone and go away."

Nathan was still high on adrenaline from the incident with his father and the motorbike. Jake always got worried when Nathan got in this state, but he also admired him and glowed with pride that he had such a heroic boyfriend. David's fellow-uniformed comrades could not contain themselves any longer. They lunged at Nathan, who unceremoniously dispatched both of them on their backs, winding at least one of them.

David looked at Jake and said, "I don't want to hurt you, but I will be forced to detain you if you don't go now."

Jake laughed and said, "Don't be a fool, David. You've seen what's happened to your lovely friends."

"I was always much stronger than you when we were kids." David made a lunge at Jake, but fared no better than his two colleagues, landing sharply on his back.

139

Jake said with a sigh, "That was a long time ago, David. Things have changed. I know how to break your neck with a single blow. Do us all a favour and quit the F.U.P. before you get hurt. I'm afraid if you don't, you are our sworn enemy."

One of the F.U.P. lads decided to have another go, but was contemptuously dispatched by Nathan, leaving him flat on his back again and gasping for air.

"Come on, let's go," David said, realising that they were only asking for more of a beating if they stayed. The three in uniform shuffled sulkily off. The onlookers had slid away some time ago when it was clear that the fight was not going to go the way they wanted. David glanced back rather wistfully at Jake as they rounded the corner, giving the impression that he wished the last few minutes had not occurred.

"Hey kid," Nathan said, addressing the awestruck youngster at the centre of the fracas, "What was all that about, then?"

"One of the guys in uniform has always bullied me since we were at school. He used to steal my dinner money and humiliate me in front of his friends. He used to tell everyone that I was gay."

Nathan put his arm around Jake and replied, "There's nothing wrong with being gay, matey. If that's the way you are, embrace it and don't let anyone make you feel guilty about it, especially not ignorant slimeballs like that lot." He then gave Jake a kiss right in the middle of the street. "Jake's my boyfriend, and I'm the luckiest guy in the world."

The young lad looked on, open-mouthed, "Gosh, you two are cool," he said with a great deal of admiration. "I don't think I'm gay. It's just that I'm weedy and don't like sport, everyone thinks I must be gay. It's a real pain round these parts at the moment. No, I have dreams about women, so I think I must be straight."

Jake laughed and said, "That's okay, we won't hold it against you. Have you got a girlfriend?"

"I'm working on it."

"Sweet," Nathan chipped in. "Do you want a ride on my motorbike? I'll drop you off at home if you like. If you get any more hassle off David Peters and his friends, just say you have Nathan's number and he knows where to find them. There you go; you can be an honorary straight member of our gay club!"

Nathan turned to Jake and said, "Listen, I've got to get this mean machine back to Rainbow House before anyone asks too many questions. You're alright getting back to Malvern on the train, aren't you? Give my apologies to your mum and the girls. Louise and Jenny can take my stuff back in their car next week when they planned to pick us up, anyway. It would be nice for you to have a few days on your own with the family, especially after today. I love you, babe."

He kissed Jake again, and then with the young lad on the back of the motorbike beaming broadly, he set off down the road. Jake could not help but feel abandoned. It had been an extraordinary day. He had attended the funeral of his father in disguise, stolen a motorbike from the most important F.U.P. official in town, had a bust up with some NPC agents and been abandoned in enemy territory by his boyfriend.

The sight of a figure dressed in black coming towards him now, suggested that the strange events of that day were not quite over yet. As he got closer Jake could see that he was a black man of Afro-Caribbean descent, tall, lean and muscular. He was in his mid-twenties and had his head shaved in a close crop.

"What the hell do you think you're up to?" The man said in a deep voice, clearly not pleased.

"...Pardon?" Jake said rather perplexed. "Who are you and what are you going on about?"

"I'm Marcus, the local Guardian and I've been watching you and Nathan all day. You two are damned lucky that all the best F.U.P. operatives are in Wales at the moment. You could hardly have drawn more attention to yourselves if you'd stripped naked and run through the shopping centre shouting 'I'm queer'."

"Okay, I guess we were a little foolhardy."

"That's the understatement of the year! ... Come on, let me take you to the station and I'll make sure you get on the train safely. Goodness only knows where Nathan's got to on that motorbike. I just hope he's not been stupid enough to go on the motorway."

Chapter 24

Darryn was having a beer in 'The Sunken Way'. He had just been reviewing the results of exercises carried out by his Guardian force the previous night. It hadn't been easy to find a suitable time to do these. They had first tried on Sunday afternoon with broom handles rather than guns, so as not to terrify the locals. However, they had attracted quite an audience, because it looked as if they were a company of mime artists doing some elaborate show. They had even got a round of applause and Darryn found some coins in his beret when he picked it up off the bench. In the end, they had to resort to doing the exercises at three o'clock in the morning, while blocking off the surrounding roads. They had developed variations to cope with an attack on any one of the establishments along the street. The only problem was that this meant an inevitable delay getting to the right place, which might cost lives in any initial assault by the F.U.P.

Darryn had an unexpected phone call from Annabelle: 'Hi, Darryn, I've got a situation here. Have you got time to talk on the videophone?"

Darryn looked at his watch. He had half an hour before his next appointment. He sat down on a leather sofa and replied to Annabelle, "Yes, that's fine go ahead."

"I've just picked up Rakshi. She was in a terrible state when I found her and I had to shoot an F.U.P. agent to get her out. I don't think he's badly injured so I'm hoping the local press are half-asleep and don't get distracted from the latest sheep prices. She's staying at Sean's in Shrewsbury for the time being, but I think we need to get her to Rainbow House as quickly as possible.

"She and Taffy were doing their usual patrol, when something went wrong. Some traps had been set around the perimeter of the camp; they were definitely not there before, and Rakshi got caught in one. There were extra guards waiting for something to happen, and they fell on her before she could do anything about it."

"Do you think Martin was involved with that?" Darryn interrupted.

"It's hard to tell," Annabelle replied. "Rakshi doesn't recall seeing him during what followed. Anyway, they took her into the camp, to the yard in front of the kitchen which I know so well. Michael O'Grady came out in a foul mood and interrogated her. He obviously asked about the Rainbow Alliance and where they were based. She gave nothing away, of course. Interestingly he also asked a lot of questions about Taffy's group who had strayed into the camp. He seemed to know we had a training camp and implied that he knew the location of it. He asked if Nathan Tasker was in the group of trainees who'd stumbled on the camp."

"We'd better warn Nathan that he's under the spotlight again." Darryn interrupted. "...Any ideas where Jake and Nathan are at the moment?"

"I think Marcus can give you an idea of what those two have been up to," Annabelle said wryly. "Now Darryn, listen carefully, I'm coming to the serious bit. When O'Grady had finished his questions, he got out a pistol and pointed it at Rakshi's head, saying they might as well start as the meant to go on. As they were going to kill several hundred deviants they might as well kill a few more on the way. He was on the point of pulling the trigger when Taffy burst out from nowhere and rushed towards O'Grady shouting, 'If you're going to shoot someone, shoot me.' I'm afraid that's exactly what he did. O'Grady shot Taffy four times, twice in the chest and twice in the head. Rakshi says that despite the profuse bleeding Taffy kept moving towards O'Grady and held him in a bear hug as he died. O'Grady was drenched in Taffy's blood.

"Rakshi says that despite the shock she seized the moment to escape from her captors, who momentarily loosened their grip, as they were even more shocked than Rakshi at what O'Grady had just done. O'Grady had two more shots, which he fired in Rakshi's direction, but fortunately Rakshi was able to find cover.

"To cut a long story short, she spent a night and much of the next day travelling over fields and through woods until she got to Corwen. That's where I found her with Sean's help."

Darryn was silent.

"Darryn are you still there? There's one other thing. As O'Grady was firing the last shot, Rakshi heard him say, 'Die like all the scum in 'The Sunken Way'. May you all burn in Hell!"

Darryn felt as if he'd been hit by hammers from all directions. James Grimwold's prediction seemed to have come true. He had suffered a personal tragedy in the death of Taffy, but he apparently now knew that the focus of attack was indeed going to be 'The Sunken Way'. He replied to Annabelle, "Keep that last bit of information under your hat. I don't want there to be any chance of it leaking back to the F.U.P. If anything happens to me in the next day or two, I'm ordering you to come and take command. Assume that what you have just said is correct. 'The Sunken Way' is the target. What did O'Grady do with Taffy's body?"

"I don't know. I think he just left him in the courtyard," Annabelle said somewhat mystified. "What are you planning to do, Darryn?"

"It's best you don't know."

Darryn terminated the call and left the bar with an unusually grim expression on his face.

***

Michael O'Grady woke the next morning. It had taken him hours to wash all the blood off, and his clothes had been ruined. Even now, there were specks of congealed dark red in his beard. He had ordered Taffy's body to be left in the yard overnight, mainly as a warning to his own followers to tow the line. He very much believed that a bullying management style was the best way to get the best out of his workers. It had rained overnight, but if it was hot today, the body would start to smell.

Having dressed, he went outside to have a look at what was going on. A small group of militiamen were gathered round something in the yard, but dissolved into other parts of the camp when they saw O'Grady appear. Where there had been one body there were now two. One of them he recognised as his own private security guard, and the other body was no longer Taffy's. Pinned to the bloodstained shirt of one of the bodies was a note. O'Grady ripped it from the shirt and opened it.

'For every one of us you kill, I personally guarantee I'll kill two in return; an eye for an eye – but only more so. You've killed a good man and a friend. I shall not forget this. You will pay for it dearly in the end. DHS'

O'Grady let out an anguished howl that could be heard across half the county.

***

A car horn beeped cheerily a couple of times outside Aunt Violet's house in Malvern. A week had passed by since the events of the funeral, and things were slowly returning to some kind of normality. Jake's hair was gradually regaining its natural colour, but he knew that his mother was unconvinced by his explanation that he'd suddenly had an urge to try a different image. He went out to see who it was and guessed, rightly, that Louise and Jenny had arrived. He told them to park the old, but extremely well-cared-for car on the drive and then come in.

Maisie and Daisy were pleased to see some new people and coerced Louise and Jenny upstairs later to talk about clothes and make-up and, in Daisy's case anyway, discuss who the latest hot male pop stars were.

Rose Holdencroft was more on an even keel too. She welcomed Louise and Jenny, showing them into the front living room, and making some coffee for them and Jake. After a few pleasantries, she left Jake, Jenny and Louise alone to get on with some housework and cooking in the kitchen. They were then able to talk more candidly to each other.

"So what have you girls been up to?" Jake asked.

"We've just been touring about, stopping off here and there." Louise replied. "We've mainly been staying at youth hostels."

"We've just come from seeing Maria and Matt," Jenny continued. "Matt's wandering around like he's Van Gough or something."

"...But he hasn't cut his ear off," Louise added; concerned that Jake should not worry.

"Obviously not," said Jenny somewhat scornfully, "but even I have to admit he's doing some nice paintings. Somehow he's got free access to Portmeirion and is doing sketches of some of the houses. He's also working on quite an ambitious landscape along the estuary front."

"How's Maria?" Jake asked.

"She's in good spirits. I think she was pleased to see us for a few days. We left Matt to paint and we went off and did other things. Anyway it's about time you told us what you and Nathan got up to in Telford. N°8 popped in just as we were about to leave and said that you two had caused all sorts of problems. Nathan had to go and see N°1, which is almost unheard of."

Jake looked worried and said, "Nathan's said nothing to me about that. Listen, you must be careful what you say in front of my mum. I'll have to own up to going to the funeral in disguise, but the stuff with Nathan must remain a closely guarded secret."

"It's not a closely guarded secret at rainbow house," laughed Louise. "He turned up on a motorbike at about two in the morning, activated the secret car park wall and coolly asked if there was a free parking space where he could leave it."

"Oh dear," Jake moaned as he clutched his head in his hands. "Nathan was a bit unhinged that day, to be honest. It was like there was some unfinished business with his family that he had to deal with at any cost."

Jake was now rather nervous about returning to Rainbow House with Jenny and Louise. Nathan had been intermittent in his communications with Jake and had clearly not been telling him everything that had been going on. He wondered if he, too, would face a dressing down from someone senior. He had no option, though. He had to return to get his AS results and besides, he had duties to perform from Monday as well as the recommencement of his Guardian training program. Gnawing away at him rather more was the state of his relationship with Nathan. He had been unimpressed at the way he'd been just left by the roadside in Telford, and he was not reassured by the infrequency and lack of candour in the conversations they'd had since. Jake was determined to give Nathan a piece of his mind when he caught up with him again.

So after a hearty lunch, Jake packed his belongings in the boot of Jenny's car and set off. There was a tearful farewell from his mother and sisters. Maisie ran up the road, waving as the car picked up speed. Jake finally lost sight of her as Jenny turned a corner and speeded away.

***

"Well?" said Jake, like an exasperated teacher.

"Well what?" replied Nathan innocently.

"Jenny tells me that you had to see Number One when you got back."

"Oh, *that*..."

"Well would you like to tell *me* what happened? After all, I am supposed to be your boyfriend and I thought we'd agreed not to have any secrets."

Nathan sighed and gave up the pretence. He flopped down into a deck chair and Jake, in more measured terms, pulled another one close to and sat beside him. They were on the garden roof having both finished a duty (Nathan had been working in the kitchens and Jake had been helping with the laundry). The sun was beginning to set behind red clouds, boding fair for the following morning.

"Okay, okay... I know I've been a bit of a moron." Nathan began. "The interview with N°1 was really weird. I didn't think I'd ever seen him before, but actually he was that old man who sometimes sits in the social area and reads the paper."

"Do you mean that guy who looks a little bit like a cross between a tramp and God?" Jake interjected.

"Yes, that's the one," Nathan confirmed. "Anyway, I went into his office on the top floor and he just stared at me for ages without saying anything. Finally he asked, 'Can I trust you?' I mean, what sort of a question is that?"

Jake refrained from saying anything as that was exactly the question he had been asking himself about Nathan for the past week. All the warnings that Ashok had been feeding him for the past year dribbled around his brain. "What did you say?" he asked.

Nathan seemed somewhat incensed that the answer was not obvious, "I answered 'yes', of course. He then asked me if I could think of any reason why Michael O'Grady should be asking whether I was one of the members of your ill-fated training expedition."

"That's very odd. You were nowhere near their camp at the time. I wonder if O'Grady has got you muddled with Tim or Ashok."

"The fact that O'Grady mentioned my name frankly scares me witless," Nathan responded. "From what Darryn's told me, he is certainly someone to steer well clear of. N°1 then asked if I planned to complete the Guardian programme. Again, I said 'yes', not really understanding what he was getting at. He then said that I was brave courageous and well-intentioned, but then added that as a Guardian, I would have to consider the welfare of others before my own interests. If it makes you feel any better, he did rebuke me for leaving you behind and causing problems for Marcus."

"Was that it?" Jake asked, clearly disappointed.

"Well what did you want him to do...Make me bend over and give me six of the best?"

"You just left me by the roadside and expected my poor mother to change all her plans for the next week. That was pretty low considering she'd just cremated her ex-husband."

"Oh, for goodness sake, Jake, don't be so dramatic. Honestly, I thought you had more about you. I left you there because I knew you could cope. I don't want a useless girl who has a fit of the vapours every time something unexpected happens. I'd have asked Matt to be my boyfriend if that was the case."

"There is a difference between that and simply being taken for granted," Jake snapped back.

Nathan shot up out of his seat and shouted back, "You can be so bloody self-righteous at times. I'm going for a run - by myself if you don't mind. I'll see you tomorrow when I've calmed down a bit."

Within seconds, Jake was left on his own, more uncertain than ever that all was well between him and his boyfriend. He was about to head for his apartment, when he was suddenly taken with an urge to see one of Matt's paintings. It was an absurd notion, but suddenly Matt seemed to be the only one of his close friends who was reliable. He remembered that Matt had recently done an abstract painting for the chapel in the faith zone. Jake descended four floors by the main marble staircase. He passed through the dining zone, which was deserted at this hour, and entered the faith zone which he rarely visited.

He expected it to be dark, but a flickering glow betrayed candlelight within the Anglican chapel area. He jumped a little as he saw a figure there, but soon realised that it was slumped in prayer. The scene suddenly crystallised as he realised that the dancing orange light was coming from four candles surrounding a coffin draped in a flag sporting a Welsh Dragon.

The figure turned around, and Jake immediately recognised the face of N^o6, sad and tear-stained. There was a moment's awkwardness as Jake felt he had blundered into a moment of someone's private grief.

"I'm sorry," Jake whispered, "I didn't mean to disturb you. I guess it must have been someone you were very close to."

N^o6 regained his composure and replied, "Yes he was a good friend to me. You knew him too, I think. Taffy Williams... He ran your Guardian expedition. He died trying to save someone else, which is how I expected him to go. He was shot by that bastard, O'Grady."

So Jake was at last aware of his third loss that summer. He'd admired Taffy in the end, and thought of him, like Darryn, as being invincible. His demise was therefore sobering as well as very sad.

Chapter 25

The twenty-fourth of August duly arrived. During the previous week, Darryn's Guardian force had been gradually more and more vigilant. Friday night had been treated as a full exercise, with all agents wearing body armour and carrying weapons with live ammunition. The bouncers on the door had been replaced by the more rotund members of the Guardian force and snipers were placed strategically on rooftops along the street. Nothing had happened (unless you count a fight between three lesbians which Annabelle sorted out).

Darryn didn't expect an attack until evening, possibly not until after ten o'clock. If the aim was to kill as many people as possible, the bars would be filling up with clubbers at about this time. Even so, they had to be alert from much earlier in the day. Already at lunchtime there were considerable numbers of people milling around. Now and then two or three people would seem to come together in a suspicious manner and Darryn's trigger finger would begin to twitch. However, these all proved innocent and explainable. Annabelle was the only other person who was fully intimate with Darryn's plans. She had been placed in charge of the team at 'The Van Dyke', but had contingency plans to mop up any resistance in the street when 'The Sunken Way' came under attack.

By four o'clock Darryn felt mentally drained and ordered his people to take a half-hour break in rotation, gambling that no attack was likely at this low period between four and six o'clock. Darryn decided to take a break himself with the first cohort, taking a cup of tea and thinking of nothing for twenty minutes. Refreshed, he went to the bar at the front of the building and carefully went over the procedure again with the manager of 'The Sunken Way'.

The Staff were to discretely try to usher the evening's clientele away from the windows and into the main body of the building. If there was a frontal assault, the bar staff were to duck behind the bar and the management were to usher the people on the lower floor into the basement dance area from where they could be escorted by Guardians through the fire exits. Darryn knew this was all fine in principle, but was still worried about casualties if his men were overwhelmed, or the public became hysterical and started rushing hither and thither.

He counted down the seconds on his watch to ten o'clock, the perspiration forming beads on his brow and his arm pits feeling uncomfortable and sticky. Still nothing happened. He and four other Guardians were positioned just out of sight in a room behind the main bar at the front of the building, looking out on to Canal Street. Ten other Guardians were mingling with the customers waiting to either draw their weapons or shepherd the patrons to safety. Guardians had also been placed outside each of the fire exits and on the roof. These had already drawn their weapons discretely and were eagle-eyed for the slightest wrong movement.

Then at ten minutes to eleven, Darryn received a call on his multi-way radio that made him jump out of his skin. It was from one of the Guardians on the roof.

"Hi, chief," the voice said, "There's something going on down here. A couple of groups of men are congregating outside by the railings on the opposite side of the street. They look as if they've got things hidden under their coats. Yes... I've seen an assault rifle."

"Code red," Darryn shouted down the radio. The serving staff ducked down behind the bar, which had been armour-plated the moment Darryn was sure the 'The Sunken Way' was to be the target. The manager, with surprising calmness, started shepherding people down stairs saying they had to comply with a health and safety fire drill. Darryn and his three companions took up their positions behind the bar as if peeping over the trenches in the First World War.

All this happened in a few seconds, which was just as well as immediately afterwards, bottles with lighted tapers and the smell of petrol were thrown through the doorway. With a whoosh associated with ignition, the petrol caught fire and set up a curtain of dancing flame between the bar and the door. Darryn maintained his concentration, looking beyond the flames to see who was entering, Suddenly all the large windows fronting on to the street disintegrated into a million shards in a cacophonous sound of breaking glass. A hail of bullets followed, hitting spirit bottles and glasses behind the bar, adding to the growing chaos. The Guardians in the main part of the building shepherded the customers on the upper floors into corners that were out of the line of fire. The reality of the event happening before their eyes was so shocking that there was no panic and only total obeisance to the Guardians seemed the sensible thing to do. Gradually Darryn could make out his assailants, a line of fifteen men moving forward, shooting indiscriminately as they came.

"Fire!" ordered Darryn. The four of them behind the bar retaliated with automatic gunfire of their own. Darryn saw two of his opponents fall immediately. The others seemed disconcerted and lost their formation. They clearly were not expecting resistance. Was this supreme arrogance on Michael O'Grady's part or did he genuinely think he had maintained utter secrecy of his plans? One foolhardy member of the fifteen dashed through the broken window, but was immediately mown down by the Guardians behind the bar.

"Annabelle and Harry, implement plan seven immediately," Darryn barked into his radio. Plan seven involved Annabelle and Harry bringing their squads down the street from opposite directions and trapping the assailants in a pincer movement. The managers of the pubs they were deserting were to lock the doors and not let anyone in or out until the conflict was over. As they went, Annabelle and Harry were to guide as many of the terrified passers-by as possible away from the conflict and quickly to safety. This was a difficult manoeuvre that had been repeated numerous times in training. Now the moment had come, they were able to make swift progress as the F.U.P. forces seemed in total disarray.

The firing became more sporadic and not apparently directed into 'The Sunken Way' anymore. Darryn grabbed a CO_2 extinguisher and tackled the fire that was threatening to get out of hand and take hold on some of the wooden fittings. Two of the other Guardians had also found extinguishers and rushed to help Darryn. The over-zealous F.U.P. attacker lay prone on the floor in a pool of blood. He was dead.

There were intermittent exchanges of gunfire from the rear of the building which suggested that an assault was in progress there too. Darryn cautiously moved to the door and saw Annabelle and Harry standing together, surveying the carnage of ten bodies littered in various poses along Canal Street. Along with the thirty Guardians, who all looked fit and well, there was a crowd on either side of shocked and bewildered partygoers.

"I'd advise you all to go home," Darryn shouted at the top of his voice. "The threat has not been completely neutralised yet and there may be some more shooting. I'm afraid we cannot guarantee your safety."

The crowd only had to look at the corpses strewn on the road to understand that Darryn was in deadly earnest. The people quickly melted into the night leaving the street as quiet as any other might be expected to be at that time of the evening. Darryn checked with his squad by radio. All efforts to gain entry had been repulsed and they had suffered only one minor casualty. The enemy, on the other hand, had either been killed or had fled into the night.

On re-entering 'The Sunken Way', Darryn was struck by the noise coming from the basement. He discovered that because the customers were unable to leave through the fire escape, the manager had asked the DJ to start his set early. This had turned out to be a smart move. The sound was so loud that the crowd had been oblivious to the gunfire and the flames upstairs, and now the party was in full swing. Darryn decided to leave them to it. The manager came upstairs and looked appalled at the damage.

"It's not too bad," Darryn said reassuringly. "You can get the glaziers round in the morning, and this black is soot rather than charring."

"Yes, but look at *this*," the manager said insistently.

"We can move the dead body for you if you like."

"No, I'm not worried about *that*, but look, there's blood all over this white carpet. It'll never come out. Do you think it's like red wine? Maybe if I use salt or white wine before it completely dries I'll be able to get it out. What do you think?

Darryn sighed and said with some exasperation, "I haven't a clue but I'm sure plenty of your customers will be able to give you advice."

Half an hour later, the scene was completely calm. The Guardians had done a complete sweep of the area and met with no resistance. They had gathered up the weapons that had been abandoned or were no longer needed by their dead owners. There were twenty corpses in all. The additional ten were placed alongside those already lying in the street; all were F.U.P. casualties.

"What do we do with the bodies?" Annabelle asked.

"I'm inclined to leave them in the street and see what the reaction of the Authorities is. It would be useful to see which way the wind is blowing."

"Fair enough, what should we do with our agents?"

"Keep a minimal presence here, and the rest of us can get a well-earned, good night's sleep."

***

"There has been so much death and destruction already," complained N°6. "And I've lost a very good friend in the process. It was very upsetting to attend Taffy's funeral having to lie about the reasons why he died."

"There would have been no funeral at all if Darryn hadn't gone and got his body from the F.U.P camp," retorted N°2.

"Well that was another foolhardy escapade to add to the growing list...and it resulted in two more deaths," N°6 added somewhat querulously. "Are you sure we should be so aggressive?"

"This is the first time we've had the upper hand. We've completely foiled their attempted terror plot. The only deaths last night were their own people. We know where their headquarters is and, thanks to Louise, we have a detailed plan of its layout. We know where their training camp in Wales is, and they will be in total disarray this morning. If we don't make the most of this moment we may not get another chance."

A small group of people were sitting in N°6's office on the Sunday morning after the assault on 'The Sunken Way'. They were tired and irritable after a tense and uncertain night following the ebb and flow of events from Manchester. Danny and two other senior operatives from the operations room remained silent. This was a moment when N°6 and N°2 had to rehearse the ethics of what they were planning and come to a decision.

"What are the media saying this morning, Danny?" N°6 asked.

"Absolutely nothing on the national news at all," Danny replied. "There was an initial flurry on social media sites last night, but those comments all seem to have disappeared this morning. Have we any news from our contacts inside MI5? Maybe there's been some intelligence crackdown."

N°2 intervened at this point saying, "The new Director General is suspected to be an F.U.P. sympathiser. Our people there have to tread very carefully these days. We cannot get the intelligence or the influence we once did. It would not surprise me if a cover-up of the operation's failure was ordered."

Danny continued, "The only reference I can find to anything at all happening last night is a local radio report in Manchester saying that Canal Street will be closed until further notice because of a suspected gas leak."

N°6 thought carefully. All eyes were upon him, even those of N°2. With a heavy sigh he said, "Well at least if we were to act now, it would be without the glare of unfavourable publicity. What does N°1 think about this? I know he normally doesn't get involved in operational matters, but what you are proposing is too big for him not to have been consulted?"

N°2 smiled and said, "You are quite right. Like you, he is uneasy, but he accepts that this is a 'now-or-never' moment. He is particularly keen to eliminate Michael O'Grady."

N°6 raised an eyebrow at this. The concept of N°1 wishing to eliminate anyone was startling. He then sighed again as if a great burden had been lifted from him. With great deliberation he said, "If N°1 is content to go ahead with this scheme, then who am I to stand in its way?"

***

Less than a week later, Darryn stood with an army of two hundred and fifty men and women, all dressed in their distinctive black uniforms with the rainbow emblems on their shirts and epaulettes on their right shoulders. By his side was Annabelle and in his immediate circle were Danny, David and Rakshi. The last fleeting embers of the day were receding beyond the western skyline. Rakshi, in particular, looked grim as she pondered her personal need to get revenge for the brave Welshman who had saved her life at the cost of his own.

They were in position near the summit of the hill, looking down on the F.U.P. training camp. There was no pretence or hiding any more. They were going openly to war with the F.U.P. as regular soldiers fighting a battle.

The camp was unlit and would soon be invisible under the darkening skies. There was a stillness about it which was also unsettling. The plan was to attack the camp, scattering or capturing as many of the enemy as possible. The capture of the camp's leaders was the top priority, but there was no doubt that if necessary, lethal force was acceptable. This engagement rule had come directly from N°1.

Darryn gave the signal to advance. The soldiers started slowly and stealthily, spreading out as they descended towards the camp. The aim was to get into positions to enable a simultaneous attack on the camp from at least three directions. Darryn had never felt so alive. The adrenaline had barely settled from 'The Sunken Way' attack and he was keenly aware that if things went awry, these would be his last twenty minutes on Earth. His senses were razor-sharp. He could feel the gentle breeze caress his skin, the light from the ice-cold stars, just beginning to appear, piercing the pupils of his eyes and the light searing the retinas behind, the faintest rustle of nocturnal animals far away booming in his eardrums and the smells of a late summer evening in Wales, pungent and exotic as those in a perfume laboratory in Paris. But most extraordinary of all, he could taste the sensations of fear and hope, joy and despair, anger and love on the very air that passed over his tongue. His psychological training taught him that this was not unusual, and he was aware that he must not let the euphoria of the moment lead him to make over-optimistic and rash decisions.

Darryn saw David out of the corner of his eye grasp Danny's hand and squeeze it. Whose hand would he most have wanted to grasp for reassurance at this moment? Would it have been Alex, his current boyfriend, or Sean who he'd recently had a secret crush on, or even Martin, his slimy, treacherous ex-partner? Surprisingly, the answer flashed into his mind that it was none of these, but instead, his old friend and close colleague, Annabelle. As she was at this moment on the opposite side of the camp, there was no opportunity to test if she felt likewise.

"Go!" Darryn ordered on his radio. He led his squad speedily into the camp. Gone were the traps that had ensnared Rakshi. They quickly reached an outbuilding, a temporary wooden hut in darkness. Darryn shoulder-charged the flimsy plywood fire door and his team burst in after him with their powerful head torches automatically coming on and illuminating the room in daggers of light. It was empty of furniture and unoccupied. They systematically moved through the other two rooms in the hut and discovered the same. Quitting the hut in organised formation, they moved to a building further in. Again, it was dark, totally deserted and devoid of any furniture. By the time the pattern was repeated on the fourth building, it was clear that the camp had been thoroughly abandoned before their arrival.

It was therefore with a great sense of anticlimax that Darryn met up with Annabelle and Jean-Claude (leading a third group of soldiers) in the courtyard outside the kitchens.

"They've obviously gone," Annabelle stated, rather unnecessarily. "It looks as if they've done a thorough job in taking everything with them too. What shall we do now?"

Darryn now realised the moment had been lost. If they could have fallen on their enemies and destroyed their military infrastructure, the disorganised rabble that was the political wing of the F.U.P. may have withered away to nothing. Unfortunately, the speedy and organised tactical retreat meant they were probably already plotting their next move.

It was only a symbolic gesture now, but Darryn still said, "Let's torch the place and let them know they haven't won."

An hour later, as Darryn was leaving the site, the wooden temporary blocks were already ablaze. Fire was not taking hold so quickly in the more permanent structures but the interiors were beginning to burn. Later that night, the locals in Bala were curious about an orange glow to the south west and they suspected a major incident when they were woken by the sirens of fire engines and police cars at about four in the morning.

By the time the fire was out, the camp looked like an archaeological ruin, beyond repair.

Chapter 26

Jake could not believe his eyes, straight A's in all his subjects. Even if the Government decided that AS grades were not going to count, they would look good on a UCAS application. He had been staring at the card for ten minutes, wondering whether there had been some mix-up at the college or the Exam Board. Maybe it was all a sick joke and he'd really got C's and D's.

Maria had done equally well, but Nathan had had a mixed bag. Yes, he had got his expected A grade in music, but he only managed a D in Maths, which Jake found quite shocking. He had always looked up to Nathan as his intellectual superior, and yet he was now beginning to look quite ordinary. Even though Nathan shrugged this result off as being 'unimportant', a gulf which had opened up between Nathan and Jake after the motorbike incident seemed to inch still wider.

Later in the day, a text came through that the Principal of young person's care and education would like to see Jake as soon as possible. Thinking that there was no time like the present, Jake immediately made his way up to the school zone. As it was still the school holidays, the area was pretty much deserted, but the school secretary was in her office typing away at a keyboard. She indicated that the Principal was in and would be free to see Jake if he were to make his way to his office.

The Principal peered at Jake over half-moon glasses, looking every inch the headmaster of a leading Public School.

"Ah, Jake, do come in and take a seat."

"Thank you," Jake replied, making himself comfortable in a leather chair opposite the sturdy desk that the Principal sat behind.

"You have some excellent AS results. Many congratulations, I'm sure your family will be very pleased. I've got some more good news for you as well. You got a 'merit' in your grade eight violin exam." He handed Jake a certificate and shook his hand. He continued:

"Now with all this academic and artistic success we must think a bit more about your future. Have you had any thoughts about where you would like to go to University and what you would like to study?"

"My results were a lot better than I expected. I wasn't necessarily expecting to go on to University. I thought I might complete the Guardian programme and work here at Rainbow House."

The Principal smiled and said, "I think you are being somewhat modest there! Have you thought about applying to Oxford or Cambridge?"

"Do you think I would stand a chance?"

"...As good as anyone else in your year group. You must get as good an education as you can, and we will support you all the way with it. You can

154

always carry out your Guardian duties later, but you will need a second string to your bow for cover, if nothing else. Consider Darryn; he is the most trusted Guardian in the service, and yet he still maintains his position as a maths tutor in Oxford. Have a think about it and let me know if you want to apply when term starts again,"

Grasping his certificate, Jake had much to think about as he left the office. On the stairs he passed Tim going the other way. Guilt again troubled him as he realised that despite his best intentions, he had not spoken to Tim for several weeks.

"Tim, how are you? I haven't seen you for ages."

Tim looked surprised that Jake should take the trouble to say anything to him, "I didn't think you'd be particularly looking out for me anyway."

"What have you been doing? Have you travelled anywhere nice?"

Again Tim looked astonished by the question, "No, I've stayed here. I have nowhere else to go and no one to go with. It's not much fun going to places on your own. I've been doing some reading and playing computer games, that's all."

Jake felt his guilt tighten like a noose around his stomach. Tim had been left friendless and on his own for the whole of the summer holiday. His intentions to be more of a companion to this sad and lonely figure had all been hot air and of no substance.

"Do you want to meet up later?" Jake asked rather weakly, hoping he didn't sound insincere.

"I'm seeing the Principal now about my exam results and future prospects. Aren't you meeting up with Nathan later?"

"Oh...yes I am. You can join us though."

"No thanks, I'd rather play a computer game than sit in a corner while you and Nathan whisper sweet nothings to each other."

Tim continued his ascent, while Jake had to admit failure to himself. Mind you, there wasn't so much whispering of sweet nothings between him and Nathan these days.

***

Darryn and Alex had arranged to meet up in Old Compton Street to go for a meal. Darryn had kept a low profile while all the business with 'The Sunken Way' and the F.U.P. camp was going on. He was worried that Alex might lose interest in him as a result, especially as Alex also seemed to have disappeared off the scene. However, on this early September evening Alex bounced up to Darryn and embraced him as if they had been meeting every day.

The restaurant was a modern affair with full glass-plate windows fronting onto the street. The clientele wore tell-tale checked shirts and jeans and looked wealthy and professional. Darryn decided to have the pan-fried sea bass while Alex chose the lentil and spinach cottage pie.

"Well, stranger, where have you been?" Alex asked with mock anxiety.

"I had to spend some time in Manchester. There was a Symposium at the University there I had to attend. What have *you* been up to, though? I've found it very difficult to get in touch with you at times."

"Ah, well, a friend of mine in North Wales had to move out of her house at very short notice, so I went to give her a hand packing."

"Oh dear, has she found somewhere else to go?"

"She's okay, she's found somewhere to rent for the time being until she can find something more permanent."

A rather good-looking waiter wandered by at that point and both Darryn and Alex turned to look at him. They both realised what each other had done and there followed some rather embarrassed and inconsequential conversation about the weather.

It was midweek, so the restaurant, which was popular, was comfortably full rather than heaving with customers. The nights were noticeably beginning to draw in and it was beginning to get dark outside. A steady stream of people wandered up and down the street.

Both Alex and Darryn decided to have a dessert. The conversation turned to what they were going to do after the meal.

"Why don't we go back to your place for a change?" Alex said enthusiastically.

Darryn frowned and said with more than a hint of exasperation, "I've explained plenty of times before why that's not possible. Maybe we should just say goodnight here and go home."

Alex looked somewhat aghast and said, "Don't be like that. I haven't seen you for weeks. We can just as easily go to mine... and continue where we left off with that naked wrestling match."

Darryn relented. For someone who worked in the Treasury, Alex was very strong and muscular. Darryn had, of course, come out on top in his previous tussles with Alex, but it had been a struggle - needless to say an enjoyable one.

***

Jake had been back at college for a week or two, and was just beginning to hear rumours of what had been going on in Manchester and Wales. He felt particularly hurt to have been kept out of the loop and upset that Darryn had not told him anything about it. He was able to vent his frustrations to Darryn directly one evening when they were both in Rainbow House for an evening meal. Sat in his favourite place in the dining room, looking out over docklands with the boats going up and down the Thames, he chastised Darryn for not telling him about the attack on 'The Sunken Way' or the assault on the welsh training camp. Darryn was very casual in response, giving the impression that he didn't understand what all the fuss was about. This only heightened Jake's irritation.

"I thought we were like family, you and I," Jake railed. "You might have been killed and I would have known nothing about it. For that matter, why wasn't I included in the army that went to attack the F.U.P. camp?"

"Don't be such an old fish-wife!" Darryn replied, beginning to get somewhat irritated himself. "I could get injured or killed on numerous occasions every year. I can't be expected to give you a blow-by-blow account all the time. Good grief, I have enough forms to fill in with my job at Oxford, without having to make my actions transparent to you as well. Anyhow, I was beginning to wonder how reliable you really were yourself, with all that gallivanting about in Telford after your dad's funeral."

"That was Nathan's doing."

"Well you ought to keep that boyfriend of yours under tighter control."

"Really ... Like you managed to do with Martin, you mean?"

Darryn looked at Jake sharply. Jake knew he'd gone a bit too far with his last comment, but he returned Darryn's gaze defiantly as he was in no mood to surrender the point. Darryn deliberately got up, without saying anything, and walked away. Jake sighed and knew he was going to have to make a serious effort at reconciliation.

Before he'd had too long to think about things, Matt came over and sat where Darryn had been. He had a parcel with him which he proffered to Jake. This was a surprise as Matt and Jake had not spent a lot of time together recently and it was not his birthday either. Jake opened the parcel and discovered a small framed landscape in oils which a few seconds later he realised was painted by Matt himself.

"Maria said you'd like one of my paintings, and as you have no artistic sensibility, I thought a traditional landscape would be as much as you could cope with." It was the estuary at Portmeirion, and one of the products of his painting holiday with Maria.

Jake was genuinely touched by the gift and he ignored the barbed sentiments that accompanied it. Rather uncharacteristically, he leant over the table and gave Matt a kiss full on the lips. "Thank you," he said. "That's one of the nicest gifts anyone's given me. I shall hang it up in my room as soon as I go back there."

Matt was unusually flustered by Jake's show of emotion but quickly recovered, saying, "Bloody hell, Jake, if I'd known that all it took was a painting to make you fancy me, I'd have done you one long ago."

Jake laughed and replied, "You're too late, matey; Nathan got there first."

Matt furrowed his brow and asked, "How are things between you two? I just sensed things were a little tense last weekend."

It had been Nathan's eighteenth birthday. Jake had bought Nathan some motorcycle leathers, an expensive present which Nathan seemed to appreciate. They had had a small party in Rainbow House, but the plan was to follow this up by going out and hitting the town now that Nathan could legally buy drinks. The fact that Jake and most of the others were still only seventeen was a mere trifle. They had started out in 'The George and Dragon' in Soho. They had a well-worked routine for avoiding the bouncers and getting served. It was a bit of a disappointment, to be honest, that Nathan could now simply show genuine ID and get served. About eleven, when Jake would normally be thinking it was time to go home and go to bed, Nathan had a notion that he'd like to go clubbing at 'Divine Hell', the big gay club at the end of Old Compton Street. Jake wasn't keen, but as it was Nathan's birthday, he didn't want to be a party pooper.

There were a dozen of them from Rainbow House and college, lining up in a queue that formed outside. Once in, they presented their coats to the cloakroom attendant and paid their entry fee. The sound was deafening as they entered the large, lower dance floor. It was dark, with powerful strobe lighting occasionally making white tops fluoresce. Nathan bought drinks for all of them, but how the bar staff could make out what Nathan was asking for, Jake had no idea.

They'd stood around for a while, bending over to shout in each other's ear. Conversations were necessarily terse as the effort to make oneself understood was immense. Gradually they'd started jigging about to the angular, percussive music and, one by one, they'd made their way to their dance area of choice. Nathan was led away by a couple of college friends, and ended up dancing energetically to what Jake thought had been described as new urban dance music.

Jake had been left as a wall flower, on his own by the bar. He couldn't help but think of Tim and empathise with his experience of feeling invisible even in a crowd. Nathan popped by every now and then for a rest. His speech seemed slurred after a while, and he was not making much sense. Jake wondered if he had been stupid enough to take something other than just alcohol.

At two o'clock in the morning, Jake had had enough. Whether it was Nathan's birthday or not he was going home. He indicated that he was going to Nathan, who responded be waving cheerily while carrying on dancing.

It had been mid-afternoon the following day that Jake had next seen Nathan, bleary-eyed and looking washed out. He had been grouchy and rather distant from Jake.

"I think things are okay," Jake responded to Matt's question dubiously. "Nathan thought that his night at the club was great and he's planning to go again this weekend."

"Yes, I thought it was a good night too," Matt affirmed, "but I'm guessing it wasn't your cup of tea? I noticed you left well before Nathan."

"No, I can't see the point in hanging around night clubs. I hate dancing. I've told Nathan he'll have to find some other friends to go with."

Matt looked a little concerned and said, "Is that wise? I hope you can trust him to be faithful."

This comment took Jake by surprise. He had not even thought of the possibility of Nathan using the opportunity to cheat on him. However, Matt's comment sowed a seed of doubt that began to gnaw at Jake more and more over the coming weeks.

Chapter 27

N°2 was once again in conference with N°6 and Danny. Annabelle was also present, as well as another couple of Guardians involved in the Manchester incident. N°2's office in the operations room seemed particularly dingy and tired, reflecting the season of autumn which was rapidly advancing.

"Well, where have they all gone?" N°2 asked. "What progress have we made in finding out what's happened to the military wing of the F.U.P.?"

"Michael O'Grady seems to have disappeared off the radar," Annabelle contributed. "He may have gone off back to Ireland. We did get an unconfirmed sighting at Holyhead. The Telford contingent has returned and seems to be simply continuing with daily life."

"Could we put the pressure on one of them and find out what happened?" N°6 enquired.

"Marcus intercepted the young lad and frightened him to death. He's pretty convinced that the ordinary recruits are none the wiser about future plans. They were commanded to pack and return home the day after the Manchester incident and simply await further orders."

N°2 tapped her pencil on the desk with a degree of impatience, "I wish we knew how much of a setback all of this was to their other plans. Who is this mystery agent from The Vatican?"

Everyone looked at each other with embarrassed faces, and it was clear that no progress had been made in finding him or her.

N°2 sighed and said, "We can do nothing about the state of the Government. The economy is going from bad to worse. Keep this to yourselves, but it is likely that a major bank is going to go bust within the next month. Having bailed the banks out once, the Government simply hasn't got the resources to do it all over again. When people actually lose their savings and deposits, there is going to be a run on all the other banks. There is likely to be chaos, disorder and civil unrest, which I expect the F.U.P. to use to its advantage. The Government is likely to lose its majority altogether, as I've heard rumours that a couple of their MP's are likely to defect to the F.U.P. in the next day or two. The Chancellor has had a nervous breakdown, and the Prime Minister has run out of ideas about what to do. It really is a very dangerous situation."

Everyone in the room looked very sober but said nothing. There seemed to be nothing to add to this gloomy prognosis.

"On another matter, we have agreed to accelerate the Guardian training programme. The Apprentice Guardians may be needed in the field before too long. We will endeavour to get them fully qualified by the end of this year."

"Is that fair?" N°6 asked, clearly concerned. "I mean, a lot of them are studying for A-levels and will be worried about their plans for higher education."

N°2 sighed sympathetically and said, "Unfortunately the times we live in are not fair. If the economic situation becomes as bad as I think it might, we will be talking about a state of affairs similar to that in Germany before the rise of the Nazis. I surely don't need to remind you who else was sent to the gas chambers apart from the Jews."

N°6 shrugged and could think of nothing to say in reply. N°2 sensed that N°6 had not been happy with one or two recent decisions, even though he had acquiesced. She felt it necessary to add, "Look, I know N°1 has agonised over some of the decisions we've had to make. I think he'd appreciate your input, N°6, if you were to go and see him in the next day or two."

This seemed to mollify N°6 and the meeting ended. As people drifted out, N°2 asked Annabelle casually about Darryn and how he was getting on.

"He's fine," Annabelle responded cheerily, "he has a new man in his life and that's perked him up no end."

N°2's right eyebrow raised a fraction and she said, "I had no idea. Is it somebody in Rainbow house? What's he like?"

"I haven't met him myself. His name's Alex. He isn't with us; I think Darryn said he was working at the Treasury."

"I hope Darryn's being careful about security. You don't know what this guy's surname is, do you?"

"Darryn did tell me... Singleton, I think. Yes, that's it, Alex Singleton."

N°2 made a mental note to check up on this character the next time she had access to the Treasury staff database.

***

"Hi, babe," Nathan said to Jake as he rushed into the social area in a semi-dressed state. They were both in their Guardian uniforms, as they were now entitled to be as apprentices.

"Come on!" Jake said in an anxious voice, "We'll be late."

They had arranged to meet so that they could go together to the briefing meeting that all Apprentice Guardians had been summoned to. Nathan and Jake made their way to the elevator. The door immediately slid open and Jake pressed the button to go two floors down while Nathan tucked his black shirt in and generally made himself presentable. They made their way to the theatre, which was at the opposite end of the arts zone to the art gallery. It was relatively small, having tiered seating for only about a hundred people. The stage was at floor level, but had proper curtains and lighting and some modest facilities backstage. There was an amateur dramatics society in Rainbow House which put on a variety of productions from Shakespeare to questionable musicals about American High School kids. It was very much their space; however, it was also occasionally used for other gatherings, such as the current briefing meeting.

Nathan and Jake sat in the second row, which was also the last occupied row as there were only about twenty Apprentice Guardians in all. Jake sensed the absence of Ashok and suddenly felt sorry that he had not said goodbye to him properly. He must see if Darryn had his address. Looking round, he saw Jenny and Louise and, sat on his own at the end of the front row, Tim. A solid lectern was in place in the middle of the stage, but at present it was vacant. At exactly the time the meeting was supposed to start a fat man with a moustache who ought to have been jolly but wasn't, and Annabelle walked from behind the curtain to the lectern. A polite silence fell and the rotund man spoke:

"Good Morning, Apprentice Guardians, for those of you who don't know me, I'm N°3, and this...." he indicated to Annabelle, "...is Ms Jacobs who will be helping me supervise the last stages of your training." He paused to gather his thoughts and then began again, "The times are treacherous and we have grave fears that the enemy may soon be able to strike us even here. N°1 has decided that we must accelerate your training programme so that you are all ready to take on the role of Guardian by the end of this academic year. I know this is asking a lot, especially as many of you are studying A-levels, but you have all shown yourselves to be of a very high calibre and we believe you can cope. If anyone wants to drop out because the pressure is too great, there is no shame in that, and you are free to do so."

No one moved a muscle and N°3 almost smiled: "Good," he continued, "Let me explain what there is still left for you to do. There are three tasks you each have to accomplish alone. The first is to carry out a specific espionage task without discovery. Wherever possible, this will be a real situation where the perceived risk is low to moderate. As part of your training, you will be taught further techniques of breaking and entering, disabling alarm systems, security penetration and hiding one's tracks.

"The second task is to spend three days out in the wild, surviving alone off the land and travelling seventy miles on foot without using public highways. You will be tested on your ability to remain unobserved and at least one attempt will be made to capture you. The third task is to show competence in a number of skill areas which include firing a gun, throwing a knife, driving a car, riding a motorbike, steering a boat and flying a glider. These skills are what most of your formal training will now involve."

Nathan's eyes lit up when N°3 mentioned that riding a motorbike was part of the assessment. Jake on the other hand, felt somewhat queasy at the prospect of having to pilot a glider; he later found out that riding a horse was an acceptable alternative, but wasn't sure that was any better.

Annabelle stepped to the lectern and said, "As part of your on-going commitment to being a Guardian, you need to maintain your fitness and take personal responsibility for it. You must continue your martial arts training. Remember, your lives may depend on it one day. Now we will continue with your exercise routine in the sports hall in twenty minutes."

The Apprentice Guardians filed out, eagerly discussing the news they had just been given. Most walked down the stairs to the sport and physical fitness zone where they got changed and ready for a session of martial arts.

Jake ended up sparing with Nathan. In between moves and counter-moves, they were able to hold a conversation.

"I suppose you are quite glad that riding a motorcycle is one of the skills you have to demonstrate," Jake said following an attempt to unbalance Nathan which failed.

"It makes it more likely I will be allowed to ride the mean machine," Nathan admitted.

"I suppose technically you ought to give it back as you didn't get the A-grade in maths you promised your father," Jake suggested innocently. A flow of blows came in from Nathan and Jake found himself flat on his back. "Ouch," he complained.

"It's not a good idea to irritate your opponent," Nathan observed, "and anyway, the AS doesn't count. I could still get an A in the final exam."

Jenny and Louise were sparring with each other and going at it hammer and tongs. Jake looked over and noticed Tim just behind them, fighting with a student of Chinese decent called Kim Wei. Despite his shy, depressed and taciturn nature, Tim was strong and agile. His arm muscles were well developed and he was more than a match for his much smaller opponent. There was anger in the way Tim went about these exercises and Jake couldn't help wonder if this was his way of releasing frustration and expression that was impossible in normal social discourse.

Suddenly Jake found himself on his back yet again.

"Stop staring at other men and concentrate," Nathan said rather sharply, Jake was embarrassed and mumbled something inaudible before resuming.

***

N°2's fears were essentially correct. First of all there were rumours of poor results at the British and Shanghai Bank, which were strenuously denied. Then a few days later the share price plummeted like a stone. The Chief Executive complained of strategic dealing on the stock market, totally at odds with the true financial position. He gave out a press statement saying the bank was in good health. After this, queues started developing outside some branches, with customers anxious to get their cash out. Again, there were statements from the directors saying there was nothing to worry about; the bank was well financed and could meet the demand for cash. These soothing words fell on deaf ears and the queues continued to lengthen until there came a day when the branches did not open at all. The queues broke rank and turned into angry mobs, hurling stones and trying to force entry. The police, already below strength due to financial cutbacks, were unable to cope and in some northern towns and the poorer boroughs of London there was open riot on the streets. Shops were looted and set on fire. Finally the army had to be called in to restore order. Martial law was temporarily imposed in the centres of Manchester and Sheffield with dusk to dawn curfew on pain of being summarily shot.

The Government was powerless to do anything about the bank. With reckless investments in virtual financial derivatives, the British and Shanghai Bank had amassed debts of one hundred billion pounds. The Treasury was already struggling to service the nation's debt, with interest rates on Government Bonds utterly unsustainable. There was no option but to let the bank collapse.

Overnight, thousands of people's lives were ruined. People in safe, professional jobs suddenly found themselves penniless. Some could not cope and the suicide rate spiked alarmingly. Others eventually found themselves out on the streets, living the life of a tramp, depending on overstretched hostels and food banks to survive.

The Chancellor of the Exchequer finally resigned saying he needed to spend more time with his family. A few weeks later rumours in the tabloids circulated that he had been admitted to an exclusive mental institution.

N°1 watched from his flat at the top of Rainbow House as dazed workers flooded out of Shanghai Towers, the corporate headquarters of the British and Shanghai Bank and only a stone's throw away in Canary Wharf. They clutched a few personal possessions, having been told at a moment's notice that they were all sacked. Some stood blinking, not knowing where to go or what to do. They were now pathetic figures, these people who only days before believed they ruled the Universe. N°1 sighed and thought about the 'let's muddle through' philosophy which now seemed to be reaching its inevitable conclusion. He knew there was worse to come.

The F.U.P. was not inactive during this crisis. In areas where they were strong, they pre-empted the imposition of martial law and used their own forces to maintain order, further diminishing the role of the police. By setting up food distribution points and cash release systems, they acquired kudos amongst their supporters and a generally positive profile in the community. Opinion polls were suggesting they would win thirty percent of the vote if an election was called. The government crackdown in certain areas gave the F.U.P. the excuse to widen their patrols and issue identity papers to residents in the areas they controlled, making it even harder for people with dissident views to express them or even go about their daily lives unhindered.

It seems odd to say that much of this national turbulence passed Jake by. Rainbow House remained a haven of order and calm insulated from the madness that engulfed much of the rest of the country. He had two main concerns in the autumn term of that year. Firstly, he had decided to apply to Oxford and was now fretting over a possible interview for a conditional offer. After much deliberation, he had decided to go for maths as he felt he was too ham-fisted to go with a practical science. Secondly, he was becoming increasingly aware that all was not right with his relationship with Nathan. They spent less and less time together, and in particular, Nathan was less inclined to stay over. Even when he did, there seemed to be no spark in their lovemaking, so that Jake got the impression Nathan was just going through the motions.

Jake felt inadequate and stressed as a result. He was noticeably snappy with everyone such that Maria had to tell him, none too tactfully, that he would have no friends left if he carried on as he was. With work, chores, Guardian training and Nathan, the last thing he needed was an order to go and see N^o2, but that's exactly what he got.

Chapter 28

"Come in," N°2 shouted from behind her office door. Jake swung the door open and marched in. N°2's demeanour changed immediately when she saw Jake, becoming unusually furtive. She indicated a chair for Jake to sit in, while she herself went to the door and had a good look in every direction before carefully shutting out the world.

"Thank you for coming so quickly," she whispered. "I think I may have something that would pass as your espionage task. It would also take a great weight off my mind without having to involve official channels." She paused and then continued on what appeared to be a disconnected theme, "How much do you know about Darryn's new boyfriend?"

Jake shrugged his shoulders, "Not a great deal," he confessed, "I've not even met the guy. I don't like to pry into Darryn's love life too much. I know he is likely to become unhinged if you mention Martin,"

"I think that's a slight exaggeration," N°2 responded smiling. "It was something Annabelle said that got me thinking. She said the fellow worked at the Treasury. Well, with all the chaos there's been lately, I've had plenty of opportunity to search the staff databases. His name appears nowhere. Call it feminine intuition if you like, but I'm just beginning to get a bad feeling about this guy. His name is Alex Singleton, or at least, that is what he's calling himself. I would like you to investigate him and find out what you can about him. I will give you the green light to break into his house or other premises to find out what you can."

Jake frowned, "I'm not so sure about this," he said frankly. "Darryn is a friend... well, more like family to be honest. It seems disloyal to be spying on the person he loves. I might end up having to spy on Darryn too."

N°2 was sympathetic and said, "I know... That is why I want to keep it unofficial. Although it will count towards your Guardian programme, you will report only to me. If Darryn catches you out, I'll take the blame and suggest it was just a bit of a laugh to see if he could be fooled. I must know whether this Alex is who he claims to be. Remember the F.U.P. has a master spy at work somewhere trying to get secret information out of one of our agents. I bet that information is the location of Rainbow House."

Reluctantly, Jake agreed. Rather embarrassingly, N°2 then passed over some photos of Darryn and his boyfriend being rather intimate in 'The George and Dragon' and added that they often met there on a Friday afternoon after work.

Jake got up to leave and was just about to open the door when N°2 seemed stricken with conscience and said, almost as a coda, "If you do have to confide in someone, please do not tell Nathan. Tim or even Matt is a much safer bet. If you want some level-headed female advice, do what you always do and ask Maria."

***

It was not how he'd originally intended to spend Friday afternoon after college, but Jake thought he'd better get on with his espionage task. He'd spoken to Darryn earlier in the week and so knew there were no plans to return to Oxford before the following Monday. There was a good chance he would meet up with Alex, and so Jake found himself wandering up and down Old Compton Street trying to look inconspicuous. The clocks were about to go back any day and the grey dreariness of late autumn turning into winter was having a depressing effect on Jake. He was wearing a smart pair of Jeans and decent shoes. As the light of day began to ebb, he zipped up his black jacket to keep out the chill that was developing.

Then at last he saw the figure of Darryn hurrying towards 'The George and Dragon.' It was good fortune that Jake had spotted him amongst the other people wandering up and down the street. He waited in a door way until there was no danger of being noticed and then followed at a discrete distance. At the entrance to the pub Jake hesitated. He did not know where Darryn was inside and could easily walk straight into him. He decided to wait a few minutes, reckoning that Darryn would buy a drink at the bar and then go to find somewhere to sit, either with Alex or on his own, waiting for him. Jake walked slowly around the block and then entered the pub, showing his fake ID to the bouncer on the door when challenged. Darryn was not at the bar, so Jake walked purposefully up and ordered a half pint of lager, showing his ID again when challenged for a second time.

"Jake!" a voice shouted from across the room. The shock was so great that half the glass of lager exploded into the air. Jake looked around to see Matt and a couple of his college friends. They were being particularly camp and squawked like overexcited parrots. Matt's dress sense was particularly alien and suggested an attempt to set new controversial fashion trends.

"Hi Matt," Jake replied, trying to regain his composure as quickly as possible. He realised that Matt would provide some cover for him and he could sit with them, watching Darryn and Alex without worrying about being seen.

Where was Darryn? Jake hoped he'd not gone upstairs because he would then have to rethink his strategy entirely. Fortunately he was in the corner by the door. Jake could not see him clearly, but his face flashed into view every now and then to leave no doubt that it was him. The back of a shaven blond head was all Jake could make of his companion.

"I saw Nathan earlier on. He said he was going to the club tonight. I said we might meet him there. George, Sebastian and I are going to make a night of it, I think." The other two giggled like children.

"I'll probably drop by later," Jake replied as if he knew about Nathan's plans. "I have something to attend to first."

As if on cue, Darryn got up, waved to Matt and Jake and then left the pub. A minute or two later the blond-haired man, who was wearing a smart city suit as if he had indeed been working at the Treasury, got up and left also. Jake rapidly made his excuses and got up to follow.

It was not easy to follow Alex. The rush hour had not really died down yet and there were large numbers of people milling about. Some were rushing; others were standing inconveniently blocking the path of those who wanted to make progress. Yet Jake did not dare get too close for fear that his intentions might be rumbled. At Tottenham Court tube station, he thought he had lost Alex completely, but he just caught sight of him heading for the southbound platform of the Northern Line in time. Jake risked getting into the same carriage as Alex, standing at the other end. There were still many travellers and the carriage was full with people standing by the doors. Alex did not seem to notice Jake or pay him any attention. He got out at Oval and, on leaving the station which was on the corner of a busy junction, turned right down the main road. He did not go far. The next turning on the right saw a grand terrace of typical London houses. They had large windows with white-painted stone frames, rectangular black painted front doors and the London brick colour which was slightly more yellow than the standard.

Alex went into one of these, number 12 to be precise. Jake waited on the opposite side of the road and noticed a light appear on the second floor. If Alex had a flat rather than owning the whole house, he could now work out how to get there. Time passed slowly and Jake began to feel conspicuous. He was getting cold and frankly wasn't at all sure what to do next. After twenty minutes, he was on the point of abandoning his vigil when, surprisingly, the light was extinguished and Alex reappeared.

Jake decided to follow him again. Back to the tube station he went, getting on a northbound train. This time he alighted at Charing Cross and walked briskly to Pall Mall. Jake stopped short when he saw Alex skipping up the steps of The Corinthian Club. It was not proof, but it was highly suggestive of a link with the F.U.P. At the back of his mind, he felt there was a connection between this man and the club that he was already aware of, but annoyingly, he could not put his finger on it.

***

Jake wasn't feeling particularly tired so he decided to go back to Soho and catch up with Nathan at the club. He was inclined to be in a conciliatory mood to try and improve relations with his boyfriend. When he tried to text Nathan he got no reply, and a call went straight to voicemail suggesting that the phone was switched off. Jake then sent a text to Matt to see if he was still about with his friends. An immediate reply came back to say they were thinking of wandering over that way now. Jake arranged to meet them and they were soon queuing outside 'Divine Hell'.

"So where did you get to tonight?" Matt asked. "You left in a most mysterious manner earlier."

167

"I had some business to attend to for someone at Rainbow House," Jake replied rather vaguely.

The queue inched forward, little by little. Every time the door was opened a thundering blast of unmelodious sound, laced with a pulsating rhythm, was released into the wild. Eventually they were let in. Jake was now used to the sensation of darkness with flashing lights and ear-splitting music, even though he hated it.

"I'll see you in a bit," Jake shouted down Matt's ear. "I'm going to find Nathan."

Jake took the staircase and found himself in a quiet oasis on the second floor, where there was a bar and some comfy chairs and sofas. Expecting to find Nathan on the third floor bouncing around to the latest fashionable dance music, Jake was surprised to see him by the bar. Beaming, he was about to go over when he noticed that Nathan was not alone. He was talking in a very friendly way to two other people who looked vaguely familiar. Suddenly he recognised them as two of the soldiers Nathan had raced against on The Malverns during the summer. As that scene flooded back, Jake realised that the one Nathan was joking with at present was the one who had slipped him the piece of paper, obviously with his name and telephone number on. Jake froze and an icy chill ran down his spine as Nathan brazenly kissed the soldier and then did the same to his friend. With an arm round both of them, he was about to lead the way to one of the sofas when he saw Jake. The look of guilt on his face was unmistakable.

A red mist descended on Jake. He flew at Nathan without saying a word and the impact took them sprawling over the back of a chair. After the initial shock, Nathan was not simply going to take this and he responded aggressively, throwing Jake across the bar. A number of glasses smashed on the floor and as he tumbled across the counter, Jake took a half-full bottle of whiskey down with him, drenching the floor tiles behind the bar and adding to the broken glass.

By now there was panic and mayhem around them. One middle-aged man shrieked to his companion, "Have some straights got in tonight?" Nathan's two army friends melted away to another floor as two burley bouncers rushed up the stairs towards the fracas. Momentarily, Jake and Nathan forgot their mutual animosity and turned their attention to the bouncers, flooring one each. Two more security guards appeared in the doorway and the whole scene seemed destined to descend into a barroom brawl in an old-style Western.

Suddenly the whole thing was over as Jake was overwhelmed by a sudden flurry of attacks which left him flat on the floor with his opponent sitting on top of him. It was Annabelle who had appeared from nowhere. As he desperately looked round, he noticed that Rakshi had Nathan firmly in a headlock.

"Shame on you, Jake Holdencroft," Annabelle exclaimed. "We were having a quiet night out and you two go and spoil it. Now I suggest you and Nathan go with the security guards and stop causing trouble."

Ashamed, the two boys meekly did as they were told. The security guards, however, were in not such a forgiving mood. Pushing them roughly out on to the street, they made it clear that the boys would not be welcome back anytime soon.

Jake finally spoke to Nathan, "Well, what the hell were you doing with those two soldiers?"

Nathan looked shifty and was on the defensive, "Chill out, babe, I was only being friendly. I accidently bumped into them...Quite a coincidence, don't you think?"

Jake was still enraged. He nearly flew at Nathan to have a second brawl with him, this time out on the street. He resisted the temptation, however, and instead shouted at Nathan, "You rat...If I hadn't come along, you'd have probably gone home with one or both of them. You've betrayed me. How many other times have you got off with people when you've come down to the club on your own?"

Nathan was clearly flustered and said, "Not many... Oh shit, I didn't mean to say that. Listen, I love you, but I'm young and want to experience a few things. I don't think I'm ready for a completely monogamous relationship yet."

"Oh shut up," Jake commanded imperiously. "You're a cheat and a liar. It's over...You can do whatever you want with whoever you want. We're finished!" And with that Jake made a dramatic exit from the scene and headed for the bus stop where he could get the night bus back to Canary Wharf. Nathan was left behind stammering and incoherent, wondering whether to run after Jake to beg him to change his mind. He didn't.

Sitting on the top deck, the adrenaline finally abated and tears welled up in Jake's eyes as he realised the consequences of what he had done and said. This was his fourth and final loss since the beginning of the summer holidays and it was the one that hit him hardest, even more so than the death of his own father who was fading from memory with alarming speed. He had assumed that he and Nathan would always be together. The sudden rupture of their relationship left him feeling empty and staring into a void of future loneliness and unhappiness. Unbeknown to him, at the exact same moment, Nathan was sat on a brick wall with his head in his hands, sobbing and muttering to himself, "What have I done... What the bloody hell have I done?"

***

Earlier that evening, after leaving Alex, Darryn had met up with Annabelle and Rakshi. Then, out of the blue, David and Danny had joined them as well. Darryn felt that Annabelle and Rakshi were getting on very well together and he approved. They made a nice couple and complemented each other well. On the face of it, Rakshi seemed to have got over the terrible

169

ordeal of watching Taffy being killed in cold blood, knowing that the bullets had been intended for her. She was laughing and joking and full of life, but Darryn knew from personal experience that you never get over an episode like that completely.

Annabelle and Rakshi decided to go to the club, as they both fancied a 'bop', as they put it. David suggested that the three of them who remained might go and see a film. Darryn consented. Now that he was happily coupled with Alex, he didn't feel such a spare part when out with partnered friends such as David and Danny. In any case, he knew that the pair was well-enough established in their relationship that they didn't need to be in each other's pocket twenty-four hours a day.

Darryn tended to avoid the cinema in central London as it was so expensive. The film they went to see was the latest blockbuster action movie. It wasn't great. Too much money had been spent on the special effects and not enough on hiring a decent script writer. It didn't matter though; it was just pleasant to spend an evening in the company of friends.

Darryn was now disembarking from the bus late at night in Canary Wharf. In automatic mode, he went through the checking procedures to make sure he wasn't being followed as he approached the newsagents shop at the base of Rainbow House.

Unusually, he was suddenly struck by a sense of unease and foreboding. He looked around. Had that rustling in the trees simply been the wind? Darryn was wise enough to be alert to his intuition and to take it seriously. He aborted his approach to Rainbow House and did a diverting circuit around the area. The sense of unease did not decrease. If anything, it got worse. Darryn kept looking around to try and catch some evidence that he was being followed. There was nothing and yet as he walked, there was the unexpected miaowing of a cat, the sharp sound of a discarded bottle falling over and the unexpected flurry of a sheet of newspaper blowing across his path.

Darryn walked casually around a sharp corner and then quickly stood with his back to the wall in deep shadow. If someone was following, they would turn the corner unsuspectingly and Darryn would be able to catch them. Darryn hardly dared to breathe. Suddenly his heart stopped, he could hear light footsteps making their way towards him. Somebody had been following him after all. The figure turned the corner and Darryn pounced.

"What the..." A startled voice shouted.

"Jake!" Darryn replied.

"What are you playing at? It's a bit late to be playing 'hide and seek'."

"Okay, Jake, I'm sorry. I thought I was being followed. Did you see anything suspicious?"

"No, I think you must be being paranoid. It seems just like any other Friday evening to me."

Darryn relaxed a little bit and then he looked more closely at Jake's face.

A couple of tears caught a shaft of light from a streetlamp and twinkled like little diamonds.

"Hey... are you alright?" he asked in a more sympathetic voice. "You look as if you've been crying."

"Thanks. Tell the whole world, why don't you!" Jake responded sharply. "I've just broken up with Nathan, if you must know. The two-timing rat was having it off with anyone he could lay his hands on at the wretched club in Soho."

Darryn ignored the sharp delivery of Jake's statement and opened his arms to embrace Jake. Jake duly obliged and burst into heartfelt sobs as Darryn gave him a protective hug.

"I'm so sorry, matey." He said, and then after a minute or two when Jake seemed to be collecting himself a bit, he continued, "Let's get back to Rainbow House and you can tell me all about it over a mug of hot chocolate."

The two of them entered the newsagents and ascended in the lift, up to the social area. Darryn kept a reassuring arm on Jake's shoulder as they went.

Unnoticed by either of them, a figure emerged from behind a tree with a broad smile on his face. He said to himself, "Thank you very much Darryn. You've now shown me what I needed to know." He then turned away and walked into the night.

Chapter 29

The next morning, Darryn was seated with Nathan in the social zone. He was trying desperately to maintain a sympathetic temperament, but lack of sleep, having stayed up half the night with Jake, was making him more and more irritable.

"Listen, if it's any consolation, Jake is just as cut up about things as you seem to be," Darryn said for what seemed the millionth time.

"But I've messed up big time, and he's the love of my life. What am I going to do?"

"Perhaps you ought to have thought about that before you started playing about with other people. What were you planning to do with those two soldiers...Have a threesome?"

"It was on the cards... but what's that got to do with anything now?" Nathan added hastily.

"An awful lot, I'd say. Didn't you think Jake would be upset when he found out?"

"I know, I know...It's just that I have needs and well... Jake can be a little dull when it comes to sex. He isn't very adventurous."

Darryn rolled his eyes and clasped his brow. The last thing he ever thought he'd be doing was acting as a marriage guidance counsellor.

"Look, there's more to a relationship than sex. I know Jake can be a bit old-fashioned and conservative in his ways, but he is a sweet thing and very loyal. Did it never occur to you that it might be a good idea to talk about what you both liked doing and try and work out some compromise? The initial excitement is never going to last. You are going to be permanently disappointed if that's what you expect every time you meet someone new."

"I know, but I don't feel I'm ready to be middle-aged like you just yet. There are things I can't do with Jake that I want to try before I die. That doesn't mean I don't still love Jake to bits."

Darryn ignored the sleight, but was more irritated that Nathan didn't really seem to be listening to his pearls of wisdom.

"You were both ridiculously young when you committed to this relationship. If you felt like that, you should have just been good friends with Jake for the time being and not made pledges of everlasting faithfulness."

"Yes, that's all very well...but what am I going to *do*?"

Darryn looked at his watch, "I have to be going. My advice is that you steer clear of Jake for a few days. He is very raw and likely to belt you one if you try to speak to him. As you are both trained to kill, someone is likely to get hurt." Darryn had now exhausted all his reserves of patience and decided to end with the brutal truth before leaving, "I'm very fond of both you and

Jake, but I have no doubt whatsoever that you are in the wrong on this one. If at some stage in the future there's a chance of getting back with Jake, it's you that's got to make the grovelling apology. But please don't bother unless you really mean it and want to live monogamously with Jake, with all the tedium and boredom that entails."

Nathan looked quizzically as Darryn got up and breezed out, leaving by the elevator which went down to the shop.

***

Jake entered N°2's office not quite sure what to expect. N°2 had one of her sternest looks.

"Can you explain why I have received a bill for £800 damage from the owner of 'Divine Hell'?"

"Sorry, I guess me and Nathan were a little careless last night."

"Oh for goodness sake" she said, passing the bill to Jake. "You're not a child anymore. I'm not going to stop your pocket money, just settle the bill yourself and take responsibility for your actions. Annabelle told me what happened."

"Sorry..."

"As a Guardian, it is important to keep your personal feelings in check at all times, but especially in the public arena. Imagine the damage to us if the newspapers decided to make a big thing of the spat. I can just see the headlines, 'hooligan gays smash up bar - no wonder homosexuals can't be trusted'. Anyway enough of that, what I *really* wanted to see you about was to see if you'd made any progress with Darryn's new boyfriend."

Jake explained that he had followed Alex to his home near the Oval tube station and then followed him again back to the Corinthian Club in Pall Mall. N°2 became keenly focused at the mention of the F.U.P.'s headquarters.

"It's not proof though. You will need to break in and see what you can find in his house. Have you been issued with your spying kit?"

Jake nodded. He had been issued with this just a few days ago after receiving a certificate of allowance from N°1. He had gone down to the operations room to get it and was directed to an area he had not been permitted to enter before that was directly linked to the maintenance zone on the floor below. He remembered seeing a very strange notice which presumably was aimed as a reminder to the supervisors. It read, 'Guns, knives, truth serum, suicide pills and sexual stimulants are not to be issued to agents under the age of eighteen.'

The Chief of Ordnance and Gadgetry himself had talked Jake through his kit, explaining what everything did. Rather unoriginally, this thin man in his sixties, with tufts of cotton wool hair and metal-rimmed glasses, was nicknamed 'Q' by those who worked in the operations room. However a more unlikely person to be involved in espionage was hard to imagine. He was nervous and twitchy, and mumbling so incoherently that Jake had to strain to hear what he was saying. At one point, there had been a loud bang in

173

the background as something was being tested. 'Q' had jumped out of his skin and hit his head on a light fitting causing such a spasm of twitching, that he had to sit down for five minutes to regain enough composure to carry on.

The kit did not contain a secret camera. As 'Q' pointed out, the camera on Jake's Smartphone was good enough to take pictures. There was, however, a miniature video camera that could be left in a room along with a miniaturised sound bug. Both of these could send information to a receiver up to half a mile away. There was also an electronic device for disabling burglar alarms, various skeleton keys to gain entry to rooms, a device for opening a safe, instant fingerprint detecting film, several false moustaches and wigs and various false identity cards enabling Jake to pass himself off as anything from a police officer to a gas meter reader. The kit was surprisingly compact in its metal case and could either be held as small briefcase or stored in a modest backpack.

"I'll do what I can," Jake said to N°2, "but I've got my interview for Oxford in a few weeks time, as well as the accelerated Guardian programme."

N°2 smiled sympathetically and said, "It can wait. I don't think the F.U.P. is going to move against us until after a General Election and even then they will need to take stock of how they've done. Concentrate on doing the best you can first, and you can worry about your espionage task after that. But do remember, any information you get about Alex comes straight to me and no-one else, not even Annabelle, and especially not Darryn."

Jake nodded again and left the room.

***

Jake was pleased to have something to keep his mind off Nathan. He had been very surprised to be asked for interview and had been spending a lot of time reading up on modern applications of maths, as well as making sure he could solve some of the knottier A-level questions. Just at the moment, there was something very satisfying about the solution to a pure maths problem. It was perfect in its own terms, unsullied by the mess of human emotions. Feelings of hopelessness and loss overwhelmed him in the middle of the night and he would often cry as he realised how empty the bed was without Nathan.

At college, the work if anything seemed to be more straightforward. His AS results, even though they were not going to count, had boosted his confidence and he was finding it easier to grasp the concepts, not just in maths, but in other subjects too.

The Guardian programme took up a lot of his time. The focus at the moment was on gun training and knife throwing, as well as the ongoing fitness and martial arts work. During November, Jake did his best to keep out of Nathan's way and Nathan took Darryn's advice and obliged by doing the same. The only awkward part was when it came to paired work in martial arts. Each of the boys desperately tried to change partners, but everyone else

174

in the group was happy with their other half and was unwilling to swap. Jake and Nathan were thus forced to work together in icy formality. For Jake, the necessary bodily contact was torture, reminding him that he knew intimately every square centimetre of Nathan's naked body by sight and touch.

Jake also continued playing in Mr Devonshire's orchestra. This term they were playing Rachmaninoff's second symphony. He was playing on the second desk of the second violins, having been promoted following his grade eight success. He had been offered a place in the first violins, but declined on the grounds that it would be too much pressure with his exams coming up. Nathan was leading the cellos and Jake could see him clearly. The first movement of the symphony took on new meaning as the dying falls of string passages at the start led to passages of almost impossible yearning. Initially, Jake had pictured in his mind's eye the composer standing on a ship watching his native Russia slip away beyond the horizon, knowing that he would never see it again. But now, it was he who was standing there watching Nathan on the shore slipping from view, with a desperate longing to be reunited but probably sundered forever. The music was incredibly beautiful, but overpowering in its intensity. Jake could only take so much of it. Nathan seemed unaffected, taking a purely professional approach to producing the sound, but Jake was interested to see a tear or two in Mr Devonshire's eyes, sat on the front desk of the viola section.

Eventually, as the weeks passed by, the time for his interview arrived. Tim was also being interviewed, but at different college, so Jake suggested they travel by train together. Tim consented without appearing overenthusiastic and so they found themselves on a train from Paddington Station bound for Oxford, mid-morning in the second week of December.

Despite the general air of gloom and despondency as a result of the financial crisis, the day was bright and cheerful. Sunlight flooded into the coach they were sat in and threw Tim's profile into sharp relief. He was sombre as always, but the light gave him a heroic appearance. In fact, to Jake at that moment he looked beautiful and highly desirable.

"What do you think your chances of getting in are?" Jake asked.

"Practically zero," Tim said in an emotionless way.

"Why have you applied, then?"

"Darryn almost begged me to, because I got a hundred percent in both my AS modules. They say Oxford is full of weirdoes, so maybe I might just fit in there."

Jake paused to think. He certainly hadn't done *that* well himself. It was always a struggle trying to hold a conversation with Tim. He was a nice lad, but he was so withdrawn and so painfully shy that he rarely spoke to anyone without being spoken to first. Jake was therefore very surprised when Tim suddenly said:

"I was sorry to hear about you and Nathan. I thought you'd be together forever."

"Well, it's just one of those things, I guess. Darryn warned me that it was unlikely to last and it seems he was right," Jake replied.

"I think Nathan must be mad. If I had a boyfriend as lovely as you, I'd be the happiest person alive. I wouldn't be looking to get cheap thrills elsewhere."

Jake was completely startled by this statement and suddenly looked at Tim carefully, but Tim had turned his head to look out of the window and Jake only caught the faintest reddening suggesting a blush.

Needless to say, after that there were only the most general exchanges of pleasantries until the train pulled into Oxford station. The two boys decided to walk to the town centre and make their ways to their respective colleges. Jake had applied to Christ Church, Tim to Corpus Christi. They arranged to meet up later and have a wander around Oxford together. There was nothing planned in either of their schedules until later in the day and the interviews were not until tomorrow.

If Jake had not already been accustomed to the marvels of Rainbow House, he would have been overawed by the grandeur and antiquity of the college. The large quad with its statue of Mercury, bang in the middle, the entrance to the steps of the impressive dining hall and the arches in the opposite face which marked the entrance to the cathedral doubling as a college chapel, were all impressive. The man who was charged with showing the hopeful interviewees to their rooms took Jake through an arch to the left where there was second impressive quad with the library along one face and a set of Georgian-looking buildings along the other three sides.

Jake was taken up the stairs in one of these buildings and shown into a room with an enormous window looking out onto the quad. The winter sunshine flooded in and illuminated the wood-panelled room furnished with a sofa, several chairs and a couple of standard lamps and two desks. There were doors in opposite walls which Jake judged correctly must lead to bedrooms.

The guide pointed out which one was Jake's and informed him that the other one was already occupied by another hopeful. The drawing room was shared between them. Jake sighed, he had not expected that he'd have to be diplomatic with a stranger and would have preferred a single room to himself. As it turned out his companion was amiable enough, if from another world. The Hon. Algernon Fortescue Templeton-Smythe greeted Jake with all the etiquette expected of the upper classes:

"I say, I'm very pleased to meet you old boy. The name's Templeton-Smythe, but you can call me Algie."

"Very pleased to meet you, Algie," Jake replied while firmly reciprocating the formal handshake. "My name's Jake Holdencroft and you can call me ... er, Jake."

"I'm up at Eton. Where are you at school?"

"I'm at school in London."

"O yes ... At Westminster or St. Pauls no doubt."

"Not quite."

Algie looked disappointed and the conversation flagged.

"Look, I'm going to meet a friend and have a look around Oxford. You can come with us if you like." Jake said, hoping his offer would be graciously refused.

"That's sweet of you, Jake, but I too have made arrangements to meet up with a few chums from school. We're having a late lunch in the Randolph Hotel. I guess I'll see you later for the formal reception."

Relieved, Jake met Tim at the back entrance a few minutes later. They set off on a random journey past colleges and through cobbled streets. Occasionally, Jake recognised a scene from a detective series he'd been watching on television. When they had wandered up past the main shopping area, Tim allowed himself to be dragged into the Ashmolean Museum by Jake, who was mesmerised by the display of violins and other stringed instruments. He stared at the famous Stradivarius, known as 'The Messiah' for a good ten minutes, wondering what it was about this instrument which made it so prized above all others. They ended up having a cup of tea in the cafe of a large department store.

"So what's your college like?" Jake asked.

"Old," replied Tim.

"Have you met anyone else yet?"

"I've just said 'hello' to a few people. The programmed events start later and the interviews are tomorrow. To be honest, Jake, I'm not looking forward to it. I shall have to be sociable to a bunch of strangers, and I'm not that good at that."

"You'll be fine. If you want to drop by later and tell me how it's gone, I'm sure that will be okay."

That evening, before dinner, there was a reception for all the candidates in the Picture Gallery. Jake felt uncomfortable and somewhat out of his depth, made worse by the fact that Algie seemed quite at home. Sherry was provided. Jake had never had this before, but rather liked it. He was astute enough to notice that you sipped it rather than gulped it down in one go. Algie appeared to be on good terms with at least half the people there, especially those with rich and influential parents. Jake looked around to see if there was anyone like him, who seemed to be lost and normal. He noted a shy-looking girl, pretending to examine one of the paintings, and decided it might be a good idea to try and converse with her.

They exchanged pleasantries and views about the paintings. Jake would have been content to chat with her until it was time to go into dinner, if he hadn't heard Algie's voice say:

"Well of course, old boy, I applied to Christ Church because my cousin is a Junior Fellow here... A chap called Darryn Harcourt-Smith. Pater thought he might be able to pull a few strings for me, but the guy's been useless."

Jake made his excuses, promising he would return shortly and very assertively muscled in on Algernon's little circle of friends.

"Excuse me, Algie... Did you say you were related to Darryn Harcourt-Smith?"

Algie looked surprised and said, "Good God, you don't know him do you?" His tone was that of someone who thought it was impossible for someone of Jake's low breeding to be acquainted with one of his relatives. Jake ignored the insult and Algie continued, "My mother's brother has a gloomy pile up north somewhere called Harcourt Towers. Darryn is his eldest son and set to inherit when the old man pops his clogs. Mind you, he's the black sheep of the family, by all accounts. He had a big bust up with the old man when he was still a teenager. I don't think he's been back home since. No one really knows what the argument was about."

Jake pondered this and realised how little he knew about Darryn's past. The conversation between them always seemed to centre on Jake's problems and issues and if they did talk about Darryn, it was always about the present and future, never the past.

"Yes, I know him very well. I've actually worked with him for the past year," Jake said hoping the statement would make an impression. He was not disappointed. Algernon looked at him with wide-eyed astonishment. Satisfied, Jake continued, "Now if you'll excuse me, I promised Olivia I would rejoin her presently."

Although it was dark outside, the weather was mild for the time of year and there was no need to put on coats or extra clothing to make the short journey to the hall for dinner. Jake walked with Olivia and another girl who had latched on to them for security. Algie walked some distance behind with his friends from Eton. As they walked up the stone staircase, Jake was sure he'd seen it in at least one film, and when they entered the hall his breath was taken away. The room was big enough to act as the nave of a modestly sized cathedral and had three lines of enormously long wooden dining tables, stretching almost the entire length of the hall. At the far end, set on a dais, was the high table where the dons and fellows presumably dined, at right-angles to the long lines of tables. Jake noticed a portrait, amongst countless others, of Henry the Eighth hanging on the wall. Surely it couldn't be genuine?

There was a degree of informality to the occasion, with some of the tutors joining the would-be students. Jake relaxed a little more as he began to realise that most of the other people there were just as nervous and just as much out of their depth as he was. Olivia was applying to do medicine and the other girl, who was called Sophia, was trying for history.

Jake was quite intrigued with Olivia's account about how she would have to dissect a real human body in her first year. He was pleased that his decision to do maths would not involve such gruesome activities, and was confirmed in his view that people wanting to be doctors or vets must be mad.

Jake wondered whether Darryn might be there, but he was certainly not one of those tutors who were dinning with the hopefuls and there was no one dining on High Table that evening. A low but eager hum was now audible throughout the hall as tongues were beginning to loosen and the excitement of possibly gaining a place at such a prestigious college was overcoming the awe of being there. Jake also noticed that Algernon and his friends were being very loud and confident. He hoped they would not be invited back for midnight revelries in their shared drawing room.

The evening ended and Jake decided to get a reasonably early night to be on top form for the interview tomorrow. He was just entering his staircase when a familiar figure came towards him from the opposite side of the quad.

"Hi Tim, how did it go this evening?"

"Ghastly," He replied, "I was so tongue-tied I couldn't speak to anyone sensibly at dinner and nobody seemed too keen to talk to me anyway. I'm not sure I'll accept a place here even if I'm offered one."

"Don't be so hasty," Jake replied, putting an arm around Tim's shoulder. "I expect you were unlucky and just happened to be sitting next to someone who was a bit snotty. Come back to my room. I think there's some coffee there."

So they went up the stairs and went into Jake's room. Tim whistled and said, "My God, you've fallen on your feet here. This is like a room in Buckingham Palace."

"I have to share it with Algernon. We each have a bedroom on either side of the room."

Jake put the kettle on. There was some instant coffee and powdered milk along with some biscuits Jake had packed before he left Rainbow House. They decided to go to Jake's room just in case Algernon came back with his Eton friends. Neither of them fancied having to make small talk with a group with whom they suspected they would have little in common. As it turned out, Algernon did not return until the small hours and he was by himself, so he and his friends must have talked the night away elsewhere.

"Did you know that this Algernon character is Darryn's cousin?" Jake said as he and Tim sat on the bed.

"I did know that Darryn comes from a posh background," Tim replied rather unexpectedly. "I gather he's set to inherit millions when his father dies."

Jake was now seated next to Tim. He was getting some fairly lusty stirrings as he was appreciating how strong and muscular Tim was. Tim's face now looked beautiful as well as sad and heroic and he was becoming incredibly desirable. For reasons beyond his own understanding, Jake suddenly blurted out, "You know you said I was lovely on the train this morning, well I think you are lovely too. If I hadn't been with Nathan, I'd have told you that some time ago."

Tim looked at Jake suspiciously and said, "I expect you are just saying

179

that because you are on the rebound from Nathan. I guess you think any single male is desirable at the moment."

"I don't think so," Jake replied, "I think it is you I find very attractive." With that he planted a kiss on Tim, full on the lips.

Tim momentarily recoiled, but then looked at Jake intently before grabbing his head and kissing him passionately.

Tim became like a wild animal, almost tearing at Jake's clothes. Jake found this all very exciting and reciprocated with a will.

Chapter 30

After the collapse of the British and Shanghai Bank, the news could not carry on being bad day after day. There was a pause, like the nation holding its breath, as the International Monetary Fund delivered a bailout which prevented the other major banks defaulting. An eerie sense of calm descended on the country over Christmas and the New Year. Those with jobs carried on going to work and even those who did not, continued to get some benefits. There was a real sense that this time the whole economic edifice could come crashing down, but it hadn't quite done so yet. It was like a man losing his balance at the edge of a precipice, but he had not fallen over just yet.

Indeed things even seemed to get better for a while. The new Chancellor of the Exchequer was a perky, no-nonsense woman in her early forties who seemed to revive some confidence in the Government. The deal she brokered with the IMF at least bought a little bit of time. Christmas was austere that year. Many towns put up no lights at all, and many families went without presents and a special Christmas dinner.

Jake decided to visit his mum and sisters. He took Tim with him and braced himself for some awkward questions about why he'd not invited Nathan. Tim had already learned to drive and had saved up for a small second-hand car. A mysterious benefactor had paid for the insurance. Jake suspected it was Darryn, but he had no proof. They therefore drove down to Great Malvern on the Saturday before Christmas.

Nathan, already upset over his breakup with Jake was absolutely distraught when it became apparent that something was now going on between Jake and Tim.

"You didn't waste much time looking for someone else, did you?" was his only comment to Jake when he caught Tim giving Jake a quick kiss in Rainbow House on their return from Oxford. Jake had been embarrassed by this incident. His ire had cooled by now, and he certainly didn't want to make Nathan suffer for his infidelity. Surprisingly, it was Maria who gave Nathan most sympathy and she was the patient recipient of much angst-ridden unburdening. Even so, Nathan decided to use the Christmas period to do his long trek. He was therefore walking along the coast, by himself, between Falmouth and Plymouth over Christmas Eve, Christmas Day and Boxing Day.

In Great Malvern, Rose Holdencroft was very excited about Jake's interview at Oxford.

"How did it go, dear? Did you answer all the questions you were asked?"

"Well, they asked about a fairly standard partial differential equation, and

I did say some intelligent things about why I wanted to do maths and how it is useful in the modern world, but I was asked a stinker about hyperbolic functions. I'm not sure whether I did enough to be offered a place."

"It would be amazing if you got a place. I don't think anyone else in the family has ever gone to Oxford."

"Well, make the most of it if I do, because I'm not going to have any children to follow in my footsteps."

Rose Holdencroft went quiet after this and Jake wished he'd not made this last comment.

Eventually Rose asked out of politeness, "How do you think you did, Tim?"

"It's difficult to tell, Mrs Holdencroft. Like Jake, I answered some of the questions, but not all. I expect I wasn't interesting enough. I'm not very hopeful."

"I'm sure you'll do fine. It would be nice if both you and Jake managed to get a place."

Tim and Jake went for a walk on the Malverns on the day after Boxing Day. A group of handsome soldiers ran by them. Tim did not even give them a second look; how different from Nathan's reaction in the summer, thought Jake. If anything, Tim was almost too attentive. He adored Jake and did everything he could to please him. Jake was beginning to find it a bit stifling.

On the last day of their stay, everyone was sat around the television waiting for the start of a Disney film, when unexpectedly an announcement came on saying that normal programmes were being interrupted for an announcement by the Prime Minister. His face appeared looking stern and serious.

"The economic situation is grave," he began, "and the Government no longer has a majority in the House of Commons. We could struggle on as a minority administration until our term is up in October, but I think in the interests of the nation rather than our party, the country needs a new Government with a new mandate to tackle, with decisiveness, the unprecedented situation we now find ourselves in.

"I have therefore been to the Palace today to ask His Royal Highness, the King, for a Dissolution of Parliament. He has graciously consented and there will be a General Election on February 1st. I will be leading my party in that election, strongly urging you to support the programme of cuts in public spending that we have already begun. My fellow countrymen and women, I know the times are bleak, but with the spirit and stubbornness that is characteristic of the British people, I am sure we will pull through to happier and more prosperous times."

"What a load of poppycock." Rose Holdencroft muttered as the Prime Minister's face faded. "We wouldn't be in this mess if the rich and powerful had thought more about the country a few years back and had spent less time trying to make a profit out of everything."

Tim and Jake looked at each other apprehensively. This was the F.U.P.'s big moment, a chance to get their hands on the levers of power.

"You'll be able to vote, Tim. I'll still be too young. Who are you going to vote for?"

Tim thought for a moment and then said, "Well I know who I *won't* be voting for. Is there much point in voting for any of them? None of them seem to have any idea what to do and no one seems to want the things I want. No, I doubt if I'll bother."

"Yes, dear," chipped in Rose Holdencroft, "I have to say I agree with you."

The next day in the morning, just as they were packing the car ready to leave, the postman dropped a letter through the door addressed to Mr J. Holdencroft. Daisy was the first to notice it. She rushed out and forced it into Jake's hand. It looked official and the envelope was not a cheap one. He carefully slid his finger under the gummed overleaf, opening the letter without destroying the envelope. As he unfolded the single sheet of white notepaper within, he noticed a colourful crest at the top with a cardinal's hat and tassels surrounding it. His heart missed a beat as he suddenly realised what this was about. He read it once, then again and then a third time.

"Well...?" Tim and Daisy said in near exasperated unison.

"I've got in! They've offered me a place. I don't believe it."

Daisy rushed in to tell the rest of the family. Rose Holdencroft and Aunty Violet, followed by Maisie and Daisy rushed out into the street and took it in turns to hug Jake and congratulate him. There were tears in Rose Holdencroft's eyes as she muttered something about being so proud of her son. Needless to say, Tim and Jake's departure was delayed while Mrs Holdencroft got down the cooking sherry and decided that even Maisie and Daisy could have a small glass to toast Jake's success.

When Tim got back to Rainbow House he found a similar envelope in his room. This was from Corpus offering him not only a place, but a scholarship as well. Tim and Jake celebrated in a somewhat different manner.

***

Jake now turned his mind to his spying mission. On several evenings in early January Jake held vigil outside the home of Alex Singleton. On the first two occasions, lights were visible in the room which Jake had identified as that which definitely belonged to Alex. An infra-red detecting device in his spy kit also showed a hot body moving around inside. On the third occasion however he was in luck. He arrived just in time to see Alex, smartly but casually dressed, shut the front door and head for the tube station. Was he on his way out for a night with Darryn? Jake thought this was highly likely.

A quick sweep with his infra-red device showed that no one was inside the darkened room on the second floor. With his heart beating fast, he got out his universal skeleton key and strode up to the front door of number 12. He had put on a novelty mask and wore the hood of his dark fleece, just in case there was CCTV that he hadn't noticed. Resisting the thought that hundreds of eyes were looking at what he was doing, he played with the key in the lock for what seemed like ages until it engaged and opened the front door. There was a light in the hallway and, as he had guessed, the house was split into a number of flats. The stairs to the second floor beckoned invitingly in front of him. He looked around quickly to see if there were any obvious cameras trained on the front door. There didn't seem to be, but nevertheless he pointed his electronic disruptor to all parts of the ceiling. He then thought it wise to remove his hood and mask just in case one of the other residents suddenly came out into the hallway. None did and he slowly and stealthily climbed the stairs. A light automatically came on as he rounded the bend in the stairs which took him by surprise. He pointed the electronic disruptor at the walls and ceiling again. The light suddenly went off and he stumbled up to the landing and fumbled on the wall for a light switch.

He reckoned carefully as he made his way down a short landing and came to the door which would lead to the room that gave out the light onto the road below. Jake fiddled with his skeleton key again and quickly managed to open the door. A second tool in his spy kit was designed to disable burglar alarms and he had this at the ready as he entered. He knew he would only have a few seconds before it went off. There was no sign of a key pad by the door and he held his breath for ten seconds, but nothing happened. He cautiously moved into the room and turned the lights on. The curtains were drawn shut, preventing him from being seen by the outside world. He waved his electronic disruptor around just in case there were any microscopic listening bugs or spy cameras.

He was in a large room that clearly doubled as both living room and dining room. There was a certain degree of elegance about the room itself with a high ceiling, intricate in its plasterwork, but the furnishing was modest. Self-assembled tables, chairs and sofa suggested that the residence was not intended to be occupied for long. Off the main room were two doors other than the front door to the flat. One led to a small kitchen, which nevertheless had an inbuilt washing machine and dishwasher as well as an oven, sink and cupboard space. The other led to a bedroom, only just big enough to fit a double bed with an en-suite toilet and shower built into the corner.

Jake considered his training for a minute. He had to search the flat systematically and also make sure he wasn't caught unawares. He cautiously looked out into the corridor and placed a device on the wall which would send a signal to his wristwatch if anyone came up the stairs. He carefully put on a pair of white cotton gloves so he would not leave fingerprints and then started in the main room, working clockwise from the window. He was a curious sight, fortunately not witnessed by anyone, half chav and half snooker referee. Twenty minutes methodical search revealed nothing. He moved next to the bedroom where he worked through the cupboard drawers, checking for false bottoms as well as the contents of the drawers themselves. Socks, underpants, ties and handkerchiefs were unexceptional, although Jake did notice they were designer label rather than from the local superstore. His training led him to check behind the pictures and mirrors, behind the cupboards, between the mattress and the bed and under the carpet.

It was only when he was doing the last of these that he noticed the carpet was loose under the bed and could be rolled back from the skirting board. Much to his surprise he found a flat sheet which looked like some document, housed in a plastic wallet somewhere between A4 and A3 size. Jake carefully removed it and placed it on the bed. The first striking thing about it was its texture; it was not paper but vellum, very smooth and soft to the touch. The second thing was that it had what looked like a string looped through two holes in the vellum held fast together by a lead seal. On the back of the seal were the faces of two idealised bearded male faces with 'SPA' embossed over the one and 'SPE' over the other.

The text, laid out in landscape rather than portrait format, was beautifully hand written, but in Latin. Jake recognised the first word as being a name, maybe in a Latin version. Then he made out the words in large letters '*Episcopus Servus Servorum Dei*' which he guessed had something to do with the named person being a bishop and the servant of the servants of God; but after, that he was totally lost.

Jake took out his smart phone and took several photos of the document, ensuring that all the writing was visible. He then carefully put the manuscript back where he had found it under the carpet, and did a systematic check before turning the light out and quitting the residence. He did consider leaving a bug or a tiny camera behind, but felt there was enough evidence to suggest he was dealing with someone who might be thoroughly trained in espionage themselves, and that it would be too much of a risk. Ten minutes later Jake was outside in the now frosty night air, head buried in his hood, heading for The Oval tube station.

***

"It's a shame we can't go back to your place tonight," Darryn said to Alex as they sat drinking a pint in 'The Queen's Head', a Bears' bar off Oxford Street. Darryn and Alex had gone there to find somewhere quiet where they could sit and chat rather than have dance music blaring in their ears all evening. Darryn had not seen Alex for some time and was feeling rather horny, hence his comment.

"Some of us have to go to work in the morning you know," Alex replied with mock disapproval. "I've got a busy day tomorrow and need a good night's sleep. I won't get that if you come back with me."

Darryn sighed and gave up that tack. He continued, "Where have you been then?"

"Well you know I went to see my parents and family over Christmas. I'm not out to them, so you know it was difficult to get in touch with you."

"Yes but what were you doing before Christmas? I was hoping I might spend some time with you then. I think the last time I saw you was one of our 'after work on Friday' get-togethers. Was it the end of November or the beginning of December? I can't remember."

Alex looked vague and said, "I can't remember either. I was probably busy with work. We're usually busy at that time of year."

The interior of the pub was old fashioned, to put it mildly. Magnolia wallpaper, probably browned with cigarette smoke in the past, was set off against wooden tables, benches and chairs. The pub was not busy. After a lull in the conversation, Alex suddenly said, "Look Darryn, I've got some bad news. I've been redeployed outside of London. I'm going to have to move to Newcastle pretty quickly."

"Oh," said Darryn, wondering whether this was true. "How does that affect us?"

"I don't know," Alex responded cautiously. "I'll get in touch when I've got settled and we'll take it from there."

Suddenly and quite unexpectedly Annabelle and Rakshi entered. Annabelle saw Darryn and made her way over to him while Rakshi went to the bar.

"Hello, Darryn, fancy seeing you in here. Who's this? Is this your new man we've been hearing so much about?" If Annabelle had been a little more alert she would have noticed all was not well by the way the two men both avoided her gaze.

"Annabelle, this is Alex," Darryn said rather neutrally, gesturing to where Alex was seated.

"Pleased to meet you," Annabelle said, extending her arm for a polite handshake. "Don't I know you from somewhere? You look very familiar."

"Pleased to meet you too...No, I'm sure I've not seen you before."

Again, if Annabelle had been alert she would have noticed just a split second when Alex betrayed that he did indeed recognise her. Oblivious, Annabelle continued, "Why we agreed to meet David and Danny in here I don't know. What a dive! The place can't have been redecorated in a hundred years."

"That's the charm of the place," Darryn countered. "It gives it an air of authenticity."

As Rakshi came over with a drink for her and Annabelle, Alex suddenly got up and said, "I'm sorry to break up the party, but I really must be going. Good evening ladies. Bye, Darryn."

As Alex left hurriedly, Rakshi said, "I hope it wasn't me who drove him away."

"No, you're alright, he had to go and get ready to pack. He's moving up to Newcastle - apparently."

Annabelle looked at Darryn and said, "Is everything alright between you two?"

Darryn thought for a moment and then said, "No, I don't think it is. I've got a feeling we just broke up."

Chapter 31

The election campaign got under way in earnest. The excitement in the media was matched by the apathy of the general public. This was no more evident to Jake than when he saw a cabinet minister out on the streets being flanked by twenty loyal supporters waving party banners, all under twenty-one and looking like the kids who never got picked for the team. An excited group of newspaper photographers and television interviewers were asking questions. Beyond this bubble of activity, people were wandering up and down the High Street going about their business not caring or interested in what was happening. The politician might as well have been on a different planet to the electorate he was supposed to be engaging with.

When the economic situation got too difficult to cope with, the MPs of all parties turned their attention to more trivial matters. Every now and then, usually just after one of them had been caught fiddling their expenses; they would become exercised with the problem of the electorate being disillusioned with politics. The leader of the opposition had had the bright idea of changing the name of his party to make it more 'voter friendly'. The other major parties, not to be outdone, decided to do the same thing. Hence the two larger parties were now called, 'Let's go, Britain!' and 'Forward Together, Britain!', while the slightly smaller party was called 'Let's be nice to each other, Britain!'

The advertising industry and the political advisors thought this had all been tremendously exciting and terribly innovative. However, the public found it even more difficult to tell the difference between one party and another, or to work out what they stood for. The impression was consolidated that none of them had any idea how to get out of the mess the country currently was in. The Family Unity Party, on the other hand, had no difficulty in projecting a very different image, certain in what it wanted to do and clear in its objectives.

There were those who spoke up and were appalled at the neo-fascist ideas that were being put forward by the F.U.P. For many however, the idea of order in society, a return to a golden age when people were prosperous and a country where the trains ran on time was more beguiling than a loss of freedom. As the campaign wore on it was clear that the F.U.P. was destined to get about twenty-five percent of the vote. The main opposition party was in the lead but only managing about thirty percent. The quirks of the 'first-past-the-post' system might allow them a majority in the House of Commons, but it was by no means certain. In public, both of the larger parties categorically denied they would do any deals with the F.U.P. to get into power.

Jake and Tim were watching the news together one evening when a clip of a speech by Lord Bernard of Agincourt came on the screen.

"*My British compatriots,*" he began. "*For too long we have lived under the yoke of Europe, immigration and the aggressive homosexual community. The pressure we have applied has loosened the ties with an over-mighty continent and allowed us to manage our own affairs again. We have plans to stop immigration completely and to encourage people to leave these shores and go and live with people they are ethnically empathetic with. Our biggest challenge which lies ahead, however, is to rid this nation of the homosexual menace that has debauched our institutions. We will scour the civil service and the armed forces and cleanse the leadership of these organisations; we will spread like fire through our schools and universities and root them out of places of influence. We will hasten the day when not one of them will feel safe to brazenly wander down the street.*"

There was wild applause from his audience and people were holding up their arms in a gesture that could have either been appropriate for an evangelical prayer meeting or a Nazi rally.

Tim got up and forcefully switched the television off, "I can't stand watching anymore of that," he said. "It's appalling that so many people are buying into that crap. You and I are just being made the scapegoats for the failure of society to manage itself fairly."

"Come on, Tim. Calm down. There's nothing you can do to change people's minds at the moment. At least we have a chance to protect people from the worst excesses of this. We should count ourselves lucky really."

Tim slumped back into the sofa next to Jake and changed the subject, "I see you went to visit N°2 the other day. What was that all about?"

"Nothing of any consequence...She's managing my Guardian espionage project and I had to make an interim report."

This was of course true and not true at the same time. The information he had to report to N°2 was of great consequence. She had been fascinated and deeply concerned about the photos of the document Jake had found.

"I wish my Latin was better," she'd said. "I'll have to get a proper Classics expert to look at this. You've done well Jake, very well in fact. Keep the information under your hat for the time being. When I know for certain what it says, I suspect I'll have to break some unhappy news to Darryn."

Tim changed the subject again and started quizzing Jake about his motor boat training and car driving. Both of these had been interesting. Of the two, Jake had found managing a speed boat rather easier than learning to drive a car. He was having trouble with the clutch pedal and was constantly stalling the car. Tim could already drive a car and so had progressed to learning to ride a motorbike. He looked very sexy in his motorcycle leathers, so Jake had taken the opportunity to click a picture of him standing next to a powerful bike. He'd then printed it out and stuck it in a frame next to his bed. Yes, Tim looked very handsome – almost as handsome as Nathan.

***

Gerald Tasker was feeling more cheerful. He enjoyed politics and the announcement of the General Election meant he could involve himself in some old-fashioned canvassing and leafleting. He was aware that there were some dubious things going on. There were plans, for instance, to sabotage the posting of poll cards in areas that were unlikely to be sympathetic, and those people that the F.U.P. had helped after the collapse of the British and Shanghai Bank had been made to give a secret undertaking to order a postal vote and hand it over, signed to the F.U.P.

Frankly, there was no need for any of this. They already had the MP for the constituency after their famous by-election win a couple of years earlier. Gerald Tasker was met with genuine enthusiasm in the poorer areas where people had lost both jobs and benefits and were grinding out an existence in increasingly desperate poverty.

Their MP was nothing special. He had been a small businessman prior to his election and had effectively given voice to the rising clamour to be rid of immigrants and gays. He did not have the wit to argue his case from an intellectual standpoint nor to develop practical policy. He would never, therefore, be anything more than a noisy backbencher.

Gerald looked back down a street he had just canvassed in the watery winter sunshine. In garden after garden stood bill boards with the characteristic purple and gold posters of the F.U.P. A sense of pride filled his heart. Less than four years ago he and a handful of others in Telford had been considered lunatics and cranks. Now they were definitely the mainstream.

***

Towards the end of January, just days before voting, Jake was summoned to a meeting in N^o2's office. To his surprise, N^o6, Danny and Annabelle were present as well. It was the usual tight circle that Jake now realised was the inner core of the Rainbow Alliance's intelligence and defence capability. Only Darryn was absent - and he soon realised why that was when N^o2 addressed them.

"I have had the document which Jake photographed examined and translated by an expert. I have asked you here to share that knowledge with me and advise me about what to do next. In view of the delicate nature of the information it reveals I am asking all of you to be sworn to secrecy for the time being."

Jake's curiosity had been whetted and he leaned forward to hear more clearly. What secrets did this document hold? N^o2 continued:

"It is a Papal Bull," She continued, "a letter which has been sent directly to the recipient from the Vatican. However it is addressed to someone called Andrew, not Alex or Alexander, so Darryn's boyfriend may not have been the intended recipient."

190

Annabelle started when she heard the name Andrew. "Oh no," she exclaimed. "I remember where I've seen him before. I only saw Alex the once, just a couple of weeks ago, but that fair hair, even though it was cropped, and those blue eyes...How could I forget those blue eyes? Alex is Andrew, O'Grady's right-hand man at the camp in Wales."

N°2 pursed her lips and said, "That explains a good deal then. The translation of the Papal Bull runs as follows:

' To Andrew, our brother in Christ, we give special licence to indulge in certain sexual acts in the knowledge that you will find them disgusting and depraved, but yet will see a greater purpose in trapping and condemning those who are our enemies and would wish to do the Church harm. We are confident that the sins you commit in the work of the Church will be absolved and forgiven as a necessary evil for the greater good.'

The others, including Jake, listened incredulous and open-mouthed. N°6 was the first to recover the power of speech and comment:

"Has this come directly from the Pope?"

"I asked my expert that," N°2 responded. "He said that the signature at the end is not the one you would expect of the current Pope. That is apparently not unusual and could indicate a powerful bishop inside the Curia sent it instead. The expert could not identify a likely candidate."

"Are we sure it's genuine?" Danny asked.

"It would appear that Alex or Andrew thinks it is, which, in a way, is all that matters."

N°2 noticed Annabelle had a furrowed brow and asked her directly for her thoughts.

"The one and only night that I briefly saw Alex, Darryn was convinced he was being dumped. What does that mean?"

N°2 tried to supply some answers: "It could mean that Alex was scared of being caught out, it could mean that he had given up his attempt to corrupt Darryn..."

"It could also mean that he had got everything he needed from Darryn and was now simply making his exit strategy," Annabelle interrupted in a less than reassuring way.

N°2 looked sharply at Annabelle but replied, "You are unfortunately right, which means it's high time Darryn was brought into the loop so we can find out exactly what has gone on between those two. I take it no one suspects Darryn of being anything other than an unfortunate victim in this plot?"

She looked round at the faces in front of her and could see that none of them remotely suspected Darryn of any wrong doing at all. She therefore continued with a sigh, "In that case, someone has to break the news to Darryn that he has been cynically manipulated by his boyfriend to reveal sensitive information about the Rainbow Alliance. Having already had a former boyfriend as a traitor, he may not take the news well. It is obviously a delicate task... any volunteers?"

191

There was an awkward silence as N°2, N°6, Danny, Annabelle and even Jake, looked at each other wondering if they should offer their services. In the end, to the others relief, Annabelle took up the short straw saying, "I know him as well as anyone and I think he'll take it from me more calmly than from anyone else."

***

Maria caught up with Jake in the dining area for the evening meal that very same day. They sat, as they so often had before, by the large windows looking out on the Thames below. It was dark outside, so the only things that really showed up were the lights of the other buildings around them. There seemed to be fewer of them than there had been a year ago, a sign maybe of the ailing economy and hope being slowly extinguished. Tim was not present so Maria took the opportunity to talk about Nathan.

"Nathan's really upset, you know," Maria said, with a good deal of first-hand experience.

"So what am I supposed to do about that? Maybe he should have thought about that before he went off gallivanting with those soldiers in the club." This came out a lot harsher than Jake had intended and he caught Maria wincing as he spoke.

"He wasn't expecting you to go off with someone else so soon, nevertheless," Maria riposted rather sharply. "When you returned from your Oxford interview and you coolly announced that you and Tim were now an item, it just about finished him off. I had him in my room until about two o'clock. I have never seen a man cry so much."

This information disturbed Jake. He had always regarded Nathan as a strong character on whom he could always lean. The idea of Nathan being in pieces gave him no satisfaction.

"Look, I didn't do it to spite Nathan," Jake protested. "Things just sort of happened and Tim is a sweet boy."

"Do you love him though?"

"I...I...I'm very fond of him," spluttered Jake.

"I thought so. Be very careful Jake," Maria warned. "You can't build a relationship based on sympathy for someone you feel sorry for."

"It's much more than that," protested Jake

"I hope so," replied Maria. "Anyway, when are you going to mend some fences with Nathan?"

Jake sighed and said, "I'm not angry with him anymore. If we can find the right opportunity I'll try and build some bridges." There was a moment's pause and then he continued, "Maria, you and I are still good friends, aren't we?"

"Of course," she laughed. "Why do you ask?"

"It's just that so many things have changed lately and I seem to be losing people left right and centre. Ashok has gone, and he was my best friend a year ago; I've lost Nathan when I thought we would be together forever; my

192

dad's died and people like Taffy Williams are starting to be killed. Promise me that whatever and whenever, we will still be friends."

Maria gave such an assurance and they hugged by the side of the dining table before going their separate ways.

Chapter 32

The day of the election came. It was a drizzly Thursday that developed into a wet and stormy one later on. Pundits were suggesting that this would have a detrimental effect on the turnout. There had been reports of intermittent bullying and malpractice at polling stations, but nothing could be later proven. There were an astonishingly high number of postal votes, which was also remarked on by the TV and press.

Jake had had a full day at college, done some basic training in the evening and then gone to an orchestra rehearsal. By the time he returned to Rainbow House a number of people, including Maria, Jenny, Louise, Matt, Tim and Nathan were sat around a large screen in the social zone, watching the start of the election results programme.

"The polls are now closed and we can reveal our exclusive exit poll which was done during the day," The announcer said excitedly. A computer graphic came up on the screen which showed, one by one, the percentages predicted for each party. 'Let's Go Britain" and "Forward Together Britain" were both forecast to get twenty-nine percent of the vote. A gasp went around the social zone as the F.U.P. was shown as coming third with twenty-six percent. 'Let's be nice to each other, Britain' were lagging well behind on ten percent and predicted to lose most, but not all of their seats.

As the evening wore on into the small hours of the night, it became apparent that the F.U.P. had managed to concentrate its vote in certain areas to maximise its chances of gaining seats. They easily retained their by-election victories, including Telford, and then at half-past two in the morning came news of a flurry of gains in the rural east of England and in the areas of suburban decay around the major cities.

By three in the morning most of the viewers in the social zone could stand it no longer and had gone to bed. Jake and his group of friends had morosely abandoned the vigil at about one. Those that remained needed a stiff drink to deal with the ever-gloomier news that came in almost by the minute.

When the dust had settled in the morning, it was clear that no party had anything like a working majority of 326 seats. The main opposition had gained 254 seats, the governing party 231 and the F.U.P. 129. There had been ugly scenes through the night in which mobs had rampaged through areas of high racial tension, causing damage to property and endangering life. The police were either overwhelmed or mysteriously failed to act in areas where policing services had been contracted out to the F.U.P.

When the Stock Exchange opened, the FTSE 100 plummeted by more than 300 points having rallied somewhat since the recent appointment of the

194

outgoing Chancellor of the Exchequer. There was little anyone could do however due to the state of paralysis gripping the Political Establishment.

***

Half term approached and Jake's eighteenth birthday now loomed imminently. Things were not as he anticipated they would be. Last year, following Maria's successful party, he imagined having something similar to celebrate his coming of age. However, with his break up with Nathan, and the general gloom that had descended on Rainbow House following the election result, such a celebration now seemed highly inappropriate.

He had therefore decided to use half term to do his 3 day trek, arranging to finish at his mum's home on the day of his birthday. Much of the week was typically grey and gloomy, not cold, but interspersed with the occasional shower of rain. As he used his woodcraft skills to build a shelter and a fire and gather food and water, he could not help but think of Taffy Williams. As he sat with his thoughts by a crackling fire, the wind at night seemed to be whispering with a Welsh accent, 'Well done, my lovely boys. Keep going and don't give up.'

Jake was surprised at how routine he now found this trek. He had become hardened to the wild and could cope with survival as well as anyone in the Guardian programme. He easily evaded the two attempts to capture him and was tempted to turn the tables and capture one of his stalkers in return. Nevertheless, he was happy of a good soak in the bath when he arrived at Aunt Violet's house in Malvern. Rakshi had arranged to be there to verify his credentials and record the assignment as having been done. Rose Holdencroft asked her to stay the night, but she declined, saying that Marcus needed assistance with his patrols in Telford now that the election had given new impetus to the F.U.P.'s clandestine programmes. Before leaving, she took Jake to one side and said, "Be careful when you're out and about. The F.U.P. has got a new MP in this area and the patrols are likely to increase. Don't do anything to draw attention to yourself or your family."

So his eighteenth birthday was a small celebration, with Maisie, Daisy, Rose and Violet. A birthday tea, including a cake with eighteen candles on it (which he blew out in one breath), marked the rite of passage. Jake realised he was lucky to have supportive family and only wished that Tim could have been there to share in the moment too.

On his return to Rainbow House, he was surprised by a hesitant knock on his apartment door just as he was thinking of turning in for the night. It was Nathan. Jake stopped himself from saying, 'what the bloody hell do you think you are doing knocking on my door at this hour?' and waited for Nathan to say something. It took a while to emerge. Finally, Nathan said:

"Look Jake, I hate it that we have to go around trying to avoid each other. Can we not at least be civil to each other?"

Jake looked at Nathan with his gaunt expression so different from the dare-devil, cheeky face that had once been so familiar. He had no wish to

195

punish Nathan further. Jake beckoned him into the room and got him to sit in one of the chairs by the side of his bed.

"Listen, Nathan," he began. "I hate the fact we're not talking either and I know it's making things difficult for our friends too, especially Maria. Let's be civil to each other and see how it goes. I hope we can restore a degree of friendship as well." Nathan's eyes lighted up at this. However, Jake continued, "But... You have to understand that I'm with Tim now. Things can't be the same as they were before we broke up."

Nathan looked crestfallen again and considered Jake's statement. In the end he simply said, "Okay, that's fair I suppose," and walked out of the room.

***

Following the deadlocked General Election and the subsequent financial convulsion, the two main parties started talks with a view to establishing a Grand Coalition. Initially things went well and the financial markets again recovered slightly. Age-old animosity and bickering over policy, let alone the details of who was going to be the Prime Minister and how the Cabinet was to be split up, led to the talks running into problems. After two weeks, it was clear that some of these difficulties were never going to be resolved and after three, 'Let's go Britain' pulled out completely.

Then the unthinkable happened. 'Forward Together, Britain' despite all the assurances which had been given during the campaign period, opened up discussions with Lord Bernard and his newly triumphant F.U.P. MPs. At the same time, The United States approved a loan to Britain to once again shore up the banking system. A surprising advocate for this assistance had been Congressman Wayne Hackett, who previously had been a staunch opponent of overseas aid.

Eventually, after two further weeks of wrangling, a deal was done. Lord Bernard was to be the Home Secretary in the new government and would also act as Deputy Prime Minister. The F.U.P. also claimed its other prize of getting the position of Defence Secretary as well as being able to demand the posts of Chief Secretary to the Treasury, Justice Secretary and Local Government Secretary. So at the ballot box the F.U.P. had achieved its wildest dreams.

***

It was the beginning of March, the first Sunday afternoon in fact. There were no signs of spring, however. An icy blast from Siberia had kept temperatures unseasonably low for the past week, with occasional blizzards leading to traffic chaos and problems for farmers. In Manchester there were the odd blobs of ice on street corners where snow had fallen and the shade had prevented the snow from melting. In 'The Sunken Way' tucked away on the first floor, Annabelle was sitting with Darryn. It had taken her several days to track him down, which made her even more nervous about what she was about to say to him. She at least had a glass of red wine to steady herself.

196

Darryn however was in full flow, and she thought it unkind to stop him just yet.

"It's grim," he said. "How can people be so stupid as to vote for those idiots in the F.U.P.? I feel we're even more on our own and vulnerable than ever. Are there any liberal voices left in the straight world that will speak out against what's coming?"

"I know, it's terrible," Annabelle sympathised. "Rainbow House is in shock at the moment. People are hardly talking to each other they are so stunned. I've heard a rumour that N°1 has summoned a 'Convocation of the Numbers' to discuss the new situation."

"Yes, I know," Darryn replied. "The senior Guardians have been asked to attend also. I'm expected to be there."

Annabelle decided that this had to be her moment to deal with her business:

"Darryn," she began, "I've got some bad news for you, dear, and I want you to remain calm while I explain."

Darryn raised an eyebrow. He knew it must be serious if Annabelle was referring to him as 'dear'. He was even more concerned when Annabelle took his hand and held it. "You're not going to propose to me are you? That would be a catastrophe!" he said.

Annabelle remained grave and said, "Listen, this is not a laughing matter. You know Alex, your partner...?"

A spark of comprehension passed over Darryn's face and he interrupted, saying, "If you were going to tell me that he was a two-timing bastard, I'd more or less worked that out for myself. The toe-rag hasn't been in touch since that night you and Rakshi came in 'The Queen's Head'. He just hasn't got the bottle to say it's all over."

"It's worse than that. He was the agent that was mentioned in the document that Jake got from the F.U.P. camp in Wales. You know... the one who had the dispensation from the Vatican. I said he looked familiar. I remembered afterwards that he was Michael O'Grady's blue-eyed boy that I'd seen and spoken to while working in the kitchens there. His real name is Andrew Judgement. I'm sorry, there's no easy way to say this; you were the enemy agent they were attempting to lure into an indiscretion."

The blood drained out of Darryn's face as he sat motionless for a moment before banging his fist down on the table. He then exploded, shouting, "Damn, I've been a complete fool. I'll never go out with another man as long as I live." He sat in contemplation for a second or two before asking Annabelle more reasonably how she knew that Alex had approval from the Vatican.

"An agent," she was cautious not to mention Jake, "broke into his apartment and discovered a Papal Bull under the carpet giving him special permission to indulge in homosexual activities. N°2 became suspicious of him when he couldn't be traced in the Treasury. Now, I know this is difficult, but I must ask you to think carefully about what he was trying to find out from you, or what he was trying to get you to do. The future of the Rainbow Alliance may depend on it."

Darryn thought long and hard and the said, "It's very difficult to know. We rarely talked about work, and I was careful to give the impression I was a Junior Fellow at Oxford and nothing else. We always went back to his place or my rooms in college, and I was careful never to carry any documents or equipment relating to my role as a Guardian." He paused again and then said, "I guess the one thing that got a bit tiresome was that he always wanted to go back to my place in London. However many times I said it was small and pokey, or that the neighbours could hear through the walls, he would still try to persuade me to take him there."

"Do you think he was trying to get you to reveal the location of Rainbow House?"

"I was careful to always use the protocols when entering the building, especially when I'd been out with Alex."

"But why did he leave when he did? I'd like to think it was because he'd given up, but I'm much more afraid it's because he's got what he came for."

A frown on Darryn's face became one of mounting concern. He finally articulated this saying, "There was one night when I returned and had a feeling that someone else was there. I did a double retake around the block and stumbled into Jake the night he dumped Nathan. I assumed it was Jake who had made me uneasy. My God, Annabelle, if Alex was there he would have seen me and Jake go into Vijay and Sameeras' shop. I must find the son-of-a-bitch and beat out of him how much he knows."

"Where will you start looking?"

"I don't know, Rome if I have to. There's no point in going to Newcastle. I'm sure that was just a cover story."

"It's a long shot," Annabelle said after a pause, "but I remember him telling me he'd come from Godalming before going to Rome. It may be that it was a snippet of truth which slipped out."

Chapter 33

In those difficult days of March, Jake had no option but to carry on with his studies, be diligent in his training and remain faithful to Tim. At least he was talking to Nathan now, and his group of friends once more seemed to be able to coalesce around him. He was sensitive to the awkwardness Tim must have felt in Nathan's presence and to be fair, however much it must have pained him, Nathan was gracious enough to slip into the background whenever Jake and Tim were together.

Jake had now done his spying assessment, his long trek and learned how to drive a car, ride a motorbike and steer a motor boat. He was making progress with his horse riding, although he still felt no empathy for the animal. The final stage now before becoming a fully-fledged Guardian was to do a hundred hours of patrolling assisting a Guardian already in place. There was plenty to do in London for the entire cohort of Apprentice Guardians, so there was no need for them to go further afield.

So bad was the situation becoming that the Apprentice Guardians now had to work in pairs and expand their work to police duties such as defending old ladies from muggers and dealing with extortion and racketeering. Jake and Tim had to deal with a gang of youths holding up a man at knife point on their first night of patrolling. In their uniforms and balaclavas they could not be recognised, and so gained some notoriety in the neighbourhood for being superheroes with special powers.

Jake thought this was cool and had some cards printed with 'Guardians of the Rainbow' printed in a fancy font over the top of a colourful rainbow. He would give these out to anyone he or Tim rescued before disappearing into the night. When N°6 got to hear of this however, he was livid and threatened Jake with expulsion from Rainbow House unless he stopped.

The issues they had to deal with were no match for their training and their senior Guardian on more than one occasion had to warn Tim and Jake about getting careless and complacent. It took a slash on the cheek requiring minor hospital treatment, however, to really get the message home to Jake.

One brighter moment came when he was able to drive out to the village of Welwyn in Hertfordshire with Maria and buy himself a new violin. He was using the two thousand pounds left to him by his father. He had felt uneasy about doing this because of the circumstances he had received it in, but Maria had persuaded him that he might as well spend it. They had booked an appointment for two o'clock. The weather for once was spring-like and optimistic. The village, with its half-timbered buildings shaped in a way that would hardly pass building regulations these days, showed a face of Britain that belonged to a bygone age. There was little sign of the economic and social crisis that was gripping the country.

The shop assistant showed them into a backroom where four violins and bows had been laid out for him to try within his price range. He had asked Maria along because she too played the violin and would be able to give some sensible advice. He thought wistfully that if Nathan had still been his partner, he would have been able to fulfil the role Maria was playing. Tim had not come along because although he wasn't completely tone deaf, he had very little music in his soul. He had a few cheesy pop albums, but that was it. This was one of the things that had started Jake thinking that maybe their relationship was not going to last. The seeds of doubt were beginning to be sown again.

Jake tried the instruments one by one. He had brought some music with him to try out. They all were much easier to play than his current instrument, but one stood out as being brighter and easier to play. He loved the feel of it and he loved the way he could make a good sound without having to make a massive effort. Maria tried the instruments too, and thankfully agreed with Jake about the instrument he preferred.

The assistant returned and told Jake a little bit about the history of the violin he had chosen. He had agreed to do a part exchange deal with his old violin. He had a slight qualm over this as he seemed to be abandoning an old friend, but he told himself not to be so stupid and sentimental.

"I think you got yourself a very good deal there," Maria said approvingly, "and I think it was very sensible to take out the insurance cover too."

"In my line of business, the chances of an accident are quite high, I guess," Jake replied.

***

Darryn was driving into Godalming. He was struck by the sign which announced that he was entering the town. In the past, it had cheerfully announced that Godalming was twinned with Joigny (France) and Mayen (Germany). Now a replacement sign simply said:

'Godalming – strangers and foreigners not welcome. Europeans should not stop - but please drive safely.'

Superficially, the houses looked the same as in any quaint town in southern England. Somehow though, there was a brooding menace that seemed to project onto the main road going through the town. As the street passed through into the more commercial area of the town, Darryn decided to park in the South Street car park, from where he could easily walk to the house owned by Alex's sister.

It was a small, unremarkable modern two-up-two-down terraced house. He knocked on the door and waited. There was silence. He knocked again and still there was no reply. The spell of spring-like weather had continued. On a small patch of grass in front of the house an ailing ornamental cherry was just beginning to flower. A few daffodils haphazardly spread around the

200

garden were also just coming into flower, but this was the extent of the effort to create a garden.

Darryn had discovered the house by checking the electoral roll for anyone with the surname Judgement. Not surprisingly, there was only one entry; the only person cited for that address and therefore probably a single woman. Further research in the extensive intelligence archive at Rainbow House had revealed the link between her and Alex. There seemed to be no parents in the area and she appeared to have an unremarkable life.

Was it worth breaking in to find out what was inside? Darryn wasn't sure. The chances of finding anything useful were slim and yet he had made the effort to come here, so he might as well see what was on offer. Using a standard-issue skeleton key, Darryn gained entry efficiently and calmly through the front door. Just as Jake had done when entering Alex's flat in London, Darryn waved his anti-burglar alarm device in the direction of anything that looked as if it might be part of a security system. There was a narrow hallway leading to a staircase and the kitchen-dinner at the back of the house. It was depressingly decorated with a dirty grey carpet and institutional magnolia-painted walls. This was a place where someone stayed, not a real home.

There was only one door off to the right which Darryn guessed must lead to the small front living room. He opened the door slowly and walked through. The cheap furniture and the sparse decor confirmed the impression gained from the hallway. There was a small television set in the corner and a computer on a desk tucked away against the opposite wall. There was no fireplace and heat was obviously provided by a scratched radiator along the long wall of the room. There was one photograph in a frame on the window ledge. Darryn instantly recognised Alex, or Andrew as everyone else presumably knew him. He was younger and smiling, but the thing that Darryn particularly noticed was that he was wearing a priest's cassock and a dog collar. Next to him was a woman, smartly dressed, who could have been older or younger, but with features that were unmistakably similar to Alex. This must be his sister.

Darryn stared at the photo for a few minutes thinking about these two people and their relationship. Yes, he knew from his intelligence that Alex had gone to Rome to carry out some studies in the Vatican and was not surprised to see him portrayed as an ordained minister; yes, he knew rather less about his sister, but knew she worked as a junior assistant manager at a local bank. However, what was the dynamic between them? They looked close on the photograph, comfortable in each other's company. They seemed the sort of brother and sister who would stay in contact and look out for one another.

"You've taken your time getting here," someone quietly said behind him. Sweat suddenly appeared on Darryn's brow as he recognised the lilt and the timbre. How the hell did he get in? He had been out-foxed yet again by his nemesis. Controlling the urge to panic and do something violent and stupid, Darryn slowly turned to face the owner of that innocuous voice. It was Martin.

"So you've appeared in person this time," Darryn said as calmly as he could. "Are there no cryptic messages or play-fights this time?"

"There isn't time," Martin retorted snappily. "You lot are so slow in deciphering my clues that the worst will have happened by the time you find the solution." Martin casually sat down on the sofa, so Darryn took this as a cue to sit in the chair opposite.

"You've been a complete plonker this time, Darryn," Martin continued. "You know I guess by now, that Andrew Judgement has been playing you for a fool."

"Just like you did," Darryn interjected acidicly.

Martin rolled his eyes and said, "Please! We haven't got time for you to get all bitter and twisted again." He paused for effect and then continued, "Why did you have to go and leave that note for O'Grady when you came for Taffy's body, and why did you have to wreak unnecessary carnage in the process?"

"It wasn't deliberate," Darryn replied defensively, "I gave them an opportunity to submit, but the idiots insisted on continuing to attack. I took no pleasure in killing them."

"Well, that as it maybe, the fact is you've thrown down a challenge to O'Grady. My God, Darryn; are you mad? The man even scares me. He is not human, he has no feelings, he shows no mercy and he doesn't forget. He's not gone away, you know. He is simply biding his time, and he is going to come for you with every intention of killing you slowly and painfully. You'd better be ready when he does, that's all I can say." Martin paused again, giving Darryn time to appreciate the seriousness of having Michael O'Grady as an enemy. He then continued yet again, "Anyhow, that is not the main reason why I've intercepted you here. Andrew Judgement saw you go into Rainbow House. Do you understand what that means? The F.U.P. now *knows* where it is. They will be coming after you before much longer. They have plans to take over the armed forces and finish taking the police under their control. They will send tanks and soldiers against you. You won't stand a chance. You *must* get the Numbers to organise some defence or you will all be slaughtered."

Darryn raised an eyebrow and said, "Aren't you taking a very big risk by telling me this?"

"Too damned right I am! The reason for the codes and the subterfuge in the past was to cover my back. Someone else would have copped it if the message about St. Bartholomew's day had leaked back to O'Grady. Now I'm putting my life on the line to save your bloody neck."

"Why?"

"Let's just say I have my reasons. By the way, Andrew's sister is a

202

complete innocent in all of this. Please do not involve her any further. She will be back from work at five-thirty, as she is every weekday. Don't leave any trace of your visit."

With that Martin leapt out of the chair like a panther, disappeared into the kitchen and was gone. Darryn wasn't even tempted to follow. He sat ruminating on the enormity of the information Martin had just given him for a full five minutes. He then got up, checked the doors and rectified any sign of disturbance before carefully leaving that sad and lonely house to its single occupant.

***

The extended 'Convocation of the Numbers' was about to take place in the Room of Benign Decision. The Numbers were sat in their places at the Great Crescent Table. The senior Guardians were stood facing the Numbers. N^o3 and N^o7 were absent, no doubt as the necessary precaution to prevent the whole leadership being wiped out in a single blow. N^o1 stood up, grave and serious, to address the assembly. He looked around, eyeing everyone in the room before commencing:

"My dear friends," he began, "The things we feared most have come to pass. The F.U.P has found its way into Government and they have also discovered our hiding place." Darryn could not help blushing as this was said, although he knew no one blamed him for the calamity. N^o1 continued, "We, here in this room, have to decide the best course of action to take in order to protect those we shelter and continue our work. We have to plan for the possibility of an assault and decide whether to stand and fight or flee. Either way, we must make sure that the young, the old and the infirm are kept out of the line of fire. Now please, we need to hear everyone's ideas and views so don't hold back."

The discussion that followed gradually became more animated. The hawks were all for making a pre-emptive strike on the F.U.P. headquarters in Pall Mall. The more cautious pointed out that any such attack would be painted as a terrorist outrage which would fuel public sentiment to allow the F.U.P. to move against them more quickly. N^o6 also pointed out that if they had the armed forces at their disposal, the F.U.P. headquarters in Pall Mall would become essentially irrelevant anyway.

The conversation then turned to the shield, which was now in place and had been successfully deployed a couple of times in the dead of night when no one was looking. The specification said that it was strong enough to withstand anything short of a direct hit by an Exocet Missile. Was it possible to take the chance? Could they just sit it out until the army got bored or ran out of ammunition?

In the end they decided to ship everyone who was over seventy to the gay nursing home in Islington. Its security was unlikely to have been compromised and the healthier and more alert old-age pensioners could assist with the extra duties of the nursing staff. One or two extremely fit septuagenarians refused to move, regarding such a move as insulting. They were permitted to stay at their own risk. The school continued to function but drills were undertaken to evacuate the building if trouble loomed. A contingency plan was drawn up to take anyone under sixteen to a place of safety. A system of lookouts was posted both along the river and along the roads to watch for the movement of navy ships and army vehicles. There was not a lot that could be done to forewarn about attack from the air except to interpret the radar signals beamed from the top of the roof.

Other than that, there was a steely determination for life to carry on as normal for as long as possible.

Chapter 34

In public, the F.U.P. ministers set about their goals of legislating for moral values, ending all ties with Europe and effectively preventing immigration. A 'Morality Bill' was high on the agenda of the new Home Secretary, Lord Bernard of Agincourt. It included measures to force shops to close on Sunday, restore religious observance in schools, prevent the presentation of homosexuality as acceptable and strengthen the law of blasphemy against the Christian religion. This was quite clever politics, as quite a few shop workers who would have otherwise been against the bill quite liked the prospect of having a day off with their families, and others equally liked the idea of a bit of peace and quiet in their neighbourhood. Hidden away in the bill however, was a clause to set up a commission to investigate suspected cases of 'homosexual propaganda' with widespread powers to arrest and fine people. The head of this commission was dubbed in Whitehall circles as the 'Witch-finder General'.

Behind the scenes there was also a tussle for control of the armed forces. While Lord Bernard might have just been seen as a front man who was rather good at rabble-rousing, the new Defence Secretary was a sharp operator who had direct links to the paramilitary wing of the F.U.P. He was angling to create a situation where the government might be forced to declare a state of emergency which would allow him, with the Home Secretary's assistance to send armed forces against the Rainbow Alliance. He now knew where Rainbow House was, and he was itching to wipe it out. He was cautious though, he knew that they would have to get their *coup de grace* right and was prepared to wait until the odds where overwhelmingly stacked in their favour.

Meanwhile the economy was hardly improving. The French had responded to some of the Government's anti-European measures by shutting the tunnel and searching all Lorries landing at French ports. The effect on British exports was devastating, causing more chaos in the stock market and a run on the pound. A number of multi-national companies announced that they were shutting their factories and moving to the continent, throwing thousands more into unemployment.

Jake tried to carry on as normal a routine as possible. He was getting very close to his final A-level exams now and spent much time on college work and revision. He and Tim were still together; Tim was clearly devoted to Jake and would do almost anything for him. Tim had relaxed and become more gregarious, becoming part of Jake's circle of friends and surprisingly becoming quite matey with Matt, Jake however was haunted by what Maria had said to him. He knew full well that he had got together with Tim on the rebound from Nathan, but hoped he would grow to love him rather than just lust after his muscular body. He kept wondering though whether the only reason they were still together was that he didn't dare break Tim's heart by breaking it off. The impending exams had produced a convenient excuse to distance himself somewhat from the intensity of Tim's attention.

As for Nathan, Jake was on speaking terms at least. However, where Nathan went or who he was seeing remained a mystery. He seemed to form no romantic attachment with anyone in Rainbow House and was careful to avoid Jake when Tim was around. Jake knew that Nathan had formed a strong bond with Maria, but did not put her in an awkward position by asking what they talked about.

The college remained a soulless place with which Jake had very little empathy. He had no strong feelings about his lecturers, who seemed to do a competent job without feeling any connection with their students. There was no sense of communal identity. The few extracurricular groups were poorly attended and half-hearted, and the sports teams only played intermittently.

In his last days there, he was disturbed to find that a few students had started an F.U.P. supporters group. Jake and one or two of the others from Rainbow House were determined this group would not thrive while they were there, and they went around taking down their posters and protesting outside their meetings. Jake knew in his heart though that the gesture was futile, because more and more of the students were openly expressing the views of the F.U.P. in a way that would have been inconceivable even two years ago.

Jake's final exam was a maths exam. The questions were all fairly standard and he managed to finish with about twenty minutes to go. Having checked through several times he spent the last five minutes sitting wondering what was going to happen next year. He and Tim would both be going off to Oxford, all being well. Nathan however was off to the Royal Northern College of Music in Manchester. Jake realised that there was a good chance he would lose contact with his former boyfriend altogether. A wave of realisation swept across him, making him appreciate that this was something he did not want to happen.

It was a hot sultry day. The last few minutes were interminable. A bluebottle buzzing on a window pane somewhere, the soft pad of the invigilator's shoes squeaking as he moved up and down the rows and the occasional sharp tap of a pencil or pen dropped accidentally on the floor were the only sounds to disturb the somnambulant atmosphere.

Then it was over. Two years of hard graft, sweat and tears were over. All that was left was to wait for the results. There was no sense of celebration or camaraderie even now. Everyone left the exam room and went their separate ways to get on with their lives. The Rainbow House students did meet up for a few drinks in 'Club Tropicana' that evening. A trip to Soho was now a distinctly dodgy business since the F.U.P. had become a governing party.

***

On the same day in Shrewsbury, Darryn was once again visiting his favourite coffee shop. Unlike in London, the day was overcast and rather cool. Annabelle was sat opposite waiting to review the reports from the local agents. Darryn looked around, expecting to see Sean, but he wasn't there.

"...Any idea where Sean is?" Darryn asked plaintively.

"I've heard he's quit his job here and moved on," Annabelle replied casually.

Darryn looked shocked and anxious for a second and then went to the counter to ask if anyone knew where Sean had gone. He was greeted with a degree of suspicion by the girl serving coffee who had no idea who Sean was. Darryn returned crestfallen and rather depressed to talk to Annabelle. Before they could get underway Marcus made an appearance and sat with them. An elderly couple stared as he entered as a black face had become something of a rarity in Shrewsbury.

"Hi Marcus, how are things going in Telford these days?" Annabelle asked.

"Well, they've not been easy for some time, as you know, but since the General Election they've become a whole lot worse. The F.U.P. has succeeded in taking the local police over. Once the law to put out all public services to tender was passed, the council fixed things to ensure the F.U.P. won the bid. Their henchmen are now all legitimate police officers and there is now a real state of martial law on the streets. When the bill to arm the police becomes law, they will be able to openly patrol with weapons and shoot people who they deem to be criminals. It will be very difficult for us to operate at all."

"Listen," Darryn said. "There's a chance Rainbow House is going to be attacked in the next few days. Stop activities and contact everyone in the area, including Digby Forester. There's a real possibility that there might be a Code N scenario. I'm putting you in charge of making sure that everyone gets safely away to join the Welsh outpost. Annabelle and I will have other things to worry about if the balloon goes up."

Marcus sat grim-faced, opposite Darryn. He said, "I can't believe you've just said that. You are talking about the end of everything we've stood for, the end of our attempts to rescue our kind and build some sort of community for ourselves."

"I know," replied Darryn. "That is why it is so important to gather everyone together, so that something of that dream may survive."

"How certain are you that it's going to happen?" Marcus asked, still not willing to believe in the calamity.

Darryn pondered the words of James Grimwold from the first time they met: *'The only way the last tree can survive is by shedding its fruit far and wide and hoping some of it will grow, there is no hope for the tree itself. It will die as all things do.'* It had meant little to him at the time and he had forgotten about it. He was sure now that this 'prophecy' applied to the

207

Rainbow Alliance, especially as he now recalled what Grimwold had gone on to say: *'You don't stand a chance. You will be up against the might of the British Government. It's what happens afterwards that's interesting. All hope may not be lost there, but the pattern is too fragmented and complex for me to be certain.'*

Darryn surprised himself by replying to Marcus by saying, "I am certain. Whether there is any hope for the future depends on what we do after Rainbow House has gone."

Annabelle looked shocked now and said, "Darryn, I've never heard you speak in such a defeatist way before."

"I'm simply being realistic. You don't know how much pain and grief it gives me to know that it was my doing, however unwittingly, that Rainbow House was betrayed."

"I'm going back to Rainbow House tonight. At least we can make a last stand. Are you coming, Darryn?"

Darryn seemed uncertain for a moment and then clarity appeared on his face, "No," he said, "I must go around as many of the groups as possible in the next few days and prepare them for the contingency plans that must follow the demise of our home."

Marcus and Annabelle looked at each other unable to say anything appropriate. The cataclysmic discussion they were having seemed so out of keeping with the gentle surroundings they were in, with the occasional clink of coffee cups, the sudden whoosh of steam from the coffee-making machine and the gentle hum of conversation in the ancient building.

"I suppose you haven't heard anything about Sean, Marcus," Darryn asked almost desperately.

"Yes, he quit his job here a few weeks ago and decided to return to Ireland," Marcus replied, rather unexpectedly. "He'd had some trouble with some youths throwing a brick through his window. He told me it was the final straw and that he'd got nothing left to stay for. I got the impression there was a love interest in the background that had not worked out too,"

"He didn't leave a forwarding address by any chance?"

Marcus looked surprised and said, "Haven't you got his number in your phone?"

Darryn suddenly realised that of course he would have him in his contacts. He could send a text at any time asking him how he was. He now appreciated how much he'd always taken Sean for granted. He'd always assumed he could find him in this coffee shop if he ever needed to see him. The remembrance of that surprising kiss came wistfully to mind, as well as his foolishness in going off with Alex instead of waiting just a few minutes longer for the sweet, good-hearted, incredibly handsome young man, who would have genuinely made him happy. He shuddered as he realised it was that decision which had brought them all to the desperate situation they were now in.

Marcus left, leaving Annabelle and Darryn to sort out their belongings before leaving themselves.

"Annabelle," Darryn said as they were about to part outside in the market square, "there's a good chance we might not see each other again. I just want you to know you've been a good friend and I do care for you deeply." He hugged Annabelle tightly.

When she could get her breath back, Annabelle replied, "Come on, Darryn, don't get sentimental. It doesn't suit you. We are survivors, you and I. I am sure we will be seeing each other before too long, whatever happens." With that, she gave Darryn a reassuring pat on the back and marched off towards the river to find her car in the large car park there.

Chapter 35

Life in Rainbow House was continuing in a surprisingly normal way. Yes, the elderly and infirm had been shipped out and a decision to transfer as many of the duties as possible to venues away from Rainbow House had led to a quieter than usual atmosphere around the place, but there was still the hum and buzz of activity about the place.

Now that the exams were over, Jake and Tim were going off on holiday with Maria and Matt. They had booked a cottage in Cornwall so that Matt could paint seascapes while the rest of them pursued other leisure activities. Jake was a little concerned about Nathan who seemed to have no plans to do anything or be with anybody. In fact he was becoming quite morose and reclusive, not unlike Tim before he had hooked up with Jake.

There was one important event to complete before they left, however. The Guardian training programme was complete and there remained the ceremony to invest the new Guardians. It took place on a sunny Sunday afternoon at the beginning of July in the Room of Benign Decision.

Jake, Tim, Nathan, Jenny and Louise, along with the other inductees stood smartly in their Guardian uniforms with their rainbow epaulettes and matching badges on their shirts. The sun streamed in through the large modern stained-glass window which was positioned behind the Great Crescent Table. The light refracted and split into a dazzling array of rainbow colours in celebration. N^o1, N^o2 and N^o3 were all in attendance, as was Annabelle. Jake was disappointed to note that Darryn was not there, but guessed he was on an operation somewhere. One by one, the new Guardians went up to shake the hand of N^o1 and receive an illuminated scroll, personally authorising them to carry out the duties of a Guardian. There was a good crowd in attendance. The large double doors had been thrown open so people could stand out in the corridor and see as well.

After the last person had received their scroll, N^o1 stood to make a speech. He began:

"Congratulations to you all! You are now officially Guardians of the Rainbow. You will need to take no further tests or exams; you will be treated as equals with the Guardian Force that already exists. After this ceremony is over, you will go down to the Ops room where you will be kitted out with your revolver, ammunition and a few other things that you were not allowed to possess as apprentices. Above all though, be proud of the uniform you wear. It is despised by people outside, those that want conformity and compliance, but to us who want diversity and independence it is a badge of honour. For many of you, the sight of this uniform was the first time you felt good about yourselves and realised you could be who you really were. For some, the appearance of that uniform literally saved your life and the wearer has become a life-long friend. Remember that legacy and aspire to follow in those footsteps. Help our brothers and sisters wherever you can. The days are darkening and night is nearly upon us, so God knows, they need all the help they can get. Do more than that, however. Be an inspiration and a light. Help any good soul who is in trouble. Defend the children and the elderly. Be honourable like a knight of old. You have been given a unique training. Use it for good."

The ceremony finished and the new Guardians trooped out to receive their firearms and a briefing. Jake couldn't help but notice how noble and serious Nathan looked as he received his weapon. He then caught Tim looking intently at him as he picked up his.

The very next day Maria, Matt, Jake and Tim set off for Cornwall. Jake had expected that they would all be required to stay and help defend Rainbow House. However N^o1 himself had made the point that Darryn had made to Annabelle, that if the worst happened, there was no point in having all the best agents caught in a trap.

It was Tim's car and he was driving. It was a sensible, economical hatchback. It had plenty of space in the boot and lots of leg room, so none of the passengers was complaining. Tim was a careful driver so the passengers felt safe and secure. They set off down the M3 past Basingstoke and then took the A303 towards the West Country. As they skirted Andover, Jake noticed a military tank on a trailer in the slow lane of the opposite carriageway. He thought no more of this until a few minutes later he saw another ... and then another. There was a whole convoy of tanks, which had presumably come from Salisbury Plain – but where were they heading? Then it suddenly dawned on him. They were heading for London and possibly an assault on Rainbow House.

"Quick," he said in an agitated voice, "pull in at the next opportunity. I must contact someone at Rainbow House immediately."

This was easier said than done as the dual carriageway permitted no stopping. A few miles down the road there was a service station and Tim pulled in. Jake's first instinct was to call Darryn who fortunately was available to answer his phone. He quickly explained what he'd seen and added his interpretation.

There was a considerable pause before Darryn replied, "You may have something there. I'll call N^o6 and he can get his boys to track them if they get to the outskirts of London. They're not going to be easy to hide, that's for sure!"

"What should we do?" Jake asked. "Should we turn around and head back to Rainbow House?"

Again, there was another lengthy pause before Darryn said, "No, I really don't see any point. Go and enjoy your holiday. Keep an eye on the news though. If it is clear that Rainbow House has fallen, do not attempt to come back. Go to your mum's house and sit out the summer holidays there. Can you take Tim with you? Keep your heads down and await further instructions. Maria and Matt can head for that holiday cottage that N°8 owns in Portmeirion. They should be safe enough there."

Jake hung up and gave the others a condensed version of his conversation with Darryn. They set off again in a serious mood, past Stonehenge, and on to their destination.

***

Darryn immediately contacted N°6 who alerted the watch guard on the southwestern approaches to the capital. The convoy was picked up and followed by two agents on the M3. It continued to the Old Deer Park, just across the River Thames and not far from Kew Gardens. The twenty-five vehicles pulled up and parked on an old athletics track, well hidden from the main road into London. They remained there overnight guarded by soldiers, unnoticed by the residents of Richmond. In the morning the two agents became aware of renewed activity. The tanks were unloaded and the trailers, one by one, left the scene presumably to return from whence they came. N°6 was kept fully informed of these events, but could not believe that even now, Lord Bernard or the Defence Secretary would have the gall to order the tanks to be driven openly through the streets of London.

As the day wore on there was a great deal of activity. The sound of noisy diesel engines, suggested that the tanks were being tested and manoeuvred. A series of army trucks came and went, some of which were undoubtedly carrying shells for the tanks. However as afternoon stretched into evening, there was still no sign that the tanks were moving from their position. The two agents, now exhausted after their continuous vigil, agreed to take it in turns to watch through the dead of night while the other one got some sleep at a local budget hotel.

At two in the morning, the tanks moved one by one, and passed through the park and down to the river as unobtrusively as possible. The agent who was watching rushed to get a better view from the bridge. Through his night-vision binoculars, he could make out a large flat-bottomed barge moored next to the path. The first tank was carefully coaxed onto the barge with the aid of a temporary bridge structure that had been hastily constructed by a platoon of soldiers. From his vantage point, the agent could tell that the towpath was being patrolled by soldiers. Any midnight joggers would have been turned away on the pretext of a serious security incident. A few minutes later a second tank rumbled up and gingerly drove onto the barge and was carefully positioned next to the first. A third tank quickly followed; then a fourth, and a fifth. When the barge was full, the tanks were covered with large tarpaulins so they were no longer discernible to the observer on the banks of the river.

After ten more minutes of activity, the barge slipped its moorings and glided slowly away into the middle of the river where it continued serenely floating downstream. Within minutes a second barge appeared and moored alongside the towpath in the exact same position. The procession of tanks continued as before until another five had been accommodated. Once again they were covered over and the barge was allowed to proceed on its way in the wake of the first. The agent was now not surprised to see a third barge appear and the cycle of events continue. By four-thirty in the morning, with the fresh dawn of a summer day already establishing itself, the last of the tanks was on its way.

Long before this, the agent had reported what he'd seen to N^o6. He had immediately alerted the river watch who had picked up and followed the first barge as it was making its painfully slow progress towards the centre of London. The second agent relieved the first at five. He spent most of the day watching the soldiers very carefully cover their tracks. By midday there were only a few tyre ruts in the grass to show that there had been any activity there at all.

**

An emergency session was in progress in N^o2's office in the Ops room. Unprecedentedly, N^o1 was in attendance. He had always made it a rule that he would not get directly involved in operational matters and leave strategy to N^o2 and N^o6, so his presence now merely underlined the gravity of the situation to the others.

"The barges will take the best part of the day to get here, if they are going to land them in the old docks area," N^o6 informed them.

"So the likelihood is we can expect the attack tonight," N^o2 reasoned. "That fits in with the speech Lord Bernard gave the other day when he said the Government were about to take decisive action against the homosexual menace."

"If we are going to deploy the shield, we mustn't do it too far in front of the expected attack or it will become noticeable to the general public. We must also take steps to evacuate the interleaved office areas before we do, or else the night owls will be trapped and not know what is going on," Danny added.

"We can set off the fire alarm from here ten minutes before we deploy," one of Danny's assistants chipped in. "That should give everyone time to quit the building, but allow us time to prevent the fire brigade from entering."

"We must make sure that we can evacuate as many of our own people as possible if the shield fails," N^o1 said.

"We have the speed boats waiting in the underground yards. They lie beneath the protection of the shield and so can be released without shutting off the shield." Danny responded.

"Good," replied N^o1, "we must make sure we have the children ready in the basement just in case. Annabelle, have you got a team of Guardians ready to drive the boats if we do need a hasty evacuation?"

Annabelle nodded in the affirmative.

N^o1 continued, "We must arrange for all non-essential personnel who do not reside here to stay away tonight. The fewer people we have to protect the happier I'll be. Now, my friends; go and get some rest. We are going to be in for a long night tonight and I want you all to be alert and sober."

The rest of the day passed agonisingly slowly. The barges halted in midstream just adjacent to the West India Dock Pier. It became clear they were going to move no further until after dark.

Nathan was called up in his capacity as a Guardian and assigned to Annabelle's team to protect and, if necessary, evacuate the children. At six o'clock he was briefed. If the worst were to happen, he was to take twenty of the fourteen and fifteen-year-olds in one of the speed-boats and take them upstream as far as Maidenhead where they had a safe house. He was instructed to check they all had life jackets and was given a list of names to check off. He was told to be stern and authoritative. There would be no time for any nonsense.

At eight o'clock N^o6 took his place in the operations room along with Danny and his team. N^o2 followed at eight-thirty and N^o1 joined them later still. The watchers were still in place out by the river, but had been given strict instructions to disappear should hostilities open. It was only as Big Ben struck midnight that the barges started to move again, drifting towards the Millennium Dome.

Then it became clear what they were going to do. They turned towards the West India Dock Entrance Lock. As the first barge approached, the drawbridge over Preston's Road lifted to allow the procession of barges through. As the bridge resumed its normal position, hundreds of soldiers under cover of darkness emerged onto the harbour quay.

As this intelligence gradually unfolded in Rainbow House, N^o1 was pensive and contemplating the best time to act. When it became clear that the tanks were now being unloaded less than a mile away, he said, "I think it's time to ring the fire bell next door, don't you?"

Both N^o2 and N^o6 nodded their agreement and Danny pushed a button on the complex console in front of him. Nothing was audible in the operations room, but in the parts of the building that interleaved with Rainbow House, providing the cover of an ordinary block of offices, a deafening claxon sounded throughout. There were very few people working that late, but one or two weary souls gathered their jackets and briefcases and assembled in front of the building to be checked off by the night porter.

After five minutes, N^o2 said quietly to Danny, "I think it would be appropriate to have a quick CCTV scan, just to check no one is left in the building. The fire brigade may get here before the tanks arrive and we do not want them going into the building before we deploy the shield."

The use of the CCTV cameras next door was a sensitive matter and strict protocols were in place making their use exceptional. Danny looked at N^o1, but he nodded his agreement, so he turned them on. A systematic sweep of the floors starting from the top and working to the bottom revealed nothing.

"Okay, the time's come," N°6 said. "Turn off the alarm, Danny, and deploy the shield."

Danny pressed two buttons in sequence, which hardly did justice to the dramatic events that were noticeable outside. Firstly the deafening sound stopped, and the half-dozen, pasty-faced workers standing outside wondered whether they would be able to go back inside. But immediately a soft whooshing sound was heard as a giant flexible plastic tent settled around the building, having been explosively ejected from the roof. The office workers had hardly any time to wonder before it inflated and hardened. One of them went up to it and knocked it. A huge booming, echoing sound was the response.

A fire engine turned up almost immediately, with its siren still blaring from having raced through the East End of London. Before the six burley fire-fighters had a chance to marvel at the sight in front of them, soldiers raced into the square demanding that everyone should leave immediately. An argument ensued between the firemen and the soldiers over who should be bossing who about. In the end, as the soldiers had guns and the firemen didn't, the fire engine reluctantly quit the scene as did the bemused office workers.

While all this was going on, the Guardians were taking up their positions inside the building. Nathan had checked his twenty young charges and had them down in the basement ready to escape at a signal from above. Everyone moved to the lower areas, ready to escape if necessary, except those manning the operations room on the fourth floor.

Finally the tanks rolled into the square, a sight as incongruous as any you could imagine on the streets of London. They took up position all around the building, except on the one side which was adjacent to the water's edge. Soldiers also took up positions between the tanks and pointed their guns towards the building.

The officer in charge stepped forwards towards what he presumed to be the front of the building. He was discomfited by the transparent hard shell that now surrounded the building, but continued with his script anyway. He held up a microphone to his mouth and said, "We have orders from the Home Secretary and the Defence Secretary to arrest those within for activities contrary to the well-being of the state. If you give yourselves up, you will be charged with lesser offences. However if you do not, we will fire on the building. Any survivors will be taken and charged with treason." The voice boomed around the square, audible half a mile away.

Rather unexpectedly a voice boomed back from the building equally loudly. It was N°1: "We will not surrender as we have done nothing that has been tested as illegal in a court of law. Why do you come at the dead of night? Why do you come with arms to arrest children? You are displaying the traits of tyranny. Where have the legitimacy of your orders come from? Even the Prime Minister himself would have to seek approval from Parliament for

215

an action such as this. I urge every one of you to examine your conscience. Killing innocent civilians in cold blood is a war crime. The argument that you are simply following orders will not save you if there is a day of reckoning."

There was some murmuring in the ranks at this, but the officer was clearly incensed. He retreated behind the line of tanks and started barking out orders. The tanks started to fire. However, the shells merely bounced off, causing the soldiers to duck for cover. They were right to do so as one of the shells bounced straight back at a tank, causing it to explode and killing the soldier inside. One tank moved right up to the shield and positioned its gun right next to the shield. This was a bad mistake as the shell failed to penetrate the material and ricocheted back down the barrel, again causing the tank to explode from within. The commanding officer was inflexible and unimaginative, but when a third tank blew up as a result of a rebounding shell, killing two foot soldiers standing close by as well as the tank driver, even he realised that continuing the offensive would result in disastrous losses. He gave the order to stop firing and ordered his forces to fall back. He engaged in an animated discussion with a superior officer on the phone. When he finished, a cruel smile emerged from his features.

Inside Rainbow House it was very difficult to gauge what was happening. The odd bang and boom were noticed by Nathan and Annabelle, deep in the bowels of the building. In Ops, there was a clearer sense of what was going on as the TV monitors on the outside of the building were still operating. N^o6 was concerned that the tanks had pulled back, but were not gone, as if they were waiting for something else to happen. It became clear what this was when the radar picked up two aircraft coming their way. High magnification identified them as 'Eurofighter' jets.

The jets swooped down in formation and then in turn fired an air-to-surface missile at the building. The remarkable material of the shield refused to break even under this assault. The first missile bounced away and impacted on the building that had housed the corporate headquarters of the British and Shanghai Bank. The high-rise building caught fire spectacularly, but as the premises had remained vacant since the demise of the bank, there was no loss of life. The same could not be said of the second missile, which bounced off the shield into the headquarters of another major bank. Even at that hour of the night, well-paid financial traders were engaged in lucrative international deals worth billions of pounds. The missile penetrated to the trading room before exploding wiping out two hundred bankers in seconds. When a third missile bounced clean across the Thames and caused the Millennium Dome to collapse, the jet fighters were hastily recalled to base.

The fire and the carnage could no longer be concealed, with ambulances and fire appliances on the way, the tanks and the soldiers beat a hasty retreat back to the quayside. The smouldering remains of the three burned-out tanks had to be left, despite the questions and the embarrassment it was bound to cause.

As dawn broke, the world's press and media were rapidly gathering to report on the tragedy at the bank. Rainbow House stood solid and defiant. The shield collapsed into floppy plastic and was retracted, leaving the building sparkling in the early morning sunshine like a precious jewel of unimaginable value.

Chapter 36

Jake looked out on a calm sea with his arm around Tim's shoulder. Tim had his head tucked in the hollow of Jake's neck. Tim loved Jake so much; Jake was not sure whether he loved Tim or not. They had just been to collect Matt from the beach, where he had spent most of the afternoon and early evening with an easel, paints and charcoal sticks making sketches, or doing more detailed work on drawings and paintings that he hoped to be able to sell. He had become much more sober in his attire. It was almost as if the success of the F.U.P. in the election had heralded the end to frivolity. His ears were healing from the abandoned gauging process and his natural hair colour, which was a mousey brown, was now prominent. He had been sitting on the beach in shorts and a plain white tee-shirt, with a straw hat on his head to keep the sun off. Jake thought Matt looked far more attractive like this and he was so pleased that Matt had failed to go through with a tattoo on his leg.

Maria had gone down to see Matt on the beach after she'd returned from an afternoon stroll along the cliff tops with Jake and Tim. She wore a simple white dress and also wore a straw hat. She had taken a book with her and lay out on a rush mat in the sand and occasionally talked to Matt when there was a lull in his concentration. Jake and Tim had taken the opportunity of being alone for an hour or so to have some intimate fun in the bedroom of their cottage. Although modest in size and of little architectural significance, the cottage had a spectacular aspect of the rolling hills and sea. The rear garden, which the owner kept well-tended, backed on to the coastal path. It was here that the four of them stood, watching as the sun grew red as it gradually sank into the west.

"Have you heard any more news from Rainbow House?" Matt asked Jake.

"Not really," Jake replied. "I don't like to bother Darryn or Annabelle at a time like this. There was a rather worrying report on the news this evening about that large American bank... you know, the one that has its headquarters just down the way from us. Apparently it was hit by a missile last night and a couple of hundred people were killed. They're saying it was some kind of terrorist attack. There was nothing about Rainbow House, though."

As Jake stood there, outwardly calm, some turbulent thoughts were going through his head. He was now convinced that he still loved Nathan, and while he liked Tim and found him genuinely sexy, he had a growing conviction that it was only a matter of time before they broke up. He couldn't do that now however. Tim would be utterly devastated and besides, how could he take him home if they had split up? He couldn't very well just abandon Tim if Rainbow House fell. No, it would have to wait until they went to University. In any case, he might lose touch with Nathan, or Nathan may not want to get back together with him. Calculating as it might seem, Tim was a whole lot better than having no one.

The red sun caressed the watery rim of the ocean and sank willingly into its embrace. As it did so, a path of dancing spots of blinding light glittered on the sea surface between the watchers and the oncoming dusk. The four teenagers watched silently until the sun had completely gone; they then turned and went into the house.

***

Darryn stood with a fellow Guardian on the roof of a building overlooking Canal Street in Manchester. It had been a glorious day there as well. The sky was a deep azure as the departed sun left hints of light at the margins. Darryn was more up-to-date with the news from Rainbow House than Jake was. He'd been told the full details of the failed assault and initially he'd celebrated. Now however, the doubts were returning. Surely the F.U.P. would try again... and then there was James Grimwold's prophecy.

He had spent the last few days checking the Guardian teams in all the major towns and cities in the North West, checking that they were resilient enough to act independently if they had to. As he looked down now, he saw a couple of happy teenagers going into 'The Sunken Way'. For the moment, people were still allowed to go about Canal Street freely. How long would it be, though, before the Commission on Homosexual Propaganda started to implement a crackdown here and in other major cities? The patrons of the establishments along the canal bank were oblivious to the protection being afforded by the Manchester Guardians, and that, in Darryn's view was as it should be. However he was now convinced that the day was coming quickly when the Guardians of the Rainbow would no longer be able to be the keepers of 'The Sunken Way' as well.

Lightning Source UK Ltd.
Milton Keynes UK
UKOW05f1154131013

218914UK00001B/36/P